Walking Marina

D. R. Hildebrand

First published by Dog Ear Publishing
4010 W. 86th Street, Ste H
Indianapolis, IN 46268
www.dogearpublishing.net

dog ear
PUBLISHING

ISBN: 978-145750-367-2

This book is printed on acid-free paper.

Printed in the United States of America

For Ms. Fran Danish,
for instilling a love of literature.

And for my mother,
for instilling love.

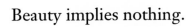

Beauty implies nothing.

Prologue

IT WAS MIDNIGHT in late spring in a condominium on Central Park. A middle-aged woman with an appetite for extremes straddled wide over her bed and a boy. She planted her knees at his waist. She paused in control. Then she lowered herself, hard, to entirety. The boy closed his eyes. The woman breathed deep. She arched her back. She moaned. The bed began to rock. She moved slowly and evenly in effortless aches until her thighs flexed tighter, her panting came quicker, and she stared glazed with a smirk in the mirror. Her breasts and buttocks bobbed wildly with enhancements as her hair slapped across her face, splashing sweat and saliva at the man filming everything beside them.

The night continued until the sheets were soaked and the woman was satisfied. Without a word, she strolled naked from the bed through the condo. She set an envelope by the door, fixed her favorite martini, then took her time in the bathroom as the man fell asleep and the boy dressed in silence. The following morning, each returned to society. The man ordered scotch aboard a flight to Los Angeles. The woman walked comfortably through Central Park. And the boy, red-eyed, unkempt, clutching a brand new portfolio, sat quietly in the corner of a casting—waiting, watching, thinking about things few would ever imagine, before bringing his envelope to the bank.

Chapter One

DANNY WAS BEAUTIFUL. In some ways because he didn't know it. In others because not much else around him was. *Beautiful* was a word he heard and learned to disbelieve. He associated it with shame. He searched it for substance. He sensed envy in its sound, the implication of inequality; and though he couldn't fathom the need he felt the struggle, the sickness, the resolve of those who uttered it to either take it or destroy it—this thing: beauty—along with a piece of him in the process.

In time, he severed.

For Danny wasn't beautiful. Perhaps the boy they saw—his skin, some disguise, the attraction in his cheeks which made monsters of women and men—perhaps he was; perhaps *that* boy was. The body he carried. The face he distrusted and refused to acquit. But not Danny. Danny wasn't beautiful. Danny was someone no one noticed.

The real Danny, he assured himself, was unremarkable. The real Danny walked with his hands pushed deep in his pockets; he went to bed with the blankets pulled high above his head. The real Danny, not the beautiful one, was born to parents he never met and lived with others he wished he never had. He lived in foster homes and orphanages and formed memories that turned to nightmares, secrets that kept him silent. The real, unremarkable Danny wasn't touched. He wasn't hit or stroked or made to believe that beauty was a belonging, that his body was an object to be abused. He wasn't a scapegoat. The real Danny didn't feel what the beautiful Danny did. He didn't feel anything at all. And yet, in the darkness of the night, he wept.

By the time Danny turned twelve he had seen much of the Midwest, and forgotten what he could of it. The week before seventh grade he moved again, this time to Indiana, where he stayed, finished high school, and got a job working nights at the local steel mill. His friend Jimmy got it for him—one of the few jobs available. And late, late each night, hours before dawn, the sound of machinery fading, the wind hissing hard across the lake, they drove home. Danny watched in silence as desertion drifted by: homeless in huddles; street lamps like fireflies; the debris, the bottles, the reminders of urgency. Jimmy drove. Danny stared. He dropped his head against the glass, his hood cowled tight, and he tried, as always, not to dream.

In the mornings he helped the girls get ready for school. He packed their lunches. He tied their shoes. He kissed them goodbye and then went groggily back to sleep until the neighbors' dogs, tethered and hungry and more depressed than the town, begged him with barks. He loved those dogs. But with the daylight in his eyes and all its declarations of optimism he found a single spot on the ceiling, and he stared.

By the afternoons he found purpose, or meaning, and made his way to the library. He liked it there—the real Danny did. He liked the familiarity, the stillness, the certainty of order. He spent hours on the floor looking at magazines, at newspapers, sounding out the words he should have years earlier when pictures seemed to suffice and imagination was still a means of hope. Then Jimmy picked him up. The practicing, the improving, the unattainable stories returned plainly to the shelves. They ate McDonald's en route; and smoke spiraled high in the distance.

Danny had been assisting on furnaces for just shy of a year. Without hesitation, he hated it. It wasn't so much the job but the future it ensured and the past it maintained. The tedium was irrelevant. The hours, the noise—he didn't care. Feeling, though, as if there were no other option, as if he were stuck because of reasons he couldn't control and would continue to be for others he couldn't foresee, as if change were just a camouflage for custom—that he loathed. Nevertheless, he told himself to be grateful. To endure. Security, however hated, was still security.

So he watched the smoke rise, or the sky disappear, and one evening in the middle of May, as beauty at last had been buried and life stood as still as a photograph, a voice, tempting like a secret, snuck unexpectedly from the radio.

"Have you ever dreamed," the ad began, "of what it would be like to be a *model?*" Jimmy slowed for red. Danny gazed out the window. The streets were bare save weeds and litter and the banners above, fluttering in the wind like streamers from beaten piñatas. A softness, some impassiveness traced his cheeks, ambiguity his eyes, no differently than the day or the week or the month before and yet now, hardly deliberate, entirely cautious, a flicker of curiosity crossed his brow.

"The biggest agency in the *world* is sending scouts across the country, and they *might* just be looking for *you!*"

Danny glanced at the radio. Then oddly, hesitantly at Jimmy. Jimmy rummaged through the bag in his lap; he dipped fries into napkins of ketchup, and licked his fingers as he ate.

"Whatever you do, *don't* miss this unique opportunity!"

Danny paused. Jimmy chewed. The advertiser cheered colorfully with infinite glee as visions of speed and success and all sorts of reasons to live jockeyed for attention in Danny's head. And for a moment, dreaming didn't seem so bad.

Then the light changed. The advertisement ended. The car crept on and Danny, somewhere adrift between the present and the impossible, as vacant and tame as a model, gazed quietly, again, out the window.

* * *

Cats were caterwauling more than usual when Danny reached home that night. The house was dim and quiet save erratic bursts of light flashing from the television, and the gales of laughter that flowed from it. Charlene was sitting upright, asleep on the sofa. Her head slumped forward, saliva at her chin. In one hand she cradled a remote control, in the other a glass of melted ice.

Danny paused, then walked past her. He crossed the living room and peered into the front bedroom. The top bunk was empty. Kimmy and Kelly slept side by side below, the sheets balled at their feet like crumpled up paper and their heads pillowed awkwardly upon crayons, coloring books, the piles of laundry left for them to fold. Danny sighed. He watched them as though they were his children, not siblings from separate parents. He leaned a shoulder against the door; he let innocence clear his mind.

Charlene stirred. She whimpered and Danny turned. He walked back to the sofa. He slid the remote from her fingers, left the glass in her grip, and bent down as he pressed his knuckles into the cushions. He formed a gully between the fabrics—the tattered robe, the abrasive sofa—then picked her up and carried her to the back bedroom, where he left her just as gently.

From under the sink he took a half-empty Night Train and with his favorite mug stepped outside. His thoughts clamored as he sat. But the wine wouldn't compromise. Danny closed his eyes. Weeds the height of wheat swayed a lullaby of susurrations and before he could help it the ad was in his ears. The charm. The zest. The vast assurance. There was a part of him that wished he had never heard it. Another that had memorized every word. He sat there with his head against the rail and the wine running rampant as he clung with an ache to the little he knew. There were *limits*. There were *certainties*. Big or small there was a difference between happiness and hope, and however beautiful, however ideal, however tempting, there were some things that just shouldn't be dreamed. Some things were simply too good. Some things were just too dangerous. What was so hard to accept?

He drank again. The wine wet his veins and he drank more. Reality be damned, he wondered what people in New York drank, what models drank, and why they ever would. *Champagne? Something better?* He couldn't fathom what else was relevant.

He needed to go. He needed to leave. He knew nothing whatsoever about beauty or fashion or modeling but he knew they existed somewhere far, far away, and that that was where he needed to be. Another world. Another reality. However far he could get.

He pushed the bottle to his lips, and he chugged.

*   *   *

Each day seemed to drag on slower than the last, until some weeks later Charlene was at work when Danny called out sick and left the house eight hours earlier than usual. His hair was clean. His nails were cut. His skin was cool with lotion. He cracked smiles as he dressed and his heart beat reawakened. He stood tall, almost confident, which took patience and practice but in his nicest clothes, his shiny black shoes, felt just a little easier than he expected.

He was finished and antsy and just about to go when the one thing he hadn't done wouldn't let him. For years he avoided it. He washed. He dressed. Every now and then he caught glimpses. Of his hands. Of his feet. Of the starkness of a knee or a thigh. But he never looked. He never stared. The real Danny had no reason.

Yet maybe now he did. Maybe now he had no choice. Perhaps looking, alone, wasn't even enough. He wondered if he should study, if he should scrutinize—his hair; his cheeks; his neck; his nose. If this was the moment to conquer his fears and himself and get proud, get arrogant, get perverted and hypocritical and all the things he associated with mirrors and admiration and unequivocal hatred. Perhaps he should touch himself. Perhaps he should pose. Perhaps he should point and shout and laugh and tease or . . . Or perhaps he should simply stand there. At last. And look.

He glanced back at the bathroom. He kept a hand on the door. For the first time in his nineteen years he knew exactly what he should do, and did the opposite.

Chapter Two

ROUNDING THE LAKE he saw the skyline. Chicago never seemed so near. He wiped his palms. He cracked his knuckles. He took out a map of the city and he studied it, repeatedly, until the conductor called his stop.

From the station it was hardly minutes to the hotel. The opulence was unlike any he'd ever known. The carpets were plush. The banisters glistened. Waterfalls flanked the foyer. From mosaics above, chandeliers like weeping willows draped in single file over imperial paintings, stately sofas, marble countertops. Business suits dotted the halls as perfumes filled the air.

Danny spotted the concierge, and there beside him a sign: EDGE MODEL SEARCH. He followed it through a web of corridors to an auditorium as silent as it was deafening. Thousands sat and none spoke. None moved. But thoughts rocketed and glances roared, sneezes and coughs and the quietest, most careful of farts blasted like trumpets at Jericho. He closed the door behind him—and it slammed shut. The waiting, the hours, the endless hours that had piled into days, weeks; those months of waiting only amplified the tension. The silence grew quieter and the noise grew louder as pockets of sweat could be heard pooling under armpits; sounds of makeup melting, nylon scratching, hearts pounding, adolescents adjusting and readjusting, frantic with uncertainty; and all the hair-combing, nail-biting, tooth-grinding, until suddenly, stridently, an outbreak of uproarious laughter ricocheted throughout the auditorium and for an instant the laws of sound and silence resumed, science governed once again, and breathing hushed to mute. Then the laughter stopped. Its source sobered. His colleagues followed suit. The three took their seats and before another moment could pass, physics failed yet again and warm, musky hurricanes thundered down thighs, echoing once more in the absence of fat.

The man on the right stood up. He seemed not to notice the thousands in torment in front of him but simply examined himself. His attire. Like a florist tidies her flowers. He rounded the table with a sigh. Then he brightened unconvincingly, and as he plumed the white chiffon scarf floating over his left shoulder he kept everyone in attendance pale.

"As I . . . *pray* you all *know* by now, this is not—hear me, *not*—a national model search. *We*," he said, his non-pluming hand circling extravagantly toward his colleagues, "are bookers at *Edge*, considered by some—by those who *know*—tobethe-world's*premier* modeling agency." He paused, paced, continued to plume. "MynameisGene," he said, an affected hand finding his heart. The agent spun a half pirouette and changed direction. "*I* am the director of the *women's* board. Behind me: Carla and Luke. *They* are bookers on the *men's* board." Carla smiled. Luke nodded. Mistakenly, the audience eased.

"*Now!*" Gene said. "No one wants to *be* here longer than they *must*. So I won't *lecture* you. Iknowhowmuchtheyloveto . . . at those . . . *rampageous* parades they call con*ven*tions." Gene threw up his arms. "*Oh*, puh*leaze!* Besides, I'msure-you'veall*been*, oryou'veheard*stories*, or you know *some*thing about them, these masquerades if you will. And if you *have*, if you *do*, then I don't need to tell you that we easily look at hundreds—ach, thousands, *tens* of thousands—of your gorgeously unsexed faces and rarely offer *any* of you what it is you come to us seeking."

Throughout the auditorium Adam's apples bobbed up and down as Danny and the countless other aspiring models raced to assess the unexpectedly harsh, statistical reality. But before any of them could calculate the odds, Gene kept his word.

"Women! All the women in the room: if you are shorter—I'll say it again: *shorter*—than five feet *nine* inches, please . . . stand."

Heads turned. Veins throbbed. Breasts perked as over-priced accessories found purpose at last. The room all but froze. Danny watched at the rear, his eyes, his nerves, his insecurity swelling. Had he been so naïve?

"Thank you," Gene said. "Now, still women—*just* women—if you are *taller* . . . than five feet *eleven* inches, will you, too, please stand?"

Fewer, but still more ladies stood up, elegant and towering and equally unaware. Danny dropped his face into his hands.

"Oh, de*light*ful! Now, allthosewhoare*stand*ing—would you kindly leave?"

Hearts stopped. Dreams crumbled. Whispers turned to shouts in a swell of panic. "*Excuse* me?" "Is he *joking?*" "Someone *tell* me he's joking."

"That's right, ladies, run *along*. I said I'd save everyone their time, did I not?"

The confusion heightened. Any remnants of peace burst into uproars of chaos. Danny stepped aside. A torrent of women and girls fled past him and out the back door, the more emotional ones whipping their hair and arching their backs, spearing ineffectual insults as they exited. "Fairy!" "Faggot!" "Cocksucker!"

As the last of the vertically unfit females snapped and stomped and snickered their way out of the auditorium, those who remained subdued. Those few, relatively few who stayed seated were left hopelessly waiting and wondering which of their unknown faults—color? curves? size? shape?—in untold categories—hair? hips? breasts? butt?—would ultimately eliminate them as well. How briefly, how benevolently would their respective stays of execution last? Dejected, the audience stared ahead. Indifferent, the agents returned their gaze.

"Men!" Gene exclaimed, no intent to relinquish the pace but purge the obvious. The women exhaled. Danny closed his eyes. Gene remained implacable, and succinct. "*If* . . . you are six-foot, six-one, or six-two . . . stay seated. The rest of you may leave. Now."

A second squall stormed east. Danny sat white with relief. And the room, at last, turned silent. Not so silent it screamed. Yet silent. Like a battlefield lain to rest. Like an ocean sung to sleep. And in the silence, the vast fatigue, the remaining candidates and their frustrated egos dispersed like ions to the outer aisles of the auditorium: the girls to one side, the boys to the other, their backs against the walls, shoulders between shoulders, eyes darting furtively about.

"Ladies first," Gene said, now pacing the inner aisle, still pluming, still sparkling. "We'll start at *one* end and we'll end at the *other*. You step *for*ward. You *e-nun-ci-ate*: name, hometown, height, age, andwhatitisyoudooo daily. You will not—I repeat, *not*—tell us about the time you posed nude for Pampers or the Cheerios commercial you shot when you were still too young to wipe your own *arse*. If it hasn't landed you in the latest Versace campaign or on a billboard in Times Square, *we . . . don't . . . care*. Period. Then, finally, a *slooooww* turn . . . *alllll* the way around . . . andbacktoyourplaceinline. So! *I* will demonstrate." He struck his hands against his thighs like a soldier, then pliéd like a ballerina and leapt forward. Carla giggled. Luke looked away and quelled a smile. "My name is Gene *Rod*erick. I come from Nueva York. I'm five feet *eight* and one-half inches tall . . . Well, not on Saturday nights I'm not!" He primped the scarf with a smirk. "My age is none of your business and you already know what I do. You! Goldilocks. Begin."

Gene returned to his colleagues and one after the next the girls stepped forward, some nervously, some superciliously, some professionally. Some said what they were supposed to and some didn't. Some turned twice and some failed to turn at all. Some smiled softly at Carla or winked coquettishly at Luke, but regardless of what they did or didn't do, none of them understood that none of it mattered.

None of it.

The agents were veterans. They knew which looks would appeal to which clients and the girls either offered those looks or they didn't. The agents also knew which of the girls' characteristics were possible to amend and which of them weren't. Poor posture, bad skin, unkempt hair, crooked teeth, an imperious attitude—each was case specific and each was subject to individual scrutiny. One girl carrying eight extra pounds in winter might be modeling a new Diane Von Furstenberg wrap dress at a Saks show by spring. Another in the same predicament, no matter what she did or how hard she tried, would never earn equal esteem. The agents deciphered one from the other and ultimately they sought the complete package. They sought poise. They sought potential. They sought eyes, lips, necks, and legs. They sought stance, motion, just the right amount of mystery. Things that couldn't be defined. And after almost five hundred half-minute appraisals, the agents graciously sent all but six girls home. Of these they discarded another three. One for the tattoo of a tiger between her breasts—"just imagine *that* on the runway." Another for refusing to cut eight inches, even four, off her hip-length hair— "what *else* will she refuse?" And a third for her senseless derisions and excessive gloating—"not on *my* board you won't; oh, *hell* no!"

Success was slim; and after watching three girls out of the original thousand-plus achieve it, the boys encountered the same scrutiny.

Danny stood halfway down the line between an under-aged bodybuilder sporting a neck the size of his own waist, and a college student at DePaul, remarkably attractive but madly hirsute, bearishly cloaked in his own fur which in itself was not a deterrent but became one due to his adamance that any form of depilation—shaving, waxing, lasering, plucking, threading or otherwise—was indisputably feminine. And feminine he was not.

Danny waited. He simply watched. He watched the agents watch the aspirants, watched their eyes drift over each face, each body, each shift and shuffle and how easily if not impatiently they detected each flaw; how assuredly they formed their judgments. He watched them jot notes, swap comments, possibly ask a question, and all the while, like the girls preceding him and the boys beside him and all the countless just as clueless to come, he never realized that making selections wasn't a science. It wasn't a process of formula or fact but a sort of art which even the top agents—Gene, Carla, one day Luke—often struggled to explain, and rarely had to.

The line, Danny noticed, was moving quicker for the boys than it had for the girls. He wondered if there were simply fewer of them. He wondered if the male features were less complex, more homogeneous, their market-value weaker, the deliberations briefer. Perhaps the agents were tiring and therefore rushing. Or his anxiousness was mounting. Or was it simply that none in this particular group was worth considering?

Three boys ahead, the umpteenth body stepped forward: name, hometown, height, age, occupation; turn. Danny noted his articulation. He returned to the line and the boy in front of teenage muscleman stepped forward, mimicked his predecessor, and returned. Then Mr. Muscles. Then Danny. Then the college kid and his irremovable winter coat. Then another and another and it wasn't until some third or thirtieth had made his appeal that Danny realized it was over. Without knowing it happened, it ended. Some verdict, favorable or not, was reached, and any attempt, any opportunity to influence it was gone. And yet had any opportunity ever existed? Was there anything he could have done, any additional impression he could have made in those brief thirty seconds that would have significantly altered their perception of him? Could Gene and Carla and even Luke have known long before he or any of them stepped forward or spoke or spun, who was a match and who wasn't, who could "make it" and who couldn't, who "had it" and who, simply, did not?

And what was this elusive "it"? And how did one acquire "it"? Was *it* intuitive? Or was *it* learned, practiced, improved in ways that even models themselves were unable to identify? Inborn or obtained, once one "had it," did one forever? Could *it* be severed, extracted, grown out of? Could it be lost?

Danny felt himself sinking. He felt his spirit collapsing. He saw himself sitting on the train, shoulders hunched, knees propped, his cheek flat and wet on the window, barreling home. He saw the smoke, the city, funereal and rotten, wishing him away, begging him to go; and all the tenacity of routine. He saw himself leaving the steel mill. Again. Riding home with Jimmy. Again. The heater huffing. The engine sputtering. Danny sleeping awake, dreaming—of something, of anything. Irrelevant, but a dream. Another morning waking up desperate yet oddly subdued, conclusive but too scared. Another morning—period. And Charlene unraveling him. He heard her, he saw her—drunk and ashamed, her baseless slurs, her torrid explosions. Her scorn and her fear and her inevitable demands, her interrogations of where he'd been and what he'd done and whom he'd seen. Too clearly, he saw her; and having no answer but his honest answer, and Charlene having no response but her only response, he saw himself telling her where he'd been and what he'd done and whom he'd seen, and he saw her falling to the floor, flailing, floundering, intoxicated with laughter, calling out his name in hysterics between gasping for sips of air.

"Danny . . . Danny *Ward* . . . in the white shirt. Over *here* darling!" Gene's voice didn't register. The bodybuilder's jab did.

"Sorry! Sorry, Mister Roderick." He turned stiff as steel.

"Danny," Gene said, affectionate at last, for it was clear that he adored the sound of his own name, adored even more anyone who remembered it, and adored more still anyone he welcomed into the agency. "Please. Come." Gene beckoned him kindly. "Everyone else . . . you may go."

Chapter Three

SLIVERS OF SUNLIGHT STILL LOITERED between buildings when at last he left the hotel. Traffic was untying. Tourists were resting. Stores began to close, restaurants to open. The evening news gave way to game shows and life, for the most part, was normal.

But Danny Ward was alive.

Trembling, choking, unable to think, he walked-skipped-tripped to the station. Then he turned suddenly to the lake. And he ran. He raced. Gusts of wind swept across his face, parted his hair, parachuted his shirt. He reached his arms wide around the world and he flapped them and soared. He swooped to the water and away, toward it and away, gorgeously, happily, happier than ever in circles and squiggles and endless figure eights. He jumped and he cried and he pumped his fists at the sky. He spun cartwheels and landed back flips and he laughed so hard that his stomach hurt. And when he tired at last, exhausted with a weightlessness he never could have dreamed, he fell back into the sand, he kicked his legs in the air, and he shouted, "Ha! Ha-*haa! Aahhhhh!*" huge and free with a happiness few would ever understand.

*   *   *

Charlene was in the kitchen when Danny opened the door. The television was on. The lights were off. Styrofoam lay scattered about the trashcan, with bits of bones and greasy napkins. Danny emptied the trash every week but he refused to consider what wasn't in the can. And Charlene refused to aim.

Danny locked the door and walked past the archway that divided the living room from the kitchen. He was past the bathroom, almost to the front bedroom when Charlene asked the window by the sink why Danny had come home so early. "Coulda been fired," she said, some attempt at sobriety on her lips. "Coulda quit. Nah, don't got *guts* to quit. Fired—that right, Danny?" She turned slowly around as Danny stepped back into view. "*Church clothes?* Where the hell you been?"

"Charlene. Please."

"*Please?*"

"Come on, Charlene. I'm tired. You're tired. Don't start."

"Don't *start?* I'll start whatever the hell I wanna start when you come here to *my* house early from work all churchy-like—"

"I'm leaving."

It was practically a whisper but he said it. And it was real. He stood there, silent, the words all but echoing as they faded. A part of him never felt so frightened.

"You're what?" Charlene didn't move.

"To—tomorrow. I'm . . . I'm going to New York."

Charlene dropped her spoon into the carton of ice cream she cradled at her chest. She set the carton on the counter. She searched Danny's face, showcased in the shimmer of reality television. She searched his eyes, his lips; she sought a sign of his deception. There was none. There never was.

A mixture of panic and some sort of agitated hate crept carefully across her face. Her eyelids twitched. Her eyebrows carved a crease above her nose. Her tongue found her gums and slid in circles under her lips, tracing her teeth like a secondhand navigates the numbers on a clock—methodically—deliberately—steadily. Suddenly, like springs, her hands snapped frantically back behind her and took hold of the first things they felt. A box of salt and a handful of plastic utensils sailed across the kitchen. Danny ducked, and she tore after them.

"Never fuckin good nough, Danny! Nothin's ever *good* nough!" She stomped into the living room and rounded the sofa after him. "Why!" she shrieked, "*Why! Why!*" The words rang like nails down a chalkboard. "What more I have to do for you, Jinx! How you jinxin me now!"

"Damn it, Charlene! The girls." He darted away.

"*Fuck* the girls! You don't care about the girls. They don't mean shit to you!"

"Quit it, Charlene! I love them and you know it."

Charlene galloped faster. She stomped harder and flailed wider, endlessly around and then halted. Violently, helplessly, she threw herself at him across the crumbling sofa. It tipped and she tumbled after it. She struck the lamp by the window and she watched from below as it came crashing down on her.

"Fuck you, Danny! *Fuck . . .*"

Like a child she cried. Sprawled on the floor beside the lamp, the sofa, her world suffocating, she cried. Danny stood motionless, stunned if not remorseful. Or just sad. Maybe that was it—just sad—standing there, looking at her, remembering her if possible. He contemplated helping her: a truce. He contemplated consoling her: a hand, his heart. He contemplated his past and he considered her future and he wished only to try harder. He crouched down. He crept toward her. He whispered her name, reached out his hand, and she pounced. Like a cat attacks a mouse—a cat with claws uncut, mascara smeared, nipples sagging and shoulders flexed and the smell of buttermilk biscuits on her breath—she pounced. Then again, and again, in vain.

Danny pulled back. Charlene groaned. She hurled curses and launched insults and as painful as it was, dragged herself on hands and knees to the other side of the sofa where Ryan

Seacrest grinned at her. She limped to the cabinet under the sink, took out the same jug of wine she opened hours earlier, and she lay there, broken, Wild Irish Rose tipped between her lips, soothing her kidneys and the blotch burgeoning across her thigh. Her knees were propped, her robe draped wide.

"You not leaving," she said, holding the alcohol at bay.

Danny gawked. "You—you don't even want me here!"

"*Fuck*, Danny! What I gone do with Kimmy and Kelly? *Huh?* What I gone do?" She pulled the bottle to her lips. She drank like it was water. Some memories, he knew, she'd never wash away. He wished he could comfort her. He wished he could hold her and calm her and assure her that life would get better, that things would return to the way they once were, that loneliness wouldn't last.

But she'd only resent him more.

"And what . . . you think . . . you gone do . . . in New York?" Her voice was flat. Her words were concentrated.

Danny looked away. "It's time for bed. Charlene."

She didn't budge. She stared into his eyes, impressive and opaque as they flashed on and off by the television. Again, he looked away.

"Model," he said at last.

Her mouth opened wide. "*Porn?*"

"Porn? Modeling! Fashion. Clothes and stuff."

"What, you—you think you're a *girl?*"

Danny closed his eyes. "Charlene, you're drunk."

"Girls, Danny. *Girls* is models. Not boys! No . . . *boys* out there modeling. Them *National Geographic*s you read. *Vogue*, Danny."

He refused to live this way. He wasn't to blame and he wouldn't be punished. He was grateful for whom she had been—had tried, once, to be. But now? To stay? There had to be more. He was certain there was, and there were choices he had to make.

"Charlene. It's time for bed."

She stared at him harder as a blanket of mystification wrinkled across her face. She should have known this day would come. She should have known it, sooner or later. Not why or how but *that* he'd leave, for there was no reason otherwise. He had become the adult and she the child, and only servility could keep things constant.

"Get out," she said, still lying on the floor, still sober enough.

Danny looked at her. He looked at the trash scattered around her feet, the wine dribbling down her chin, the robe falling off her shoulder. He looked at the knots in her hair and the folds under her eyes, the mascara that had funneled into them now drying. He looked at her hands—clenched without her realizing, shaking without her feeling—and he remembered how they had held him, how they had hugged him, how he let them. Seven years was a long time. He had never considered goodbye. Not like this, so simple and terse, so silent and final. Not goodbye without goodbyes; goodbye without the girls. Without reason, without requirement, without any at all, he loved them. And in a way he loved her too.

Charlene let the bottle roll indifferently from her hands and pooling every ounce of inebriated energy pressed her palms into the salted kitchen floor. Her torso climbed. Her knees trembled. She closed her eyes and groaned heavily with a fury and frustration and despair that echoed from every arc of her body. The house seemed to be darkening. The seconds moved like hours. He couldn't bear her misery. He stepped toward her, started to speak. He thought of trying—of anything—to save the night, to level the wine, to restore posture and sense and hope and all the life that could still be lived. But it was only that, a step. And with the torture of time she said it again. "Get out . . . the *house!*"

For a moment their entire past ballooned before him as she looked devastatingly into his eyes.

Then she roared: *"GET OUT, GET OUT, GET OUT!!!"*

And it burst.

Chapter Four

THE BUS STOPPED in South Bend, Elkhart, Howe, Cleveland, Milesburg, Newark, and shortly past noon, Memorial Day Weekend, warming but the urine not fully thawed, Danny entered the lion's den. New York: the lyric noir. A lingering haze turned the tops of skyscrapers to a blur as Midtown teemed manic, brusque and outrageously animated. Pizza parlors were packed, Macy's at a standstill. Taxis battled tour buses for attention and street maps sold faster than honey-roasted peanuts in winter. The onslaught of lights, the bombardment of sounds, the abundance of extraordinary advertisements turned heads and cameras and entire communities up and around and in every direction across streets that were wider and fuller than any he'd ever known. He took his bag from under the bus as he tried not to stumble between ticket counters, escalators, all the subway signs about. He asked for help and he received it in Spanish. He asked again and he got it in Sign. English that sounded like Chinese, Russian, Arabic, Swahili only confused him more but he asked again and again until he heard words he understood. He found his way, at last, to an alphabet of blue bubbles, the A-C-E, Brooklyn-bound. And he boarded, and he sat, and he stared.

A blind man. A string quartet. Bankers, and a woman reading poems to children. Conversations in Yiddish. Emos in all black. Love affairs that flared and the many more that faded. He lost himself to manifold worlds of purpose and finesse and independence, awed but at ease when moments later every sign read WEST 4TH and reality returned anew.

Shoved and jostled and all but carried en masse up the stairs, he found Bleecker and tracked the addresses west to an apartment three floors above an L-shaped restaurant known city-wide for its risotto. A poster shop neighbored it, fruit stands across the street, jewelry stores, costume stores, incense shops with velvet curtains duplicitous at the back inhabited every intersection; tattoo parlors in between. A French bakery sold croissants, baguettes, pastries, *pain aux noix, pain aux graines, pain de blé au levain* down the street. And Danny could hardly contain himself.

The entire neighborhood breathed. The streets were narrow and Bleecker bustled. It was throttled by pedestrians going to and from the health food shops, the T-shirt shops, the sex shops, all the overpriced apartments above. It was lined with vivacious awnings, artsy windows, globs of bubble gum dating decades and the specs of glass that beautified them. Drivers in Hybrids yielded to bikers on Raleighs and there were brownstones and there were ginkgos and there were flower pots filled with forget-me-nots.

It was spring. Sleeves were short and shorts were shorter. Favorite piercings and drunken tattoos, forgotten moles and newfound roles emerged suddenly from hibernation. Once more it was spring and once more the scent, the touch of the wind was scintillating; once more the cafés opened their windows, the robins their voices, butterflies their wings, and the thrum of skateboards crossing mangled streets was bearable, even missed.

Besieged but awakened, Danny checked the address and a buzzer with the names Jeremiah Jonker, Xavier Legard, Sasha Adams—exactly as Luke had said. He pressed it and stood back. Three windows up a screen slid open and a voice like that of a long-time friend called down. "One sec, Danny!"

There was a faint hum and he stepped in. Something felt like home. Like being, like finally finding home. The mail-boxes on the wall? The smell of a wholesome meal? The earth-toned tiles that lined the foyer, or the way the stairs squeaked as he climbed, how his arms hardly ached carrying everything he owned? This amazement of comfort! He wanted more, much more! He reached the second floor smil-ing, the third with a hop. He came to the fourth and thought he'd knock down the door but he waited in wonder. This life! This dream! Practically seizing with disbelief he leaned his calmest to the door and just as he did it opened, with Xavier (6'2"; 173; 40L; 16-34; 32x33; 12; brown; blue) standing stub-bly and statuesque inside the frame. He wore an undershirt and sweatpants with the words **Columbia University** stamped in light blue letters across the thigh, and an aura of care and virtue. Slight folds collected across his temples when he smiled. His eyes met Danny's, and he smiled.

"Come in, come in! How was the flight? You want some water? I'm Xavier." He offered his hand. Danny returned the greeting, speechless and unknowingly relieved. Everything felt natural. The sun shined patiently through the curtains; its hems brushed against braided ficuses, miniature bonsais about the windows. Spotlights fell on leaves, on coins, on the dust balls cowering in the crevices of the room, quivering on the floor with each exhale of the wind. The sofas, the tables were plain, peppered with notebooks, with blankets, with buddhas. Danny breathed.

"Drop your bags wherever," Xavier said, sounding markedly American. He took a cup from the cabinet. "I'd show you the place but Kinzie and Remmy are still sleeping. Rough night I guess. What about you? Did you sleep on the plane?"

"Who?" Danny set his bags respectfully by the door.

"Sorry. Kinzie is Sasha's modeling name, and Remmy's just short for Jeremiah." Xavier handed Danny the water. "Here, I'll show you my room."

The space was small, a converted study with a queen-size bed that all but filled it. There was no dresser. Only makeshift shelves ensconced in a deep-set, carved-out closet. On the window sill, behind the pillows, there stood a black-and-white photo of its owner and a brunette, she somewhat younger, her lips at his ear, their eyes closed and innocent. Not an advertisement. A guitar stood between the foot of the bed and a door-less closet. A series of bookshelves bearing cryptic texts in foreign languages, each underscored, annotated, and dog-eared to shreds lined the wall dividing Xavier's room from Sasha's. And along the opposite wall, against which the bed was pushed, painted in a bloodlike, purplish plum, there was a poem:

> feed the models, fast the models
> build the models, break the models
> love the models, lose the models
> drink, drug, and dream the models
> fuck the models, fault the models
> buy the models, be the models
> shine the models, shun the models
> crowd, kiss, and kill the models
> feed the models
> please: feed the models
> **DO NOT FEED THE MODELS!**

Danny felt himself chill. He glanced at Xavier. Then back at the wall. He'd stare if he stayed and the moment he turned to leave a door opened beside him and out stepped Sasha (6'1"; 162; 40R; 15-34; 30x33; 10; brown; brown) rubbing his eyes unresponsively and tottering across the flat to the bathroom outside Jeremiah's room. The faucet ran and moments later, dripping, he stumbled just as blindly back to bed.

"That was Kinzie," Xavier said. "I doubt you'll see him much on the weekends." Danny nodded as though well acquainted with the damage a New York night could cause as a groan or some morbid whimper seeped from Sasha's room. Another, warmer breeze floated into the apartment. Xavier suggested taking a walk. "Get you a map, some food. I used to play 'host' all the time."

Xavier changed clothes while Danny sat waiting, buoyant and spirited but laden with questions all scurrying through his head like rats in a sewer and increasingly aware that curiosity has no choice but to reveal itself. His room, foremost—did he have one? And Edge—near or far? When would he start modeling, and how? And would he meet other models? Central Park, of course! Was there really a zoo? The Statue of Liberty! The Empire State Building! He had to see—

"You must be Danny." The voice was broad and imposing, but honest and kind. It hovered somewhere between baritone and bass like a volcano beginning to breathe, like a didgeridoo in the night. Dulcet. Decisive. Magnetic if not mesmeric. Danny gazed up and saw Liam (6'0"; 168; 40R; 16-33; 31x32; 11; bald; black), shirtless, hairless, calm, skin the color of Law, black as a judge's cloak, wearing nothing but a pair of white pima underwear, standing there staring back at him. A slice of sunlight elucidated the slopes along the left side of his body— quadriceps; smooth; obloquies; smooth; pectoral, nipple, collar bone, jaw. Smooth, smooth, smooth, and smooth.

"I . . . am." Danny stood. "And you're . . . Jeremiah?"

Liam smiled. "Liam," he said. "Pleasure to meet you."

Danny was confounded. And equally unnerved. The body before him—the sight of another's skin, a peer, a male, so unabashedly exposed, so undeniably beautiful, artistic, pure and even proud yet polite—it stunned him.

The toilet flushed and Danny turned promptly to the bathroom to find Jeremiah (6'2½"; 151; 38L; 15-34; 29x34; 13; red; blue) walking toward him, as naked as Liam save freckles, boxer briefs, and a faint track of hair stretching south from his bellybutton. He stopped beside Liam, sleepy and completely fascinating. Danny's eyes tick-tocked: Liam to Jeremiah; Jeremiah to Liam. Xavier watched from his room. The toilet released a long, spongy sigh. And silenced.

"This," Liam said, the depth, the transparency of his voice hypnotic, "is Remmy. The most important person to know in New York."

Danny smiled, unsure why.

"Come on, baby, don't embarrass him." Jeremiah gave Liam a generous glance, then turned back to Danny. "You need something, just call me. Anything."

"Thanks—thank you," Danny stammered. "Definitely."

Jeremiah shook his hand. He studied him casually. Danny felt oddly observed. "Well then," Jeremiah said at last, as though pleased or impressed or ever more curious. "We're going back to bed."

The two disappeared down the hall. Danny raised a brow as Xavier stepped out of his room wearing ripped jeans and another white T-shirt with the word **fashionism** scrawled across the chest. Again, Danny tried not to stare, and even harder not to ask.

The two models stepped outside and were met by robins and butterflies, sex shops and costume stores, *pain aux graines* and *pain au levain*, bikers on Raleighs and Hybrids and skateboards and favorite piercings, drunken tattoos, tiny glass shavings shimmering in globs of bubble gum, brownstones, ginkgos, flower pots filled with forget-me-nots. The touch, the scent of the wind was scintillating. Danny was fatigued. He was restless and scarcely aware, saturated with silence and adrenaline and the novelty of everything, with questions he could no longer contain.

"Xavier?" Just hearing his own voice was a solace.

"Hm?" Xavier's eyes were closed. His head was tilted back, the sun on his face, another semester complete.

"Where—where am I sleeping?"

Xavier turned. "In Remmy's room."

Chapter Five

XAVIER, WITH HIS FRENCH ROOTS and German upbringing and his years of education in Linguistics and Aesthetics and everything that came easily, was supremely meticulous. He called their weekend *Essentials 101* and delivered something of a semester as Danny struggled to recall any long weekend having ever been longer. They combed the city and though Danny didn't always understand Xavier's digressions—modeling and academia being uniformly bureaucratic? both of them merry-go-rounds of pomp and polemics?—he listened intently as the soon-to-be-professor taught him the subways and their systems, the neighborhoods and their dispositions, the subtleties that distinguished the East Side from the West and the parks and the landmarks and the boroughs beyond. They strolled along Delancey and through the Whitney and back and forth over the Brooklyn Bridge. They pinballed through Rockefeller Center and stories upon stories under Times Square. They ate samosas in Little India. They loitered at poetry slams in the Lower East Side. They stared stupefied at the city from the Statue of Liberty, and again from Ellis Island. They smoked hookahs and caught a Mets game and browsed Juilliard and Grand Central and the gentrification of Harlem and at one point The Ansonia as Xavier went on about Babe Ruth and Saul Bellow and Beaux-Art, mansards, air conditioning, copper cornices, and how Bette Midler and Barry Manilow both started their careers singing underground at the Continental Baths before it turned straight. Chinatown. MoMA. Outside the U.N. and in it. They spent hours that felt like days people-watching. Anywhere. Whenever. Broadway from dusk till dawn.

All the while, Xavier talked modeling. Danny listened to every detail thinking there was some contest or exam or all-important moment that didn't seem real but was. "Real as tomorrow is remote," Xavier said. "Preparation implies future but in modeling there is no future. There's only now. And now is never-ending."

He pulled Danny into a supermarket. "Food: it will consume you—if you let it," Xavier said. "Don't. Nutrition labels: read them. The more words you can pronounce and the fewer there are, the better. Organic: Monsanto makes Phillip Morris look like Mother Theresa. Calories: your diet is something you maintain; it's not something you 'go on' and 'go off' willy-nilly. Shams: tell me, how will more fat make you *lose* fat? Does one plus one equal half? Vitamins, minerals: take every pill you want but a salad always wins. What was it Edison said? A blade of grass? Animals, *meat*: maybe you do but I don't know many models who eat them."

They passed gyms and peered into windows and watched women bench hundreds and men squat more, bars bending, backs breaking, veins bulging blue and eyes popping pink as grunts and groans roared hellacious. Juicing at the lockers, flexing in the mirrors, their muscles swelled to preternatural proportions as their sexual organs shrank to equally unusual extremes. Biceps turned to quadriceps swaying clumsily from strained sockets. Necks expanded until they disappeared. Clothes ripped with every step, turn, and bend, and Xavier refused. "Never. Even if Tom Ford *wasn't* in."

At bookstores and magazine shops they browsed trendy campaigns, artistic nudes, commercial advertisements, and the most avant-garde editorials. Xavier noticed a friend on the cover of *Another Man*. He opened to the spread and dissected it. Body positions. Facial expressions. Clothes, hair, and makeup. The story told. He pointed out contrasts in lighting and angling and in the shadows and textures they formed and the perceptions they produced. He recreated the photographer's instructions to the models, his demands of the assistants, his freedom from clients and directors and technicians, and everything that they, the viewers, couldn't see: strobe lights, power packs, fog machines, umbrellas, fans, anything on set that the team of a dozen or more had dutifully removed, or couldn't, but didn't have to—"spoiled," Xavier said, "by the lies of technology. Plato would have loved the fashion industry. It's the ultimate Allegory of the Cave."

With every anecdote and insight and unassuming caveat, Danny questioned more. He'd never thought so many thoughts or pondered so many possibilities and while he was eager and open, he was deluged and tiring. Xavier, though, was like a train—the cars just kept coming.

"What people don't realize," Xavier said, "is that shopping doesn't imply buying. It doesn't imply needing or wanting or even understanding, but appreciating. Our bodies. The clothes. We tell ourselves that understanding is the foundation for appreciation, but it's not. Not with clothes. Not with necessities."

"Does it even matter?" Danny said, hoping for a break but not about to ask for it, and in a way, enjoying his new friend. "Clothes are clothes. It's all the same."

Xavier smiled and leafed through a rack of T-shirts. "Here, try this on."

"I just mean it's—eighty *dollars?* Xavier, I don't have eighty dollars."

"Did I say look at the price?"

Danny shrugged, then took the shirt into a fitting room. Xavier waited outside. "See, fashion is just etiquette," Xavier said, "with some profound psychology mixed in. Go deeper though, go inside—there's artistry, there's unbelievable craft."

"Clothes, Xavier. Some thread, some dye, a button . . ." He opened the door. "Eighty dollars?"

"Wow. If there were two of you. What do you wear, kids' sizes?"

Danny stepped back inside. "I just want to model, you know. Show up. Shoot. Go home. That's all. You make it seem so complicated."

Xavier shook his head. "So—so what would you think of a teacher, of a legislator or babysitter who just 'showed up'? What would you think of a musician who was blasé about her instrument, the conductor, the venue? Modeling might seem simple but only when it's brilliant. Trust me." Danny stepped out, and they headed at last toward home. "Look," Xavier said, "no one expects you to know every detail of a Meisel or a Leibovitz or to chart the evolution of Chanel. But you can still appreciate them for what they are. You can still look at a photo or try on a pair of pants and think, Wow, who shot this? Who designed this? Of course you want to model, but ultimately you have to *be* a model. You have to appreciate. The clothes. The location. The photographer and the stylists. Anything less, you're wasting your time."

In the apartment Xavier got more personal. He brought Danny into the bathroom, stood him in front of the mirror, and told him to undress.

"Do what?" Danny didn't move.

"Take off your clothes," Xavier said.

Danny stared at him, speechless, wondering if he'd mistaken his new friend.

"Look, Danny, there's nothing you have that I haven't seen and nothing you have that I care to. You'll be showing skin every day. If not now, then later."

"Then why now?"

Xavier was gentle, but frank. "Because. You're scared."

"Scared? I'm not scared. What am I—"

"Yourself."

Danny tightened. He didn't know if he was struck more by what his roommate asked of him or sensed in him. There was a hard, endless silence, and Danny just stared. Then swallowed and turned away.

"Danny, how often do you look at yourself? Naked. In the mirror."

He shook his head, stiff like a child. "I don't know what you're talking about." And in a single step he pushed his way out of the bathroom.

Xavier turned, still standing at the door. "A lot of people *fear* themselves, Danny, but they don't go out and become models. They don't sell themselves to the world." Danny stopped midstride. "If you hate yourself, that's fine. It's practically the first requirement to modeling. But you can't fear yourself. You can't avoid yourself."

Danny turned. He looked at the floor, the walls, trying to listen.

"I know it seems vain," Xavier said. "But it's an act. It's a persona you create. Some models don't even use their real name. The pretense might last a moment or a day and it's exhausting, but then you go back to being you. The only thing is: who *are* you?" Xavier shrugged. "I don't think you know. And if you don't know—if you don't know the *real* you, then you'll never know your persona. You'll never know the difference. And you won't know who to hate." Danny folded his arms, still avoidant, but listening. "You're a product," Xavier said. "What are your strengths? What are your weaknesses? What should you emphasize and what should you improve? If it were a car or a house or a necklace you were selling, wouldn't you know every detail?"

Xavier looked at him patiently, and Danny's eyes and uneasiness began to settle. Xavier had warned him that he could get carried away. He was finishing his dissertation, *A Psychoanalysis of Beauty in the Post-Supermodel Age,* and everything he did lately seemed governed by it. Danny was grateful for the guidance, but stunned.

"Listen," Xavier said. "I'm stepping outside. I'm closing the door. I want you to go in there and *look* at yourself. *Know* yourself. Head to toe. If you want—if you can—talk to me. Describe what you see. Hate all you want, but don't fear."

Danny glanced at him, and walked back into the bathroom. He stared at the lock. He thought of turning it. He thought of his childhood. He thought of the myriad stories he used to tell himself, the games he concocted to help him divide. Beautiful Danny, Real Danny. One day a toy, the next so numb he could have been a heartbeat from dead. Beautiful Danny was cool and free and selectively amnesic, and he could hurt more times than Real Danny could bear. Real Danny thought he'd said goodbye to Beautiful Danny. He thought, he believed, he was now one. He never imagined it was all just practice.

Minutes had passed when at last he moved away from the door. He stepped onto the bath mat and turned his back to the mirror. He reached his hands above his shoulders and pulled his shirt, quietly, over his head. He untied his shoes. He took off his socks. He unbuttoned his jeans and he slowly, benignly, unzipped them. The lump in his throat only grew. He turned his palms to his sides and lowered them evenly into his underwear, then stared with a vacancy as his thumbs looped limp at the waistband. He lowered them more, and the underwear slid to his ankles. He stepped out of them, absently, and turned. And for the first time in years, stood square in the mirror.

For a moment he saw a stranger. He saw eyes, gray, blue, the early part of night. He saw a nose, slender if not slight. He saw the texture of two lips, the glide of a chin, the exactness and shame of the most understated cheeks. He saw the slope of a forehead and the secrecy of a neck and though no single feature looked familiar he saw a timeline, broken, of a person he knew.

Slowly, he stepped back. His thighs left the sink and his image stretched. He saw his collars, his nipples, the crests of his ribs. He inhaled and they rose. He exhaled and they fell. He inched back again and he saw his navel, his hips, his pubic hair unexplored. He moved back once more. His heels touched the tub and he saw down to his knees and he paused. He looked. No memories. No fears. Just a body unadorned and no judgment to place upon it. He stepped back to the sink and pulled another, smaller, maneuverable mirror out from the wall. He took his time, motionless, staring at the scars on his back, and finally, gently, without thinking of Xavier or anything but himself, he spoke.

"My hair. It's brown." He tilted his head. He moved it up, then down, profiling and combing with his fingers. "It's thick. It's messy. Like dirt." He meandered more. He searched more. And he fell deeper inside himself, turning, looking, closer and slower and seeing nuances he'd never known. Patterns in the roots. The coarseness at the back. Every follicle he owned. He studied the whole of his body from his fingers to his toes to the places he had to twist to see, and those more visible that he had habitually ignored—the public, the private, the hated, the beautiful—everything embarrassing and exceptional and entirely plain until he had little left to see or say and an incredible mixture of fatigue and novelty and catharsis cooled him.

Xavier was reading when Danny emerged. The stillness between them was kind. "Maybe . . . you'll take some pictures?" Danny said.

Xavier nodded placidly.

Danny knew even less about what he looked like on film than he did in a mirror. His childhood didn't encourage it, for a photo serves only one of two purposes: either to enlighten us of the pain felt by others, or to remind us of the joys we call our own. Danny's joys had been few. And his photos were fewer.

He stood by the window in the living room. The curtains were open and streaks of light ran across his hip where an oversized T-shirt met loose-fitting jeans. He paused, then took off the shirt.

"Nice," Xavier said. "Right there. Just hold that a minute." He unfolded a tripod and started walking around the room as he configured the plants, the curtains, his camera, and told Danny to pretend it was film. "Really, you shouldn't even be allowed on digital until you've proven yourself on film. But all anyone wants these days is fast fast fast, product product product. Models, photographers—they couldn't care less for patience, for practice. It's all try and forget. Re-try, re-forget. Throw enough darts and one's bound to stick. *You* are going to learn."

Danny nodded. "Almost ready?" His arms were dulling overhead.

"It's sad," Xavier said, fiddling with the lens, "so few of the top photographers still test on film. But the rawness, the *edge*. I mean, it *is* a test. Digital's improving but the resolution still sucks and the depth of field, the light contrasts—where's the potency, that rich, grainy mystery? If it's mystery that makes the model alluring then wouldn't—" Xavier looked up. "Why'd you drop your arm?"

"It got tired."

"Tired? Is that what you're going to tell Steven Klein when Dolce & Gabbana's dropping ten or twenty grand for you to model their latest watch, and you can't tough it? My arm got tired? What, like we're in a yoga class? You rest when you're told to rest. It's not the eighties anymore. These people are for real."

Danny repositioned his arm. Xavier returned to the lens. "It was higher," he said. "And angled out more. Exactly, right there. Now, chin down. More. Little more. Stop! Your left triceps—flex. Good. No, relax. Flex again, but just the triceps, not the biceps. And loosen the hand. Better. Now clench the jaw. Squeeze it. Bite down in the back—the molars. It squares the jaw which draws in the cheeks and accentuates the cheekbones. Triceps, Danny. Slight part in the lips. No, not that much. No teeth. Look at me . . . Exactly, but what about the jaw? Clench the jaw *and* part the lips. Both. Together. Yes. Nice! And the triceps? The chin wasn't that low. Turn the head just a few degrees left. Your other left. A few more. Not the eyes. Keep the eyes still. Find a spot behind me, lock in on it, *then* turn the head. Good. Triceps, Danny, triceps. Now draw out the chin. Keep it down, but draw it forward. Lengthen the neck. Less. Don't move the shoulders, just the neck. I know it feels odd. You have to trust me. That's it, good, just don't knot the eyebrows. Relax. Relax the eyebrows. Yes. And the bottom eyelids—narrow them. Good! Very good! Annoyed but seductive. More seduction, less annoyance. Nice, Danny, triceps, triceps! Chin, molars, lips!"

Click.

Danny exhaled and collapsed about the window sill.

"Whoa, whoa!" Xavier said. "I didn't say relax. You hold *through* the photo. That was just one picture from one look. This is film, remember; it's artwork. Precision. Let's set it up again."

Danny glanced out the window. He felt empty, numb; straining when he thought he should feel effortless. Effortless, compared to moving across the country. Effortless, compared to fear and hope and the vanity of struggle. Effortless, compared to a weekend in New York and all its impatience and superiority and hyper-diversity, all its masochism and pollution and rampant happiness. Effortless, simply to stand.

There was a heavy silence. Then Xavier suggested they switch. Danny agreed. He took Xavier's place at the camera. Xavier took his by the window. And the novice watched as the veteran sculpted. He set his feet, like Danny's. He raised his right arm, like Danny's. He flexed his triceps, relaxed his biceps, angled his head, lengthened his neck, lowered his chin, squared his jaw, parted his lips, narrowed his eyes, all, unerringly, like Danny's, as if one had left a mold into which the other stepped. "How'd you . . . All this time I . . . And you just . . ."

Xavier smiled. "Why do you think we're practicing?"

*   *   *

He was drained past empty, and he was filled beyond full. He closed his eyes and he saw clowns. He saw pigeons and hot dogs and flowers, statues and sightseers strolling through Battery Park. He opened them and saw the time: 12:33.

He curled fetal and closed his eyes and saw cars a mile or more like Critical Mass but slower and smokier and stuffier, crossing the Brooklyn Bridge. Coming. Going. Honking. Hot. He opened them again: 1:19.

He climbed down from the loft above Jeremiah's bed. He fumbled for his wallet. He took it back up the stairs as he tried to recall the last time he felt happy. Not euphoric. Not like a week ago. Just happy.

He opened his wallet and took out his only picture: Bo, Linda, Danny in between. They were smiling and he was smiling and he remembered how he smiled that entire day, his birthday party with all the bowling balls and presents and the cake and the candles, ten plus one for good luck. And his friends, how much they liked him and accepted him and never questioned, never pried, but simply welcomed and befriended him. That day. That entire year. He was happy. With Bo, with Linda. He still cried and had nightmares and got nervous that they might see him undress, but he was happy.

He smiled and wiped the tears from his cheeks. He heard Bo's laugh like a song and smelled Linda's hair like lavender and he wondered how two people could bring him so much happiness and so much pain, how they could appear so suddenly and disappear just as fast. He recalled the nights he wanted nothing more than to have been with them, driving and crashing and soaring, going to wherever it is that one goes. Not returning, again, to another orphanage.

He tried his best to stop crying. He tried to smile as he looked at them, their joy, their love, their dreams still so vivid in a photo bound to fade. He slid it back into his wallet and he wondered if they could see him, everything turning out alright.

Chapter Six

EDGE MODEL MANAGEMENT RELOCATED that spring from Park Avenue to Broadway. Martin Noy, the company's President, told the *New York Post* and other publications that the agency was looking to revise its image, and that the move was intended to help. "Soho," he said. "It's not Gramercy, not Flatiron. It's funk. It's edge. It's who we *are*. We all agreed it was time for a makeover."

It was true: the new neighborhood had funk; and it had edge, too. The new office, however, had neither. It was downier, swankier, and more urbane than its predecessor—the entrance more imposing, the layout more intimidating, the lighting more unforgiving. Martin claimed not to notice but as the elevator reached the Penthouse Danny stepped out into a semi-circular waiting area which Martin called "the foyer" and gawked. The walls, the ceiling, even the floor were all white to omission. Four black boxes—sofas?—stiff, sleek, as hard as park benches but built without backs and clad in taut, imporous leather, waited pensively in pairs at both sides of the semi-circle for someone to perch on them. A flat-screen TV posed squarely over each sofa. Coloring the screens, girls who would never bear children and boys who looked like them marched rank and file before a fusion of critics and celebrities—to the camera, from the camera, off the camera—deliberately, expressionlessly, fascistly—as an experimental blend of German techno and Italian opera pulsed from the speakers and an ambush of spotlights shined overhead.

The fashion shows, which at the moment presented the collections of Elie Tahari in New York, John Rocha in London, Love Sex Money in Milan, and Yohji Yamamoto in Paris, all showcased the forthcoming *prêt-à-porter* fall designs. Danny found himself fixated on the screen closest to him, enthralled or unnerved, or envious, but unsure why. Was it the modishness of the garments? The robotics of the models? Their absence? Their emptiness? Their remarkable dearth? Perhaps it was the combination of the two—clothes and models—the way fabrics flowed on frames like costumes draped on hangers. Was that his aim? To be a clothes hanger?

The Love Sex Money show ended. The finale concluded and Lorella Signorino emerged from behind the dividers blowing kisses to the crowd as the audience exploded with delighted applause. Danny stood in silence. And a new show began.

"Are you here to see someone?" The voice sounded bored. Danny turned toward the height of the semi-circle where three young women sat behind a plum-colored desk with the word EDGE, epic, above them. The receptionist on the left removed her headset. The others continued taking calls. Danny approached. The receptionist rolled her eyes, and smiled.

"Hi . . . I'm Danny? Danny Ward? I'm a new—"

"Of *course!*" she suddenly exclaimed. "Carla's expecting you! The fifth aisle from the left. Or third from the right. End of the hall." She picked up her headset and within moments rejoined in her colleagues' indignation. "Edge Models, please hold . . . Edge Models, please hold . . ." Danny continued on.

Behind the receptionists, caffeine was waking the agency. Voices were growing. Models were arriving. Junior agents crisscrossed the halls. The office itself fanned out into seven enormous corridors. The front of each one hosted a private conference room where out-of-town clients held in-house castings, and where weekly open calls resulted in innumerable rejections—admittance to Harvard the likelier. Danny passed four corridors and turned down the fifth. The room he passed was empty, except for a thick black table with matching chairs and two mightily framed photos filling the walls. One was of a boy about Danny's age sporting Christian Lacroix on the cover of *L'Uomo Vogue*. The other was of a young man suggesting an eerie likeness to Sasha, though healthier, and happier, gracing *Details*. Danny walked timidly ahead.

The sheer volume was unlike any other. The behemoth of the modeling agencies, Edge's Men's board alone employed thirteen agents who represented some six hundred models. The exact number fluctuated, often daily, as models were signed and released. The total, however, never included the male models in the agency's other divisions—Kids, Classics, and Celebrities—who accounted for hundreds more.

On the Men's board the agents sat facing each other at a table that ran lengthwise from the conference room to a hall at the end of the corridor. Between every two agents there was an empty chair. The organization, in theory, was meant to offer models access to their agents, and to offer agents the opportunity to collaborate. Martin called the setup hopeless and juvenile, but before the agency had moved and the agents were freed from the thralldom of their cubicles, Monika, director of the Men's division, along with Gene and seemingly every other agent, vowed to resign if they weren't going to at least decide how they sat. Martin yielded; and the divisions formed identical designs.

Monika was the only agent on the Men's board who didn't face one colleague, but all twelve. She sat at the far end of the table in the furthest of its nineteen chairs. Mostly, she paced, as she did when Danny approached, and from the opposite end of the hallway heard her barking across the Atlantic. "I'll say it *one* more time, Bernhard, and don't act like your English isn't good enough to understand me. You tell Louis I want the other—which *Louis?* What do you mean *which* Louis! *The* Louis, Bernhard. You tell *the* Louis to cough up the other twenty-five grand by Friday or I'm boarding the next flight to Paris and I'm ripping off every last one of his diamond-studded fingers. *Compris?* I'm fed up with the bullshit, Bernhard, now get me my money!" She stabbed the receiver and before Danny could breath she transformed. "Ah! Our new Danny!"

Danny turned as red as Monika's fingernails, as Carla and Luke, who sat closest to her, and every other agent glanced down the hall. Cautious but poised he walked down Carla's side of the hall with half the models' composite cards beside him. Carla stood up and met him halfway, greeting him with more affection than he preferred and in moments began introducing him to her colleagues. There was Geraldo, who sat next to Carla, and transferred from their office in Rio, then Kosuke and Surya who handled clients overseas. There was Jen who booked Edge women until just last month and Derek who spent years as a casting director in L.A. Across from Derek, and furthest from Monika, was Beth, who was as old and sharp as the industry; and then Oliver, one of Beth's first models. "Anika and Peng work with Suk and Sur on Asia and Europe," Carla said respectfully. "Luke you already met. And Monika, well, Monika's Monika—all of us times ten."

They each smiled or nodded or waved, or they gestured discreetly with approval as they continued their phone calls, their emails, pulling pages from stacks of magazines, as Danny fought not to stare at the speed, the clarity, the assurance of everything about him. They rounded the table to the D's and Carla pointed to where his cards would go. "Right here," she said. "After Danny G. Or do you prefer Daniel?"

"No, no. Danny." It was all so surreal. "Or Danny W?"

"Certainly. Danny W." And she continued walking, continued introducing, continued exhibiting her newly found model as though Danny, he, it, were a prize she'd won or an invention she'd created as her colleagues were left wondering how she always, *always* found the best.

They reached Luke's desk, the K's behind him, and Danny spotted Sasha's cards. He took one from the stack standing upright on the metallic shelf and he scanned it. "Kinzie looks different. He looks younger."

Carla seemed stung. "Kinz—Kinzie loves the camera," she said professionally. "And the camera adores Kinzie. I only send my models to the very best photographers." She smiled, so Danny smiled back, wondering why he suddenly felt awkward. "Well," Carla said, louder than necessary, "*you* need a haircut." She reached past Luke for a pen and paper, writing down everything she said. "Ask for Debbie. She knows what I want. Then come back. Luke will take your measurements, your digitals, go over paperwork. You have a busy week. Three tests in three days . . ." She hesitated. She studied him. Then shook his hand. "Welcome aboard, Danny W."

*   *   *

It was a short walk to Yuri's on 14ᵗʰ Street where a bistro was being gutted below. The photographer was crouching over an Affenpinscher bouncing hysterically at his feet when he opened the door. Dreadlocks tumbled everywhere out of a frayed headscarf and an outstretched arm exposed a network of tattoos. "Spring" from Vivaldi's *Four Seasons* catapulted past him. The energy was chaotic and quirky but it was real. And Danny's nerves began to ease as Yuri stood.

"Rock *on*, man! Come *in*." Yuri flipped back his locks and stepped to the side, clearing whatever wedge he could into a hovel the size of a prison cell. "Your digitals are on point."

"Thanks. Thank you." Danny ducked as he entered.

"It's a box," Yuri admitted. "But it's me." Danny stepped wide and was halfway into the apartment. He turned around and saw the kitchen, the office, the bed built above and a closet to the side. Thumbtacks held clippings, sketches, a mishmash of inspirations that made everything in the studio seem strangely powerful. Yuri put down the dog and fixed his scarf. "You want some wheatgrass?"

"Water?"

Yuri found a cup and filled it from the sink in the bathroom. "So listen," he said, handing Danny a glass. "I'm not that non-stop photographer-type snapping hundreds of shots an hour, testing ten guys a day. I like to chill first. Get to know each model a bit." Danny nodded stiffly. "Oh, don't get me wrong! I don't mean that Bruce Weber crap—everyone standing around naked on their head. We're not all perverts. I just mean a chat, you know, seeing what we have in common."

Danny picked up the encyclopedia-sized portfolio beside him. "You mind?"

"You should."

The book was bound in black. Yuri started saying something about the company that made it—"best fake leather"—but Danny wasn't listening. He skimmed his fingers over the letters of Yuri's name, branded at the bottom and felt some odd sense of respect, not only for what lay within but for the effort required to achieve it. He wondered if that was the awareness Xavier meant. Appreciation.

He opened the cover and was immediately gripped. A girl, naked and wet, helpless but accusatory, stared back at him. Her hair hung in clumps past her breasts, past the lens, as limp as an afterthought. Water like glue clung to her lashes, her nose, her nipples. The grooves in her ribs glistened in it. The cups in her collars collected it. Some dazzling mix of rainfall and tears.

Danny turned the page and the story unfolded. The photos switched to color but stayed swarthy and soft. The girl was in a forest, a jungle, inundated by trees soaring hundreds of feet high. And a boy, also bare, stood beside her.

"We shot that last year in Peru. I've never seen such gorgeous light. The water, the leaves—spectacular. McDonald's has probably torn the whole place down by now, covered it all up with grass and blood and—"

"Yuri." Danny looked at him. "Your work. It's amazing."

Yuri shrugged. "I've had some pretty amazing models. We won't be doing anything quite so experimental today." He reached to his office and pulled out a second, equally over-whelming portfolio. "This is my more traditional stuff, what I get paid to do. Still edgy. But kosher."

Yuri drank his wheatgrass and reached from room to room chatting garrulously about a book by Anne Wigmore as he took out cameras, lenses, film, mirrors, cosmetics, an iron, a blow dryer, a light meter, and at least as much more that Danny never noticed. He continued talking as he rummaged through the suit-cases—one full of Sasha's clothes, the other Xavier's—pairing items from each with accessories of his own until Danny became himself, Yuri became intrigued, and the light became ideal.

"I'm all set," Yuri said, closing the bags.

Danny studied one more picture, then closed the portfolios. "Me too."

Moments later, the concertos silenced. Yuri browsed his computer. "Requests?" Danny shrugged, and something lounge-like filled the air. "The arts might be brothers, but music is my master." Yuri walked to the window. "Come stand over here."

Danny obliged. Yuri inspected his skin in the light. He compared his complexion to the hues in his gamut; he moved him again, and again, and looked closer. "Your skin," he mut-tered. "It's flawless."

Danny didn't move. He stood there—no shoes, no shirt, no belt or underwear, only jeans—waiting in another world, some place that wasn't real, as Yuri manufactured his hair, glossed his lips, worked with intensity, care, and restraint. Sun dripped through the window and Danny's body, slim but sculpted, responded to every drop.

At last, Yuri picked up his camera. "It's time to work," he said. And Danny held poses he never imagined.

If Xavier was boot camp, Yuri was war. An hour had passed before they changed looks and Danny now sat on the floor. He wore linen, with one knee propped and his arm like a petal draped across it. Stillness, not motion, was the quintessential challenge, and as fifteen minutes of shifting, shaping, ever-so-slight tweaking turned restively to twenty, Yuri still wasn't satisfied. The look, he said, was off. But he couldn't indentify it, and Danny's back began to quiver. Yuri squatted in front of him. He repositioned his neck. He realigned his shoulders. He rearranged his hair, his hands. Twenty became thirty. Danny's buttocks began to numb. Yuri stepped back, he stepped forward. He lay beside him on the floor. Danny's hips felt like they'd crumble, his spine like it would snap.

"It's not working," Yuri said, without assigning blame. "We'll try the next look."

The room was tense and Danny wanted to shout but untangled his contortedness in silence, then shot page-stopping portraits as he stared into the sun.

It was early afternoon when they broke for lunch. Yuri treated Danny to his first falafel sandwich and his first lecture on art.

"The way I see it," Yuri said, "the goal for every artist, the challenge of every art, is to create a product that most closely resembles a vision. You have this amazing idea, and it's perfect. As long as it stays in your mind it's perfect. But then you start creating and suddenly it's not. It comes into being as something else. What happens in between? What happens from dream to reality, from vision to product? *Art.* Art *is* the in between."

Danny wiped the tahina from his lips, wondering if his legs would ever stop twitching. "Everything is art," Yuri said. "Inventing. Dancing. Teaching. But not every inventor or dancer or teacher is an artist. It's the sentiment that matters, the feeling in the process, the artist alone who strives within."

He was still discussing it with hints of encouragement when they reached an alley in the middle of the Meatpacking District.

Danny, however, was fighting to focus and had just realized the outfit he wore looked like the one on the life-sized cover of *Details*, lauded in the agency. He wondered if the *Details* model also had his tie taped to his shirt, the tips of his shoes padded with toilet paper, the back of his suit clipped down his spine like a dolphin's dorsal. He wondered if the *Details* model also shot on location in front of pointing passersby and if he also balanced for half an hour on one foot and countless other scenarios, when Yuri startled him.

"Danny! Focus. And you're knotting your eyebrows again. Relax."

The sun was unbearable. He wore a chocolate brown, three-piece suit in wool and a white shirt with violet twill, a tapered waist, barrel cuff, and a tie bursting gold or lava, knotted thick at his neck. He had a fob watch affixed to his lapel. He held a Montecristo in one hand, wore a rock on the other, and sweat soaked his stomach. He wanted to quit, but Yuri was determined.

"*Feel* the clothes." Yuri leaped toward him. "Make . . . me . . . *want* . . . you . . . Be a gangster, be a pimp, be a spy; be the CEO of a Fortune 500. Whoever, I don't care! But be *someone*, Danny, and for Christ's sake, make me salivate. I see a million dollars looking like a dime and I'm bored. *You* are the art; *make* yourself." He took out a mirror and angled it up and down in Danny's face. "I'll be damned if we don't get the shot."

They got the shot. Danny channeled spy, stunningly, then they walked to another alley where Yuri held up a bed sheet and Danny changed looks, and they shot again.

They shot eight looks in all. Danny could hardly move by sunset. He sat dressed and packed, sipping tea as Yuri marked film, too tired or polite or overwhelmed to leave, but just as desperate for Yuri to stop talking.

"You know what the oddity of our art is?" Yuri said. "The fascination with it?" Danny shook his head, his body torn. He couldn't fathom feeling so veteran and young. "It's that a picture is a story, told in the absence of time. How seriously awesome is that? The picture doesn't escape time. But the story within it does. The picture stops time—click!—frozen! But the story evades it. The story goes on, it unfolds. It lectures or loves or horrifies, maybe it dares or accuses but whatever it *does*, it does it out of time. Free. Forever. Completely eternal. The picture itself preserves a past, as the story within it cancels all future."

Danny nodded. He yawned. He tried to sit up, but exhaustion was winning.

"*You*," Yuri said, turning and ducking and putting away every item he had used, "are the focus of the picture. *You* tell its story. But you're not an actor. You're a model. So any actions you perform and any words you speak—they're gone. They're gone from the story but they're present in the picture because in pictures, though there are no actions and there are no words, there *is* a performance and there *is* a message. That's the allure. The stillness of it. The silence of it. And yet all that intensity. The picture I take of you is time captured. The story you tell us is time released."

Chapter Seven

HIS ENTIRE BEING ACHED. His neck, his shoulders, his calves. The arches in his feet. More so his thoughts. He did three tests in three days with three different photographers, adapted to each of their styles, their visions, their contrasting demands and adopted some twenty looks in the process. One after the next. Persona after persona. Becoming them and being them and *believing* he *was* them until he had nothing left to give and was gone. Real Danny, not Beautiful Danny, modeled. And he paid. Yuri worked him. Eryl more. Simon touched. Cool, natural, perfectly implicit like Danny's career depended on it—and Danny didn't know what to do or say or think or feel except quietly to die so he did. And now he hated himself. Like a child again, he hated himself. He raced up the stairs. He bolted into the bathroom. He tore off his clothes, blasted the water, and threw himself in the tub as the air steamed and his thoughts multiplied and his skin ripped and burned and scratched and swelled and all but pruned like grapes in the boil. Red, purple, black—it could have peeled and popped and blistered and bled and still he wouldn't have cared. Still he would have stayed. Mashing his legs, writhing his hips, pulling his hair raging *WHY?!* as he swept his hands in spasms over every inch of his body, rubbing, scrubbing, squirming, fighting, and the water spraying and his veins throbbing and nothing but fury and confusion and loneliness and loss and sickness beyond description surging through him as he curled his fingers into fists, sank deep into the tub, and kicked and shrieked and trembled and cried.

*   *   *

Danny had been in New York for a week. He went on a smattering of go-sees, primarily to photographers who said more than they thought, and whose every adulation he relayed excitedly back to Carla. Nothing had come of these meetings, but he knew plenty would. Exciting trips. Important jobs. He'd earn money and be free and his life, at last, would begin. By the time he'd been assigned his first casting he was on the verge of feeling smug, even powerful. Then he got there, and froze.

Models were everywhere. More than he could count. The studio was packed and everyone in it held an aura of honesty and ease and some shade of darkness in their eyes that whispered, "You wouldn't dare." The atmosphere was as amenable as it was taboo, though why or how was unclear. A girl at the door changed out of a dress into a tank top and jeans. Another fixed her hair as she mentioned a couple she met from out of town, and what they did when she got to their hotel. Some sat alone with books or magazines or talked on the phone with an agent. Others—many—kept busy in ways that made them seem more salient than they were, with a front, with a façade, with some slick exhibition of certainty that made anything seem possible.

Danny never felt so out of place. He moved discreetly along the wall to the floor. He felt meaningless, embarrassed. And for reasons he couldn't change. He couldn't buy a brand new wardrobe. He couldn't buy a one-of-a-kind bag, an iPod or gadget or friends to make him cool. When he turned eighteen and Charlene stopped receiving foster care, he started paying her half the rent and all his own expenses. And even though the agency "paid" for his move—advanced him the money, for he'd be billed every cent the moment he worked for them; he simply didn't know it yet—he could barely afford food or basics. Building an image simply wasn't an option.

He pulled his knees up to his chest like the flat-chested girls chatting in Russian beside him and looked about in silence. He wondered how it would feel to be known. Not beautiful-known. Just real-known. Really *known*. Believed. Understood. Special. He wondered if anyone knew the difference. And no sooner he heard his name.

Danny sprang to his feet as Sasha and the girl he arrived with smiled just enough to be nice but not enough to be accused of it, then pressed their nostrils like coke addicts and sniffed. Sasha wore his signature black V-neck with G-Star jeans and calf-high boots and hair bed-head chic; his lady friend entirely the opposite.

"I see you're all set," Sasha said, and gestured loosely to the portfolio tucked tight under Danny's arms. He pressed his nose, and sniffed again.

"My book!" Danny beamed. "I just picked it up at the agency. You want to see?" He handed it to Sasha, then grinned at the shadow beside him. "I really like *this* one," Danny said, leaning over his roommate's shoulder and pointing to a portrait in sepia.

"Mmm." Sasha leafed casually to the back. He pulled out a card and flipped it. "You're a 28-waist?"

"Carla said my measurements are great, I'll get a lot of work. You think?"

There was an arid, complicated silence. Sasha sniffed. His shadow straightened. Danny wondered what he had said. "Could I see your book, Kinzie?"

Strapped to his back like a sword, Sasha rotated his bag and removed something huge, like a binder. The corners were ragged. The spine was feeble. The covers were spread wide with nearly every page filled, as the physiognomy alone conveyed strength and experience and layers of character. Without even opening it, it suggested a passport of proof stamped with universal approval, an anthology of international campaigns.

In some ways, Danny identified with Sasha. Not his late nights or wearied look but aspects of his upbringing. He came from a broken family in a no-name town out west and wanted more. He didn't care for the army so he enrolled at a community college and halfway through his first semester withdrew, to New York, forever. It was ten years ago or more, a lifetime in model-years, and as Danny stood there, stunned by Sasha's work, he realized something was off. The work was dated. Sasha was aging. His allure wasn't transforming into one more dapper and debonair, but corroding. His youth, once so kind and unrestricted, was waning. Yet Sasha, Danny realized, had only, ever, been a model.

"Maybe you can look at it online, Danny. They're almost up to our numbers." Sasha motioned behind him. Then swiped his nose and sniffed yet again.

"Numbers? What numbers?"

Sasha and his still-unnamed appendage looked at each other. They had arrived some two hours earlier, signed in, and left. The waits were simply too long, too crowded, yet the castings—for some models, many models—were too necessary.

"What numbers?" he said again, hesitant to hear the answer.

"Every casting will have a sign-in," Sasha said, steering Danny through the maze of attractions. "It's like waiting in line at the DMV, except there's no electronic display. You have to keep track or get someone to text you."

They reached the back and Danny saw the piles of pages that were already full. He wrote down his name beside the next number: 404.

"What's—what's your number?" He dreaded the response.

"258," Sasha said. "They're going about a model a minute."

Danny's jaw dropped as Sasha and his someone shrugged and pushed further through the mob. Danny sat down with a size sheet wondering what he would possibly do all afternoon cooped up in a room full of strangers all hinting distant and glamorous and at last turned to the boy on the floor beside him and asked if he could borrow a pen. The boy reached for his bag. Danny noticed the sketch book in his lap.

"What are you doing?" He prayed for conversation.

The boy handed him a pen as he drew. "Sketching."

"Models?"

"My teacher said it might make for an unusual exhibit. She said all the homeless were getting depressing. I said models might depress her more." Danny looked around. The boy continued to draw. "You're new?"

"Yeah, how'd you—"

"Never tell anyone that you're new." He massaged his thumb into the paper. "They already know. What they want to see is how well you can bullshit. It's a game. You'll see. One big psychological nightmare." Danny furrowed his brow defensively, wondering how many models would agree.

"Don't be intimidated," the boy said, inspecting his work, then facing him at last. "Most cat-calls aren't this big. And you'll have requests, too, which are usually smaller." He turned back to his drawing. "See how you feel the first time you walk into a room of a dozen Doppelgänger all twenty-eight thirty-twos, fourteen-inch necks, short brown hair, nineteen or twenty years old; six-one on the dot. Then enter the casting and try to explain to the client why you're right for the job—without opening your mouth." He smiled. "Don't worry, you'll get used to it."

The boy returned to his work. Danny wished he wouldn't. He felt lost and willful and wanted desperately to talk, to ask countless questions and relieve himself of curiosity but didn't know what, if anything, was considered acceptable; only that it seemed silence and trivial banter were fine and fashion forbidden, unless in some languid, impassive tone or you were Heidi Klum and had transcended the unspoken pigeonhole.

"What's with the dogs?" Danny said after a time. He had noticed them as soon as he arrived, a sea of Maltese Terriers, Chinese Cresteds, baby Japanese Chins all poking timidly out of enormous purses. "It's fashion?"

The boy shook his head and drew. "Don't get me started."

"Well, I've got all afternoon."

"Yeah, and you'll need it."

"Well, I love dogs," Danny said.

"So do I. And cats, birds, elephants, every other animal."

Danny looked confused. The boy put down his pencil. "It's hypocrisy," he said. "It's double standards. For animals *and* for people."

Danny looked at the models, then turned back more perplexed.

"Those bags they carry them in were carved out of deer. That lipstick they throw in with them was tested on rabbits. The very height of the industry is a killing campaign, yet they go skipping around with their Pomeranians and Shih Tzus like they're each some innocent champion of love. You think they don't know? Fashion adores it. Designers, their assistants, they see these models and their little purse-dogs and suddenly they forget all about those Scandinavian furriers who won't stop courting them and bribing them to find a place for yet another gorgeous slaughter in their collections that the whole world will see but never buy. And they do. They use them. Because they get them for free and they think it makes them look like geniuses and they can't remember the last time anyone stormed a show or plastered de la Renta with tofu. So they think no one thinks it's wrong even though deep down *they* know it is. They know they're doing something crueler than any animal ever could. So when they see some girl and her Chihuahua all cute and loved, of course they can't help but drool at the thought of some good-hearted face repping their label. Oh sure, there's the occasional clueless model, but believe me, most play the game so well you'd never know it. That's what *I* want to see— a designer be as bold as a model and actually create something so honest we think it's real. Use some heart. Be sensitive, be progressive, be *responsible*. Not just mope around chained to the norms of greed and all the selfish industries that couldn't care less about art. Or *life*."

The boy leaned his head against the wall. Danny looked at the dogs. He felt ill, and vexed, and for the umpteenth time snatched from his shell.

"But the boys don't carry them."

"Yeah, because a boy carrying a dog isn't part of the game. A boy can love a dog just as much as a girl can, but if he's carrying one around with him you can rest assured he's not working. He could be the baddest bad-ass there is, but if he's holding a Poodle in his arms? What client's going to hire him?" The boy packed up his sketch book.

"Where—where are you going?"

"They should be up to me soon. Seriously though, just listen to the conversations. Think about what you see. Look at how everyone acts. The girls. The boys. The game. It all has a purpose. Models are only stupid when they're expected to be."

The boy walked away and within seconds someone new took his spot on the floor. Danny looked at the mob, lonely and stunned, wondering if they could have been friends. Maybe that wasn't what models did. Become friends. He couldn't decide if it was worth losing his place by the wall to find out. So he stayed. And while he waited—for hours—he looked and he listened and he thought. Casting after casting he watched and reflected, and it didn't take long before he noticed certain patterns.

Girls discussed their hair. They discussed their clothes and their handbags and how nicely they held all their makeup and their mirrors, their tampons and their contacts, their pepper spray and lotion and Kleenex and comp cards, their breath mints, their iPods, their iPhones, their Stilettos and their Chinese Cresteds. They never talked about work. They never talked about how satisfied or dissatisfied they might be. They never grilled each other about castings or jobs or agents or money or anything vaguely competitive that patriarchy would frown upon, but kept ladylike as a rule until it was safe to act otherwise. They dressed their best. And they never told the truth.

Boys, meanwhile—cool, neurotic, sour and insecure—were voluble and loud and starving to be known. They conformed to their own sorts of spuriousness, their own lies. They referred subtly to their client pool or talked nonchalantly about their social life or complained interminably about their agent not pushing them correctly or anything that helped to maintain the appearance of (still) being dissatisfied with having (seemingly) everything that (virtually) everyone else in the world—model or not—(assumed they) wanted. He was always working more than everyone, yet the market was never strong. He was always at odds with his agent, yet he never sought a new one. He was always partying and traveling and spending excessive sums of money, yet never earning his due. And he was always talking, and talking, and talking, yet never holding a conversation.

Both knew the game and played it appropriately. The only difference from reality was the very basis for the game: *he* was powerless; *he* was worthless; *he* was misplaced and disregarded and an afterthought at best, an alien to a manmade industry that selected Beauty a woman's domain. And she? *She* worked. Billboards to buyouts to spreads to campaigns, she worked. Showrooms, she worked. Covers, she worked. Fashion shows to catalogs, she worked. The female model was a working model, never some wishing, waiting, wanting model. *She* was wanted. *She* was The Man. *She* was the breadwinner and *she* was the bedrock. *She* was known and he—*he* was her knower. The men who emulated her were few. The ones who dared were many. Her world was everything his wasn't and in an industry of heightened anomaly, failure was the male model's certainty. And yet, as though adhering to some unstated, some misogynistic rule, both kept face.

She: handbags, dogs, oblivious to success.

He: wanted, working, the definition of it.

Chapter Eight

BY LATE JUNE Danny hadn't been booked. Carla reassured him with her optimism. Xavier said it was the industry's nature to be fickle. Sasha reminisced about his own sluggish start in the business. The comments, though well-intended, were hardly helpful. Danny wasn't concerned about his ego. He was concerned about his survival.

He called Jeremiah. He hadn't seen Jeremiah since the day he arrived. He slept in Jeremiah's room in the loft above Jeremiah's bed, sometimes browsing his closets or colognes or trying on a tie with a chuckle, but otherwise maintaining every bit of order. Ever since Liam had moved back into the city, Jeremiah's room, even with Danny in it, had gone idle.

Jeremiah, however, was never idle. Night after night he went from event to event: fundraisers, openings, banquets, birthdays, as well as a variety of others he didn't discuss, always gracious, always good-looking, always kind and calculated. He still modeled, too, on occasion. But only as a tool. Or a favor. Or when the money was exceptional.

The invidious and the ill-informed credited Jeremiah's status solely to his parents. They scoffed and said he was merely born into his rank, or "naturalized" into it as he was practically a teenager when his parents left Johannesburg. But never that he earned it. And they were as correct about the little they said as they were cautious about the more they didn't; for it was true that his parents' alliances had introduced him to the necessary New Yorkers, yet it was equally so that his own dexterous charm vaulted him to a class well, well beyond.

Danny had overheard hints of this. He knew Jeremiah wasn't the average model, that he likely never had been. But he knew neither the detail of his network nor the depth of his notoriety, and when he called him one night in late June already a month after their first and last encounter, he couldn't think of what to request because he had no idea what his roommate could offer.

"Pretty much anything," Jeremiah said, pouring them wine in Liam's apartment. "What are you looking for?"

Danny shrugged. "Whatever'll get me some money?" He had neither a clue nor optimism and aside from assisting on furnaces for a year after high school, no experience or résumé to fake it and no connections but Jeremiah to circumvent it. He was skeptical and equally naïve. For even without Jeremiah's aid he had assets. He had intelligence that he failed to articulate. He had beauty that he didn't comprehend. He had innocence that he couldn't conceal. For New York, he had plenty.

"You want nights," Jeremiah advised. "Keep your days free. Castings. Shoots. Lunch dates. The aim is to not have a real job but still be, still *seem* as busy as possible." He leafed through his notebook. Someone was always looking to hire. A boy. Pretty. The newer the better. "I could have a bartending job for you next week. Gay or straight, but gay is where the money is."

"Remmy, I've never even been to a bar."

Jeremiah smiled and drank his wine. "Then definitely gay. I'll get a party going for Saturday. You'll get more practice than you'll ever need."

*   *   *

Jeremiah had everything delivered—the alcohol, the mixers, the ice, the cups. Danny unpacked everything as he quizzed himself on the drinks in the bartending book he picked out at the library, then spent the rest of the day stashing Buddhas and Bonsais safely out of sight and cleaning whatever he could to keep from getting anxious.

Night fell, and the apartment teemed. Guests arrived with their own guests and the party swelled into a *Who's Who* of New York's most illustrious models. Many had just returned from shows in Paris and Milan. Others were preparing for trips to Tokyo or Singapore. Some were simply passing through— Copenhagen, L.A., a break in between. Danny listened to them talk. Not about handbags or Shih Tzus or the market someone's booker couldn't master. Not about lip gloss or night clubs or some campaign they should have booked. But life. The world. Ideas and interests and the Arts; and he envied them. He envied their opportunities, their experiences, their education and vast sophistication. They weren't the models he saw at castings, the ones who systematically attracted bevies of attention with every sly and planted, premeditated action—fanning themselves widely if not theatrically with their composite cards as though the air conditioning wasn't plenty; reorganizing their portfolios hurriedly if not distraughtly as though their agents' choices weren't informed; assessing themselves repeatedly if not continuously as though their last dozen engagements with the mirror weren't precise. They weren't the models who talked, and talked. About nothing.

They were the models he didn't see, who were never seen save when it counted. They were the models who opened fashion shows for Dior and shot calendars for Pirelli. They were the models who signed contracts with Tiffany's, lured shoppers to Guess, mused for Lagerfeld, and graced covers of *Elle*. They received write-ups in the *Times*. They got ranked by *Forbes*. They booked ads for Gap, worked Diesel with Richardson, reminisced about Avedon, and sat understated at castings—if they even attended them. More likely they were working; every day associating with another director, designer, photographer—

adapting and adopting forever as necessary. They spoke their languages. They knew their cultures. They acquired any persona and modeled to any expectation. They redefined cosmopolitan; they faked ease second to none; they impressed socialites, mystified the media, and never hinted elitist for they had little to prove with words that they hadn't already with actions. They were mild-mannered and kind and listened more than they spoke, and often viewed themselves the least intriguing at any party.

And they partied. For weeks if not months they worked meticulously, constantly, location to location, client to client, persona to persona, and when the time came to relax they rioted until they crashed. Gin-and-tonic. Vodka-Red Bull. Dos Equis by the pack. Ecstasy like jolly ranchers. "Danny, dude, your look—New York must be all *over* you." Sasha and his someone fled like phantoms into the bedroom. Madonna to Nickleback—the volume pumped. The lights dimmed. Talk of Selby and Aronofsky, a tip jar circled. Was that an Olson by the door?

"Danny, Danny, *Danny!*" Xavier spread his drunken arms wide to reveal a plain, self-scribbled T-shirt that read **silicone-free** across the chest, then swung them around his new roommate. "Dan-*ny!* I want you . . . a meet . . . three of . . . of . . . dearest . . . Thissss Tamar." (5'9½"; 114; 33; 23; 33; 2; 8; brown; blue) "Tamar . . . with . . . Next. She comes . . . the Holy, Holy . . . where the pomegranates . . . the pomellos . . . women!" She patted the *chamsa* at her neck and smiled humbly with *tichelet* eyes. ". . . is Albina." (5'11"; 121; 33; 23; 34; 4; 10; black; black) "Gha—Ghana, with Q." She offered a long, delicate, silver-lined hand and ordered martinis for each of them. "And *thiss* . . . is Isis." (5'9"; 117; 34; 24; 34½; 2-4; 9; brown; brown) Xavier sobered. "Isis is from Colum*bia!* She's at the very . . . the *very* prestigious New York Models." He slid an arm around her waist and whispered softly into her ear, "*y realmente una diosa, por no decir algo más.*" Her tawny copper cheeks lifted faintly and glowed. Danny had seen her. Billboards? Magazines? She looked at Xavier, and he knew. The photo in his roommate's room.

Vodka-soda, Vodka-lime, shots and shots and shots of tequila. Patrón? Milagro? The volume pumped more, Outkast, Pink, The Roots. "Was that your spread in *10 Men*? Just wait until Smith sees you." Pushkin and Tchaikovsky and the Russian Romanticists. Sasha and his mime meshed boisterously into the throng. A Cabernet, a Merlot, a Malbec by the bottle. A Jack on ice. Coke, and the lights dimmed further. Who if not an Olson?

"So! This is Danny?" An older, heavier, giddier man had followed Jeremiah through the mire of models and nodded approvingly.

"Danny," Jeremiah shouted over the noise. "This is *Alan*. Your new *boss*."

Danny turned away from the sea of guests and the wave of requests they flooded upon him and shook hands with his smiley employer.

"How about a drink?"

"Love one," Alan said. "Long Island."

"Oh, no Triple Sec tonigh*iiiiii* mean why not a double!"

Alan laughed. "I like this one."

Danny mixed the drink and bullshitted until Alan drifted away. Then Manhattan, Becks, Vodka-cranberry, Vodka-OJ, lights, music, Wordsworth, Dickens, snowboarding, scuba diving, pollution, famine, deforestation, coke, obesity, coke, Obama, coke, doctors, health care, food, coke, music, music, music, *more, more*, and he escaped to the bathroom spinning, spun, slow, fast, upside-down, ears throbbing, eyes burning, feet like bricks and desperate to pee, and as he opened the door he halted. He gaped. The light was blinding. The stench was revolting. Vomit filled the sink, the bathtub. Water fired from the faucet. Towels were soaked and strewn. The shower curtain dangled, ripped from its hooks. Sasha lay limp. His face wet. His nose bloody. His companion just as well at his side.

*   *   *

Aqua was a new bar, in the heart of Chelsea. The space was turquoise and dim and had acquired a reputation for its water-lined windows and liberally arranged urinals. Danny started out working Tuesday, Wednesday, and Thursday nights but after an eternal second month without a booking, and Carla snappier than he recalled—"What can I do, Danny, *magic?*"—he asked for Fridays, too.

"You won't want Saturdays," Alan said with a chuckle. "I can tell you that right now. Five nights a week for a straight boy in a gay bar is more than you could handle. Besides, Saturdays is just a bunch of high heels and tube tops. This one chipped a nail. That one lost her tiara. Why won't the DJ play Raining Men? All drama and no drink. No *money.* Some girls carry more baggage than a goddamn airplane."

Danny worked his first Friday on the last night in July. He was tired from another hopeful yet lackluster week of waiting, the resilience of the heat, and Aqua's loud, saucy nights that lingered long into the mornings. Every day he assured himself, stubbornly, that better was to come. He didn't know when, but until it did, at least he was working, he was earning. Sometimes as much as a thousand dollars in a single three-day week. And though it wasn't doing what he came to New York to do, he didn't dare complain. The money was more than he had ever earned and the inordinate tipping amused him. Patrons often left twice the cost of a drink and then thanked him for allowing them to. He told his roommates about it and Xavier explained that gay men were often wealthier than straight men, that they had fewer friends in high school and college so they spent more time studying and got better jobs. Unbridled tipping, he said, was their attempt to buy society's respect. Sasha said it was more basic. He said gay men simply had a fetish for paying for what they knew they'd never have. Jeremiah said neither.

But Danny never asked and while he found their actions extreme, he had no intent to deny them. Until Friday. The crowd changed. The atmosphere lost its aqua-cool feel and acquired a fervid, restless, bawdier one. Patrons' clothes matched the sexual tensions they brought with them and their tips—even more wanton than usual—held implications they didn't on the nights Danny was used to working. A hundred for a shot might relieve a bartender of his shirt. Two hundred, his pants. Plastic, if charged eagerly enough, was, on occasion, returned the next morning wrapped in a phone number.

Danny knew none of it, or of the man fixated in front of him. He was short and muscular with buzzed brown hair and an impenetrable goatee, his face a mix of alcohol and sun—scarlet against his bleached white, skin-tight T-shirt. He was out with friends, gym buddies by the looks of them, and was the sponsor of the night's activities.

Danny served them as he did all his customers. He accepted their banter in stride and he returned it appropriately. But despite the leads from his co-workers and the pleas from his patrons, he refused to undress. He had adjusted to doing so in front of mirrors and cameras and occasionally casting directors, too. But he rejected it outright at the bar, regardless of the tips he was told it would generate. The man with the buzzed brown hair and Stop sign-red face, however, was drunker and more determined than any. He ordered his trio's fourth round of shots and fourth Dom Pérignon Oenotheque and grinned, glad, once again, to drink most of it.

"Someone celebrating a birthday tonight?" Danny opened the bottle as though he had opened thousands.

"Just another Friday night out," the man said, and smiled, his goatee expanding. He lifted the glass to his nose and breathed deep. "Why've I never seen you before?"

"Maybe you don't know the right nights to go out." Danny set three fresh shot glasses on the counter in front of him and reached for the Chinaco.

"Then maybe *you* should enlighten me." The man leaned over the bar and gave Danny a playful, yet purposeful, pat on the cheek.

Danny's demeanor cooled. He clenched his jaw. He turned square to the man without attracting attention. "Don't you ever touch me," he said, dropping his voice and enunciating every syllable. "You got that?" He held his gaze but the man only smirked as he lowered his hand to Danny's chest, tweaked his nipple between his shirt and fingers and smothered him with his breath.

"What—scared of what might happen if I do?"

A tempest seethed within. Something gripped him and overcame him, and raged. Something, everything, a violent, belligerent, mocking string of thoughts and memories and emotions of fear and hate and disgust and depression and unconditional darkness all stormed and subsumed him like vengeance or a cure.

Yet he restrained.

Then the man smirked happier. He chuckled hornier, pinched harder, and twisted. "That it? You're scared? Of what'll happen?"

Sensibility crumbled. Danny turned and snatched the nearest glass of ice water, chucked it at the man's blistering forehead, then reached back and slammed his fist into the bush growing on his chin. Something cracked. Danny froze. The man tumbled back and nothing made sense. Nothing connected. Patrons looked everywhere, dumbfounded. The man's friends rushed after him. Bartenders stopped and stared as the music pumped and Danny's chest pounded and his thoughts blanked and burgeoned and apologized and blamed and silenced and stormed from touch to touch to touch to touch that for years he absorbed and never deflected in the longest seconds he'd ever known. Then he breathed. He blinked. His senses returned. Everything clarified more than he could accommodate and he felt an onslaught of stares, a swell of voices, some increasing commotion as shock turned to terror,

terror to pain, pain to nausea, guilt, shame, the confusion of acceptance, and without knowing it he slid slowly, madly, hopelessly in a ball to the floor.

*　*　*

Jeremiah stopped pacing at last. "So let me make sure I got this," he said again, still stern and amazed as Danny sat in silence on Liam's sofa. "You ask me to help find you a job. I do. You're at this job for four weeks. *Why* just four weeks? You get fired. *Why* do you get fired? Because you clobber someone. A guest. One I *happen* to know—not that I'm particularly proud to say I do. But still, you *punch* him. You knock him out *while* working at the job *I* got you. The next day you call me. You ask me for a *new* job. Another one. As though the first one never happened. Just like that—the end. Is that it, Danny, or did I lose you somewhere along the way?"

Danny could barely hear himself speak. "No. That's it."

Jeremiah shook his head. "So why on *earth* should I say yes? So you can break more jaws? Cost me more contacts? There are boxing rings, Danny."

Danny laid a bag of ice on his hand. There was no use explaining, no use trying. There was nothing to say. Nothing that could defend him or acquit him or restore him; nothing that might make Jeremiah understand that as paroxysmal as his behavior seemed, it wasn't his norm. He wasn't violent. He wasn't cruel. He wasn't a risk or a menace. Just desperate. Just overwhelmed. Just incredibly frightened.

"Remmy, please, anything. Bell boy. Dish washer. I don't care, I just . . . I . . ."

"Do you honestly think I got to where I am by taking second chances on thugs? Do you have any idea how hard it is to build rapport in this city? Not to mention keep it? Do you, Danny? Any at all?"

His mouth was so dry he couldn't talk. He just sat there—penitent, cross, stunned by the little he knew and chilled to no end by Jeremiah standing there staring back at him. He looked away. The silence was vexing. He thought of all the boys he met, the models who earned their money every conceivable way they could but rarely, actually, modeled. And he wondered if he was one of them—if that was what was happening or already had. He swallowed in torment. He looked at Jeremiah gazing cross-armed out the window. There was a sense of unrest, some numbing, nagging discontent between them as though neither were sure of what to say, yet neither satisfied to end the conversation.

"I got a call last week," Jeremiah said at last. "There's . . . this woman I know. She's British. She's rich. She's very rich. She lives up in Lenox Hill and she's looking for a new—I forget what she called it. Basically, an exercise partner. Someone young. Someone energetic to . . . well, motivate her. The pay is decent and the hours are early. You'd be done around nine, then have the rest of the day free." He rubbed his neck. "What do you think?"

"All I do is . . . walk with her?"

Jeremiah paused. "All you do is walk with her."

Danny got a pen and paper. Jeremiah read off the telephone number.

"I'll tell her to expect you. Her name is Marina."

Chapter Nine

THE F TRAIN RAN LATE that morning, and Danny reached the condominium sprinting. A middle-aged man, reddish and tomato-shaped with overcompensating posture, stood at the door. He wore a stone gray suit with shiny gold buttons and a pin over the lapel that read WILLIAM, and with hardly a glance he raised a hefty leg to the side and let it fall gracelessly in Danny's way.

"Marina?" Danny said. "I'm here to see Marina." William stood like a wall. Danny fidgeted, breathless. "Please?"

The doorman stared, then rocked stiffly aside as Danny zipped through the foyer. He hardly noticed the rugs, the floor, the gilt-framed mirror or 19th century oil paintings but went directly to another, thinner, older gentleman, attired like the first with a badge that read HAROLD.

"May I help you, young man?" He spoke slowly as though omniscient or bored. Danny calmed and asked for her again. Harold nodded, then gestured opposite him. "Please, sir. Sit."

Danny wiped the sweat from behind his ear and sat down on the further of the two matching settees. He glossed the fabric with his palm, the Italian damask, the pale silver lilies, burl wood at the sides. He noticed the delicacies of the rug in mauve at his feet and the Longcase clock standing masterfully against the wall, and for a moment he wondered. About beauty. About wealth. About desire.

"Yes, Madame . . . Certainly, Madame . . ." Harold hung up the antique receiver and stuck his thumb into a panel of buttons beside it. A rush of cables and cords racketed skyward as a string of buzzes penetrated the lobby, until the elevator was distant and only silence remained. Danny turned to the panels and to two screens the size of CD cases above them. One was blank, scratchy and opaque. The other was just as turbid but clear enough to see a door slide open and a figure appear. All he could see was a silhouette, the face indiscernible, the movements slight, and as the buzzes and racket returned Danny stared even harder at the screen, at the ambiguity and the oddity and at this woman who would pay so handsomely, so readily, for a companion.

The elevator reached the ground floor. The door opened and the figure exited. There was a brief lapse from the time the image on the screen returned to its standard, spacey state to the moment the profile appeared from around the corner. Then she did. Stately, she stepped into the corridor, her back erect, her breasts afloat, some intimidating display of certitude or indifference or mocking resolution librating across her shoulders as she surveyed him. Her eyes were copper and rich, the color and character in harmony with her hair, and while neither looked particularly tired or lonely they were both easily, impatiently desirous. They wanted something. Something beyond the morning hour. Something beyond a day, or two, or even three. Something, if possible, beyond reality. The want was all about her. It trailed the canals in her ears, the crevices of her lips, down the slopes of her brows and the canvas of her neck and it pulsed from every ebb and flow of her body, invisible bursts of pheromones spouting from her thighs, her wrists, her hips, from every turn in her navel. Danny stood up. And swallowed.

"*Dani*el." It was a word; but it was enough. She was forward, and she was firm.

"Marina. Hi. Can I . . . call you Marina?" He stepped forward, offering his hand.

"It is my name, is it not?"

He raised his hand a little higher. "Well I actually prefer to be—"

"Daniel *Ward*," she said, her hands on her hips, her eyes lodged in his, her words circling the lobby in search of something hollow to absorb them.

"You can just call me—"

"Shall we, Daniel? Or must the sun rise *and* set in vain?"

"The sun?" He raised a brow.

"Well, do not just *stand* there. I have not hired a mannequin. Truly, leash me up and let me out. For heaven's sake, *woof!*" Marina opened her eyes as large as golf balls and nailed them to Danny's. He congealed in confusion as she inclined her head at him, snapped it forward and back and Danny broke from his catatonia with a bolt to the side. She pulled her hair into a pony tail and spun it into a bun keeping her eyes moored to his and her posture exaggerated just enough to reveal a single, negligible deposit of pudge where the bottom of her form-fitting tank top approached the top of her low-rise capris. "Will the fat burn itself?" She marched through the hall, glanced sharply in the mirror, addressed the doorman with an apathetic nod and a vacuous "*Will*iam," then turned north along Fifth Avenue, opposite the zoo, leaving Danny bewildered at her heels.

Lenox Hill was serene but vivacious with babysitters born in Warsaw now living in Astoria, house cleaners from San Juan commuting from Far Rockaway, dog walkers from Stamford by way of Paris all scurrying from block to block, grateful for a summer without ten-year-old girls in plaid skirts and their twelve-year-old brothers in clip-on ties capering contentedly to school or to their nannies' new Benz.

Danny drew even with her as she neared the first traffic light.

"Oh, Daniel!" she said, as if pleading for him to cease some onerous conversation in exchange for more mirthful one. "*Tell me something. Tell me something splendid! Tell me something supreme!*" Danny looked at her. Marina looked at the traffic light. Red turned to green and she stepped into the street, leaving him, again, in the distance. Again, he caught up.

"Really," Danny said, "you can call me—"

"Something *mar*velous, Daniel. Something utterly refulgent. I am just so truly supine today, so listless you see. Aurelian, Daniel! Tell me something Aurelian!"

"Marina, I don't—"

"Lucius Domitius Aurelianus? You do not know him, Daniel? Do you jest?"

"Jest? No, I just—"

"Oh, pray tell, what *do* they teach you poor Americanos these days? Dreadful. The great Aurelianus, Daniel, was Emperor of the Roman Empire. *Restitutor Orbis.*" She circled her hands high and wide. "Tell me, you *have* studied Latin. Or are you—" But she was stifled by a spate of honking taxis. "Bloody hell! At this hour? And we call ourselves civilized? I *do* contravene!" She lifted her bosom, straightened her posture, and huffed. "Daniel Ward. Truly. Must I beseech you? Something grand already. Something bra*vur*a. Thrill me! Shock me! Titillate me!"

But he was speechless. He was lost to such sensationalism, such magniloquence, and why she kept calling him Daniel. He didn't know half her words or anything Latin and started wondering if it was all just a game she played, some addiction she nourished, a test she administered to each of her prospective partners for it couldn't possibly be real. And assuming it was— a game, an addiction, a test—he wondered to what extent he was willing to sport, to feed, to pass, and if it even mattered. His options were numbered and money was money. Nothing could be easier and Jeremiah wouldn't stay patient forever.

"I . . . I . . ." He quieted, and sighed. They walked on in silence as the city fell farther behind and only the sound of the leaves pacified the discomfort between them. Then Marina started clearing her throat. Loudly. Repeatedly. They passed the Dene and the East Green and she kept doing it and as they passed Mother Goose and the Falconer and King Jagiello she did it more. Danny began to jell, aggravated and embarrassed and at least as bewildered, scrambling for something, anything to say, and without knowing why or how he thought of his magazines and blurted out, "The tongue of a Blue Whale weighs as much as an elephant."

Marina hardly flinched. Her lips, her cheeks, her chin all exalted, she strutted on. But like a student cheating on an exam she strained her gaze at him. He was mortified, dumbfounded. He blushed at his feet wondering what sort of fool he was trying to make of himself and how long it would be until she laughed yet said, "They're a hundred feet long and have veins big enough to swim through," and thought he would melt.

"Ahh! Ah-ha-ha! Oh, Daniel, you are simply marvelous, just brilliant you are. The tongue of the Blue Whale weighs that of the elephant? Well, I do say, just envisage being licked by *that* beastly fellow. How exquisitely sultry! How sensually suffocating! Tell me, Daniel, what else do you know of tongues?"

He was more baffled than ever and stammered to please. They continued deeper into the park passing monuments and museums and talking at length—Marina, mostly—to Danny's infinite bewilderment, about tongues. Then lips and teeth and biting, and they reached the bridal path and Marina made a confession. "You see, Daniel, I find little else in this tenebrific world of ours more magnificent than food. How I utterly de*light* in it. All of it! The textures, the tastes. Their salmagundi of scents at the reaches of my throat. Ambrosial. Simply am*bro*sial! Oh, Daniel," she said, sighing ethereally, "I am a woman of desire, you see. Of epicurean delights. Sybaritic stimulants. *Need* is for the masses. But pleasure, Daniel, *pleasure* is for the privileged. That, of course, is why you are here.

Not to curb or quell my cravings. Oh goodness no! God itself could not accomplish that. No, Daniel, you are not here to help me eat less but to *burn* it, these calories I consume." Then abruptly she paused, and as though heeding a voice inside her head she turned. "Goodness, Daniel, faster. What is this, a bloody parade?"

She lifted her elbows and broadened her clavicles, added inches to her torso and over-rotated her hips as Danny doubled his pace with ease. They merged into the traffic of exercisers all rounding the reservoir and it didn't take him more than a few steps and the sudden strength of Marina breathing beside him before he sensed it. The monotony. The universality. The collective identity of the pageant they joined. Ages, races, sizes, shapes all varied and yet everyone seemed the same. Everyone seemed unfulfilled. Everyone looked as though they were trapped in a sort of paradox they couldn't conquer or even understand, yet would never dare, or desire, to escape. He saw it in their eyes. He saw it in their chins. He saw it in the way they pressed their shoulders behind them and shrugged and laughed and placed each foot with tension on the ground, and breathed. He saw it on the face of their dress, the Under Armour, the Everlast, the Oakleys for him, the Patagonias, the Reeboks, the Y-3s for her. He saw it in the comforts they created—the way clothes are calculated to do—and he saw it in their every contradiction as well, all that was veiled and all that was revealed, the little disguised and the plenty disclosed. He saw it, too, in their every movement. He saw it in their necks and in their thighs and in their aggrandizement of exertions like acrobats probing for applause with every action, yet staring strictly ahead like models on catwalks praying that fixation meant invisibility. He saw it all about them, in their every attempt at self-deception, and they looked unwell. Psychologically. Emotionally. They didn't seem themselves, whoever they in fact were. Confident *and* naïve. Trendy *and* unique. Signs of sophistication and control mixed with simplicity and candor. They didn't want to be there. Yet did. Just not as they were. And neither as they weren't. They all aimed at perfection and invariably they succeeded, and in the process failed. The eternal paradox.

Danny was intrigued. Marina was saying something about the tragedy of struggle talking more to the wind than to anyone in particular, and Danny was distantly intrigued. These people he'd never known. These people who didn't know themselves. Outwardly they looked so complete, so flawless and ideal and self-assured, and yet inwardly so torn. They longed for something. For the same thing. A thing they would never define, yet would define them forever. They yearned for it. They demanded it. It was amorphous and ambiguous and an unrelenting necessity. It was as migratory as the wind and as vital as water. It was cultural and ephemeral and as changing as the setting sun, as elusive as the midday shadow, and somehow they each knew it better than they knew themselves.

Beauty.

What exactly beauty was Danny didn't know. It wasn't that he didn't recognize it or understand the idea of it but simply that he never formed a notion of it. And certainly never sought it. He never contemplated the details of his face or his body or considered ways to highlight them. He never compared himself to others or aspired to chance ideals. He never exercised beyond play or bathed with exceptional products and though he never ate very much either, it wasn't his intent, nor anything he related to aesthetics. He never chose to go to bed hungry.

Somehow it seemed everyone rounding the reservoir knew this. It was as though they sensed his indifference or ignorance or extraordinary laissez faire demeanor just as he sensed their struggle to fake it. For they looked at him. They gazed and they glared, they studied and they denied, they admired and resented and turned questioningly away with their expressions still strangled in a cross of desire and shame and befuddled envy. But they looked at him. They had everything and wanted

more, and whether it was ego or greed or both, they were cha-
grined; and Danny was intrigued. One after the next they fascinated him: all perfect and displeased; all perfect and
dissatisfied; all abundant with work and wealth and family and
friends and houses and cars and things they could buy, and all
snug in every way possible save the one imperative way that the
public dismissed but privately craved, that they felt shame for so
passionately desiring and seeking and needing and needing and
demanding but missing as they walked faster and swung wider
and breathed deeper and stared harder and tried miserably to
curb their perpetual conflicts amid looks of manic-depression,
synthetic-realism, beatific-visitation, and in a hopeless, senseless, invariably self-sustaining sort of way, sado-masochism.

Beauty. The bitch of it.

". . . but it is all so de*lect*able," she said, still talking, tangent
to tangent, as Danny faded in and out unsympathetically. "So I
eat and I drink and it does not *look* like a lot, not at the time it
does not, but it most certainly *is*, Daniel, it *tis* for by the end of
the night I have eaten handfuls, dozens of their bloody bite-
sized finger-foods, and it simply does not matter the occasion,
these unimaginative, unimpressive, unwilling caterers always,
but I tell you *al*ways serve my most favorite hors d'oeuvre and I
absolutely loathe them for it. I loathe them! If I died today,
Daniel, right here and now and you sliced me open and probed
inside, do you know what you would find? Figs, Daniel, *figs*—
countless figs, each wrapped in finely cut strips of the choicest
prosciutto, stuffed with almond-scattered mascarpone, and
bejeweled side-to-side with warm mists of caramel. *I eat them
whole!* Oh, Daniel, how I loathe them!" She dabbed her fingers
against her temples, patted her palms against her neck, and lowered her head as though lamenting an unforeseen death; then
revived. "Of course you might think someone as titanic as *I* has
no place walking—that I should pick up my satchels and run.
But I will have you know, Daniel, that running burns glycogen
before it burns fat and I do not aim to burn glycogen. I aim to

burn *fat*." She slapped her size-six hips, gripped them and tugged. Danny wondered if it were true, or if she simply wanted it to be. "Daniel, you need not contort yourself. I am well aware of your opinion. To you we are whales, all hippos and seals with dysfunctional thyroids, I know. But what do—"

"Marina, I never . . . When did I . . . No you're not!"

"But *what*," Marina insisted, "do you know of *fat* anyway? Just look at yourself! You are a bloody scion! Just how thin are you? What *do* you weigh? No! But no! Inquiry annulled. I do not wish to know . . ." She placed one hand gently on her bosom and waved the other abstractly in front of her. "Oh, bloody hell, tell me! Go on. Say it. One fifty? One forty-five? *Ten stone?*"

"Ten stone? What are you—"

"*Less?*" She turned and stopped and seized him as a train of exercisers surged by. "Arms up," she said, easily authoritarian, then bunched the sides of his T-shirt and pulled. The fabric squeezed against his skin revealing an outline of torso. Danny looked away. Marina gaped, then released her grip and suppressed a grin as she rejoined her colleagues in orbit. "I dislike you, Daniel Ward. I simply dislike you." She sucked in her stomach. "And purchase some bearable attire. Something halfway fitting. What is this dishabille? You look like a clown and I am not entertained."

Marina pulled back her shoulders and quickened the pace. Danny tried to ignore his overwhelming embarrassment but couldn't keep his fingers from finding every stain and hole in the mass of material he wore. He felt cheap and wanted to escape, to vanish, or at least apologize for his poverty and lack of education and undernourished upbringing and these rags he had worked nights to afford. Furtively, needlessly, he glanced at her. She gazed ahead—expressionless; blank; statuesque—her eyes transfixed on something that didn't seem to exist. He was certain he had ruined it. He didn't know how but was certain he had. The relationship. The job. The money. Even if he hadn't he was sure they were a failure either way. How different, how enormously incompatible they were. Still, he wished he could salvage it. He wished there was something he could do or say or reverse to retain it. She had everything he needed. And yet what, exactly, was she seeking?

They completed the lap around the water and retraced their route through the park back to Lenox Hill. A few steps outside the condominium, William opened the door. Marina mumbled his name, then checked herself in the mirror as Danny trailed anxiously at her feet polishing and re-polishing his atonement with such sincerity and concentration that it wasn't until she stopped abruptly in front of him and he collided into her that he even realized they were back.

She lunged with a grunt.

"*Dan*iel!"

"Marina, I'm sorry! I wasn't . . . I didn't . . ."

She straightened and glared at him, heated and hard though not entirely disturbed. She held him there with nothing but her eyes and the rhythm of her breath, for a moment that felt like a million, then picked up a thin white envelope from the table at Harold's hip and presented it to him.

"Marina, I—I'm sorry if I—"

"This," she said, "is yours," handed him his due, and about-faced to the elevators. Danny looked at the envelope, then back up at Marina, puzzled and foreign to everything the morning had been and just as amazed by all that it wasn't. He didn't know if it was the brevity of their goodbye or not knowing if he should return that confused him more, but as if she heard his thoughts she stopped and turned. "Next time," she said, a richness, a fullness, a mild humor in her voice. "*Do* be punctual. Tardiness is *most* unbecoming." Then she continued around the corner and became a blur on the screen above.

Chapter Ten

A T PRECISELY SEVEN the next day, Danny greeted William at the door, then Harold in the foyer.

"Morning, Harold."

"Good morning, Mr. Ward."

"Marina, please?"

Danny sat down on the further of the two settees as Harold phoned Marina and the Longcase clock chimed. A rumble leaked from the elevators. The buzzes began. Silence came at last and a door on one of Harold's screens slid open. A figure appeared. The door closed. The raucous returned, then stopped, and Marina, clad in gleaming white Reeboks and a brazen red combo, stepped perfectly from around the corner.

"Harold."

"Madame."

"*Dani*el."

"Marina . . ."

She swept over the runner, glanced in the mirror, mumbled "William" at the door, and turned north along the park amid the house cleaners and babysitters and dog walkers. Her shoulders were back, her clavicles high. Danny broke the silence.

"I'm wearing a new shirt," he said expectantly. "New shorts."

"I feel so im*proved* today, Daniel. So remarkably improved. I feel . . . I feel . . . I feel like Aphrodite, rising from the sea."

He glanced at her.

"Yesterday was so violently hot, Daniel, so thanklessly infernal. Oh, but today! Listen to the birdies carol. Listen to them call. The Cape May Warbler—where are you, my little mustard-rump chick? Tsi-tsi-tsi-*tsi?* Tsi-tsi-tsi! And there, the Scarlet Tanager, a female no doubt with such a brief and pulpous cabaletta. How guiltlessly she chirps, like an ailing baby robin choked by tonsillitis. Sing! Sing, my queasy coniferous ave. Sing me your paean. Chik-burr! Chik-chik-*burr!*"

"I don't—"

"Oh, Daniel, summer in the city *could* be quite lovely I suppose, yet everyone vacates and the result is simply vapid. Like an amusement park filled with broken rides. What a yawn. Of course, Jonathan and I venture to Rye and the Hamptons with the rest of hoi-bloody-polloi but the *traffic*, Daniel, the traffic is so utterly bullying, so brutally hectoring that I—that *we* much prefer the Poconos instead. Have you been, Daniel? Have you been to the Poconos?"

"No," he said. "I haven't."

"Oh, but you must, you certainly *must*. The trees. The mountains. The privacy, Daniel. I do refrain from lauding it to too many, naturally. I prefer that it remain as is: my own little Canopus for me and my dearest coterie. And apropos coterie, how *is* my magnificent Mr. Jonker?"

Danny was looking at a homeless couple lying on blankets under an archway, wondering why he'd spent so much on a T-shirt.

"Daniel."

"Huh?"

"Mr. Jonker. How is he?"

"Oh. Um. I don't know. He's never home." To please her? To appease her?

"Well, Daniel, Jeremiah *is* a busy man. I suppose I do see him from time to time. Just last week I believe. Oh, where were we? The theater? Stella's? Yes, yes, I saw him at Stella's. She was hosting a trunk show or a gala or some immaculate affair as always, and he was there. He looked well, quite valiant indeed. And that *Liam!* Oh my word, the twosome they are— the incarnate, the avatar of the chocolate-covered strawberry. How utterly delectable! How tauntingly delicious! Truly, Daniel, every time I see them together I want nothing more than to pluck, dip, and swallow. Yum, Daniel, *yum!*"

Danny rolled his eyes. "That's wonderful."

Marina turned. "I beg your pardon?"

"Nothing," he said.

"No, Daniel. You said something."

He paused. "Why'd you even ask?"

"Ask?"

"About Remmy. About how he is."

"It is called conver*sa*tion, Daniel. Must I defend mere colloquy?"

He'd never heard the word but muttered "No" as they reached the end of the lap and turned away from the water. He glanced at her, erect and at ease and he wondered what she was like in public, the "private"-public, the places she went that others didn't, the events she attended that others couldn't, those glitzy functions at which invitations were required and paparazzi trolled and passersby craned their necks with envy and pride as though simply seeking out a friend from the pageant of lights and smiles and cocktails, gazing straight past the security guards, the maître d', the paparazzi, directly at Marina. And what did they see? Did they see a woman provoking and offending the other guests with her icy narcissism, her vainglorious detachment? Did they see her interrupting? Diminishing? Disregarding? Did they see her histrionic gestures and extraordinary deportment and recognize her imperial timbre? Or did they, perhaps, see someone else? A Marina adored and exalted. She among admirers. Or better yet, did she go unnoticed, buffered by the multitudes who in effect were no different? A Marina among Marinas. Was that it? They were all the same? Yet Jeremiah—was he one of them? A Marina? Was he always, or only when he was with them? Was there some disguise he donned, some performance he played? Would Marina not see through it? Was she an actor too? Was it all just one big show?

"Yes, yes, yes, it *was* a trunk show. How could I have forgotten? I saw the most exquisite strapless dress, silver chiffon of some sort or another but thinner and even more translucent and I simply *had* to have it. I had to, Daniel. It was the perfection of fashion, *any* girl's dream, but . . ."

He hadn't realized he was listening. "But what?"

"But . . . but my breasts." And she raised her hands to prop them.

"Oh." Danny swallowed.

"Well," she said, "I suppose bigger isn't *al*ways better. And to think how much I paid for them!" She chortled, more to herself than aloud. "Of course my girls have not inhibited me before, so I did what any scrupulous fashionista would: I stood Stella aside and I said, Stella—mind you, Daniel, I might have had one Bellini too many by this time, but who hadn't?—so I said, Stella, my British sister, my fellow daughter of Her Majesty the Queen—I *said* I was besotted, messy as a dog's breakfast!—anyway, British sister, fellow daughter, whatever else I said and surely need not have, Stella dearest, I beg you, an alteration, what can be done; for your prim pleats shall never hold these dirty pillows. Right there, Daniel! Right there at Stella's show I called my breasts a pair of pillows and as surely as the sun shines some cold, edacious, utterly obdurate dicksplat quoted me in the rag the next day. The poor bastard would be unemployed if not for me! Forget him. Stella is making the necessary adjustments and that, Daniel, is grand."

Danny turned toward the reservoir and closed his eyes.

"Truly, Daniel, you *are* exhausting."

He nearly laughed but restrained, and they walked on in silence. Every sound seemed heightened—Marina's breathing; the stones crunching; the wind and the leaves and the alternating arias of Cape May Warblers, Scarlet Tanagers; the children playing; the dogs panting; the taxis honking. Still quiet, amazed, he followed her into the foyer. She handed him an envelope, and she smiled in a way he didn't understand.

*   *   *

The temperature cooled again that night and the following day Danny met Marina at the same seven o'clock hour amid the same plush seats of the same Lenox Hill condo. She looked spritely as she approached him, changed but with such subtlety it was unclear. It could have been her hair that was treated or her lashes that were lengthened, or that she was a shade browner than yesterday's bronze. If it was her teeth that had been whitened or her lips that had been filled, he wouldn't have known which, yet whatever the change and however illegible, the impression of one was certain.

"Did you sleep well, Daniel?" She finished arranging her hair as they walked past the zoo, then casually adjusted her electric-yellow top as they entered the park.

He forced himself not to look. "Yeah. You?"

She glanced at him, then kept adjusting. "Occasionally."

He felt it again—that pull, that trap, so stealth.

"It depends," she said. "On the circumstances."

He stared ahead. "They . . . change?"

Marina straightened. "Do you have a girlfriend, Daniel?"

He turned to her. "A girlfriend? What's that have to—?"

"Yes, Daniel, a girlfriend."

He paused. Then looked away. A girlfriend? There were no girlfriends in Gary. Girls in Gary were selfish. Girls in Gary were loud. They were uneducated and pregnant and cared more about Welfare than wellbeing, more about Beauty than being beautiful. They allotted untold hours that

turned to afternoons if not nights minding the synthetic collections of hair and nails they masqueraded as their own,
happy to bury the natural and the genuine below the artificial
and the illusory, eager to enhance their falsity spending entire
days at salons paying for pampering they couldn't afford
while orating about boys who couldn't afford them. Boys
they didn't even want. Only what was a part of them. Jason
and his arms. Kevin and his smile. Everyone they could
name and for any reason in reach. Danny and his silence.
Danny and his mystery. Danny who never desired them but
whose disinclination attracted them. They speculated wildly
and wantonly about him, about his basest wants and these
"games" he played with them and every detail regarding how
he was packaged. Everything they would do to him and all
the more he'd do back.

They wanted him.

They wanted his.

But he didn't want them or theirs or anyone's and he was
done with being wanted. He was tired of being a toy. He was
bled of his availability. He knew he wasn't normal, that his feelings, his dearth of them, his numbness and dormancy and
seemingly hopeless asexuality wasn't normal. He realized it
about the time he was reaching adolescence and arrived in Gary
and everything from the agreed vocabulary to the standard pas-
times was mutating. Words like *cooties* had turned to *coochies*.
Anything *nice* was now *naughty*.

Danny distanced himself. He didn't disappear or reject his
classmates or do any of the things they said he did. But he
inverted. He hardened. Like a glacier in the ocean, an island
in the sea, all the world revolved about, flowing as it did, lust-
ing as they would. And he watched. He disregarded aesthetic.
He disregarded norms. He disregarded girls and their fronts
and all the boys who baited them. He knew enough about
"attraction," enough about "nice." He knew enough about
naughty and coochy and candy and cock, and about secrets

upon secrets of nightmares and crying and all the things his peers were just then exploring. He wanted, only, to heal.

"*Well*, Daniel, either you do or you do not," Marina persisted.

He suddenly hated himself. "No. I don't."

"Is that so, Daniel? Indeed, I am surprised. And why not?"

"What, is there some law against it?"

"No, Daniel, but there is a *norm* encouraging it. There—"

"Yeah, and what do you know about norms?"

She turned.

"I . . . I'm sorry . . ." He looked away.

Marina adjusted her posture. She raised her chin, her collar, her breasts—her pair of dirty pillows. She inhaled and exhaled precisely and audibly and quickened the pace as Danny cooled. He stared strictly ahead. He refused to acknowledge her, to permit her, but couldn't escape her. He couldn't understand how simply she invaded him yet knew nothing about him. Nothing of his hurt. Nothing of his fears. Nothing of his confusion or desires or longing to forget and develop and be. To become. Nothing of anything and yet so callous and entitled, so quick to attack and never retreat.

"Tell me about modeling, Daniel." She smoothed her hair.

"What about it?"

"What jobs have you worked? With what photographers?"

He sighed. "I haven't been booked."

"Oh, how unfortunate. Not even once? Is that so, Daniel?"

"Yes, Marina. It is so."

"Well, why do you reckon that is, Daniel? What do you—"

"Marina, come on! Really?"

"Really what, Daniel?"

"*This*. This discussion." He knew she didn't mean it. He knew she wasn't cruel or trying to be but he couldn't figure out how she could make him feel like it was his aim to fail, as if he hadn't been picking himself apart ever since he arrived—day

after day, casting after casting, searching every flaw, taking
every criticism. If he knew what was holding him back he
would have already fixed it. But what was he supposed to do
when one agent told him to grow his hair and another told him
to cut it? How was he supposed to react when one client said
he was too thin and another said too fat? His teeth weren't
entirely straight but no one wanted him to smile. He had a
mole on his neck but Cindy had one on her face and if clients
asked photographers to edit out entire tattoos, rashes, and scars,
not to mention enhance jaws and abs and shrink waists to nothing, how hard could it be to remove a single mole? He was
aware of his pigmentation, too—his virtual lack of it—yet
everyone advised staying out of the sun. "Prune isn't in . . ."
His features, clearly, were anything but masculine, but what
teenage Prada or Gucci model's were? Besides, he didn't care
about the coveted campaigns. A back-to-school sale at Payless
was plenty. Maybe it wasn't the ideal, but it was work. It was
something. It was decent and far better than nothing. He knew
he wasn't perfect but he never thought imperfection alone
could keep him from working.

"What's there to say? Why'd they even bring me here?
They just throw me into this ocean and if I swim they're
golden, I sink no one cares. They'll find someone else. They'll
scout till they do, till they find someone who'll soar." Danny
flattened his hand and sliced it like a plane, dejected through
the air. "It's not fair. Sink, you sink alone. But do something
good and suddenly everyone did something to help."

Marina held a hand to his face. "I will have *no* more of this
hogwash, Mr. Ward, this analytical poppycock. If you think I
have hired a Socrates you are most categorically mistaken. The
sun is invigorating and your joylessness does not comply."

"Just frustrated," he said, and resisted the temptation to
judge her, or emulate her. She paid him well. She slid her
palms over her sports top like a corset, lifted her posture, and
continued on with an air of satisfaction. "And the girls just

make it so much harder. Look at what *they* do. Then look at what *we* do. What we *don't* . . ."

"And yet," Marina sighed, somewhat pleasantly, "you do not have a girlfriend."

"Marina, *please*. What's that have to do with anything?"

She schooled him with a glance, then returned calmly to the absence ahead of her. "*Join* the very force you cannot beat, Daniel, that which you cannot contain. Socialize. Fraternize. Consort. Gain acquaintance with your colleagues and show them that *you*"—she jabbed a finger into his arm with unanticipated power—"like *they* . . . must be met." She paused. Then padded her tone. "Girlfriends help. You mingle, Daniel, do you not? You attend bars, lounges? Similar establishments?"

It all sounded strange. It sounded cryptic and exaggerated and in a way belittling. And yet true. "You're telling me I can't model on my own?"

"I am *tell*ing you to be *seen*. And that a woman, Daniel— girlfriends—shall help. One never knows who might be watching." She turned to him. And he turned to her. They veered away from the water and headed back to Lenox Hill, Marina all but glib, and Danny absorbed in her counsel.

*   *   *

The next day she showed the same subtle verve and wore the attire to enhance it: white spandex shorts that barely covered her bottom; a white manguito tied at her bosom; white Asics; white socks; a white headband in her hair and a white vintage Swatch watch on her wrist, with her nails painted pink. Danny stood as he watched her exit the elevator and nearly lost his balance a moment later as she turned the corner in front of him.

"*Dan*iel." She handed the envelope to Harold, who gulped and looked away.

"Ma—rina."

She turned and pranced down the hall leaving Danny to tag hurriedly at her heels. She stepped outside and as he sped up to even with her she cast her arms wide with glee. "Oh, this day, Daniel! This life! Do you feel it? The wind, the sun! Heaven on the lips like a warm chocolate soufflé, piles of powder, sprigs of mint, raspberry sauce to eternity. Yes—and a *late* harvest Chenin Blanc."

He glanced at her.

"Entertain me, Daniel. Tell me a story. Something light. Something amusing. Tell me about your life. Mr. and Mrs. Ward. From where doth Daniel come?"

He stared ahead. "That's . . . complicated."

"Well, I am not seeking a synopsis of human reproduction." Her lashes fluttered. "A novice I am not, Daniel."

"I wasn't suggesting you were."

"Were you suggesting the opposite?"

"What? No, never mind, just never mind."

"Never mind indeed, Daniel. Now, Jeremiah tells me you come from Indiana—Gary in fact." Danny rolled his eyes. Marina cleared her throat:

If you'd like to have a logical explanation
How I happened on this elegant syncopation,
I will say without a moment of hesitation

"Oh, the pure hell, the sheer calamity I have heard the place has become. Just the thought of such vice, such iniquity . . . And you were born there, Daniel?"

He stared quietly into a stand of distant maples wondering how he would explain. How he would answer one question and not answer the next. He kept thinking, trying, wishing, but couldn't sugarcoat his past or figure out how it had gotten so dysfunctional; when it went wrong or why it had to be.

"No," he said at last, his gaze drifting to the leaves. "I wasn't."

"Oh, thank goodness." Her relief sounded genuine. "Where then, Daniel?"

Squirrels jumped from branch to branch. "Houston," he said.

"Houston? A cosmopolitan fellow? Oh, and here I mistook you for a vagabond, just another peripatetic boy journeying dolefully nowhere." She ran a nail over her collar and down the declivity of her neck. Then straightened. "And what *of* Houston, Daniel? Do you advise a holiday there? Do you endorse its museums, its operas, its restaurants?"

"I . . . I was still young when . . ." Explaining seemed hopeless.

"You were still young when what, Daniel?"

"When I left."

"And moved to?"

"Roswell."

"Roswell?"

They never fell. Those flimsy little branches, and they never fell.

"At what age?"

"Three."

"Because?"

"Because . . . Well . . ." He disliked her energy, her interest. These memories she refreshed. He had started over and restored himself and there was nothing else to say. "Because my mom wasn't . . . ready to raise me. Because she—"

"Oh, no, no, *no!*" Marina raised a hand and halted. "You will *not* dampen my day with your sob stories."

"*Sob* stories?"

"I do not wake up with the rest of the working world to paddle about in your pool of tears. If I ask about your mum or your childhood or the Big-bloody-Dipper, Daniel, what makes you think I want to hear Broadway's latest Macbeth?"

"It's just the way it is! It's the truth!"

"The truth? Damn the truth! I would have died a thousand deaths if I collected the truth. For whom do you take me, Daniel? For what? The bearer of your burdens? The towel for your tears? I do say, a reassessment is speedily due." She snapped and turned and continued talking as he leaped to catch up to her.

"You asked me about my *life*—"

"—a reality check, as you Americans say—"

"—and I was just trying to explain—"

"—as though I asked to psychoanalyze—"

"—you just—just wipe me way—"

"—bloody sing-song about Mummy and her . . ." But she stopped. She gasped. She reached out her hand, clenched Danny's wrist, and like a child yanked from a street he flung about-face with his unfettered hand landing hard on her hip and his nostrils sunk deep in her cleavage. "Look, Daniel. Do you see?" He turned as quickly as he could.

"Those," she said, still frozen and oddly enthralled, "those are Coton de Tuléars." He followed her gaze to two little dogs on alizarin leashes led by a tall and muscular man who looked like a bodyguard. Danny hadn't been there a week but he noticed the oddity immediately. From Havaneses to Bergamascos, Shiloh Shepherds to Yorkshire Terriers, the Stabyhouns, the Chinooks, the Hungarian Greyhounds and Peruvian Inca Orchids all walked a dozen deep. And no matter how much their respective keepers claimed to love them, not one had a bodyguard.

"The breed," she said quietly, almost covert, "originates in southern Madagascar. Intelligent creatures. Alert, affable, affectionate. Presumed relation to the French Bichon and Italian Bolognese. Yes—the black snout, the wide-set eyes, the lofty, triangular ears. Those brawny necks and chests pressed low. The moderate tuck up. The tapering tail." She drew a hand to her cheek. "Why, I've not seen a Coton since my Snuggles passed."

Danny cocked his head and stared at her. It wasn't that he expected her empathy or even wanted it but that he never thought two random dogs would acquire more of it. She had never even met them. *They* had never met *her*. He couldn't believe how easily she pushed him away and glowed: "Oh, what *champions* of the canine world!" she said. "Breeding at its utmost! Grooming without equal!" She started slowly to bow. She bent at the waist, her heels joined, hips thrust back, her breasts falling dangerously forward. They were about to tumble entirely when some gravity-defying force contained them, quivering like Jell-o at the top of her manguito. The man looked down. The collars lured her closer. "And *these* are divine! Sevan himself could not cut stones this exquisite."

She reached out a hand and in the bat of an eye the man swept both beings under one burly arm. "Madame . . ."

She righted herself instantly. "Oh, dear, I meant no ill," she said, sweet as candy, and trailed a finger about her bellybutton. "Admiration is *all* I intended."

The man kept his grip but relaxed his gaze. The dogs looked as small as squirrels against his arm and Danny could no longer tell which specimen Marina looked at more. The bodyguard twinkled. He moved one animal to the opposite arm, propped them high at his chest and tested her. "Do you have any idea how prized these puppies are?"

Marina didn't miss a beat. She set her hands at the base of her back. "Do you?"

And they were lost in flirtation, the dogs their agent, and Danny refusing to listen. He wished those two little fur balls would roar like lions in her face or piss rainfalls down the man's arms but they did neither, nor anything, and Danny turned away wondering how an entire city of dogs could be better fed, better dressed, better educated than he was; more loved than he was. The Mastiffs. The Akitas. The Azawakhs and countless other uptown sweethearts that made Danny think of the boy at his first casting and the fashion he critiqued and if any of it was honest. If these dogs, whose walking and pampering and medical bills could end hunger, were nothing more than status symbols of society's elite, and really no more regarded by their supposed "companions" than the creatures they ate and the rest they wore. He looked long at Marina, the bodyguard, the dogs they ignored. The man said something witty and she laughed like gold glistening in the afternoon sun. She no longer kept a pet. Yet her status was well beyond.

*   *   *

Friday couldn't have come soon enough. Danny was desperate for a break from the endless waiting, the routine failing at yet another week of castings, and from Marina as well. Her volatility. Her ease. Her power.

He sat down and Harold called up as scheduled.

"*Si, Lucia* . . . Then *wake* her . . . *Si, despiertela* . . ." Harold hung up the phone and nearly an hour later a contour unlike Marina's appeared in the haze of the monitor. Harold glanced up, and just as soon looked away. Danny stood as she turned the corner. She wore a T-shirt and fleece pants and stale, muddled makeup, her hair hanging heavily. She walked by without a word, down the hall without a glance, and stepped outside without any reaction save a flinch as the sun struck her face. Danny followed behind her, impatient and angry and determined not to talk. They were halfway around the reservoir walking inch by inch like geriatrics out for an early summer stroll when Marina moaned: "I have a headache the size of an earthquake."

Danny cringed, but could feel himself yielding. "Did you go to bed with it?"

Marina raised a hand to her head. The sun shined magnificently across the water. "Had I gone to bed with it," she said, "would I not have taken the suitable antidote *then* so I would not feel like a bloody train wreck *now?*"

He couldn't fathom why he cared. "My roommate says never take pills."

Marina sighed. "Shock of the century. Mr. Xavier Legard?"

"You know Xavier?"

"He has met me."

Danny bit his tongue. "Well, he says the key to good health is just three things: water, water, and water."

"How very novel," she said lethargically, but began to walk faster, and gradually to open her eyes.

"First is the water we ex—the water . . . in *which* . . . we exercise." Danny turned. Marina twirled a finger. He felt compelled to impress her. He spoke slower, and clearer, and in a way happier. "That means swimming. Xavier says it's the best exercise there is. Second is washing. Never make the water too hot and never, *never* use soap on the face. It makes more pimples than it blocks. And third is diet. Xavier says to drink eight cups of water and eat ten fruits and vegetables every day to clean out the body. Maybe—well, maybe that's what you need, Marina. A cleansing."

She shook her head as a hint of energy returned to her lips. "Your juvenescence is simply inimitable, Daniel. The man is a philosopher. He is a vegan and a masochist. He calculates his environmental footprint and wears a shirt stating **before *and after*** across the chest. He considers modeling an *art*, and you suppose I cleave to his counsel? His erstwhile theories of goodness and naturalism? Are you mad, Daniel?"

"Xavier has fun."

"Xavier is lame."

"It was just a suggestion, I mean, it's *water*. It won't kill you."

"One," Marina said, standing straighter, talking louder, gesturing now even wider. "You will not see me swim in *any* body of water—holy, salty, chlorinated, or otherwise. Two, to bathe without facial sanitizer is incomprehensible, not even fitting of comment. And three, if I want my Cristal, or my Almas, or any of the sparse joys of this blunt world then I shall have them, and I shall have them without limit or fuss or *any* care of *any*thing but that of the moment and I will *not* dilute my few precious pleasures with your catalog of Xaverian measures. My triptans suit me just fine and I will enjoy them as I please."

"I never said you couldn't."

"You implied temperance."

"I suggested the obvious."

"You insinuated censure."

"I was just trying to be *help*ful!"

"You were in*tend*ing to belittle."

"Are you always this impossible?" He faced her directly and for the first time felt any sense of confidence before her. "Or am I just lucky?"

She walked erect. Her cheeks were soft. Her lashes were light. She set her hands on her hips and looked full, cleansed as though recovered, as though there was something about these confrontations she enjoyed. The tension. The arousal. The testing of limits and in turn excitement. A game? A goal? They exited the park and she breathed deeper; they entered the foyer and she stood taller. She glanced narrower and smirked stealthier and as she handed Danny his daily envelope she seemed whole and healthy and sharp. "Yes," she said. "I am." Danny reached for the cash. But Marina quickly retracted it. "And yes. You are."

Harold studied the wall.

Chapter Eleven

MOST OF THE AGENTS had already gone home when Beth called with the good news. Danny was at the library reading a tattered *Warriner's English Grammar* between issues of *National Geographic*, trying to ignore the daily 5:30 phone call when he would check in and find out that his chart was clear or that an option had come off or that everyone, again, was too busy to answer one simple question and he'd hang up the phone feeling like the ultimate loser of the most thankless industry imaginable. But as he was leaving the library after a stifling week with Marina and two numbingly static months as a model, "Edge" appeared on his phone and he stopped, unenthused, in the stairwell.

"Hello." He couldn't bare another agent calling to know if he could canoe or ski or ride a horse and then hang up the phone thinking a booking was surely imminent but never hear of it again. It was like online dating, without ever getting a date.

"Danny, it's Beth. Just a quick head's up, sweetheart. *W* confirmed for Monday. Call-time is 5:15. I've already emailed you your details. I'd love to chat but we're—"

"*Wait* . . . Beth! I'm . . . ? Am I . . . ?"

"Are you what, Danny, it's just Derek and I and we're trying to get out."

"I'm sorry, it's just . . . it's my first booking . . ." There was silence on the phone as visions of independence spun summersaults in his head. "Beth?"

"It is?"

"Beth, thank you! I'm going to—"

"Danny, didn't you sign . . . in the spring?"

"Yeah, something like that. End of May? Why?"

"Just . . . just checking."

"Beth, I'm going to make you proud—really, really proud."

"Good. That's good. And Danny. Get some rest this weekend. Monday will be a long—a *very* long day."

*   *   *

He passed the weekend on water and adrenaline and erratic bouts of self-doubt until on a dank, sleepy Monday morning he came to a trailer the size of a bus in the heart of Tribeca. He reached for the door, timidly, and a man carrying a walkie-talkie looking fresh as flowers darted out. "Hey, Danny, vanity's still prepping," he said as he walked. "Just relax." And he went on down the street as Danny stepped inside where from a litter of more walkie-talkies he heard the same vibrant voice. "We have Danny on the mo-ho. We have *both* talent on the mo-ho."

It was quieter, steadier than he expected. Pens and papers and half-eaten muffins lay scattered about. Music played quietly as a man in high tops examined curling irons and the woman beside him covered a table with cosmetics. Two girls, each Danny's age, steamed clothes more expensive than cars. A third consulted her boss about hats, gloves, various scarves. Danny decided not to interrupt. He put his bag on a sofa and sat down, he assumed, unnoticed, and listened to whispers and sighs about anything from Jean Yus to Giorgio Viscontis, violet Tufas by Manolo, someone's boyfriend who had cheated, which agencies were going under, and the driver everyone wished would stop snoring.

"Zoë?" The walkie-talkies all blinked. "How's Una?"

The stylist stood by the bathroom. She went to knock on the door when it opened, and a girl (5'11"; 123; 33; 24½; 34; 4-6; 9; burgundy; auburn) with the most delicate lips and ears and cheekbones like bridges between them stepped out.

Zoë paused. The hairdresser continued his arranging. "You feelin OK, sweetie?" He studied her sideways. "Cause if you gotta heave, girl, you go right back in that cubby and you *stay* there till them pretty pipes be clean, you hear?" She looked at him plainly, from behind a long rack of gowns. "You ain't so special, sweetie, these clothes make me wanna puke too, but I ain't chokin." He puckered his lips; then cracked a smile.

The model, svelte and striking, eased past the hangers. Zoë's assistants fumbled to help, but she sat down alone under an arc of light bulbs and stared oddly at the mirror in front of her. Everyone watched. She closed her eyes. "I'm fine. I promise. I am." And as if to prove it she turned sharply to the hairdresser. "Now Oman, how many times we work together? You know if I had to puke I'd aim straight for your pretty little perm before I hit any of your precious products." She winked. Then subdued.

"Girl! Sit up and stop your playin. Come in here lookin damn near scary as death givin Mama a heart attack. Oohwee." Oman ran his fingers through Una's hair, lifted it, massaged it, contemplated it, then selected the appropriate supplies and started the saga of how he met his latest paramour. Una just sat there, quiet and soft, tired if not pensive as Danny approached the breakfast table and caught a glimpse of her profile in the mirror. He wondered what she thought, what she saw. She looked reflective. She looked serene. She glanced occasionally at Oman and the arrangement of the pins he planted in her hair, but otherwise stayed focused on herself. Danny looked at her, the stillness of her image, and he felt calm. But sad.

A hand went up beside her and the woman next to Oman patted the chair next to Una. "Ready for you." She smiled at

Danny. His heart suddenly hammered. He forced himself to grin in return and felt the heat from the vanity like fire at his face.

"I'm Danny."

"Jessica," she said, and wrapped a Velcro sleeve around her wrist and up her arm. "Have a seat. Your skin is amazing. You must hear that all the time."

Danny blushed. Oman stopped preaching mid-sentence and turned. "Danny."

"Yeah?"

"Oh sweet Jesus, sista would *kill* for some skin like that. You moisturize what—three, four times a day? Estee Lauder? Olay Regenerist? Some *au naturel* humectants? Olive? Shea? It's quillai, I know it's quillai. Honey? Avocado? Don't be *shy*, sweetie, we all family up in here." Oman leaned over, still holding Una's hair. "Now tell Mama all your secrets."

Danny thanked him demurely and sank down at once into the neighboring chair. He dried his palms on his pants, then met Una's gaze, genial and composed in the mirror. "Here— here's some fruit," he heard himself say. He passed her his bowl with a shrug. "If . . . you're hungry."

She studied him closer. There was an honesty he knew, like benevolence or pain. "Thanks. I—I love blueberries."

She reached delicately for the bowl. Neither left the other's gaze for an eternity that ended a moment later when Una smiled and rolled her eyes toward Oman. "I'd turn, but . . ." Danny mimicked her in a hurry and they continued talking by way of reflection with nothing but their eyes and lips and chests in motion.

"So what agency are you with?"

"Edge," he said quickly. "You?"

"Willy," she said. "But I'm switching as soon as shows end. I'm just *tired* of it. Always pleading for my money. Like it isn't mine." She groaned and said something about ethics, about games and runaround and giving credibility to industry stereotypes, but then stopped and sighed as though she didn't see the point. Suddenly she looked up. "Not a word, Oman."

"Sweetie, who I gonna tell? You can't trust Mama?"

"So where will you go?" Danny asked.

"At first I thought Edge. Then I realized I'd just be going from bad to worse. Maybe not with money but with intimacy. You're just numbers there, aren't you?"

Danny shrugged.

"You're right. You're absolutely right. It's not worth discussing. I'm going with Women or IMG and that's that. They're as enthusiastic about me as I am about them and in this business that's the bottom line." She glanced at the berries. Danny didn't move. There was something brilliant about her. Something assertive, strong, yet unpretentious. She chose one and ate it. "In any relationship, I guess."

"Oh, no doubt, sweetie, it is, it *is!* It's like what happened with me and Eduardo, that Spanish fling I had goin on last summer until *one* day I wake—"

"*Oman.*" Jessica smiled with a glare. Oman whipped his head, and winked.

"Maybe that's the trouble for me at Edge. There's all these bookers and I haven't really connected with any of them."

"How long have you been there?"

He held up a peace sign as Jessica dabbed balm at his lips.

"Two years? Move on. Our careers are too short."

Danny shook his head. "Two months."

"And before Edge?"

"No one."

Jessica spun him around before he could see the look on Una's face. She nodded as she inspected him, her work, the product. "You're good till Oman's ready for you."

Danny turned back around, to Una opening a book. He looked at it. Then at her, looking at him, at his reflection.

"What's—what's the book?" He never felt so out of breath.

She held it up. "Know it?" Danny shook his head. "But you know Kerouac . . ." He shook again. He felt awkward. Una closed it in her lap. "So where are you from?"

"Everywhere," he said. "You have a pen and paper?"

She rummaged through her bag. "What for?"

"The title."

"The title?"

"I'll get it. At the library."

Una paused. She lingered on his reflection. Then she tore a piece of paper and hardly looked at what she wrote. "If you like *The Dharma Bums*, and even if you don't, promise you'll try *On the Road*." Danny nodded as Una went on: Burroughs, Ginsberg, Cassady, underlining every word and eyeing him in the mirror.

"Now that's enough note-passing for one morning," Oman said. "Girl, *sit* still. All this hair you got. Worse than a goddamn buffalo!"

An hour later, Danny was standing in a sea of lights, in a lounge across the street. Una walked in like fireworks wearing a kaleidoscope of aqua, indigo, amber, and cream, a patchworked silk georgette with Sergio Rossi pumps and an arm of gleaming bracelets. The room silenced. Danny stared. He felt trivial in his tuxedo.

"Could you imagine if people dressed like this?" She stood next to him, revived, yet suddenly soured. Danny turned. A man with a ponytail and a camera and conceit across his chin ambled toward them. He was short, but talked like a giant.

"Well, hello, Una," he said, looking up at her.

"Hi, Jevon." She hung her head to the side. "Are we here to work today, Jevon, or should I prepare for something less professional?"

"Una, do you wake up with an attitude or do I just bring out the best in you?"

"Neither. I guess not everything is as it seems—or everyone as *he* seems."

"Or she?"

"Just give us our assignments, *Jev*, before I start gossiping with Zoë and Oman." She glared at him without a flinch until the photographer cleared his throat, and shrank.

"We're shooting eight, hopefully ten looks," Jevon said, speaking strictly to Una as he explained the story. "It's called 'Woman's World.' Shopping. Dining. Traveling. Various scenarios of a socialite, including being attended to." Still, he looked at Una. "We're starting with an evening look. You're awaiting your aperitif. You feel the server scoping you. No eye contact though. Not with the camera either. The world is yours, and you have no limits. I'll guide you as we go. Any questions?"

Danny opened his mouth. "Yes," Una said. "What's his name?"

"Whose name?"

Una scoffed. "Some things don't change, do they, Jevon? *His.* The other *model.* The server scoping me." She looked at him. "Oh, for goodness sake! Jevon, Danny. Danny, Jevon."

Jevon shook Danny's hand and turned back to his crew. "Here we go, people! Can I get readings? I need you back, Danny. More. More. *There.* Una, over a little." He looked through his lens and the lounge was alive. Someone appeared with a meter and called out numbers. Jevon asked for marks on each of them. Someone else laid tape as every stylist stepped in. Oman nipped at Danny's hair. Jessica combed his eyebrows. Zoë made adjustments to Una's gown, then tugged on Danny's tuxedo as Oman detailed Una's curls and Jessica powdered her face.

"Sweetie, you look better than gold," Oman said. "Got envy written all over me."

"Today," Jevon said.

"Natasha who? Lily who? Work it, girl, *work* it!"

"We've got a schedule, people! *Oman.* Jesus Christ, Oman, to*day.* *Thank* you. Danny, angle it out more. And away. Can we get him a tray? Eyes on Una. Always. You're a server, the place is upscale. Five-star. No. Not staring. Just concentrating." Jevon clicked the camera. He glanced at it, clicked again. "You're concentrating on her. You're preparing for her. Good, but not so close. A few steps forward, a few steps back. Forward, back, forward, back. Never closer than those chairs." Click. Click. Click. "Can we get some music going? Please? Una, that looks great. Just what you're doing. Danny, slow it down some. Tray at your side." Click. "Other side." Click, click. "Una, eyes over here. Up and right. Up and left. Show me the bracelets. Left elbow out. Oh, God yes. Good! Amazing!" Click, click. Click, click, click, and an oddly electric blend of heavy metal and seventies porn music filled the room. Click. The energy intensified. Zoë stepped on camera. She smoothed her hands around Una's dress below her breasts and back to her shoulder blades, then readjusted the clips behind her and tiptoed away. The digital technician said something about blur and Jevon walked over to the computer. Oman raced into frame and checked the pins in Una's hair. Una's eyes fluttered tiredly. Danny watched and wondered, and fell out of character. "We're looking good, people! Una. Hips. And turn toward me some . . . more . . . a little more . . . stop!" Click, click. He moved in as he shot, navigating his way through velvet chairs and pentagonal tables. "Danny, rest a minute. Una, legs just a little wider . . . right knee bent . . . chin down . . . eyes over your shoulder . . ." Click. "More." Click. "Nice!" Click, click. "Love it!" Click, click, click. "Amazing, Una, amazing!" Click-click-click-click-click.

A few minutes later Jevon moved them to the bar, Danny behind it, Una in front. Jevon stepped back. He called orders to an assistant. Everything seemed to accelerate. Danny took off his jacket as Zoë instructed. Jessica told Una to look up. Zoë stepped behind Danny and slid a hand down his pants and he stiffened. Jevon asked if they could move any slower. Oman mumbled something snippy and kept plucking at Danny's hair. Zoë tucked the shirt down tight with a sweep and a fondle. Danny froze in disbelief. Jessica and Oman switched spots.

Zoë pinned Danny's shirt. The music turned to rock and there was a moment of calm as the stylists scattered away. And Danny remembered to breathe.

"It's going to be a long one," Una said, gazing distantly. "Fifteen, sixteen hours. One look at time. Just one at a time . . ."

"You're OK?" Danny said.

"If I wasn't, would it matter?"

"Great, here we go," Jevon boomed. "We're looking good—really good, people. Una! Una, the lounge is packed. Everyone's eyeing you. You're waiting for your drink. I want angelic but mysterious. I want feminine but indifferent. Show me that cover you know I like. *Ohhh, yeah,* and we're shooting!" Click. Click, click. "Don't stop, Una. Danny, chin down, eyes up. You're mixing but you're scoping. Less mix, more scope." Click. "Move in some." Click. "More in line with Una. And the camera." Click, click. "Turn out a little." Click, click. "I don't know how you do it, Una!" Click, click, click. Zoë darted into the frame. Una remained precisely in position as Zoë operated her gown, then disappeared. Click. Her eyes met something invisible. Click, click. She owned it. Click, click, click. The posture looked painful and altogether perfect, and slowly, gently, she kept her elbow turned out as she rotated her chin. One Mississippi, click-click-click. Two Mississippi, click-click-click. Three Mississippi, click-click-click. Everyone stared. The music jammed. Lights flashed and her eyes never moved, her arm never twitched, her intensity never faltered. Oman fanned himself frantically. Jevon spewed accolades. Danny did as he was told, and realized he was working with the best.

Jevon orchestrated two more variations of the same scenario before announcing they got the shot. Zoë, Oman, Jessica, and their assistants sped back to the motor home. The models followed after them, Una with her pumps in one hand, her gown in the other.

"So I guess you're still pretty new to all this," she said. "Still enamored."

"I guess. Kind of." He peeled the tie from the shirt, the tape left dangling.

"Let the stylists do it. The clothes are too expensive. So, why did you start?"

"I thought it would be a good way to leave home. Finally start my life."

"I thought you said you're from everywhere. How can you get away from home if home is all around you?" He glanced at her. "I'm teasing."

"I lived in Gary, Indiana the last seven years."

"Music Man? The Jacksons?"

"Them and a steel mill. A pay check if you're lucky. I had just turned thirteen, summer before seventh grade." Danny opened the door. Una stepped in.

"So that means your birthday's soon? You're a Cancer? A Leo?"

"Damn, sweetie, you walk slower than my great aunt Gigi Mae—and she's *dead!*" Oman was under a table sorting through a suitcase of hair supplies. "Well, come now! Get them million-dollar rags off your skinny little ass and sit yourself center so Mama can see you. All the times we work together and I ain't *never* seen you so distracted."

*　　*　　*

They shot three more looks, then broke for lunch. They shot another three and broke for dinner. After that they shot three more. It wasn't much before midnight—though long after Danny's feet began to blister and his adrenaline to abate—when they wrapped. He sat down beside Una as she massaged her calves by the vanity.

"Can you check if this is right?"

Una glanced down, his booklet of vouchers pristine. "No one ever showed you?"

"Should they have?"

She pulled out a booklet of her own and skimmed what Danny had written. "No, that can't be," she said. "One twenty-five is the day rate. Editorial is never hourly."

"My email said one twenty-five. That's not . . . per hour?"

"It's editorial," she said again, as if this time he'd understand. "Some editorials don't pay anything. And if they do it's never more than one twenty-five. A day."

His jaw dropped. "Overtime?"

She sighed apologetically. The silence was rhetorical.

"Then why—why in the world does anyone *do* it? How do we make any money! We just work for free? We just—"

"Danny." She was stern and hardly loud enough to hear. "*Don't* raise your voice at a job. Ever. A client can destroy you. And no—you don't shoot editorial for money; you shoot it for pictures, for your book. To get catalog work. *That's* where the money is. Not in fashion. Sometimes . . . it just takes a while. You have to be patient."

He dropped a fist on the table and turned away. What had he been if not patient? Finally, the relief of a booking, the euphoria of achieving a goal—once if never again—and it bit with a rip and a burn. Be *more* patient? Was the work not perpetual enough? How many times could he hurry up and wait? How often could he get excited and stop, get ready and stop? Go go go and stop. Rush rush rush and stop. Wait. Wait. Wait. Hurry-rush-go and wait . . . wait . . . wait. Race and wait. Race and wait. Indefinitely? However long necessary? Just be prepared and available? Be perfect and stay perfect? Be present in energy and character and time, and forget himself? Hungry? Impossible. Thirsty? Nonsense. Exhausted by all the manic uncertainty? Don't sit or you'll wrinkle. Don't scratch or you'll smear. Don't lean or touch or do anything natural that might not be perfect. Just stand. Still. And wait. Hurry up and wait and be ready. And perfect. Expect nothing because nothing is earned. Don't be you but the model we've made you. Don't think or feel, but express our beauty. *Our* creation. *Our* completion. Beautiful? Forget beautiful. Be *beauty*. Just be it. Be ideal, be model, our art. Perfect and exact—the vision and the execution and you, ours, the model made. The model manipulated. Perfected. Sold. And forgotten.

He stared at himself in the mirror, his first booking an eighteen-hour day for $125. Minus commission. Minus taxes. And that, she said, was normal. That was expected. But what if the shoot had lasted even longer? What if it was twenty looks instead of ten, or there weren't any meals, or the agency didn't like the photos? Or what if the magazine chose not to run them? What then? Were there no standards? No rights or guarantees? Was there no union? No security? Just exploitation at will? Was it the same for actors? For writers? Photographers and stylists? This wait? This patience? This poverty?

"Listen. What are you doing for your birthday? I'll celebrate with you!"

Danny shook his head. He tried to appreciate her enthusiasm. "Nothing," he said. "I don't even know anyone. Just my roommates and one's in Chicago, another's in Paris, the third could be anywhere." He wanted to revive but simply mumbled and shrugged. "Don't think I really care anyway. Besides, we're under age."

"Oh, don't worry about that part. I'll take you out. Will you let me take you out? You're not one of those macho-type guys are you? You know: Haha, hoho! Man work! Man feed! Woman clean stay home make baby!" She held her arms wide, her chest full, then deflated and burst helplessly into laughter. Danny joined, uninhibited.

Oman caught Jessica's eye. Jessica ran her thumb and index finger across her lips like a zipper. Oman snapped his head from side to side and they cheered in silence from their respective sides of the trailer, and continued packing their belongings.

The models caught their breath at last. "You can't sit at home on your *birth*day, Danny. It's like, illegal! You *have* to go out. Celebration is required."

It felt right. Saying yes felt entirely right. Taking the invitation and celebrating his birthday with someone who wanted to celebrate it even more than he did felt nothing other than right. And yet he was terrified.

"OK," he said, trying his hardest not to shake or shine. He took out his phone and dialed her number as she recited it. A chime rolled out from her bag and his heart raced, his hands warmed, his every sadness washed away.

Chapter Twelve

FROM GREENWICH VILLAGE to Lenox Hill, everywhere, something seemed different. Maybe the air. Maybe the trees. Maybe the F train was just a little cleaner, not as shrill. He passed bakeries and the bread smelled sweeter. He crossed corners and the drilling sounded softer. From the juice he drank to the shoes he wore he didn't know what it was or that it was anything at all, but he sensed it. Something.

"They do some landscaping over the weekend?" he said as they entered the park. "It looks . . . fresher."

Marina glanced at him. "Have you been smoking, Daniel?"

"Well, something's different, that's all. Something's definitely different."

"I do say, Daniel, something most definitely *is* different. *You.* How gyratory you are today. I envisaged a bit more lassitude following such a protracted day—with Jevon no less." She lifted her chin. "I more enjoyed the placid Daniel, him of old."

"Marina, you've known me for a week."

"Oh, blither blather, Daniel. *You* have known *me* for a week. There is quite little for me to know about you." She marched like some sort of model-soldier-gymnast mutt, and he refused to let her deflate him.

"How was your weekend?" he asked patiently.

"This gig, Daniel, this job—was it worth your time, the tumult? Did it pay well?"

He glanced away. "Yeah. Pretty good."

"Of course," Marina said, "I would hope we might establish some consistency, some reliability between us?" She straightened even more. "Indeed, it would be a pity to have to find a new . . . partner. So soon."

"Marina . . ."

"The pay—it is enough?"

"Yes, plenty!"

"And the hour—not too early?"

"No, not at all!"

"And this route we walk—it suits you?"

"Marina, I'm sorry, I won't cancel again."

"Noted." And in an instant he felt like a child. They kept on in silence with guilt relaying between them and Danny determined not to accept it. He fiddled with his shirt. He kicked at the gravel. Marina sighed, and without a word kept him repenting.

"You know this book," he said at last. "*The Dharma Bums.*"

She sighed again. "I was raised with tutors, Daniel."

"So you do?"

"Oh, and they say even inference can be taught."

"I thought I'd read it."

"Read it? Daniel, you are a *model*." She laughed dismissively. "Why *ever* would you *read*?"

"Well—well, why not?"

"Well, for one, Daniel, clients are not seeking sages, are they?"

"Sages?"

"Perhaps it would be more practical to blend tan lines instead? To tone your tits? After all, Daniel, you are not a bottle of wine; you are a stick of butter, bound to expire."

Danny turned. "I'm not trying to be a brain, Marina."

"And you, Daniel, would need much more than Kerouac to make you one."

He looked back ahead and forced himself not to respond. He didn't understand. Why should she care? Why should it matter? If he wanted to grow, if he wanted to try, what difference did it make? Xavier was almost a professor. Jeremiah read constantly. Sasha hardly knew the alphabet but he painted and built sculptures that were impressive. Maybe Marina didn't know it. Maybe clients didn't either. But it seemed every model he'd ever met had a talent or passion for something. No one was *just* a model.

They had slowed behind two old ladies and were trying impatiently to pass. "What's so wrong with it anyway? It's a book."

"You *do* amuse me. So innocent you are, so blank." Marina raised her arms. "Oh, Gnostics, beware! Bodhisattvas, take heed! The great Daniel Ward hath arrived!"

"Body-*what?* You know, I know models smarter than you."

She waved a hand. "Read. Read it all. Read everyone. Read Dickens, Joyce. Bloody hell, read Homer and Hesiod, Sappho and Solon, Virgil and Seneca."

"Marina, I don't—"

"*Yes*, Daniel! Dante and Boccaccio! Goethe and Schiller! Tolstoy and Achebe and Rushdie and Camus! Read Kawabata! Read Marquez! Read it all and more, Daniel, but do not implore *me* to educate you!"

"Implore? These words! What's that even mean?"

"How now brown cow! The rain in Spain stays mainly in the plain! Oh, oh, *oh*, set a yardstick in my hand and by Jove I shall *swat!*" She smacked her hands at the sky. He stared at her amazed. "Patience, Daniel. I lack patience. Children disturb me."

"But . . . but I'm not a child!"

Her arm movements stopped. She turned to him slowly. She smoothed her hands over her hips and she straightened. "You are legal."

* * *

Danny left his only casting of the day—a three-hour wait for a three-minute slate, profile, and turn, and ultimately abortive dialogue—and walked cross-town to the library. He'd been thinking about her the entire day, how patiently she smiled, how energetically she laughed, the unassuming way she accepted him. He was thinking of her, still, as he entered the library, and without realizing it veered from his daily path to the magazines, his pages upon pages of nature and freedom, and went instead to the novels. Excitedly, he searched. He heard her in his head. He scanned every aisle, skipped his fingers across thousands of spines, old and new, translated and original, eternal ideas until he reached it, and stopped. He slid it off the shelf. The corners were creased. The cover was cracked. The pages were spotted with scribble and the back was textured like ancient parchment, worn from all the hands and tables and shelves that had held it. He opened it at the back and fanned to the front. *Dedicated to Han Shan.* He paused. Then took out a notebook from his bag and between the Stephen King and Rudyard Kipling collections on one side and a host of Millers on the other he sank to a half-lotus on the floor and wrote the words *Han Shan*, steadily with a twinkle and a smile. Then he positioned his finger and began: "Hopping a freight out of Los Angeles at high noon one day in late September 1955 I got on a gon—a gon—"

Gondola. He copied it carefully under *Han Shan*. He thought for a moment and under *gondola* wrote *dharma*. He drew an asterisk beside it and continued gradually on. He followed each word with his finger and each sentence as though it were his own, and one by one, like secrets, they escaped. He didn't know half of what he read but he knew he had to try. He whispered and he enunciated and he grinned every time he sounded out another word that he recognized, or finished another page, or thought about the day when he'd impress

Marina and impress Una and perhaps even write a book of his own and tell everything he had ever experienced including all the things that no one wanted to know, like the abuses and the modeling and all the alcohol in between and he would promote it and he would sell it and he would discuss it, and be smart.

*   *   *

"Describe your ideal day, Daniel. In detail. You know I a*dore* detail."

"My ideal day?"

"Yes, Daniel, from wake to weary. What would you do? Whom would you see? Where would you go?"

He thought a moment. "I guess I might get up early. Maybe watch the sun rise. At the beach. I've never watched the sun rise or been to the beach, but I'd like to. I'd see whales and dolphins. I'd swim with them and with sharks and seals and turtles and—"

"Daniel."

"We'd all—"

"Daniel, e*nough*. Your asepticism; it infects me. Truly, how sterile can one be?" She lengthened her neck. Danny glared at the water. "*I*," Marina said, the same hand pressed patiently to her neck, "would rise to the late spring breeze. Bay windows ajar. Satin curtains afloat. A young . . . a glabrous . . . a help-lessly insatiable *man* at my side. We would kiss and caress and he would beg me—he would *beseech* me to make love but I would deny him. I would send him away with his loins in knots and thoughts in rage! 'Tonight, Frederico! Tonight!' He would leave and I would change and I would *plow* through the park, the barberries and magnolias and the lemon yellow daylilies in bloom, the Carolina Wrens all achirp and the wind so fresh and so vernal and so sweetly electric with its panoply of perfumes—the cut grass, the piquant sweat, the raw and zesty traces of last night's . . . oh, I digress." She smoothed her hands across her hair, patted the bun at the back, and dabbed at the

111

moisture beading down her neck. Danny had just started drifting to Una, her smile and sincerity and the excitement he felt about them celebrating his birthday together when Marina again used words that caught his attention.

"What's vernal?"

"I would bathe and then I would *eat!* Like a teenage boy. Infinity times infinity. Apple wood smoked caramelized bacon. Cheddar cheese strata with worlds of paprika. Créme fraîche strawberry crépes. Passion fruit! Melon slices! Mimosas for everyone!"

"Krem fresh?"

"By noon I would have a massage. Immanuel would come to me with his oils and his accent and those exquisitely large hands and he would grease me up and rub me down and . . . well do not be so sexist, Daniel, you libidinous men are not the only ones entitled to your hip-happy endings. A woman's options in this city are horrifying, simply vapid!"

"Libidi-what?"

"But all is well. Immanuel practices lomilomi. Oh, Daniel, I just *love* lomilomi. And I love the way Immanuel performs it. The way he would. On . . . my . . . ideal day. He would know exactly how to . . . touch me. I would lay there and let him . . . work me. It would last only an hour but it would feel endless and supreme like heaps of hot fudge cascading down mountains of vanilla ice cream but without *any* of the calories. None of the stomach pain or torturous bowels. Just pleasure! Torrents of pleasure!"

Danny turned. Marina sighed.

"Of course, I would bathe. Again. With *soap*." She looked at him with concern. "Then I would set to my art. My medium is—well, it is somewhat untraditional, I admit. It is rather akin to photo-mosaics. But more abstract. I shall show you sometime."

Danny looked at her, startled. "Sure . . ."

"*Then!*" she boomed, "I would shop!" Danny rolled his eyes. Marina gleamed. "A jewelry day! I would start at Van Cleef. The emeralds, the diamonds, the platinum. Just walking into one of their boutiques is like entering some Garden of Eden of Jewels. They have the most exquisite tiaras you have ever seen, Daniel—not that I *wear* tiaras." She chuckled. Danny didn't. "Surely, I would visit Danielle B as well, for what would an ideal day *be* without Charriol? The Flamme Blanche collection is simply peerless. The sapphires at least. Perhaps not the residual glitz. Oh, but La Jolla! One of *each!* And of course how could I bypass Cartier? Daniel, should you ever contemplate a gift for me, some gesture to express your joy for this . . . arrangement . . . please, do consider the Panthère de Cartier necklace—eighteen karats of yellow gold beset with diamonds, onyx, garnet. Could you *die?* I have one, naturally. But I would not deny another."

"Show me the money," he mumbled.

"Amusing, Daniel! That was droll. I fancy the merriment, now cease disrupting. After shopping I would primp and preen. I would listen to Balakirev or Tchaikovsky and browse my gowns, slip into a Missoni or a Galliano or—yes, Daniel, a *Galliano*; and no, I have *not* seen *Zoolander*. I quite enjoy the extravagance of the designs and have read no law requiring one to always don black merely because one lives in New York. Truly. In any case, I would opt for the Missoni, one sleek and ethereal and nude at the back, and as the sky turns timid I would meet Federico at Masa. No! *He* would come collect me. It is *my* ideal day. Carlos, the little Janus-faced stoolie, would not be working that night. He . . . he would be ill. In hospital. And Federico would fetch me freely and we would arrive at Masa together. The simplicity of the décor is quite arid indeed, even stultifying, but if one desires sushi with*out* toting to Japan one has no other option. It is simply so. The Suzuki with Shisho-leaf sauce is frighteningly orgasmic and the Kobe sukiyaki is well beyond the English lexis. Federico simply *whips* with envy just watching me eat it!" Marina sighed in distant delight, no longer couched behind useless subjunctives but blunt. "And then we return home, Daniel. And we tease and we frolic and we conclude the day the following morning, drunk on riotous rounds of Sake and sex." They exited the park and Marina nearly buckled from exhaustion as she let out a "wooh!" and an "uhh!" and an "oh my!" and barely missed puncturing Danny in the ribs with her elbow.

"And that's really so different from any other day?"

Marina turned. "I beg your pardon?"

"Aren't you married?"

"*Dani*el!"

"Ma*ri*na!"

"My married life is—"

"*Are* you?"

"Occasionally!"

"*Occasionally?* And on your ideal day? Are you married *then?*"

"Daniel *Ward*!"

Every taxi seemed to honk as they walked out of the park in unyielding silence. Moments later Marina handed Danny his daily envelope and turned toward the elevator. Danny watched, still dumbfounded as she disappeared. Then turned to Harold for a pen. Harold didn't have one, and neither did William.

*   *   *

"So where in England are you from?" He refused to hear any more of her sex life. Marina, though, looked worn, not nearly as crisp as the day before.

"You know it, Daniel? The geography?"

"Well, no. I don't know the U.S. much either."

"The City, Daniel. I was born in the City."

"London?"

Marina sighed. "Londinium, Daniel." She looked burdened by life, by the world. "Yes, London. But Lond*ini*um. Primordial London." She waved a hand without reason and said something about Claudius, Boudica, a city within a city.

The Royal Exchange. Mansion House. Christopher Wren by and by. "Londinium makes London go round." She couldn't have sounded any less enthusiastic.

"I see," Danny said, and they walked deeper into the park, further from the welter of taxis and tourists to where children and dogs and grass were all on their best behavior. They walked under overpasses where temperatures plunged and homeless parents sang. They passed trees that had witnessed world wars, first kisses, shooting stars, and kept the secrets that others couldn't. They reached the water and all the ripples that coiled gently from the ducks that dispatched them. They walked the same path they walked every day and that millions more would walk after them and for a time Danny forgot about Marina beside him and he composed. He created. Stories about summer. Stories about travels. Stories about anything he heard or smelled or saw that reminded him of the ones he read in his neat little book which he couldn't wait to continue.

"Actually," Marina said, breaking a lengthy silence. "We spent little time there. We kept a villa near Valencia. The grandest on the Po. We had nurses, tutors; we never set foot in a classroom. Mum and dad were rarely together. Or with us." Danny turned. She sounded pensive, even calm, as though yielding or dying behind a forgotten gaze and he seemed suddenly to comprehend. He knew what she would say but he couldn't decide how sorry he could feel for her—this ill, affected woman he had tried so hard to imagine once crying out for milk or playing with toys or skipping merrily across fields of flowers who now said everything and more. She talked about dinners and debutantes, "Season," she said, the various charities they attended. She talked about the centuries of merchants, her ancestors, all men, and how she got her name, Marina, by default. She talked about her father's drinking, her mother's jealousies, about how competitive her brothers were—swimming to rowing, archery to equestrian. Fencing, she said, and talked quietly about her collections of dolls, her coins, all the hours they spent learning Latin, Greek, History, Art, and how their math tutor sometimes looked at her and talked to her and touched her the way he did her mother when they assumed no one would see. How he resembled her. Or she him. How it was never discussed . . . She kept talking, almost drunk or delirious or scared but calm and unaware like a sleepwalker, and Danny wished he could wake her. He wanted to, badly, but didn't know how without making everything awkward and real. What could he say? What could he do? He wanted none of her past, like she none of his, and as if a prayer had been answered, she stopped, inadvertently it seemed, and Danny, without knowing why or how, forgave her. For everything.

"I . . . I'd like to go to England some day."

She looked at him. "England? Oh. Yes. Indeed."

They reached the lobby and Marina relayed the envelope from Harold to Danny, then very evenly, very placidly wished them both a pleasant day. She rounded the corner and entered the elevator and became a blur on the screen above. Danny pulled out a pen from his shorts and wrote *Londinium* on the envelope as he tried to recall others from the morning's monologue. But none came to mind.

Chapter Thirteen

UNA CALLED later that afternoon. Danny was still in the library sitting cross-legged on the floor with his notebook and dictionary beside him. His list of words had spilled onto the second and third pages. For each word he defined he found more he didn't know and looked them up with the rest. His back had braided itself into a rope and as he sank into a new position, too engaged to find a chair, the phone in his pocket began to vibrate. *The agency*, he thought. *A booking?*

Something expanded inside him. It was warm and it was light and it swirled deep inside his chest. He sensed it stronger each time he spotted their book, and then again, only more so, when he saw her name on his phone.

"Hel-loo?" His voice cracked.

"Danny. It's Una. From *W*."

He already felt high.

"Hey . . ."

"Hi! Are you busy?"

A vein throbbed in his ear. "No, now's fine. Now's . . . good."

"So why are you talking so quietly?"

"I'm in the library."

"Wow, you really do like those wildlife magazines. I mean, that's awesome. Everyone should be passionate about something."

"Actually, I'm reading your book." Then he thought of how Marina would say it. "I'm reading Kerouac."

"*The Dharma Bums*? You like it?" He could hear her smile.

"I do. There's this one part. It's so—it's just really . . . Here, I'll read it to you." He picked up the book off the floor. He spoke softly, slowly, like a child sounding out each word, unsure if what he said was correct, or if the sounds were coherent and clear. And yet he felt their every meaning. "'But it seemed that I had seen the ancient afternoon of that trail, from meadow rocks and lupine posies, to sudden . . .' That's a bean plant," he said. "And a posy . . . Sorry, you probably know all this."

"No, tell me," she said. "What's a posy?"

"It's a bouquet. And a Bodhisattva—Kerouac writes a lot about Bodhisattvas—they're Buddhist people who find enlightenment but sort of wait and postpone it to help other people find it, too." She smiled again.

But it seemed that I had seen the ancient afternoon of that trail, from meadow rocks and lupine posies, to sudden revisits with the roaring stream with its splashed snag bridges and undersea greenness, there was something inexpressibly broken in my heart as though I'd lived before and walked this trail, under similar circumstances with a fellow Bodhisattva, but maybe on a more important journey, I felt like lying down by the side of the trail and remembering it all.

"And this part I really . . .

The woods do that to you, they always look familiar, long lost, like the face of a long-dead relative, like an old dream, like a piece of forgotten song drifting across the water, most of all like golden eternities of past childhood or past manhood and all the living and dying and the heartbreak that went on a million years ago and the clouds as they pass overhead seem to testify (by their lonesome familiarity) to this feeling.

"Sometimes all I want to do is climb a mountain. Or walk in the woods."

"I don't think anyone has read to me since I was a child."

It wasn't a beaming smile. But soft. Shy.

"I'm writing down the words I don't know and looking them up in the dictionary. I want to get smarter."

"Smarter? Danny, words don't make you smarter. Thoughts make you smarter."

"But you can't have thoughts without words."

"Sure you can. Animals have thoughts and they don't use words."

"Well, we use words to show our smartness."

"And we also use emotions and expressions and actions. Words are overrated. You're a model, you should know that. Intelligence is thought and thought is creativity and creativity—well, that's essentially the process of making something generic original. Stimulating, pragmatic, whatever. Like when you get in front of the camera, your goal isn't just to create something but to create something new and inspiring and exceptional. And for that you need intelligence."

He had never thought of it that way. He had always thought if he just knew more words he would have more to say. But now she talked about books and imagination and vicarious moments, about journeys through distant places, other eras, thoughts kept alive and all the lessons they taught. Danny wanted to equal her, to say something intelligent to impress her or complement her or just to know what it should feel like to talk like her. Instead he brushed his fingers through the carpet. He sank further into her every word, into her honesty, her energy, the way her voice swam through his blood.

"Do you ever people-watch?" she said. "Do you ever just sit somewhere and observe and process, what looks natural and real versus forced and cold? Some of it is instinct but some is learning. There's nothing we're not asked to mimic. No movement. No emotion." He wanted to watch her.

"I do," he said. "I enjoy it."

"So what do you think? Is it even worth it or is the industry just dumb to reality? Because some models think there's nothing for them to do but be. They think modeling is passive and innate and sometimes mere chance."

"Well, I haven't been doing this as long as you. But remember I told you about my roommates? The one in Paris right now, Xavier, he's real scientific about everything, about modeling. I mean, he thinks it's an art but preparing for it is a science. To Xavier, everything's practice. It's all cause and effect. But Kinzie, the one in Chicago, he does tons of drugs and eats what he wants and says what he wants and I'm sure he doesn't ever people-watch or exercise or think anything he does makes any difference to modeling. But they both work. They both get booked. I think."

"So what are they doing there? In Paris and Chicago."

"It's just for summer. Xavier's researching for a book and Kinzie's modeling."

"So maybe if Xavier is abroad doing research for a book, he's not really as OCD about modeling as he seems. And if Kinzie is spending a whole season out in Chicago, maybe he's not as insouciant as *he* seems."

"Wait. Spell that? In-soo-see . . ."

She smiled. "I'm impressed, Danny."

He put down his pen. He combed his fingers through the carpet. They sat silent, for a long, telling moment, then asked simultaneously, "So where do you people-watch?" Neither answered. "You first." They laughed. They spoke in unison again but this time Danny said, "Central Park," and Una said, "Anywhere."

"I like Central Park," she said. "It's mostly a bunch of exer-cisers and dog walkers but those can be some pretty revealing types, too."

"Yeah, revealing indeed . . ." He paused. *Indeed?* He switched the phone and pulled his knees to his chest, leaned back against the metal stack, and combed.

"They're just so inflated. They're better suited for actors to watch. You know—all distraught and insecure, thinking they're fat but feigning thin. They walk in circles wishing no one noticed them yet they puff and swagger like peacocks demanding a mate. You *know* they were all rugby players and prom queens in high school and now they're just dying to have their bodies back. And their mirrors. And the kids they used to tease. Yeah, they reveal alright. They've got psyche written all over them. But it's so staged, you know. So the-atrical. They're too obvious for us, too manic. Models need subways. We need lunch breaks and bookstores. We need the people who don't have the slightest idea they're being watched and not the slightest inkling of why anyone would want to."

Danny didn't understand. He didn't understand how any-one could make him feel so comfortable. He didn't understand why anyone would want to or why he deserved it, what he had done or how it all started.

He opened his chest and felt his shoulders spread across the books behind him. He furrowed his fingers through the carpet. He tried in earnest to concentrate. He heard everything she said and he wanted to emulate her, or at least to try, but he was consumed by what he didn't understand.

"Maybe we'll people-watch together sometime," Una said. Danny tried to reply, but nothing came. "Or maybe . . . you prefer to alone. That's OK. Alone is OK."

"No, no. Yes." He dug deep into the rug. Something sharp punctured the lining under his nail and at last he had a pretext to cry. It was a relieved cry, warm and smooth but muted and faint, and distant like the remnants of a passing storm, distant like the sort he had known as a child.

"Una." He was barely audible. "Where are you?"

"In L.A."

He closed his eyes.

"I'm shooting."

He inhaled, quietly.

"Just today."

He nodded. Alone.

"Danny?"

"Yeah?"

"Are we still going out? For your birthday?"

"I think so."

"My treat . . ."

Seconds, maybe minutes passed. They sat in silence, like at the depth of a pond or in the midst of a cloud where time was unknown, where everything moved in harmony and not even the wind was a disturbance, but the most beautiful reminder of clarity. And Danny felt like he'd found home.

"Danny?"

"Yeah?"

"I—I have to get back on location. But I'll talk to you soon. I'll see you soon."

He wiped his cheek with the back of his hand. "I'll see you soon."

* * *

He called the next day but she didn't answer. He thought she might be working; perhaps in the air. Another day passed and he started to worry, another and he wondered if he should try yet again. He didn't want to seem desperate or psycho, but neither aloof. He told himself to forget about her; he told himself to call. He told himself to go to sleep and to pick up the phone and to move on and to try again. He dropped a fist with a groan on the mattress. He rolled over and whimpered. He smothered his face in the pillow, drummed his feet against the bed and wished someone—anyone—would appreciate him. He picked up the phone. He set it down. He picked it up and opened it and closed it and set it down, over and over, up and opened, closed and down, and then finally he dialed it. Then smacked it shut. He tucked it tight inside his fist and tossed and cried and punched and shook and moaned.

His birthday came. Just as painfully, it passed. He watched the clock on the wall. Each second ticked by slower than the last, each minute more quiet and more remorseless like a sunburn seeping deeper into the skin. He sat there and he watched. Both hands reached vertical. They stood like mountains, like trees, like stars in a dark, dark eclipse. And the second hand passed proudly by. Still, he told himself she'd call. He told himself it wasn't too late. He told himself unlikely meant possible and a birthday hadn't passed. He told himself he hadn't mistaken her and new wasn't old, he didn't dislike her and time wasn't real, no one was so cruel and clocks weren't clapping, clocks weren't clapping, clocks were not clapping!

He picked up his phone. He groaned and he cursed, he punched where he could. And this time he launched his fist at the floor. But this time, time stopped. This time, time divided. For somewhere between Danny's grieving fist and the hardwood floor, somewhere between such dissimilar things that at any other time, on any other day, when time was surely time and seconds were in fact seconds and birthdays were nothing more than a complete calendar of days, when emotions weren't nearly so cumulative and confidence not nearly so low, when loneliness was just another day rather than a demon or an hourglass of hope and a single hello could jumpstart the soul, neither he nor anyone would notice the relationship—his fist; the floor—even as they were distinctly connected if only by the giving and the getting of a telephone: for somewhere between them it rang.

He heard it.

Then watched it shatter around the room.

Chapter Fourteen

BETH HAD TAKEN TO DANNY, and Danny to Beth. Beth had been booking the world's top male models for as long as there were male models to book. She'd known thousands and met more, and Danny had become a favorite. *W* bestowed praise. For Beth, though, a client's kudos didn't suffice. She formed her own impressions, and he refreshed her.

Beth sat opposite Derek at the front of the Men's Board. She was the first person models passed when they entered the hall and while most said hi, most knew the politics, and kept walking.

Danny was less informed. He went to the agency more often than ever and sat down right beside her. He thanked her for *W* on every occasion and swiveled innocently with his back to the Board as they talked about various clients or castings or what he did over the weekend. They talked about books. They talked about fashion. They talked about the 70s and 80s and Studio 54, the effects of AIDS on the industry and the wealth of homophobia that still blemished it. They talked about art and about beauty and about exhibits at the Guggenheim, how the color blue was so diverse. They talked about tactics in first impressions and in securing a client, and whenever it was feasible she guided him. She made suggestions about his posture. She improved his diction. She reminded him about eye contact and body language, and inquired into his goals. He tried not to reply with too much about modeling, but when he did there seemed to be an understanding between them. Certain specifics that were better left unsaid. Certain individuals who were wiser not named. He never stated the loyalty he felt toward Carla—or the irritation he felt in return—but he conveyed it, left it, and went on swiveling, talking about music, talking about magazines, talking about whatever interests they shared until he continued down the hall and stood patiently, professionally, briefly and insecurely and modelsome next to the agent who just a season earlier made him feel hot. They talked about nothing and he wondered if it was the same for the rest. For Xavier. For Sasha. For Jeremiah. This high. Then low. This loved-and-unloved abyss.

A week had passed since Danny's birthday, days since he got the guts to tell Beth about a girl—a girl he liked, a lot—on the *W* shoot. He told her about the way she spoke and the things she said and about his birthday, about their plans. About the excitement, and the disappointment, and even about the telephone. It wasn't long after he told her all of this that he was back in the agency feeling lost and anxious for advice when he turned down the hall and found someone else sitting in Beth's seat. There were two new tables and four new chairs and some man looking juvenile and meddlesome, sitting at her desk, typing on her computer, wearing her headset, and stopping him cold.

No one noticed. Monika paced. Carla pulled cards. Models chatted with agents in hushed foreign languages. Luke tore pages from magazines as others emailed and ate, and Danny forced himself not to panic.

"Um . . . Derek?" He tapped the agent gently on the shoulder. Derek turned—"because the rate is too *low*"—he raised a hand—"because you're asking for five *years*, Joan"—he motioned to his head set—"compromise on *what*; it's a joke, it's insulting"—then rolled his eyes.

Danny smiled in fear.

"Something *I* could help you with?"

He looked across the table, at the man he wanted to maim. "Where's . . . Beth?" It was of course, possible, that things weren't what they seemed.

"Oh, you mean the woman who used to work here? Yeah, she doesn't anymore."

Maybe it was the caution of his smile or the repellence of his laugh, or just Danny trying to reverse time, but the words didn't register. Then his heart plunged like a rock and he felt stranded and confused. He felt nauseous. His throat locked. He nearly roared *Who are you!* but somehow sobered, focused, and breathed. "Well . . . where is she?"

"Yeah, that's a question for Monika." He shrugged with a nod. And a smile.

Derek hung up the phone. Danny heard him say something but he kept staring, struggling, waiting for Beth to appear or someone to laugh and tell him it was all a joke. He turned to Derek at last but kept staring as he did and when he finally brought himself to speak, the phone rang yet again. "Edge Models, this is Derek." The hand. "Joan . . ." The motion. "Usage?" The grin. "And the rate?" He pumped a fist and he spun.

"Take a seat," the man said.

"I'll stand."

"How are you, I'm Terry."

"Danny . . ."

"I know! It's my *job* to know, yeah?" His laugh was repulsive and Danny pooled all his strength to grin. "Two more bookers are coming, but I don't know more than that. Just got here Wednesday. And you? You've been with Edge a while, yeah?"

His thoughts spun like a fan. Was that the way it was? Agents came and went? As fickle as the wind? No loyalty? No stability? For the agent or the model or anyone? But how long had she been there, and why would she leave? Would others? Should he? Did he even want to? He was tired of leaving. He was irritated and directionless and needed a chance to stay. But all he ever heard was: "Go with the agent, not the agency." Did anyone do it? Was it so easy—this round-robin, this Hopscotch? And even if it was, where was Beth anyway? What if she hadn't gone to another agency? What if she left the industry entirely? What if she hadn't but her new colleagues had no interest in him or his contract didn't permit him. *Could* he leave? What were the terms? Had he ever even read them? What else didn't he know? Who was his agent? Was it Beth? Was it Carla? The Board as a whole? Carla found him but Beth was the only one to have booked him. Did any of it even matter? Did he?

"Sorry," he said suddenly, "I have a casting," and headed in a daze for the lobby. He held his thumb to the button between the elevators, then smashed it in until it burned. The secretaries deliberated behind him.

"I still can't believe she waited so long."

"One of them was bound to go sooner or later."

"One of them, schmun of them—Monika never would've waited *that* long."

"Oh, right, and I'm a size zero. Edge Models . . ."

"There's long, and then there's stupid. Long is loyalty. Any longer is just stupid. Beth books; she gets it done. But she's old. And who has time for old? Fashion is image and image is youth and Beth just *isn't* youth."

Danny felt frozen. He couldn't see them or know if they saw him but wanted nothing more than for the doors to explode.

"Even though she books?"

"*Even* though she books."

"*Because* she books! Because the last three boys Carla brought in *Beth* booked. And Carla hasn't. And you *know* how Carla—Edge Models . . ."

"I still say it was age."

"And I still say envy."

"You'd *think* money."

"Money? Men don't make money! *Women* make money. Where have you been? This is modeling."

"Edge Models . . ."

"Edge Models . . ."

"Edge Models . . ."

The elevator opened and Danny stepped in. He turned and faced the secretaries. His eyes were solemn. His cheeks were subdued. His neck was idle and slack as though his head just barely balanced. His eyes met the secretary's furthest to the left, the one he first encountered some three months earlier and the one who now cachinnated: *money? men? modeling?* He looked at her. He stared at her. Melancholy, ache, inanition filled his eyes. Some plea for compassion. They glistened, lonely and tormented in a lost, vacuous stare. The secretary gazed back, trapped in the tornado of his thoughts.

Then the elevator closed and for a moment he continued to stare. Then it plunged and he felt himself rise. He closed his eyes, just as everything disappeared. Modeling. The agency. The pressures and uncertainties and all the esoteric expectations. Beth, too. Her grammar lessons, her wardrobe advice, her smile and freckles and friendship and memories of Elvis and the Kennedys and Fashion prior to computers—they were gone. Her anecdotes about scouting, grooming, selling decades of brilliant and short-lived faces and all her examples, her warnings, things Danny didn't want to hear but knew he had to. Gossip. Truth. Lies. Egos of agents and the network of insiders from photographers to casting directors to clients themselves who spent indefinite phone calls criticizing models they'd never seen, asking about others they never intended to book, scoffing amateurism as they paraded details about who had slept with whom, which ones had eating disorders, how they looked without their underwear, what this one or that one must be like in bed, scandals, cheats, alliances, rivalries—a type of fear that breeds subservience.

Everything she wanted him to stay clear of.

The elevator flew. He felt high with disconnect, soaring, floating, like a balloon leaving everything behind. A dizziness, some faintness filled him. There was little more for him to feel or know than the forgotten sobriety that flattened his lips, and the gravity that was gone from his feet. He could have stayed that way forever, flying, unresponsive, but the elevator suddenly stopped and he felt the weight of his head press upon his neck, and his neck upon his shoulders, and each upon the next, cantankerously down to his toes and he wobbled, shuffled, and stood.

The elevator opened. How he longed not to see:

The stories-high billboards and their unachievable standards. Their charisma. Their classicism. Their unrelenting distance.

The stretches of windows so bright and airy. The exuberance and abrasiveness and the mannequins unrefined. The clothes inconceivable and proud.

The newsstands all endlessly routine, all clearly mendacious. The magazines and the myths and the two-faced deceptions of comfort and control and the life to be sought.

The restaurants. The gyms. The spas. Their patrons and the things they believed and the little they knew. The excess they knew.

He was a steelworker-turned-model. And he was as idealized as he was envied. The world saw him pretty and they assumed him complete. They saw him golden and plentiful if not the apex of attainment, and they wanted whatever he had— all that he was. But what did they know? What did any of them know except the dreams they needed? Beauty begets attention. Beauty attracts love. Beauty is power and predictability and joy and the gloss behind which purity lies. Beauty is the answer, the end, the savior to which everything essential must fly. Beauty is boundless. Beauty is decisive. Beauty is one.

He was a model. And the world had its assumptions.

Chapter Fifteen

AUGUST WAS SUDDENLY COLD. The sun was bright but the wind was strong and clouds collected ominously in the distance. The Mexican Petunias still burst brilliance, and the European Starlings still sang love, but the paths were starker than most mornings. Minus the dogs, dozens deep, as usual.

The twosome moved swiftly. Marina was talking easily about Danny and Danny was impressed yet just as annoyed. He kept waiting for her to dismiss him or forget him but she kept discussing him with zeal.

"But *hear* me, Daniel: you are *trying* too hard." She smoothed her palms across her hair, from her forehead to her bun, then back to her sides as the wind curled quickly under her arms.

"What do you mean *too hard?*" He felt sour and mistaken and gallingly curious. "How's that even possible? What's that even mean?"

"It *means* excess exertion, Daniel. Supererogatory application. It means *this*—this straining, this striving to know."

"No I'm not."

"Oh, but you are, Daniel! You are, indeed!" She smiled faintly and swirled her fingers in loops, twice, thrice through the air. "You are trying too hard at your castings. You are trying too hard with your bookers. Indeed you are trying too hard with this, this, this Una—is that her name?—this Una and all that Kerouac you read for her."

"I am not!" He turned to her flustered; then looked sharply away. "I'm reading it because I *want* to. I just do. And my phone is busted. I already told you. I have a new phone and new number and I don't know where she is or what she's doing so how is that trying too hard? What's so super-er—supergyratory?"

Marina crowed. "Oh, Daniel, how riotous! Bloody riotous you are! What a lark! I do say, Daniel, *gyratory* you are not. You are stiff as stationary."

He dropped his head with a groan and wondered what he said that was so absurd. "You're the one who said I should have a girlfriend."

"Oh, Daniel, you are like snow in spring; let the flowers bloom."

"Why are we even having this conversation?"

"Because it amuses me, Daniel, that is why. Now, tell me more about this Una. Describe her. What is it you fancy about her?"

The wind swept wide. It smelled damp, like rain. Danny breathed deep and wished it would. For days, for weeks. Penetrating and silent. Everything cleansed.

"It's like, when I talk to her, everything is good. I don't need to be next to her. Just talking to her. Her voice is so . . . nice. She talks and I listen. *I* talk and she listens. I don't know what I say that's worth listening to but she—"

"Well that *is* a pity, Daniel."

He turned as though awoken. "What?"

"I said it is a *pity*. That you no longer fancy her."

"Well, I do, but . . . it's just . . . Can we not talk about this?"

"Oh, certainly, Daniel!"

The wind cut colder and sharper, and neither said a word. The sun disappeared. The pace seemed to quicken. A chill seeped through Danny's skin and he stiffened with a shudder.

Marina commented casually on the weather and on her displeasure at having not yet broken a sweat, then proposed they continue longer, and harder, until she did.

"Another lap, shall we?" He told himself it would pour. "I *will* compensate you, Daniel. Naturally."

Half an hour later they reached her building in a dash. Marina handed Danny his due, then headed past Harold toward the elevators.

"Well, come, Daniel. I *said* I would compensate you."

Danny looked at Harold. Harold stared at the wall. He looked back out the door. Outside, it started to rain.

*   *   *

It was still raining the next morning when Danny left his place in the Village, and at least as hard when he reached Marina's in Lenox Hill. He stood shivering in the foyer with his hands cupped tight over his lips. His hair and lashes were disheveled with water, the beads on his neck nearly icing as they dried. The central air blew above.

Marina reached the lobby twenty minutes later. She wore a fulsome white robe which swirled plush over alpaca fur slippers, and found Danny standing next to William, hugging himself outside under the awning.

"Daniel!" She opened the door and halted. "Daniel, it is *freez*ing! Are you off your trolley? Loitering out there? In a bloody *T*-shirt?"

Danny stepped inside. His hands were wedged into his arms; his molars clicked. "Y-y-you're not going out like that, are you?"

"My word, you really are off your trolley! *I*, Daniel? *I?* I am going nowhere. But *you*—why on earth are you here?" Surely, one couldn't fake such sincerity.

"W-w-why am I here? I'm here because you want me here! I'm here because I'm always here!" The wind smacked the door shut behind him.

"Daniel, there is rain enough to flood a desert!"

132

He had been rubbing his hands rapidly over his arms, and stopped. "So . . . s-so we're not walking?"

"No, Daniel, we most certainly are *not* walking."

His mouth fell agape. Every feature in his face asked the questions he couldn't. *You couldn't have called? What am I, a mind-reader?* He turned for the door.

"Daniel!" She gripped the top of her robe. She seemed, for a second, unprepared. "You—you cannot *possibly* go back outside. Not without first warming up."

Danny turned, ready to retaliate. But she was already halfway through the foyer, turning the corner as Harold examined his fingers. Danny stood dumbfounded, watching, then raced after her. Thirteen floors up, he stopped cold at the door.

"Well what, Daniel, you suppose I am going to *bring* you the towel? I shall not. You may decline entry for payment, for something earned," she said. "But for warmth? For something offered? Come in this instant before I rescind my civility."

Still shivering, still silently irate, he stepped at last into her fairy tale of opulence. He resolved not to stare. His eyes shot wild like gun fire, grazing rugs, hitting tapestries, lodging into armchairs, ricocheting off picture frames. Crystal door knobs sparkled in the glitz of a chandelier. A mirror hung massive in bone. Life-size busts stood mounted atop marble plinths— grandparents of grandparents glistening in a remarkable luminescence. He thought he had stepped into another century; he thought he had entered another world. His eyes subpoenaed his every understanding but his mind wouldn't grant the testimony he deserved. Reality? Whose? In what game of consciousness? He stalled in a stupor, and Marina planted herself in front of him. "This way, Daniel. The bath is *this* way." And he remembered, shivered, and followed.

She led him past a library built of rosewood, a sitting room flaunting a Cézanne, into a window-lined bedroom with an ottoman and an armoire, antique yet still pristine. Danny walked straight to the window. Immediately adjacent, Central Park spanned wide, and unified the city below.

"I *do* wish it were for sale," she said, parking herself right beside him and joining in his admiration of the view. She gazed forward as she placed a benign, unexpected arm around his shoulder. "Oh my word, Daniel! You are colder than a snowman! Come."

He stood there, static at the bathroom door as she set the soaps, fixed the water, arranged the towels, this way and that all oddly, improbably motherly. Finally, she left, and Danny undressed. He pressed the button by the faucet and stepped into the Jacuzzi as cold clashed with hot and his skin turned to needles and nails. He itched, he twisted, he struggled and strained until he exhausted himself so entirely that he dropped his head on the cool, custom-cut stone, and wondered if his life were a dream. Luxury, alone, surrounded him. Dignity, unparalleled, beheld him. Abandoned baby. Abused boy. Astronaut at sea. Sailor in space. Flying or falling. Sailing or sinking. Nowhere to go, nothing to be. Never to know and forever unknown. Aware of all of it, aware of more, this baby, this boy, now dozed peacefully in a Jacuzzi in a condo in Lenox Hill.

In the distance he heard her. He heard his name, her voice, nervous and motherly. "Danny? May I—may I come in? I heard you crying and . . . and I . . ."

Then he heard his own voice. But younger and throttled with hiccups and tears. "Suh-sorry, Linda. Pluh-please don't hurt me. I won't cry."

The door opened and Linda, the only mother he had ever laughed with and loved, rushed in, shaking and halting and wanting desperately to hug him. "No, Danny, never! It was only an accident. I wouldn't ever." She sat down beside him. Her eyes welled with tears. Her hands trembled at her mouth with every effort not to reach for him and without looking up he fell into her arms. They sat there rocking in the corner of the room with his coloring books and building blocks scattered about them, Danny apologizing, Linda soothing, until at last they calmed and she suggested a bath.

He breathed deep, and let go. He turned off the faucet. He turned off the motor. He listened as the bubbles quelled and the bathroom silenced and he combed his fingers through his hair as the water trickled off his elbows. For a moment he remembered her—where he was; how bizarre, how unlikely, how limitless it had become—when suddenly the door flung wide and she trundled in. Danny turned with a jolt. His backside slid forward and he disappeared under the water, his feet surfacing, flailing, before quickly plunging and landing and sending him surging. Wet and hairless he shot up. He gasped and shook and in one large, contiguous motion, he gyrated. A wave rolled forward. Water rushed over the edge. Marina laughed as though adoring some frolicking dog. Then stepped over the puddles between them.

"Oh, Daniel, you need not be alarmed. I have brought you a tea. Would you like a tea, Daniel?" She spoke so casually and maneuvered so professionally he hardly knew what was happening. "It *tis* my favorite. Tieguanyin from China. Surely, you know it. Guan Yin was a Bodhisattva, Daniel, a Bodhi*satt*va. I reckon Kerouac drank Tieguanyin. Or would have wanted to. Well, drink, Daniel, this is not a staring contest."

"No. Thanks. But . . ." He restarted the motor. He sank deeper, crouched tighter and came closer until a jet pressed hard into the declivity of his pelvis. "No, but thanks. I'll get out. I'm warm. I'll get out as soon as . . . well, whenever you . . ."

"Daniel? Does my presence abash you? Do I distress you?" She sipped tidy and she looked at him. She shifted her robe. And she looked at him.

"Well, no. No." He shook his head. "W-*why? Why?*"

Marina raised a brow. She kept one hand on her robe and her eyes on Danny's. She held him with her gaze, with the transparency of the situation. It felt like an eternity as the jet continued to blow and the sweat grew on his neck, his breath a distant memory when all at once she sipped again and floated to the window. Danny moved with her. Another jet worked his hip and she shook her head. "Hurricanes in the islands? So soon? This rain, Daniel, this tempest—one cannot *possibly* cross it." And she looked at him. He swallowed and he stared and he sweated and he froze; and she looked at him and she looked at him and she looked at him. The jets blew, the bubbles burst, and nothing could keep her from looking at him. There was calm in her face. There was fire in her eyes. There was decree and grit and a dash of delight, and without falter she looked at him. "Nature," she said, more casually, more evenly, more carelessly than he had ever heard her say anything and yet more assertively, more sensually, more incongruously, too. *"Nature,"* she said again. "Nature overcomes every contest." Then she gathered her robe and walked to the door, past Danny, stunned and dripping and naked in her tub.

* * *

When he woke the next morning the wind had subsided but the rain still fell. Danny took the umbrella Marina sent him home with, and returned to a foyer that felt colder than ever.

"M-m-morning, Harold. You l-l-leave it on all w-winter, too?"

"I beg your pardon, Mr. Ward?"

"N-never mind. M-m-marina?"

He paced in circles in the lobby but never escaped the chill. He rubbed his arms and blew his knuckles and eventually walked back outside next to William.

"Wild weather," Danny said.

William gazed ahead. The rain fell evenly as though pacing itself; the drone against the awning eased their silence.

"Think we'll ever see the sun?"

The doorman didn't move. Danny lowered his eyes. He crossed his arms over his chest and began to twist to keep warm.

"Used to work on the West Side," William said at last. Danny continued to twist. "Never believe the things I seen. Through them monitors, all them elevator monitors. Could write books. Straight out of movies. Tits on tits. Blow jobs. Guys twice my age fucking girls half it. Pussy. Cock. Ass. Freaky stuff. Married fifteen years, I'm talking stuff we never done in private. Bedroom, bathroom, car." He turned solemnly to Danny, as round from the front as from the side. "It's hot? Like in movies?"

Danny's movements had been slowing, and now stopped. He forgot the cold. He forgot the rain. He forgot his lips and his ears and his knuckles and nails, Marina and the park and their walk and his wait, and he stared.

"No. No, you don't under . . . That's not . . ." He shook his head. He felt hated and envied for something that wasn't true, yet overwhelmed by the insecurity that it was. He shook no—*no*—ardently disbelieving, just as the door opened quietly behind him.

"Madame requests you. Upstairs," Harold said, and faded back into the building. William turned back to the park. Danny stood speechless, stunned, still shaking *no* when he passed Harold staring at his feet in the foyer.

The door was open. Danny knocked anyway—loudly and abrasive until Marina arrived in the same plush white robe and alpaca fur slippers and smiled.

"*You* said we were walking. Last night on the phone, you *said* we would walk. Rain or shine. Don't tell me I'm off my gourd, Marina. I haven't lost my stupid marbles. You said it! You *said* it and I'm *here* and I'm *freezing*. This whole building is *freezing!* And I'm not coming in. I'm not. Just tell me if we're walking because if we're not, I'm leaving. This is crazy. It's crazy!"

She looked at him blankly. He halted at her boredom.

"The bath is running, Daniel. Warm yourself. I have something to show you."

"To show me?"

She turned and walked back into the kitchen. Danny stood baffled at the door. "Oh!" she called, her voice as shiny as a chandelier. "And your envelope is by the bath. Tea will be ready in a tick."

He threw up his hands and bolted back to the elevator. He jabbed at the button. He paced and shivered and cursed and jabbed, but then looked at the door and stopped. Maybe it was the cold. Maybe it was the cash. Maybe it was the fear of unemployment or some need to be known that he would never admit. But he panicked and surged and before he knew it he dunked himself into the Jacuzzi. He twisted and squirmed, tingled and swelled, raged and calmed and quickly dried off. He put on the same clothes he came in, stuffed the money into his pocket, and was just sliding on his second sock when Marina walked in carrying tea.

"You have somewhere to be, Daniel? A casting? A shoot?" She walked directly to him. She sat down in front of him. She took hold of his wrist, turned over his hand, and planted the mug in his swollen fingers. She looked up. "Do you?" They both knew the answer. But she asked it again. "Do you?" He tried desperately to avert her. Still, she asked it again. "Do you?" She sipped her tea and she suspired and in a voice that hardly seemed real, that hardly seemed valid or fair or in any way concerned, in a voice that didn't even seem to be answering a question or confirming a suspicion or relieving or suspending a struggle, in a voice that wasn't a whisper but was quieter than necessary and quieter than customary and stroked his hair and shook his spine and made everything confident cowardly, she said, "You don't." Then she raised his mug to her lips, cradled it in her hands, fondled it with her fingers, and blew, gently, the steam into his face. "No," she said. "You don't." And he wondered how he could stop something he hadn't realized had started, had always been, and would likely always be.

He followed her into the study and up the spiral stairs. "By spring," she said, "certainly by summer we shall have the floor above this one, too. That *should* suffice—the top three floors of the northwest quadrant. Jonathan is an avid collector. Trains, Daniel. Have you *heard* of anything so hackneyed, so truly passé? I would sooner scoop doggy doo off Fifth Avenue."

"Where is Jonathan, anyway?"

"In the back we have the guest rooms. I am the courtesan to the dinner party and I could not possibly permit my guests to—ah! That reminds me! Apropos dinner parties, we host one in the Poconos every autumn, Columbus Day Weekend. Are you available?"

He looked at her, perplexed. "A dinner party?" He hadn't even met her husband. "Well, I guess . . ."

Marina reached the top step and spun. "I know it is still weeks from now, indeed. But a thousand for the weekend?"

He needed a moment to comprehend.

"Cash," she said. "As always."

A knot tied inside his chest and he hardly knew he had nodded.

"Brilliant, Daniel, that is brilliant! Now, where was I? Yes, yes, three bedrooms in the back, and *here*," she said, her arms stretched proud, "here is *my* room, my warren."

A part of him had given up, but as his eyes cleared the landing he looked ahead. The space was open and loft-like, all naturally lit with rain-spotted windows. There was a work table in the middle and bookshelves to the sides, stacks of magazines and her art all about. Danny glanced at her.

"Come," she said, and led him on a tour of her work. She took him from piece to piece using words like *emulsion* and *bracket* and *solarization*, and others that he repeated to himself until he could no longer contain any more. "I call it a synthesis of magnified re-creation and mystified distortion! Is it *grand?*"

"Collage?"

"Daniel!" Her face fell. "My work is not child's play! It is highly researched. Highly detailed. Alex Cao I am not, but mere collage, Daniel? Indeed, I expected a more munificent first response."

He looked in earnest at the pieces on the wall, then turned kindly back to Marina. "I just think you're trying too hard."

There was a remarkable stillness.

"Daniel?"

"I'm not saying I don't like it. I'm just saying it looks . . . forced."

"Daniel."

"It's good, Marina, it's unique. I just think—"

"Daniel *Ward*. Are you mocking me? Is this some sort of apish mimicry?"

"What?"

"Do not feign *deaf*. Are you *mock*ing me?"

"No! I—"

"Because I will not tolerate it. I will not—"

"All I said was I think you're . . . Oh. No, Marina, I didn't mean it . . . like *that*."

"Then how *did* you, Daniel?"

"Just . . . that you can . . . do even better."

"Scores, Daniel, some hundreds of individuals have seen my work—my *collages* as you call them—educated, inclined individuals, and never has one offered but a morsel of instruction." Composed, even curious, she ambled around the table. "So, Mr. Ward." She folded her arms. "Enlighten me. What can I do better? What do *you*, Daniel, propose *I* do better?"

He tried to speak. He turned to the piece that was next to him. He knew what wasn't right about it. He knew where she was trying too hard. She was too set on reality, on perfection—on her idea that any exact re-creation of reality *was* perfection. She was concerned only with proportions and colors and with the photos in place of the reality, with the photos *as* the reality. The pieces had merit and were in some ways exceptional, but only because of distracting attempts to make them so.

"I'm not sure. Maybe it's a hunch."

"A hunch?"

Danny shrugged.

"Yes. I see." She stood poised, even loosened—her robe. "Daniel?" He turned. "Daniel." He waited. "Daniel, I would like you to be my subject." He stared.

"Your what?"

"I would like you to pose for me, Daniel. Would you pose for me?" She turned back to her worktable and slid a well-moisturized finger across the edge of it.

"I don't think—"

"Would you pose for me, Daniel?"

"It's just that—"

"I only ask for a fraction of your time."

"I know but—"

"Five hundred dollars? Two hours?"

He lowered his eyes. She let down her hair.

"You *are* a model, Daniel."

The word, so misused, begged to be defined.

He wrapped his arms around his chest; his T-shirt crumpled over his ribs. He felt suddenly cold again, helpless again, trapped or lost, somewhere in the world of his youth. She had too many offers, too many needs. She had too many games that he didn't want to play but couldn't afford not to.

He took off his shirt. He went to the window. She took out her film and prepared for her pastime. Danny watched her and wondered if life, if his life, was merely a series of patterns—as predictable as the morning sun.

Marina looked up from her camera. "Thank you," she said. She smiled politely. Then she laid the equipment on the table and picked up an assortment of paints. "I find them stimulating. The reds particularly." She pressed her finger into something carnal and ran it gently, motherly, in streaks down Danny's collar, then sternum, then stomach, and he shuddered.

"Are you cold?" The voice in his ear was as soft as the finger on his trunk.

"Are you tense?" The strokes were eternal and delicate and penetrating.

"Are you always so reserved, so taciturn? Whilst modeling?" She streaked past his navel and paused. Then again and paused.

"I'm . . . I don't . . ." His head burned. The rain fell lighter like miniature pins and needles dancing on the window. "Marina?" He looked up. He had forgotten how close she was. "I . . . don't like the paint."

The room was silent. She looked at him. She studied him. Slowly, she smiled. "You amuse me, Daniel." Harmlessly, she smiled. "Yes, you amuse me." Delicately, she smiled. "But tell me, Daniel, what do you reckon makeup is? And what of shoots? There must be far more paint—more makeup at shoots. And all sorts of pinching and plucking and prodding." So sweetly, she smiled.

Something ripped within. Something tore. His intestines. A kidney. His liver. Not his heart. Something collapsed or burst or shut down. Something ached. Violently but with numbness. Something was broken. Something was lost. He asked for so little. Essentials. Dignity. Decency. Yet he'd rarely been granted much of any of it.

"So shall we call it a shoot, Daniel?" Unconditionally, bounteously, she smiled. "You are the model. I am the others. The paint is makeup, the process clinical. A pinch. A pluck. A prod." She patted his hair. Maybe his ear, his neck, an arm. He wasn't sure. And she smiled. Then she switched to yellow, and she continued lower, and gentler, and more motherly. Slight creases shifted painfully in his shorts. Something splintered. Something caved. He closed his eyes and he tried his hardest not to be.

* * *

Later that morning, he stepped outside. He held a crisp wad of bills rolled tightly in his hand. William opened the door. Neither said a word. Danny gripped the money; and through the film building up in his eyes he saw the sun breaking through the clouds in the distance.

Chapter Sixteen

FASHION WEEK WAS EVERYWHERE. Buses carried advertisements for Mercedes Benz. Maybelline bought every billboard. The sidewalks and subways were more eclectic and longer-legged than ever; the taxis were more dangerous. The city was rested and revived in the post-long-weekend but every agent, every photographer, every designer and editor and each of their assistants and boyfriends was overworked, overpartied, overanxious, and bitchy.

At Edge, Danny worked twice in two days. Jen booked him for a quick editorial that required him to wear women's clothes, while Kosuke got him a job riding dirt bikes. Little else, though, was worth getting excited about. The new ones, Shania and Megan, were quickly proving their ineptitude. Monika said she couldn't be bothered. Derek was taking more of an interest in Danny but Danny felt increasingly uneasy in front of Terry. Luke swore that he was quitting, though whether the agency or the industry no one knew. And Carla was having her period daily for the last three weeks. Danny spoke only when spoken to. And then, always, succinctly.

Castings multiplied. The competition soared. Danny spent long, undesirable days surrounded by the world's most recognizable models waiting to be inspected by the city's most illustrious designers. Like the majority, he was never booked.

He did, however, still find his way into the Tent. Weeks earlier—before he knew what Fashion Week was, or had any inkling that he should; before he had been booked back-to-back, and started wondering if he would ever be booked again; just when he had earned the extra cash from Marina and accepted her bid to earn more, and saw his life turning into something worse than it had ever been—days after he smashed his phone—he ran into Jeremiah researching properties on Spring Street. Jeremiah looked well and asked about the apartment, about the agency, about Marina. And Danny smiled and lied as though his roommate weren't the savviest person he had ever met.

Jeremiah postponed an appointment and took Danny to lunch. Danny ate faster than he could breathe and feigned mirthful to no end, talking erratically about Una and *W* and his birthday and why he had a new number—something about dropping his phone in the toilet which sounded no likelier than a dog eating homework—then more about Una and *W* and the phone all over again.

Jeremiah let him talk. He ate his Panini and drank his Pellegrino and hardly said a word as Danny said the same thing fifty times. It could have all been true or false or part of a dream, but whatever it was, it was clear he was desperate. Jeremiah paid the bill and scribbled a name and number on a piece of paper. He slid it across the table and looked Danny in the eye. "It'll get better. I promise." A minute later he was gone and Danny sat staring at the note, relieved that he didn't have to ask.

Fashion Week arrived and he ushered. He walked each morning from Marina's condominium in Lenox Hill to the white chiseled tent in Bryant Park and he waited there in silence for a critic or a celebrity or some heiress to omnipotence to lose her way among the alphabetically-marked seats. He remained grateful for the job and for the opportunity to watch the shows, but with each day he became increasingly distracted by the division between his colleagues. Girls modeled. Boys didn't. Male models were everywhere—except on the runway. Some, like Danny, were ushers: dummies at the edges of the floor. But most worked well beyond it, in the foyers and conservatories and in the park itself, disseminating previews of everything from fashion magazines to mints and moisturizers, lip glosses and candles and cute little cards wrapped in ribbon that said, "It's fashionable to say thanks." They were as ubiquitous as they were un-booked, and to the women and men who attended the shows they were eye candy—ideal for distributing the innumerable samples of items they already owned but whose jobs or egos demanded they reacquire. "Oh, thank you, darling. Just one more . . ." and three fell to the bottom of her handbag. "Suh-*ho* kyuh-*hoot!* This one is for a friend . . ." another five fell to the bottom of his. Once every boy and his product had been sampled and assessed, they continued casually on their way as though it were natural to toddle into a tent the size of a baseball field in the middle of Manhattan and discuss horror films or UNICEF or veganism with Liv Tyler while waiting, to Danny's astonishment, for some two dozen, same-faced, same-bodied, same-styled, same-stepping girls to saunter perfectly past them at eighteen-second stops in Erin Fetherston formalwear or Gottex bikinis.

Danny had already watched more shows than he could recall: Terexov, Abaeté, Tony Cohen in the Salon; Luca Luca and Dennis Basso, Vivienne Tam in the Promenade; Lacoste, of course, DKNY and Miss Sixty and Diesel Black Gold in the Tent. It was past midweek and he was starting to tire—from the glamour, from the reminder, from things he couldn't identify. He entered the Tent, as always, at the back, and had hardly flashed his badge at the security guard when he found himself, again, amid a potpourri of lights, mirrors, cameras and beauty products, handbags and shoes and racks of replacements, water bottles, bagels, fruit baskets and hair stylists, makeup artists and designers and assistants and assistants' assistants and models in every direction.

Half-naked girls. Completely naked girls. Discretion lost to indifference. Commotion mixed with calm. Patience and stress. Pressure and precision. Conformity begging security, and emails, texts, telephones set to vibrate. Clocks. Interviews. Outside world and real world and the infiltration of misunderstanding. The tension of all things critical. Extensions. Eyeliner. Appearance and disappearance and gowns all bold. Cerise. Sangria. Scarlet. Some lavender for relief. Perfection predicates practice. A dissertation on every detail. He put the badge back in his pocket, and headed for the buffet.

He had hardly been there a moment and was still trying to break a stem of grapes without injuring etiquette when he thought he heard his name. Something accelerated. He heard it again. That voice. That cloudless, crystal, sky-blue voice. He turned around and suddenly elation made everything hyper as she held him and he held her and words he couldn't connect overwhelmed him. "Where have you been?" Una said. "I left you all these messages. Did you ever get them?" She had held him. And he had held her. And he wanted to again. "I'm really sorry I never reached you. I hope you went out." That bountiful, beautiful, clear-as-day voice. That piles of pillows, that billows of sheets, that lusciously quilted voice. "Was your phone off? I need your email. Wait. Danny. What are you doing here?"

She might have said more. She might have said less. Danny got that tingle again, that warm, light, swirly sensation. And he no longer cared about anything. The birthday. The divide. The darkness that followed and felt like it would never end. It just vanished. At once. "Una," he said, "you look like a Barbie doll!"

She let out a startled laugh and giggled with delight. "Sh-sh-shhh! The *designer!* How did you get in here anyway?"

"I'm ushering." He showed her the badge. "They *want* you to look like a doll?" He glanced about. Every model's hair was pulled, looped, and tethered hard to the right, jutting out like a horse's mane and hanging halfway between her shoulder and her elbow. Danny had already gathered that uniformity was the unanimous fashion, that the viewer was meant to study the modes, not the models, and that homogenous accessorizing aimed to facilitate this. Still, he couldn't help but question Fashion's rather contradictory ideas of minimalism and inconspicuousness. If the focus was clothes, why hire models?

Una took his arm and led him away from an amplification of nerves to the spot where he entered, and bit into an apple. "Suh whas this uzjering?"

Danny shrugged. "I don't know, I stand to the side and wait for someone who can't count to look confused."

Una munched. Then lit up. "Ij you inish *Arma Ums?*"

They laughed at the sound of the smush in her cheeks.

"*Dharma Bums?* Yeah, and just started *On the Road.*"

"Ooh, ooh, good, good, *good!*" She seesawed her shoulders and swayed her hips, a stationary dance that made her ponytail bop and Danny grin. "We have so much to talk about!" Yet she silenced. The whole tent seemed suddenly to silence. Una's enthusiasm met Danny's delight and they blushed and stared and tried their hardest just to breathe. But never spoke. They didn't have to. They were literates, then and there, of a language neither had ever known.

Without warning, the spell was broken. Someone called Una's name and they talked hurriedly, smiled anxiously, and as if they had never learned or couldn't remember or had forced themselves to forget, they hesitated, awkwardly, and hugged.

*   *   *

Only fifteen minutes behind schedule, the lights went out. The guests silenced. Salaciously, the music began:

Bowm . . . ba-ti-da-ba-da, bowm: A black-bound toe with a single-strapped ankle shot forward; a white China silk jersey brushed aside. Bowm . . . ba-ti-da-ba-da, *bowm!* An incandescent light, like from the doorway of death, flooded the makeshift partition. In white on white a name appeared upon the inner wall, NAEEM KHAN, bleached by the glow but outlined by its shadow. *Bowm* . . . ba-ti-da-ba-da, *bowm!* An indistinguishable blend of beats—the precursor to a country brawl, the scheming of a skillful seduction—boomed from a circumference of speakers: *Bowm* . . . *ba-ti-da-ba-da, BOWM!* The light beamed forward. It stretched to the end of the runway, precisely as a perfect rectangle. A heel hit the ground. A knee pumped high. *BOWM . . . BA-TI-DA-BA-DA, BOWM!*

Straight down the middle of the runway, blinded and unblinking, head erect, shoulders square, hips forward, arms steady, face austere, cross, cross, cross, she walked. The gown swept over her shoulder, creased diagonally across her laterals, her ribs, hips, thighs, tucked behind her leg with a twist and draped around it with a flare. She reached the end of the runway. Paused. Shifted. Turned. And already pacing hard from the exit, a silk white jersey T-shirt with a crème, silver, aqua, peach, great waved embroidered palazzo pant swirled forward. *BOWM . . . BA-TI-DA-BA-DA, BOWM!*

One after the next the models appeared from behind the divider, passed under the designer's name, and marched automaton-like, android-like down the middle of the aisle, posed at the end, and returned dead to the right. Each wore her hair like that of the next. Each wore her makeup like that of the next. Each conveyed as little as that of the next. Staring. Glowing. Expressionless. Surreal. Disconnected and inexplicable and gaunt. And though Danny had been critical of what he'd seen backstage, unable to understand it, the point of it, the rationale behind it; and though he was irritated, increasingly, by beauty and what it was and who said and why and for what reason if any, and how it might not be today what it would be tomorrow or once was before or never at all, not to mention trying to find his place within it; and though all of these things, all these confusions and frustrations and desires disagreed with him, the artistry he saw before him, the garments, the creases, the stitches, the colors, the cuts, the weaves, the way they all made his eyes swim, his lips part, his thoughts pale, he couldn't deny, was exquisite.

Even genius. Each item was more impressive than the last, so masterful the attire seemed suited not for the analysis of critics, not for the entertainment of the lay or the cursory thrills of undeserving socialites, but for fewer. Like a Rani. Like a Maharani. Danny glanced about in the dark. Perhaps one was there. Or the season prior. And if not a genuine princess or queen, then perhaps some other diva or devotee instead—a Mariah, a J Lo, a Beyoncé nearby. Surely *one* of them had worn a Naeem Khan—or two. Maybe the black floral lace column with the diagonal beads and exposed shoulder. Or the plum chiffon gown poised with crystal-trimmed cuffs. Easily the ink marbled-paillette sheath with the jet beaded neckline. Oprah, to be sure. And the inventory only continued. Funnel collars. Ikat prints. Python sequences. Black and bronze jacquard panne velvets; gold leopard-embossed matelassés; bootcut silk faille pants; magnificent caftan gowns, peony embroidered. Certainly the black iridescent coque feathered cape, how it tickled the thighs and left room at the elbows.

But that was spring, when the fashion was fall; and this was fall, and the fashion now spring. Blacks, bronzes, golds turned to whites, reds, and the kaleidoscope between. Fabrics cooled. Cuts loosened. There were obi belts and satin Thai pants. There were bubble skirts and chic caftanettes. There were halter dresses with lightly fringed hems, cherry blossom dusters with embroidered Mandarin collars, three-quarter-length sleeves floating airy and lithe. There were strapless sheaths and strapless pagodas. There were origami dresses and origami gowns. There were phoenix garden ruffle skirts hiked high above the knee and a silver confetti bodice with fire at the feet. There was a Maltese crystal encrusted collar, a chrysanthemum floral paillette, a coromandel gilet, and a cinnabar beaded georgette. And more stunning than any of them, there was Una.

Danny's eyes peeled wide. She cleared the split, and owned the tent. Her lips hung full. Her heels pumped heavy. She moved with agility and ease but neither motive nor arrogance. She held an aura of strength and indifference, conveyed in everything from her posture to her pace to the effortlessness in her cheeks, the grandeur of her garb. She wore a silk jacquard combination consisting of a strapless cloud mini dress under a great wave embroidered three-quarter length sleeve coat held open by her hands resting comfortably in the pockets behind her hips. The fabric was woven with silvers, browns, fuchsia and lilac and ube twisting and twirling from shade to shade, while through them, these distinct yet transient hues, as ephemeral as Uluru under the setting sun, petals upon petals crisscrossed in red—scarlet and shining and lavishly red. The coat's inner lining was red. The dress itself was red. Her lips and her neck and her collar bones were bare, her legs were distracting and bare. But everything, otherwise, was red.

Everything was precise. Everything was choreographed. The order, the lights, even the music matched the clothes which transitioned fluidly with the silks and scarlets from the opening country-brawl-meets-city-seduction to an odd sort of bad-ass, new-age, deep Euro hip-hop featuring English-speaking rappers with French-sounding accents; then something hummed, something Turkish or Lebanese. Una emerged and it segued again, this time from an intimidating Goth-like blend of House and Chant to a smooth, sax-less jazz. She could have been entering the ballet. Or a palace.

It was polite of course to stare. But Danny stared differently, dumb, with his heart like a gavel in his ears and his lungs like wings in his throat. He sensed nothing more. Even as she was gone. Wondering, simply, how she did it. No one could follow her. She walked on heaven, in garments nonpareils.

*   *   *

He wasn't supposed to leave between shows, but they found a spot on the stairs facing Fifth Avenue and started devouring all the carrots and cantaloupe and rice crackers they could carry, and a bag of M&Ms for fun. Una tossed one and caught it in her mouth. "I can't tell you how glad I am to be finished with them," she said, massaging her scalp. "All I want is my money. They think I care about their gimpy little Fashion Week party? I'll go to IMG's if I want. What are you doing tonight? Did Edge have its party?"

He rolled his eyes. "Last night."

"What—same shit, different day?"

"I wouldn't know, I never got in. I didn't even want to go. Not alone. Xavier and Isis went to her agency's party. Remmy's never there. I told Xavier I didn't think I'd go and the next thing I know Kinzie's calling saying be ready by nine. Ten o'clock rolls around and still no Kinzie. But I'm all ready to go. So I do. The Double Seven. You know it?"

"Of course, but no *the*. Über-chichi. So Meatpacking. *Sooo* Edge. Here. Eat. This cantaloupe is amazing. So you go . . ."

Danny shrugged. "That's it; I went and never got in. It was like 10:30. I must've tried for an hour. A whole bunch of us. All guys. Just standing there. Waiting, waiting. My name was *on* the guest list. They said they were over capacity, fire safety. Girls kept getting in though. Girls not even with the agency. One was escorted right over me. Lindsay Lohan? I don't know. Forget it. Let's not talk about it."

Una grinned. "You're getting so . . . New York," she said.

"So New York?"

"You're still you. Just with more . . . mettle. More edge."

"Edge?"

She tossed up another M&M. She caught it and winked. "Come with me to Cielo tonight. I promise we'll get in. I hate going to these things alone."

Danny circled his finger over his knee, pensive and patient and dreading returning to work. "Where . . . where were you? When it was my birthday? What happened?"

"Danny, I called. But your—"

"I know. I know you did. My phone—it broke. I wasn't able . . ." He looked up. "I mean your message. What did you say?"

Una lowered her eyes. A few strands of hair fell quietly from the chaos.

"I just was wondering. You know. What you said."

"I apologized. I said sorry. If I let you down. That I know how it feels. But . . . but sometimes . . . You know what it's like, how unpredictable everything is."

Danny shook his head. "How unpredictable what is?"

"Modeling. One minute I'm in L.A. waiting to get back to New York; the next minute my booker calls and I'm flying to Hong Kong."

"Hong Kong? *That's* where you were?"

"It's not like it's every day. Not like I wake up each morning in a different city. Even if it feels like it sometimes . . . But how do you say no? It's the first direct booking my Tokyo agency has gotten me. Thanks but no thanks? Give it to someone else?"

Danny looked at her, silent. His life wasn't at all the same. They could have been operating in two separate industries: she, working; he, not. She was there and then gone and though he was ready for it—this swift and endless jaunt—it simply wasn't the reality. It wasn't his life. He didn't live in the air, thirty, forty, fifty flights a year. He didn't hop from one shoot to the next, removing makeup every evening just to have it reapplied by another artist in another studio for another client the following day. He didn't walk onto a set and forget, genuinely *not know* why or for whom he was there. Delirium, persona, money, excess? His life was as humble as it had always been.

He glanced at his phone. Una caught his eye as they stood. Something felt odd again. Pleasant yet odd. Self-conscious. Adolescent. They could feel relaxed as others. They could feel at ease among strangers. They could find security in front of cameras, tweaked and painted, critiqued and discarded, instructed and lit and ready to fake all of it if necessary. Yet as themselves? In their hearts? The world their witness?

"I—I have to go," Danny said clumsily. "I'll see you tonight."

*   *   *

Little West Twelfth Street bustled with rank. Everyone from escorts to assistants to the drivers of their cars and the dogs they packed into purses—models who could coat entire walls with campaigns; celebrities who came to New York to "get away"; socialites who attended fashion events for distraction—everyone was someone. And knew it.

And Danny? They reached the door. Una drew him in. A woman in all black asked for her name and she said it, cogently, amid the mass of multi-lingual socializing, the basses stimulating, the appearing and disappearing of countless taxis and paparazzi and all the fashionable litter of New York noise.

"Plus one," she said, "Una, plus one," and greeted the defensive line semi-circling the front door. Danny followed with nods, shakes, snaps, a pound, as if he were suddenly a member of an unspoken fraternity whose intimations he unknowingly acquired.

Without a word they stepped inside. Una waved at acquaintances. Danny looked with ease about the club. He felt his adrenaline explode and he ignored it. He scanned. Nothing around them happened faster than indifference would allow and yet the music saturated everything it touched. The lighting was hypocritical. The geometry was fixed. The entire club was hostage to a perfection that everyone fostered but no one noticed. Models were everywhere: girls and boys, women and men, others ambiguous between. They mingled among agents, among editors, among the predators who paid handsomely for their admission and whom insiders called "freaks." They mingled without words. They mingled without trying. Bodies and bodies imported from every nook of the world and all their faces exported back. Each distinct. Each elusive. Each intrepid and desired and soulful and sleek. Malleable. Addictive. And more.

Beautiful?

They had eyes cerulean, eyes anthracitic, eyes big and effervescent and dangerous when they latched. They had cheekbones pulled high like volcanoes that refused to settle or waves that wouldn't fall, in ivory and magnolia, soil and sand, olive and amber and brown that was all but black. They had foreheads spread long and wide, flat as runways and landing pads, and lips all bursting or absent, jaw lines proud or absent: for extreme was the essence of arresting, and symmetry alone was the valid exception. Each nose, each nostril—from bridges above to the philtrums below—spoke the ultimate symmetry. Every tooth teased perfection. Every ear defined balance. Necks like streams, waterfalls, ski slopes tucked and turned at all the right spots. Hair brought begging; skin pleading. Postures gripped and nails, knuckles, dispositions, subtle glances and countless nuances from hips to hats to a Flute, a Capharinia, a Singha in hand, effortless and understated and unaware of all of it—the flawlessness, the rightness, the excellence, the perfection—that all of it together produced some inexplicable portrait that none of it really was.

Beautiful?

"So what do you think?" Una leaned in and shouted. Her lashes skimmed his ear. Her breath warmed his neck. "Love the décor; sort of seventies in a postmodernish way. *And this sound system!* It's like having ears all over your body." She waved again. "You want a drink?"

It was the music. The models. The ambiance of indifference. The beauty of it? He wondered who agreed. And it was the weeks, the months, the season and its tensions, all his failures and dearth of successes and earnings and accolades and the trying and constant trying to be right, to be ideal, to be perfect for everyone and sought by everyone and *be* everyone that clawed at him. Standards he couldn't articulate were choking him. Boundaries and definitions and the most basic understandings of self and satisfaction, innocence and hope were becoming as mixed in his mind as he was in others. Watching. Imitating. Lost yet certain, utterly certain that the best models were ultimately, simply, themselves—unaware, only, that some selves were multiple, some mercurial. Adroit and suave and resourceful. Chameleons beyond any master. Quicker than the Fashion that Danny couldn't grasp.

"I'll get them." He felt some masculine need to affirm himself, to spend foolishly what he didn't have on a girl whom spending didn't impress. He didn't realize of course, that the drinks were free. Nor what they would have cost if they weren't.

It was nearly an hour before he returned. Una was gone and the mob had grown. Danny finished his drink as he searched for her. He finished hers, too, and went back to the bar and drank his third and fourth and was on his way for a fifth when he turned and found her carrying champagne and a scent of cigarettes, and a smile he didn't recognize.

"I was looking for you." He felt fuzzy and deaf. He couldn't tell if Una heard.

"I ran into my new booker," she shouted. "She was talking to editors at *Bazaar*. It's all about the networking . . . Oh, there's this photographer here you should meet." She looked around. Danny felt bothered. "He's here somewhere. Mostly shoots girls but he might like you."

"Go look for him. I have to pee."

He made his way through throng after throng feeling his eyelids sag as he waited what seemed like days for a toilet. He barely noticed the vomit as he sat, or heard noses vacuuming coke off pocket mirrors. He leaned his head against the divider but never felt the bodies pressing back against him, or wonder if he was in the right bathroom. He sat motionless except for the alcohol and the music and all the models deep inside his head for some merciless time until he stood at last and thought faintly of Una. He stepped out beside a wall of sofas. The club was now packed. The music swelled. He felt neurotic and warm like he was being watched. He wasn't sure but he searched and he tried to hide but couldn't move. All he wanted was himself. All he wanted was to breathe. Someone was watching him and he couldn't help but feel crazy and beautiful and sick with shame. A myriad of emotions tore across his face and in a heartbeat he crushed all of them.

The man approaching him grinned. Danny looked away.

"Were you leaving?" His voice was deep, like whiskey or war.

"I wasn't sitting," Danny said.

"Would you like to?"

"Excuse me?"

"Would you like to sit?" He gestured confidently at the sofas.

"I'm looking for someone, thanks."

"Not yourself, I suppose."

Danny sobered.

"I'm always looking for someone," the man said, and stared at him with ease.

"Do I know you?"

"Gábi," he said. "I shoot fashion." He continued to stare as he removed a card from his wallet. Danny glanced at his fingers. They were long and svelte like a pianist's or surgeon's. He slid the card into Danny's hand. "Call me. We'll test." And suddenly he seemed softer than Danny first realized.

"Sure," he said, as the man turned to leave. "I'm . . . I'm Danny. With Edge."

The man smiled, slowly, and Danny remembered himself— the novice he was.

*   *   *

They left when everyone left, and took a taxi down to Tribeca. Una had been invited to the same party she was invited to every Fashion Week, hosted by a man whose name she couldn't recall. "I don't know, Danny, he works on Wall Street like everyone." Mostly, she adored the view. It was a penthouse, the view panoptic.

"And you can't remember how you met him either?" He looked at her, steadily, wondering if he were the drunker of the two. "You're sure I can come along?"

Una gazed out the window. She slid further into the seat, her hair pushing high above her head. "People like this don't count, Danny. Numbers mean nothing to them." She rubbed her face, and he wished they wouldn't go. She grabbed her purse, annoyed, and started rummaging as he watched with confusion. "I must look like shit," she said. "I *feel* like *shit*. I can't believe how many M&Ms you let me eat. I'm the fattest girl up there and I'm stuffing myself with M&Ms. Where is my *mirror?*"

Danny glanced at the driver. Then back at Una. He felt like he was concentrating and didn't know why. Like everything was happening incredibly slowly and explosively and pointlessly with a stranger he had known forever. She had this way of searching him, inspiring him. He felt absorbed in her every detail and wanted nothing more than for her to look at him.

"So what's he have to do with models?" Perhaps he shouldn't have asked.

Una stopped rummaging. She turned to him softly, as if to apologize. "Nothing," she said. "There's just . . . these people, Danny, these insanely wealthy people who . . . can *buy* anything. So they do. They buy friends."

She looked drained and unemotional. She looked like she had seen the world, and didn't care to discuss it.

"It's refreshing. How innocent you are." She laid a hand on his.

Danny looked out the window. "I'm not innocent."

"Yes, you are."

Danny leaned his head against the glass. He moved a finger from under her hand and laid it across her knuckles. And felt her contentment fill the car.

"I'm going home next month," she said slowly. "In Canada we do Thanksgiving in October. It's quiet there, in Selkirk.

Which is nice sometimes." Danny turned to her, her hair mashed and forgotten against the seat. "You can come. If you'd like."

Everything felt calm. Everything about them felt still and silent. Her hand on his. His spirit returning. The absence of time and the drone of the engine, idle. The words didn't register at first but then the driver tapped hard on the glass and the world burst in. Una stepped out. Danny paid and scrambled for the door. "Maybe—maybe we could talk about it tomorrow? When we're—well when we're not so—"

"Danny, I can't go in like this. Look at me . . ." She moved the mirror in closer. She jostled her hair. She evened her makeup. Danny turned as the taxi pulled away, taking their conversation, it seemed, along with it.

"We're going in *here?*"

Una picked at her hair. "It's one of those post-September 11th revivalist projects. Ian Schrager. Robert DeNiro. The view is totally surreal. You can see all the way down to the Statue of Liberty and up to Times Square."

She snapped the mirror shut and tossed it into her bag. In the lobby they handed their IDs to the man behind the desk. Una typed a code into a keypad and the attendant stood up for what seemed the hundredth time that night and led them past rows and rows of mailboxes and unmarked doors to a single elevator at the back. He stepped inside and swiped a card over a plastic shield, then walked away without a word.

The elevator opened at the only floor it could. A boy, a model Danny recognized stood at the entryway holding hangers and ticket stubs, and envy in his jaw. He nodded, and Danny nodded, and Una paused in front of a six-foot platinum-framed mirror and gazed oddly with resolve. Danny tried not to notice, and a moment later felt her hand on his shoulder, his confidence soar, and the music surge. They stepped under a door-less archway into a living room the size of Danny's apartment hosting speaker-lined ceilings fifteen feet high, walls of glass, scents of myrrh, floors russet wood with streaks of ecru. The condo splayed as sofas, low like daybeds and stunningly white, hugged the walls, jutting out back-to-back opposite low white tables with large, white, empty bowls. Everything felt ignored. Models in Jimmy Choo mixed with investors in ill-fitting linen in an air of casual tension, slow and enigmatic, like jellyfish drifting through the ocean.

Alcohol was plentiful, subtlety supreme. The ambiance was intimidating and artificial and Una led Danny through all of it to a small group of models and Ivy-educated men standing outside on the balcony. She was welcomed by her colleagues with kisses, hugs, jostling by the men, as Danny, like the music, like the view, like the walls, went ignored. He kept as close as he could. He sought favor in association. But as he glanced around he realized the only other boy in there was the one at the elevator, and that these men, their attitudes, while outwardly so sophisticated and clean were in fact cultureless and self-absorbed and too horny to be human and growing crueler with every glance at him, as though wealth were a pedestal, and innocence a threat. The models remained neutral but the bankers sneered and after a few callous gestures he found Una's ear.

"Why are we here?"

She dropped her head with a smile and set her chin, politely, to Danny's shoulder. "The men can go fuck themselves. Would you mind getting us drinks?"

Danny looked at her, stunned, but she was already re-engaged. He made his way to the kitchen where he poured bourbon and drank it and stared at marble, stainless steel, pictures of exotic places. The alcohol hit him harder than any he had had that night and he wanted desperately to wipe every last bottle off the counter and straight into the sink. But all he could do was gaze at them with every ounce of approval, and wish someone would understand.

Everything had gotten uncomfortably quiet in his head until two models walked in and two investors followed, like the assholes they were. Danny poured another drink and drank it, and realized he couldn't make sense of anything they said. Whether the models spoke Russian or the investors spoke yachts or he was simply losing more of his senses, the only thing he knew was that beauty was a waterslide, to a pool full of sharks.

They shot Patrón. The men poured more. The models moved in a way that made their collars stretch and the bankers smirk and Danny watched, and drank, and in flashes thought of Marina.

The kitchen began to fill. More models walked in, followed by more investors, more drinking, more moving in ways that Danny could have confirmed from the moon and more smiles he wanted to smack. He thought of shaking them all sober, exorcising their egos and uncovering their dreams and bringing reason back to reality but slammed his glass on the counter instead and walked back to the balcony, bracing himself against the walls and trying to remember why he was there.

The balcony hardly informed him, though the view offered hope. He felt his eyes like stones, his feet like bricks, and if the ledge had been higher he might have jumped. Two models lay tangled and tongue-tied, two more propped comatose against a daybed. Danny stared at them, phlegmatic and silent until after a long delay he remembered her. He walked back into the living room and sat slowly and dizzily on something square that blended with the room. His veins throbbed, his cheeks burned, his thoughts ran in circles as he watched the models, the investors, every illusion meet reality, and then he saw her. Hovering. Slow. A long white line storming straight up her nose.

Chapter Seventeen

OUTSIDE HIS APARTMENT he vomited at last. He'd been sprawled there, motionless, an hour or more, peacefully in pain. Night was yielding to day and even half-conscious he knew better than to be late. He rolled himself off the steps, crawled to the closest tree, and rammed a finger like a sewer pipe down his throat.

Everything was still hazy and slow hours later, but Harold, he was sure, had told him to go home.

"You have been sleeping since you sat, Mr. Ward."

"I'm waiting," he said groggily. "For Marina."

"She is not home, sir. I called when you got here."

But Danny just sat there, coddling his book bag and waiting patiently to respond. Yet he was too numb or nauseous to try.

He spent the rest of the day in the dark. He watched—he heard Project Runway, Tadashi Shoji, Chado Ralph Rucci close the week, and he budged only for the bathroom.

Una called in the afternoon. Sabyasachi was ending in the Salon. The audience cheered and dispersed and as the silence spread, she texted. Danny sat down. He studied the runway. He'd been recovering gradually, at last, but the more his hangover subsided the more his memory returned, and the more hurt he felt. He wondered if she even knew. He wondered if she was calling to apologize, if he'd accept, if there was anything to say. He knew what he saw. He knew how he felt.

He closed his eyes. He slid the telephone back into his pocket.

She called again during Omnialou, and once more as he was going underground. When he resurfaced he read the texts and listened to the messages. She was leaving, Sunday, for Paris and Milan. Could she see him? Could they talk? She didn't know where he had gone and she was worried.

He opened his door and climbed into bed. He didn't shower. He didn't change. He just lay there, daylight in the window and the shows, the parties, the week, the work, everyone's success and delight and disregard and all the things toward which he strived racing through his head without the slightest direction. How often could he be rejected? How often could he be faulted? How many times could he be told such subjective and necessary and contradictory things and not look in the mirror and grow cynical? He was stagnant in one of the fastest industries imaginable and he was sinking lower and lower into the underbelly of all of it. Yet no one seemed to notice. No one seemed to care. There were no boundaries, no definitions, no actions that supported words but a labyrinth of disguise and some resilient, inexplicable faith in the newness of each day.

He texted her at last, and fell asleep before she could reply.

*　*　*

They met the next morning at a park near their apartments. Danny arrived first and watched as Una neared.

"Hi!"

"Hey." He didn't move or make an effort to stand. Una took off her sunglasses and reached into a bag.

"I brought you something. It's from the farmers' market in Union—"

"I'm not a dog," he said harshly.

"What?"

"I don't jump at treats."

Una dropped her hands in her lap. Her eyes narrowed but her voice remained fair. "Danny, what is this? What did I do? I thought you were having a good time and the next thing I know you're gone and not picking up your phone."

He looked at her, amazed. "What did you *do?* Are you kidding me?" He'd been wondering how the topic would be broached. If she'd simply apologize. Ignore it. Lie. Play model as only she could. "Where should I even begin? Oh, I know. Why not with the fact that you brought me to some rich perverted stranger's house and you sat there snorting coke!"

"*That's* what this is about? *Cocaine?* Are you serious?" She nearly laughed but stopped. "Danny, this whole *city* does coke. The whole industry! What difference does it make? Who cares?"

"*I* care!" He stared at her, silent and scared and in a way even mournful, finished. "I didn't ask for this. I didn't come here to fuck up my life and I'm not about—"

"Fuck up your *life?* Who said anything *about* you? No one, Danny, *no* one forced you into anything. You're an adult. You can do what you want."

"Yeah, so I left."

"And your apartment?"

"What about it?"

"Don't act dumb, you told me about Kinzie. Are you leaving the apartment, too?"

He didn't respond.

"Well what's the difference?"

But he couldn't answer. He had never thought about it, and the first difference that came to mind overwhelmed him. He looked at her. He felt something he never had, for anyone, and was too overwhelmed to say it.

"I didn't choose Kinzie," he said. "Look, I'm not hanging out with coke addicts, Una. I'm just not."

She stared at him wide-eyed, humored and shocked. "Coke addicts? You think I'm a coke *addict*? And who are you, Captain Planet? I'm not calling you an alcoholic just because you got smashed. I did a line, Danny. *One*. You drank what you weigh and could've had alcohol poisoning but *I'm* a coke addict? Funny how that works, isn't it? Why'd you get so wasted anyway? Maybe you *are* an alcoholic. Maybe I mistook you. Maybe you're just like every other Midwesterner here—one more disillusioned binger, running away to wherever you blend in. Is that it? Is it, Danny? Or are you different? Maybe you're different. Maybe you just needed a night. To say fuck it. Fuck *all* of it. Fuck fashion, fuck the industry, fuck the standards. Fuck everything I put myself through and every asshole who can't deal with it. Everyone leave me the *fuck* alone. Let me live. Let me be. Is that possible? Is that so bad? One night to just forget about the fact that you can no longer remember what got you here. Why you were ever so eager to get into this business and why in the world you find it so difficult to get out." She looked away. Danny was silent. "Maybe that's what I needed too," she said. "A night. To say fuck it. To feel good. Feel pretty." She tried to smile. "Happy."

Danny didn't move. He didn't even try. Una closed her eyes and he felt helpless in every way possible. He couldn't fathom how he knew her so well, yet hardly at all, and felt so loved just being beside her.

"I think you're pretty," he said.

She forced another smile. A tear pressed through her eyelids. "And do you think I'm happy?"

He inhaled and let out a long, low breath; then moved an arm around her shoulder and eased her cheek to his chest.

* * *

He returned to Marina the following week. He didn't mention her absence or ask about the various "delights" from which she suffered. He put it behind him and assumed she would too, but when he opened his envelope after his first day back with her he found double his daily pay, and wondered how sick she really was.

The consistency, the reliability of the cash flow only made addressing it harder. He had been thinking all weekend of how he would tell her. He practiced consistently, experimenting with every possibility: "Marina, remember when you mentioned . . . Marina, I was wondering if you still needed . . . You know the party you're throwing—it's actually the same weekend . . . Well she's from Canada and their Thanksgiving . . . It's that it conflicts with . . . My point? My point is . . . I can't work your party . . ."

"What do you mean, *can't*, Daniel?" She pronounced it so strictly, so differently than anything he had prepared for. "Undoubtedly, you *can*. Surely, you *can*."

He should have asked. He should have lied. Some outrageous excuse.

"How much did we agree upon, Daniel? One thousand for the weekend?"

The number sounded so much larger than he recalled.

"Shall we say two thousand?"

"Two thousand?"

"Oh, Daniel, make it *ten* thousand, I do not care. Just *be* there. What is so bloody byzantine about that?"

If it were modeling he could explain; something legitimate and he could justify it. Like she did, repeatedly—"how do you say no?" But there was nothing here to be named and with every word she spoke he felt another piece of him crumble, his dignity fade. Everything he thought he had come for drifted lifelessly out of reach. He sought himself for answers. He counted what he could control. There was never supposed to have been a Marina. He never wanted this sort of work. His contract said nothing about need, about failure, about outlandish offers from the barbarically wealthy or how he might feel once his autonomy had been taken.

"Marina, you don't understand. I was invited—"

"No, Daniel, *you* do not understand. I am hosting a weekend fête in the Poconos and I am paying you to help."

She swallowed him with a glare, and he fought his hardest to be grateful.

Chapter Eighteen

I T WAS NEARLY NOON when the driver called. Danny had been reading all morning and still hadn't packed. He had finished every Kerouac book the library was carrying—all on the same patch of carpet—and decided it was time to switch authors. The next day he passed a book vendor on the street and there on top was a title he recognized, tagged and marked with the number 5. "We'll make it four," the salesman said. Danny looked at the aging Bohemian sitting on a nearby milk crate, then back at the book and paid for it promptly—the first he'd ever bought. He started reading it that night and was reading it the next morning when the car arrived.

He expected something refined, something chic and modern and überly Marina, but nothing like what he saw. The driver opened the door and Danny about-faced to sit. The rear quad of seats mirrored each other in pairs, inverted as on a train or in the cabin of Air Force One, furnished just as plentifully. Each seat was accompanied by a ten-inch, high-def, flat-screen, swivel monitor, separate stowaway keyboard, and individual media device complete with movies, music, and the Web. There were fold-out desks, heaters for the seats, electronic shades, and a chassis built to withstand everything from shotguns to hand grenades. The interior was made of the softest skin, with the cabin divided from the driver by a vertically-moving window, too turbid to see through, but which Danny would have preferred to face. He sat down backward, and with the Pullman complete, Keith, Blake, Bryce, and Danny headed promptly to the Poconos.

Keith sat opposite Danny, Blake diagonally, Bryce to his right. Keith and Blake, the former taller, the latter blonder—literally and figuratively—were strikingly similar. They had been classmates and teammates and friends from a lonely town just halfway between Lincoln and Cheyenne, where Colorado intervenes. They were all-Americans, in practice and appearance, from the dimples in their smiles to the gusto in their greetings to the mountainous shape of their shoulders. They stood just above and below six feet, and they bench-pressed their combined weight. Both were signed to PGK at R&L but both were on the verge of losing their contracts. They had become too thick, too titan, even for Abercrombie and soon *Men's Health*. They ate extraordinary servings of tuna, egg whites, chick peas, peanut butter, and spent endless afternoons calculating glutamine, nitric oxide, creatine ethyl ester, and all their branched chain amino acids. They obsessed over their physiques and over those of others. They counted and criticized every flaw. They divided nights with biking and exercise routines. And because they lived together, exercised together, double-dated together, and worked many of the same non-modeling "model" jobs together, they could obsess, constantly, together. Some called them vexing. Others said bromantic. Danny couldn't tell them apart.

Bryce was a different spectacle. He was a shade more mature, equally muscular, but trimmer and stealthier and not as consumed by pop culture. Unlike the blondes—their faces bulbous, their noses dense, their grins wholesale and juicy—Bryce straddled fashion. He had lank brown hair, hazy blue eyes, inconsistent stubble dotting a triangular jaw. He knew his angles and proportions and he showed it in the tilt of his chin, the part in his lips, the indomitable way he walked not only in bombers and boots but in denim—*on* denim—as if he should be and everyone would be, and the dictatorial way he wore his underwear. There was the scar over his left brow, the slope of his trapezoids, the arc in his spine, the contour of his ears. There was no single feature, but all of them combined, that unlike Keith and Blake, offered Bryce versatility. It offered him mystery, and nearly celebrity, except that he was six-foot-four if not taller, and slouching was unbecoming. According to his comp card he was, of course, a welcomed six-two. Agents at Fusion weren't idiots. Even so, fashion, for Bryce, remained elusive. For even with a firm jaw and a doughty swagger, even with hazy blue eyes, numbers never lied.

From the moment Danny saw them he knew they'd be chatterboxes. Not Bryce, but the duo—two big fish from one tiny pond—and he sought the car's amenities instead.

"So what about you?" Keith tapped him on the leg. "Who are you with?"

Danny glanced up. "Edge," he said, his tone nondescript.

"Edge? You're at Edge and you're working weekends out of town?"

Danny shrugged. "What, is that some sort of anomaly?"

"I mean, we've been here, what, Blake, two years, working these gigs just as long, and we sure never worked with anyone from Edge."

"What gigs?" Bryce said. "Marina's? She hosts often?"

"These *kinds* of gigs." He pulled a plastic fork and two cans of tuna from his bag. "I never met the woman."

"You're eating two?" Blake looked forgotten.

"Chill, one's for you." Keith turned back to Bryce. "So, what, you just model? You get by? You don't work for any party companies?"

"Just model? My chest is that flat? I bartend."

"So how'd Marina find you?"

"Bartending. Fashion Week. Edge had its party at Double Seven."

Danny turned. "Marina was at the Edge party?"

"The place was packed. Total madhouse."

Danny looked out the window. They entered the tunnel and all he could see was a smear of tiles and streaks of fluorescent light.

"So, what, some woman just walks up to you at the bar, orders a Martini and says, 'How about a weekend in the Poconos? Dinner party. Five hundred in cash.'"

"Pretty much. Except it was a Negroni. And a grand."

Danny wondered if this bar was anything like Aqua, and if they were hiring.

"Dude, you're getting a *thousand* for the weekend? We're five hundred a piece."

"Yeah, cause this party company she got you through probably takes half right off the top. Besides, anyone dropping fifty for a twenty-dollar drink knows I don't need to leave the city to make five hundred in a night."

"That's insane." Keith shook his head and opened the can. Danny couldn't help but stare. His fingers, his entire hands were wildly mesomorphic; his wrists were almost as large as Danny's biceps. He lowered the window and squeezed the juice into the air. "What about you? Five hundred? Which company?"

"What are these companies?" Bryce insisted.

"No idea," Danny said.

"No different than working at a bar. They keep us alive."

"Who? Models?"

"*Guys*. Girls are models. We're . . . something else."

"You can say that again." Danny opened another gadget.

"Not the foreigners," Bryce said. "Asians, Europeans, the Brazilians—they work. South Africans, Israelis. Americans though—we're too big."

There was a brief silence, and everyone glanced at Danny. Danny wasn't too big. Danny was thin, he was un-Americanly thin. And he was working a private dinner party. He was, of course, no longer a résumé-less model. He shot an ad for a west coast client the previous week. Nevertheless, he certainly wasn't the sort of model one might expect to be looking for extra income.

"I'm still new," he said. "Not even six months in."

Keith looked at him curiously. "You ever tried supplements? Dextrose? Whey? You know what ZMAs are?"

"I don't lift," Danny said.

Keith finished his tuna and handed the fork to Blake, who offered it to Danny. "You want some? You hungry?"

"I stopped eating meat."

"It's fish."

"I know."

There was another silence, and Bryce persisted. "So would you tell me about these party companies? Catering?"

Blake's lips curled errant and impish. "Catering?" The word sounded juvenile.

"Not catering," Keith said. "Those aren't what I would call *par*ties. Actors cater. Dancers cater. Models don't cater. I'm not walking around going table to table in a tux for eighteen bucks an hour saying, 'Chicken or fish?' 'Red or white?' 'Yes, Madame?'" Blake laughed. Keith sneered. "Fuck that. I'm talking parties. *Real* parties."

Still, Danny was clueless, and wondered if Bryce was too.

"Just tell them," Blake said.

"It's not all just sex and drugs."

"You get paid to go to sex parties?"

Keith straightened. "Not always. Sometimes crash a wedding. Get paid a few hundred bucks, show up for awhile and get everyone dancing. Sometimes Bar Mitzvahs, but mostly just weddings. Sweet sixteens. Most of them you just hang around shirtless, let the girls giggle or point or touch, flirt a little, maybe embarrass them. Parents tell you: greet, get in pictures, dance, ride around in the limo a bit; let whatever happens happen. Bachelor*ette* parties—they're a little trickier. More pressure. See, parents don't pressure their sweet-sixteen-year-old daughters. They just give them what they ask for, you know. But the bachelorettes. Their friends. What you get paid to do and what they expect you to do—it's not always the same."

Danny was dumbfounded. He wasn't sure if he was intrigued, distressed, cynical, or entertained, or simply intimidated by the possibilities, but as he sat there and listened all he could think was, *Marina's not sixteen, Marina's not a bachelorette,* and repeated it until it mattered.

"These parties—they look wild. But they're not. Just a bunch of prudes hoping for an excuse to do something they're too scared to do without one. It's a game for them. They tell themselves that whatever they're doing is what they're supposed to be doing, that that's why they're there and that's how you celebrate. The next day they're all giddy about it, thinking they're cool for doing a few Jell-o shots and touching some guy's dick that doesn't belong to their boyfriend, but still feel safe that if word gets out they can just pat their pleats and cheeks and braids and say, 'Oh, but I didn't *mean* it. I mean, I *had* to. Everyone *was* and I just . . . I thought . . . you know— that's what you *do*. I had no *idea*. I'm not that kind of *girl*.'" He leaned in to Bryce. He pushed out his lips and he batted his lashes and in some Little Miss Piggy-like voice squeaked, "Really!" then rocked back and laughed. The others did too. Then he cracked his neck. He cracked his knuckles. And with some rogue, frolicsome shimmer in his eye, he said, "They have no idea."

* * *

The twenty-foot-long S600 with run-flat tires, a self-sealing fuel tank, on-board fire-extinguishing system, 5.5-liter twin-turbocharged V12 engine, 517 horses, and ample room for fondles and footsies rocked gently left, and up, and passed through an iron gate with the inscription AD INFINITUM above an MM, then steadily decelerated over a blanket of snow-covered stone.

Danny rubbed his eyes and stretched his arms. He lowered his window, waking, and squinted at the sheen. Torrents of light came flooding in. Too blinded to stare but too beautiful not to, he reached beside him and tapped. "Wake up . . . Guys, wake up."

The limousine ascended slowly up the driveway to a remote summit where the air was brittle and life undisturbed. Far, wide, everywhere there were mountains, billowing and criss-crossing like quilts without end. They vaulted high, high into the atmosphere, then tapered to the ground. They traded valleys and swapped streams and they cajoled every corvid, every junco, every robin to sing as they glided like kites across glens and swales and over supine lakes that mimicked them wing for wing, as no ocean ever could. Waterfalls raced to the ground. Rocks smoothed like slides. Streams kissed the wind with purple, bronze, gold, and green, the oaks, the maples, the birches all about, and Danny stared. The sun shined selflessly as little wisps of mist floated out from his lips. He breathed in, deep, autumnal and fresh, and he held it as it hardened within his lungs until he could no longer contain it and a long, heavy cloud disappeared into the world. *Ujjayi.* His breath met a million trees and a million trees breathed back without knowing or being known but simply appreciating the necessity of release. Another ego undone.

Namaste.

For a moment he thought of Kerouac. For another of flying.

The car eased right, then shifted left and hugged a busty, chalk-colored fountain. Danny didn't see it behind him, as something more prodigal, a sort of mansion or manor replete with indulgence and every expression of inconceivable grandeur, crept into view. He wasn't sure if it was threat or enthrallment or hilarity he felt, or maybe just disbelief, but like a child in some phantasmal factory of unending chocolate, eager and amazed and altogether addicted save only respect for gluttony's pain, he saw it, and mouthed a deep, quiet, *Noooooooo*.

It—the château?—was three floors high, four at the back, and colossal in expanse. It was built from Pennsylvania fieldstone, a patchwork of grays and whites. A colonnade to the right wore a porte-cochere some dozen feet high that reached beyond Danny's view to the back of the estate where the same scene of knitted mountains, rocketing trees and reflecting lakes stood in plain sight from all of the four observatories. A porch projected from every level, each stretching the length of the estate with ceiling fans for summer, heat lamps for the fall, iron railings, parquet floors, dropdown shades, and an assortment of elegantly padded sofas, loveseats, and lounge chairs in rattan of Australasia.

The car stopped. Danny and the other—other who?—models? aids? boy-toys?—Danny and the others stepped out. The snow packed beneath their feet. The air expanded in their lungs. Slowly, they turned, they stared, and they gaped.

The mansion. The mountains. The echoes of isolation.

Then Marina burst through the door. The foursome turned to find her dressed in what Danny knew to be her standard, accentuating exercise attire, her hair bunned high. A towel hung around her neck. Sweat stains spread stylishly under her arms and breasts and at the peak between her thighs. Her cheeks glowed cherry in the early afternoon sun as her bosom rose broad with each inhale. Danny had never seen her so. He knew she exercised most afternoons, that she had other instructors, actual trainers who sapped her of her breath and barred her of her reveries of crème fraîche, lomilomi, tsavorite garnet, and Mimosas for all—essentially of any talk or attempt. He knew this, and never more so than seeing her then: sweaty, sultry, hotter than he had ever made her.

"Oh, was it *fun!* Was it?" She hugged herself as she skipped, stomach exposed, still absorbed in some unidentifiable mirth, looking more at the car than at any of them. She was elated, amused, oddly informal, talking as though they had, just an hour before. "I saw it in one of Jonathan's periodicals last month and I thought, Oh, I must! I must!

What a *lark* it would be. So I *did!* Was it fun? Were you entertained? *Did you play?*" She spoke to them, but walked through them, to the vehicle, inspecting it, absorbing it, enjoying it. "It *is* sniper-proof you know, bumper to bumper. The dignitaries ride them. Oh, but what a lark! If Stuttgart only knew!" She opened one of the doors and as though tasting something decadent and unexpected, entirely novel and yet equally disobedient, she exclaimed, "Oh! Oh my! Oh my word! *That* is divine." And disappeared inside. Blake turned to Keith. Keith turned to Bryce. Bryce turned to Danny. Danny shrugged. The novices were speechless. Danny attempted to feign the same. "*Well,*" Marina said, rejoining her crew and petting the limousine approvingly, "they most certainly did not make toys like that when I was a child. We devised our own sorts of fun." She paused, and two fingers skated about her neck. "Daniel! You are here! How very marvelous! And Bryce? Yes—Bryce. And you must be Kieran and Blake."

"Keith," Keith said.

"Right. Yes . . ." She looked at him, her chin just barely rising, her lips parting, dry. "Boys—gentlemen!—it is brisk and I am torrid and my exercise is not yet complete. Come, bring your shambles inside. Supper is—please, do not soil the house with snow. Supper is being prepared in the kitchen. Alcohol, save wine of course, is in the larder. Flowers shall arrive in an hour. Jonathan will receive them and instruct you as necessary. Guests are shortly underway as well, and shall be here by and by—seven, a quarter past. Be groomed by six thirty? *Splen*did!"

She turned and walked back inside. Without moving they looked at each other. Not excited. Not intimidated. No sign of exhilaration or apprehension or even disbelief. No sign of anything. They just looked. Flat. Uniform. Flabbergasted without realizing until suddenly, lithely, she reappeared at the door. "This *is* a soirée tonight, gentlemen. Please, do behave. Accordingly . . ."

* * *

The guests arrived, precisely delayed. They kissed and they hugged and before too long they were drinking and mingling, praising and pleasing with subtlety and charm. Danny and Bryce mixed cocktails behind the bar. Keith and Blake passed hors d'oeuvres as instructed. Classical music played ignored. Scents of Escada mixed with Ungaro and with the flames, the oils, the spices of an educated kitchen. Purple, too, some wisteria or lilac warming with the walk-in fireplace, mixed with a pee-colored yellow over an Erdem double duchesse. A Trussardi 1911—Old Etonian at the cuff, one half lillet blanc— fringe-fronted suede bomber jacket approached; eyes only. Garlic and Rachmaninoff and a silver tubular ankle-length stretch dress by Marios Schwab toasted Trovata's wide-wale mulberry corduroy, untailored and understated, as a Balenciaga scrolled peplum leered. Jonathan sipped scotch in Bottega Veneta. Marina wore a fascinator. She drank Pimm's with indifference and flair, and when the time came, she seated her guests with glee. Danny abandoned the excessively stocked bar and watched from a room away.

"Everyone, everyone," Marina said, her accent heightened. "Please, a moment." The collective murmur quieted as the guests cluttered the table and turned their attention. "Let us— yes, let us have Jonathan there at that end, I here at this." She stroked the broad outer slope of the gilt chair she claimed, the back of which reached as high as her bosom, then proceeded with ease in orchestrating the arrangement.

First: Donald and Helen. She placed them to her left, Donald most immediately. He was a Vice President at a Wall Street firm, sported a full head of salt-and-pepper hair, an Ivy League smirk, and an extensive knowledge of wines, wars, and sail boats, some of Marina's favorites, in addition to an insatiable appetite. Helen was an exceptional cook. She was also an inspiration of sorts to Marina; an envy of one as well.

Next, she assigned Davide and Fiammetta to her right, Davide inside and across from Donald, Fiammetta across from Helen, for of the two she spoke the better English. And because Helen had patience and Donald did not and because Fiammetta would talk verbosely about their business and Davide would not. And because Davide, like Donald, knew war, and was beautiful. Marina translated suspiciously.

In the middle, on the left, beside Helen, she sat Angela, and beside her, Jared. They didn't know one another, but neither did they know anyone. Angela was a jeweler and a bachelorette. Jared was a widower and self-proclaimed food critic, a golfer as well. He wore an antique set of cufflinks. Angela first examined them at a lonesome distance. She was the youngest of the guests and Marina watched her.

Santos and Phil she seated fourth, Santos beside Fiammetta. Spanish and Italian weren't entirely dissimilar, though Argentine wasn't exactly Spanish. Phil paid for the night classes and Santos learned quickly. His wife, his Green Card—Phil's first cousin—certainly helped. Being a state senator was hard enough. Phil thanked his family daily, and he thanked his hostess, too. He owed her.

Back to Marina's left and between Jonathan and Jared, she placed Jane and Mel. Mel was the CEO of a luxury hotel and Jane was the prim socialite who married him. Mel was uxorious and Jane kept him so. Jane won a beauty pageant when she was eight. She won another when she was nine. Jonathan handled her superbly and Marina held glances with him to be sure. Mel doted.

Finally, Nikko and Caroline. She sat Caroline across from Mel and next to Phil, and she sat Nikko to Caroline's right. Caroline was a three-time Temple graduate, and was a partner at one of the big Philadelphia firms. She was svelte in every way possible. Nikko was a self-employed dentist. Marina traveled to him to have her teeth cleaned. His, she insisted, was a special sort of whitener. They met in Japan.

Jonathan, of course, was Hollywood's principal cosmetic surgeon.

Chairs shuffled. And as assigned, they sat.

Danny poured the water. Bryce poured the wine. Keith and Blake served the soup—salsify, carrot, ginger, *pâte de feuilles*—and stood aside.

The volume in the room began patiently to rise. Voices blended like mixed drinks as conversations diverged in sundry directions. Napkins unfolded onto expensive laps. Glasses swirled under reconstructed noses. Chins nodded as Trellis spoons sank gingerly into burgundy-lined bowls and lips closed smart. Culinary compliments were bestowed upon no one, and received by all. Rachmaninoff danced the rafters. Agapanthus toured the halls. Outside, though none knew, it snowed.

Danny clutched his wrist with the opposite hand behind him. He breathed deep, and exhaled slow. The party, the atmosphere, the conversation—it was all beyond him. And yet impossible without him, exactly as he was, standing there, watching, available. He didn't feel ignored or disregarded, but simply less present than the music, the flowers; more like the snow. Just as it fell, so the water poured. It happened. The ground patted white, the glasses filled high, and between rounds of Bordeaux, they sipped.

They didn't ask. They didn't wonder. They simply lived in their worlds, strictly and exclusively, and Danny stood aside. He had been unnoticed before and at times wanted nothing more, though at the moment he had to wonder if not attending would have been more alarming, if they would have sooner seen his absence than his presence, the oddity of vacancy before the assumption of being. Or if this scene had nothing at all to do with him. If it was merely that they, the hosts, the guests, their extended coterie, *were* the very models of indifference, if they

were the indicators of its exalted ambiance, and if he was no different to them than the statues by the door.

"Florence?" Helen said. "Our son Evan is there right now.
For the weekend."

"Actually, no," said Jane, "I don't believe I've *ever* worked."

"Santos, enough." Phil lowered his voice. "No one will say
a word, I promise."

Danny poured more water. Bryce poured more wine.
Keith and Blake served familial vegetables—cardoon, violet
artichoke, sunflower tuber, mixed celery branch—*persillade d'O-
lives Niçoises*, and again stood aside.

Ambiance: was it invention or intuition? A blending of
both? For every detail, every sound, every scent and every sight
was constructed—which as union, relation, intention, seemed
entirely invention. Yet the feel of it, the insight of it, the orches-
tration of it, collaborating in harmony like eyes, lips, shoulders,
hands, not simply each in itself but as a whole, how to move
them and coordinate them, jointly, seemed wholly intuition.

But ambiance, invented or intuited, has made models its mea-
sure. Models are not its master; they are its muse. Models are not
its creator; they are its carrier. Models are interpreters—interpreters of the ambiance of indifference, of that which is called
beauty, and that called *beautiful*. Models are models not because
they themselves are beautiful. They are models because they
mime. Because they mimic ideals, notions, expectations that others conceive and acclaim. They are beautiful, perhaps, but if their
eyes can't gaze through a lens like a soul, if their lips won't comfort and curse simultaneously, if their shoulders don't shrug or fall
or twist or roll like the wind to the waves and the mariner who
struggles to engage them, then they might still be beautiful, but
they are not models. And they might try and try again, but if it is
not within, still, they are not models.

Jonathan smiled politely. "Yes, but celebrities have sensi-
tivities too."

"Phil"—Jared paused—"*Senator*. Have you ever dined at Le Bec-Fin?"

Marina sighed. "He says he has not yet drunk enough to believe you . . ."

Danny poured more water. Bryce poured more wine. Keith and Blake served the main course—baked langoustine and striped bass; confit tomato agnolotti; bouillabaisse consommé and curry emulsion. Attentive, indifferent, they stood aside.

That model *look*: that's what they called it. They, the masses; never its initiators. And it was that look to which they aspired. To weight. To height. To hair. To colors and shapes and aesthetics of inexhaustible sorts and yet to something well, well beyond: enigmatic, insoluble, inexplicable. Ambiance. They aspired to legs and hips and noses, no doubt, to necks best suited for gold. But they aspired, unequivocally, to ambiance. They aspired to some undefined totality of the incessantly idealized that likely *did* make them "beauty," likely *did* make them "beautiful," but more so made them models.

Masses aspired to it—to them, to beauty, to ambiance saturated by indifference—and yet they aspired to models who merely mimicked the very aristocracy to whom their clients marketed them. The celebrities. The socialites. The Marinas. The clients knew. They knew who bought. They knew who could and who couldn't but would without fail, their dispositions, their desires, their obsession to mix with like, to dress as like, to look like like. They knew indifference, too. They knew the ambiance of it, the staging of it. They knew that indifference sold because indifference bought, and that indifference had become a trend. Indifference at its origin was an ambiance which only the truly wealthy could afford, which only they could invent and only they might intuit. Yet current clients knew and fed the distorted trend—indifference to self. Eyes *like* another's. Breasts *like* another's. Skin *like* a model's which was *like* an actor's which was *like* so beautiful. Imitation to a science. Copies of copies and an ass to take home. Handbags and makeup and everyone's alike, everyone's grand, everyone's a celebrity. Everyone's like everyone and no one knows the difference. No one *is* oneself.

But this aspiring: was it beauty? And this aspiration: was it beautiful? For what was real? What was unique? What was itself, alone, and proud?

Caroline cleaned a molar with her tongue, just as Jane looked up and saw.

Angela cleared her throat. Then giggled and Jared continued.

Santos glanced furtively. At Keith. Then Blake.

Danny poured more water. Bryce poured more wine. Keith and Blake served dessert—aerated chocolate sponge; gooseberries, whiskey, walnuts—and they were still rounding the table when Marina raised her voice. "Oh, Phil, darling! I nearly forgot. Nikko and Caroline are members of your constituency. They hail from the historic city of . . . *agápē*." Marina chuckled; then sobered. "Although, Phil, when men are shooting each other in the cinemas . . ."

"I'm sorry, dear, from where? Who was shot?"

Marina dabbed the corner of her lips as Bryce passed behind the Senator, and the lawyer who nearly voted for him. "Philadelphia," he said. "It was a bad joke."

He couldn't have said anything more casually, but that he said anything at all caused a startling silence. She hardly flinched or shifted but with a flash of authority few models could match, her domain suddenly swelled. "An educated lad?"

Danny halted. Bryce paled. Confidence and virility turned to unrelenting shame, pure emasculation. It meant nothing that he was sober and she was drunk, that he was tall and she was short, that he was standing and she still sat. She governed. She commanded. This ability she had to dwarf. "I just . . . I . . ."

Marina raised a brow without raising one at all. Bryce silenced, like a baby fed. Phil downed his glass in a gulp, and right then, Danny realized.

*　　*　　*

Rather than sip coffee and klatch for hours as Danny had told himself they would, Jonathan led the guests away and Marina took her boys to the bar. "Drinks, gentlemen?" She stood behind it, the foursome in front. She pulled Rocks glasses from the shelf but rather than set them on the counter she lined them just below. No one seemed to notice. Bryce had turned to Danny in comforting conversation, and Keith and Blake were giddy with the news that they were off. "So drink," she said. "Shower. Change your clothes. Make yourselves comfortable." She watched the glasses as she spoke, then set the first, chaperoned by an envelope, on the bar before Keith—"Kieran"—then Blake—"Blake"—next Bryce—"*Bryce* . . . and . . . of course"— she now looked higher than the bar, higher than the buttons on shirts and the pectorals behind them, but at, and into, eyes— "Daniel." She lifted her own glass and grinned in a way he'd never seen her. "Cheers!"

They drank, grinned, and Marina went to the kitchen, Keith and Blake to shower. Bryce poured seconds and thirds and took them to the conservatory. Danny sat down on a bar stool and steadied himself. He eyed his glass. It doubled diagonally. He stared at it and his stomach fell. What had she given him? He thought of eating but was too woozy. He thought of fresh air, of a shower, but he couldn't even begin. He . . . he was drunk? He wasn't sure. Time slowed and he thought he . . . he wanted . . . thought he needed . . . whatever would come . . . as . . . as . . . as he closed his eyes . . .

*　　*　　*

One hand hung heavy over the side of a bed. The other lay limp by his thigh. Through the window there was only blackness, the stars. A glow caressed the walls from the door left ajar. The linens were exceptional, the pillows plush, the mattress supreme. He lay there, flat, not a stitch or feather disturbed.

Hours passed before the first finger twitched at last. He opened his eyes. He saw the ceiling, registered shadows. He felt mislaid without knowing why or where or how he had come. There were no answers without thoughts to think.

He turned, and something pulled. Something stretched. Then cracked like clay down his collar, his chest, his stomach.

He turned again, and more, and the pulling, the stretching, the cracking continued. He ran the hand that hung from the bed up along the quilt until he felt a lamp beside him, fondled it and flicked it on.

The light was invidious. He turned swiftly away. He pulled his elbows up and in, he lifted his head, and he looked.

His shoes were on. The laces were tied. He felt them before he could see them. His belt was unbuckled but still looped to his pants which crumpled taut about his knees, his underwear inside. His penis hung flaccid across his pelvis. His shirt was unbuttoned and flung wide, still on but off with his shoulders exposed and his sleeves kept fastened. His skin, his body, from his belly button to his neck, only some of which he could see, was dotted and streaked, dry, white, and crusty.

Danny gawked. His adrenaline surged as he scrambled for modesty. His clothes kept him tangled. He could feel himself panic and quieted to concentrate, to remember, but couldn't. He had no thoughts. None connected to the present. He never felt so void, so utterly undone. He was about to veer his feet to the floor, to sit up and regroup and think harder when he saw his book bag slumped in a parlor chair at the front of the room and remembered putting it there earlier in the day.

The Poconos?

The dinner party?

His breath quickened and he remembered more. The drinks. Not feeling well. Wanting to eat or shower or walk outside. Had he? Where? He remembered the stairs. They looked easy enough to climb, the way they rose from the ground, arching, curling, lifting like a wedding dress. Had he climbed them? Alone?

He stepped into the bathroom. He put on the clothes he arrived in and went out into the hallway hoping anything would inform him. He came to the stairs. They fanned as they fell. He swept wide with the banister and as he approached the landing he saw the dining room, spotless, in front of him. It was silent and austere like a museum display or a mansion made into one. The table was pristine. The floor was too. The chairs were spaced equidistant with the music still playing and the flowers still standing, and Danny, halted, was stunned.

Then he heard her. A cackle. A shriek. A whoop or a hoot or some combination of all of them. It was strange but he was sure it was she. He paused, then heard it again, clearer and louder and realized it came from below. He walked through the dining room, the sitting room, the parlor with the bar. The outbursts continued and as he entered the kitchen he was nearly speeding and stopped. The room was bare. No signs of anything. No pots or pans. No antique glassware. No aprons or timers or utensils. There were no bottles of wine or recipes or blood, but only order, emptiness, and curiosity.

He turned beside a pair of stainless steel refrigerators and looked down to where part of the floor the size of a bathmat was folded over, the light from below at his feet. He crept carefully down. The sounds amplified. He ducked and entered a wine cellar. He went on and reached a room of humidors; further and a gym; further still and a pool; until situated as deep in the sub-snarls as possible, lined with plush sofas, downy carpets, hand carved tables sprawled with priceless couture, bottles of Chivas and buckets of ice, glasses and ashtrays and half-smoked cigars, boxes of condoms, plates of cocaine, dildos and toys and lubricants and Viagra, he entered the scene through which he slept.

Everyone was naked. Jared and Angela lay twisted and wet, as disheveled as rags on the floor. Nikko's face ran deep inside Jane's legs, Mel's over her breasts and belly. Jane pinched a joint, her grin catatonic, her hips aquiver. Caroline hunched over a table. She closed her eyes and a nostril and inhaled hard, then leaned back, quiet, with a smile. Davide, Donald, Phil, and Santos formed a square on the floor. Their legs jutted out. Their necks strained sideways. Their mouths were wide and full. Fiammetta and Helen lay parallel beside them. Fiammetta lay face-up, Helen face-down, their moans in sync with Blake and Keith straddling them firm, gyrating and turning and kissing each other. Bryce sat opposite them. Marina sat on top of him. She plunged her nails with a growl into his skin. She gripped his chest. She gripped the sofa. Her eyes swam uncontained. She clenched her teeth as her hair, her breasts, her diamonds and loquacious commands rocked wildly in every direction. Sweat spilled. Saliva sprayed. Muscles, tendons, veins all throbbed. And Jonathan, with one hand hard and shifty, recorded it.

Chapter Nineteen

THE WALKS RESUMED. Danny got up at six and reached Lenox Hill before seven. He waited for the clock to chime, for Harold to call, for the elevator to grunt and Marina, casually, to descend. Outside, the temperature dropped. The leaves changed color. Nannies moved indoors and squirrels dug hastily in the dirt. The dogs continued to walk; and Marina looked healthy in pink. She held her stomach firm, her shoulders back, her elbows obnoxiously wide. She talked about shoes and gowns and emeralds and wine, "and the mint chocolate cheesecake, Daniel, oh my *word*, the caramel, the raspberries . . . the boy *serving* it . . ." Danny listened, and spoke, only per imperative. Hello. Goodbye. Yes when it was appropriate. He thought constantly about the weekend and though he refused to bring it up, he couldn't stand it any longer that she hadn't. Their Friday lap was ending. Marina was saying something about Etro or Malo or the way silk felt in blue when suddenly she stopped.

"Is something the matter, Daniel?" She sounded caring yet cold.

"I don't know. Should there be?" He turned with exaggerated innocence.

"Do not play games, Daniel. You have been laconic all week and your attitude has grown ornery."

"*My* attitude? And you, Madame hostess?"

"I beg your pardon."

"Did you even *notice* I was missing? Did you care? Why'd you even have me there anyway?"

"Daniel," she said, slow and deep and with detailed foreboding.

"My name is *Danny!* And don't *act* like you didn't know I was missing all night. I passed out in *your* house, working at *your* party."

She turned to him steadily, almost robotic, almost sinister, knowing and unfazed. "First, Daniel, you will lower your voice and you will restrain your temper." She paused, comfortably, then charged. "And *second!* Who are *you*—who are you to interpret *me?* What do you know of me? What do you know of acting? And *what*, pray tell, do you know of the acts that occurred whilst you slept? Nothing, Daniel. You know nothing. And do you know why? Do you?" She quieted, she grinned, she stared, and Danny's chest filled his throat. "Because I drugged you."

He stopped cold. Marina turned a few paces ahead.

"You what?"

"I drugged you, Daniel. Rohypnol. Roofies. I drugged you and I stripped you and I wanked you bone dry." She smirked as though she had obtained something at last that was rightfully hers. Danny's thoughts went blank. He could hardly sound a whisper.

"Rape . . . ?"

Marina sobered in disgust. "*Daniel*. Your language. How crass. How vulgar."

He stared absently at the ground. His stomach coiled in knots. Images of his fate flashed vivid and bare. He'd told himself it was the senator, his lover, one of the models taking a dare; the Rémy Martin he gulped without a crumb to catch it. He'd told himself he ascended unassisted, he navigated by a miracle, he found his bed, at least, on his own. He'd told himself—

assured himself—it was better to have been blank and unable than conscious and opposed, that he never would have abided what he watched underground. Yet as she gloated in front of him he felt a sickness born anew. His feet felt cemented. His neck locked in place. The wind broke like helicopters in his ears and as he fought to keep the only word he could create from forming on his lips, he glanced up at Marina and thought he would heave.

"*Rape?*"

She approached him swiftly. "I did not *fuck* you, Daniel." Her tone was resolute. "I could have. I should have. You know it is what you wanted. You *asked* for it, Daniel. You *knew* what awaited you—and you came. You came and you loved it. Every minute of it. Your entire body, your entire being shook with pleasures you have never known." She stood directly in front of him and grew suddenly benevolent. She grazed his ear. She traced his neck. He clenched his jaw and looked away. "Is that right, Daniel? Pleasures beyond compare?" She was inches away. Decisions neared. Loneliness, fear, dignity, hate, ease, chance, optimism all battled infinitely within. She reached his collar. She reached his shoulder. She trailed along his arm to his wrist and his hand and in a test or stroke of clarity he snapped it free. And walked away.

In the distance, amid the avalanche inside his head, he heard her laugh.

*   *   *

They talked sporadically that month but Danny grew increasingly disenchanted as the story always changed: something unexpected came up; he was out of town that week; he'd been shooting fourteen hours a day for the last five days and was behind on editing, eating, and sleep. After weeks of enduring excuses and ever-evolving impediments Danny decided his persistence was in vain and gave up. He had seen Gábi's Web site. He'd seen the models and celebrities Gábi shot, his client

list, the quality of his work, and he couldn't think of why anyone of his clout or caliber would offer him time for prints. Yet
one Sunday afternoon at the end of October as the rest of the
city gathered hung over for brunch, Danny found himself
between the Bowery and Alphabet City twelve floors up a
guard-monitored, key-coded building in Gábi's condo, shooting.

He had already shot in black knee-high boots sheathing
beige jockey pants, something like a cardigan tucked tight in
the front, unbuttoned to well below the navel, hair disheveled
precisely. He had already shot on his knees, brown leather
moccasins laced up to his calves, a silver pendant around his
neck and a bluish, collarless dress shirt tugged taut between his
legs. He had already shot—rather impressively—in a slim,
plum, pinstriped suit and a top hat, quarter profiles, moving,
bending, hips and knees electric. He had already shot in Cavalli,
too—Cavalli on the loveseat; torn velour by the balcony; a hel-
met in his hand.

He was back in front of a white backdrop, the side lighting
furtive yet punchy wearing champagne satin suspenders that
doubled in length and russet wool pants that belled at the bot-
toms, a distressed felt cap tipped up and turned sideways, Gábi
lauding. It was the way he moved with the suspenders, the lines
he created with them, the shadows and angles and definitions
they exposed. *"Good,"* Gábi said, "Now pull back. More. Hold
that! Nice, *nice.* Forward . . ."

He felt good—unusually, incredibly. He felt confident,
photogenic, and changed. Perhaps it was Gábi, orchestrating,
advising, extolling. Perhaps Una. Perhaps Marina. Perhaps it
was the Vodka Red Bull he drank when he arrived or the Vodka
OJ thereafter. Perhaps it was New York—New York and its
masquerades; New York and its billboards; New York and all its
successes and smiles, all its struggles and loneliness, its love and
charisma and incessant teasing. Perhaps it was the music, the
memories, the experiences and expectations compounding.

Perhaps it was the rarity of the occasion, some desire, some determination or desperation to impress. Or perhaps it was all of them, a watershed step toward adapting to the novelty, the industry. The guise. The game.

He dropped one strap to his side and pivoted conversely. A shadow lined his jaw. He lowered his hand to where the fallen strap rose from inside the pants and laid it there as the fabric slid willingly over his hipbone, and sloped. He moved the other hand inside the opposite strap and exposed his pectoral—his nipple, specifically—but nonchalantly. Gábi shot, and shot again.

The atmosphere strained. The music persisted. Danny pulled his elbow back and slid his palm over the outer, upper part of his ribs. He twisted his torso. He slit his lips. Gábi shot again. Danny raised his back heel, bent the same knee. Slowly. Leaned on it. Carefully. Gábi would stop him. Gábi would tell him. He leaned further. His pants sloped further. Gábi shot. Gábi would stop him. He set his eyes and weighted his lips and he balanced, twisted, back, nonchalant, unaware of the day, of the outfit, his hands, the spectacle, the utter editorialness of it all. Gábi looked up. *"Don't . . . move."*

Gábi moved him.

Maybe Una did too, her smile, her spirit, her captivating, unmannered honesty. Maybe Marina moved him, the way she goaded him so fluently, to speechlessness, to ire, depression. Maybe it was the inebriation or the energy or something entirely independent that had built inside him. Maybe it was restlessness, curiosity, the little he had to lose.

But Gábi, at least, moved him. His focus, his artistry, his technicality moved him. His explanations and instructions and intentions all made sense to him, encouraged him, even freed him, and like any photographer would want to, and try to, Gábi praised him. And Danny fed.

Danny liked it. He liked the way Gábi addressed him, the way he bolstered him, even if every word of what he said was mere, flatter-some bullshit. It could have been. Some photographers worked that way, directionless, simply building, constantly building, flaws compounding, until the model operated entirely on intuition, experience, and ego, devoid of any guidance from behind the lens save simply for "yes!" and "just like that!" and "don't stop, don't stop!" all almost sexual, almost erotic, hot and horny and inflating yet uninformed and uninformative. The medium was digital. And there was Photoshop. And when the final product pleased the photographer was praised; and when it didn't the model was blamed.

But Gábi wasn't adulating redundantly and he wasn't one who had to. "Danny, don't move. Don't move, Danny. I'm just switching my lens, just switching my lens. Ten more seconds. Don't move, Danny. Five. Don't move. Don't move. Here we go." Gábi shot. The atmosphere strained more. The music silenced between songs. Danny exhaled entirely and his stomach muscles surfaced forming two parallel rows of knots and added tension. Gábi shot, and shot, and instructed, and shot.

It was the last look. Danny unfastened his suspenders as he stretched his stomach and rolled his shoulders, with Gábi, for a moment, still shooting.

"Come look at these," he said, scrolling through the pictures.

Danny peered over Gábi's shoulder, unsure of how much sentiment to reveal. Quietly, but excitedly, he smiled as the pictures passed.

"*This*," Gábi said, stopping at an image of Danny resting heavily on his heels, one knee down, the other wide and parallel to the floor, "will be the new front of your card."

Danny motioned for the camera. He held it close to him, examining it. His pose, his expression, the lighting, the composition—everything compelled. Danny glowed. "It's . . . *wow* . . . I . . . I like it, I *love* it."

"Of course you love it! Look at the textures. Look at these angles, the contrasts. Fuck, Danny, look at *you*, your eyes, your cheeks. Amazing." Gábi continued scrolling. Danny continued smiling, and for a moment he felt a sense of exhilaration, of affection, for the product but also toward its producer. He felt a sort of euphoric, indebted gratitude that he couldn't express but knew he would if there was a way. "I think this might be one of the best series I've seen in a while," Gábi said. He held the camera in front of Danny. "Look at the light on the suit, the lines, the purple and the black. And your expressions, your attitude. Look how you moved your feet, how much energy there is. Still, each shot is totally different from the next." Gábi looked at Danny. "Come here. Give me a hug. You were awesome."

He knew he was. And he was atingle that such a famed photographer agreed. Danny imagined the possibilities. "Maybe—maybe you'll show some to your clients? Maybe they'd want to use me?" As soon he said it, he regretted it. Impatience. Avowal. Zeal. It wasn't his place. He crossed a line. He sat down and untied his shoes.

"Yeah. Sure."

Danny looked across the living room, dining room, and through the pass-through at Gábi shelving dishes in the kitchen. He paused, staring uncertainly. His eyes drifted to the sequence of spines of encyclopedia-sized photography books stacked fashionably in front of him. Cherry, Gábi's mini Kyi-Leo, climbed into his lap. "Have any plans?" Danny said. "For the rest of the day?" Perhaps he'd have images by morning.

"Shooting. Again. An old friend. He's trying to revive his look, find a new one. He was big years ago. That wave's been falling for a while though. I remember when—oh! I almost forgot!" Gábi stepped out of the kitchen and collected his camera. "Come."

"Where?" Danny stood up. Cherry leapt to the sofa.

"The roof."

"The roof?"

"I shoot everyone I test on the roof. Come. Just a few quick shots."

Danny followed Gábi to the elevator and up to the twenty-third floor, then down the hall to a flimsy metal staircase where the wind curled endlessly in circles.

Gábi strapped the door to the wall and walked out onto the flat silvery surface. "Just leave your pants and shirt on the stairs," he said, "and stand inside the frame."

Danny hesitated, then laid his clothes on top of his shoes, off the patches of rust. *Just a few shots*, he thought, and stepped into the doorway.

Gábi walked toward him a few paces, then crouched down. "Turn your feet left," he said, "just a bit. Now twist from hips to head back to me, your whole torso." He shot. "Drop your chin." He adjusted the lens. "This light couldn't be better. Shift to the right? Slide your thumb into the waistband?" He paused. He stood. "No."

Gábi walked over to Danny. He positioned him as though he rested on the frame. "Lean, but don't touch, don't press." He tilted the crown of Danny's head, his shoulders, and repositioned the arm opposite the frame. He squatted down and turned one foot out, bent the knee, then tugged on the lower seam of his briefs, just outside the thigh, and walked back to his original place on the roof. He looked back at Danny, still motionless. He walked back to him again, jostled his hair, and in one swoop dipped inside the fabric instead of out, pinched the same seam of underwear, but ran his finger to the inner thigh and tugged again. "Sorry," he said, his face hardly a foot from Danny's, "just don't want that catalog look."

"Right." Danny's voice was dry. Gábi's fingers were cold, the contact swift and unexpected yet faint as a feather. Danny sensed his briefs shift but ignored it.

"You look good," Gábi said, and patted him on the arm. "Just a few more shots." He took a few more shots, then returned to him again. "Can you move to the other side? And raise your arms?" Gábi stood a few feet in front of him and watched. "Pull the right elbow out in line with your head. Let the left elbow relax, but prop it with your shoulder. More. More." Gábi set down his camera and maneuvered both elbows appropriately. He did the same to Danny's head and the small of his back, then his pelvis and knees, and finally his underwear. He tugged it down once more and walked away.

The position was uncomfortable, it was painful. Danny could feel his neck numb, his spine sting. His shoulders winced. He breathed deep but slow, his form unruffled; his body, his mind controlled. He exhaled. Gábi shot. Gábi shot. Danny breathed deep, again, and exhaled. Gábi gave an instruction and Danny followed it without a thought. He breathed deep. He breathed low. His shoulders softened, his chin fell. Gábi paused. Danny exhaled and straightened and as Gábi returned once again, he reminded himself that he was almost finished, that his book would be the better for it, that Gábi's contacts were invaluable, to forget about the past, about the foster families and the orphanages and the test in late spring—not with Yuri or with Eryl but Simon—and to forget about Marina too. For anything Gábi had done, or would do, or could do, couldn't possibly compare. He pretended he was still tipsy. He pretended that he was still loose and uninhibited and open-minded at least. He pretended that because a time-for-prints wasn't at his expense, it was therefore out of his control. He pretended. He pretended that boundaries existed even if they never had, that Gábi surely knew them and respected them and upheld them, even if he didn't. He pretended that the future was too important and that the present was already past and that this was the break he needed and that none other might ever come. He pretended that the agency would laud him for such unprecedented pictures and that they'd view him keener and push him harder and love him more. He pretended that his body was not really his own, that his thoughts and emotions and reactions were really only in response to things that touched him—touched but didn't affect. He pretended he wasn't affected; he pretended he wasn't touched. He pretended his soul was still intact and that they were still shooting and that he had to stay still, had to stay stoic, had to allow the photographer to adjust his shoulders, his hips, to tug at his underwear even if one particular tug were too tough or too close or too revealing, even if the second were more so, the third entirely, increasingly shameless and violating; even if his neck numbed and spine stung and shoulders winced; even if his breath shortened; even if his spirit crumbled; even if his heart wept. He pretended that this was work, what professionals did, what they allowed to be done. And he pretended it would never happen again.

* * *

An hour later he was walking in a tremble of circles around Tomkin's Square when he realized he had forgotten his glasses. They weren't the sharpest but he bought them as a gift to himself for booking *W* and he liked them. They reminded him.

Going back though, was not an option. Gábi would send images to the agency and that would be the end of it. No more contact. No more embarrassment. No more "unique" opportunities.

But he wanted the glasses.

He rehearsed in the elevator. He pictured the scenario. Gábi would be shooting. Music would be playing. Danny would be polite and firm and know exactly where to find them. He'd take them and he'd leave and that would be the end of it. In and out. Hello and goodbye.

He turned down the hall repeating his approach. He was all but convinced of it until he stopped in front of the condo and found the door left ajar—not as he anticipated. He knocked hard. The music was loud. No one answered. He sighed and stepped in.

The first thing he saw was a pair of black boots and a plum-colored portfolio. The boots could have been anyone's. But even upside-down the portfolio was obvious.

He stopped mid-stride. He'd figure out another way. The situation was already debasing enough. The last thing he needed was another model to confirm it.

He turned in an instant and out of the corner of his eye he saw them. He glanced across the room. Most of it was out of view. He remembered his instructions to himself and was going for the coffee table when the music faded and he heard a voice in the hush. He turned to the bedroom. The door was cracked, the sounds indecipherable. The music burst back on. He grabbed the glasses, bolted to leave, had a hand on the door and turned as something moved in the bedroom. He told himself to leave. Curiosity overcame him. Who else did Gábi "photograph?" Who else did he destroy? He stepped past the closet. He laid a hand against the door. He forced himself to go, but pressed an eye to the frame.

The room was idle, eerily as though abandoned. There was a dresser to his right. The top drawer was open. A clock and a Rolex. He leaned further, hardly, and a camera lobbed across the room. He pulled immediately back. Then eased in. He saw the camera on the bed, the sheets unruffled. A tray. A wallet. A credit card. Dollar bills expanding over residue. He pushed further and saw clothes, more and saw Gábi. He saw his back, his buttocks, movements he recognized. The slightness of them. The economy of them. The furtiveness and the transparency of them. He recognized the tension associated with them, the emotion felt by them. He recognized the silence and the chaos, the tranquility and the fight. He recognized the proximity and the distance, the removal, the substitution of place and time, of thought and self. He recognized himself. He recognized struggle. He recognized outrage. He recognized pretending and disappearing and an outpouring of self-hate. He recognized motives and insecurities that weren't his and he couldn't see, but sensed unequivocally, and as the photographer fell slowly to his knees he recognized the model, his roommate, Sasha standing bare.

Chapter Twenty

WORK IMPROVED. HE BOOKED EDITORIALS, small shows—enough to keep him busy but not enough to keep him secure. Rates were abysmal. They were so low that models had earned more money for the same work twenty years earlier, before Danny was born. And as the economy imploded, they tumbled even lower. Pay checks were sobering. The subtractions were manifold: the commission; the expenses; the guesstimated taxes. The remainder was paltry, and yet that was only when the client paid. As the economy crashed, the agency stopped advancing. Rather than compensate its models within two weeks of work—whether the client had paid the agency or not—Edge rewrote its policies and cut checks only upon payment, which commonly exceeded the standard ninety-day window. With clients tardy to the point of delinquent and models throughout New York considering "life in the real world," Danny weighed his options. Bartender? Bellboy? Secretary? No one was hiring. No one was even interviewing. He tried to stay positive but he tossed in his sleep, he daydreamed at castings, he tickled knives at his wrists and starved himself and binged and it was only a matter of time before he swallowed his pride and felt the paradox of angst and relief as he rode, at last, back to Lenox Hill.

"Daniel."

"Marina."

The wind was cool. It was fresh like a waterfall in summer. But summer was gone. October was ending and the trees, the squirrels, the warblers all knew it. The park was quieter than Danny remembered. It was lonelier too.

Marina wore neon. Her leggings were black but her fleece was like a flashlight rounding the reservoir. Danny worked hard not to think. It wasn't his place to initiate discussion, and Marina took her time engaging him.

"Have you modeled?" she said offhandedly at last.

"Modeled?" He had nearly forgotten she was there.

"Daniel, the parroting . . ."

"Some," he said politely.

"Some?"

He looked at her. "Some."

"What is *some*, Daniel?"

What is modeling! he nearly snapped. "Editorials," he said. "A showroom."

Marina extended her neck. She flared her nostrils as though smelling something. They walked in silence with the gravel crunching under their heels.

"Are you reading, Daniel?"

"Am I reading?"

"Daniel . . ."

"Yes," he said, sighing. "I'm reading. I just finished some novels by Burroughs, and now I'm starting some of his—"

"Daniel."

"—poems and short—"

"Daniel, I did not ask *what*."

He looked at her, amazed. Then exhaled and looked away. Marina straightened. Another silence tiptoed between them until she broke it once again.

"And the girl?" she said, as cavalierly as jejune. "What of her?"

Danny rolled his eyes. *"Una.* She was in Europe. For shows."

"And?"

"And now she's back. She got in last night."

"And?"

Danny turned to her sharply. He waited and stared as she smoothed back her hair, her eyes fixed ahead. At last he looked away. She patted her bun. "And?"

He threw up his arms. "And *what?* We went out! We had dinner!"

"It is a holiday, Daniel, but will twenty-five suffice? For Thanksgiving?"

"Thanksgiving?" He shook his head. "Twenty-five what?"

"True." She circled her shoulders—once, twice, backward and forward, relaxed and unmoved. "True indeed, Daniel. Three thousand then. The Poconos, most probably. We shall confirm soon, as I must select my attire according—*Dan*iel. I did not tell you! I purchased the most comely, the most im*pec*cable garment. It is errorless, just errorless. Pulchritudinous to say the least." And suddenly everything seemed well. She carried on about every detail of the outfit, the material, the cut, the feel, how it fit her like a sheath, she said, like a scabbard to a sword, and how red and how brilliant and how splendiferous and unmatched. She went on about attraction and design and how she felt like a queen when she wore it and Danny simply stared like a rock at the ground. She was everything he wasn't and yet he knew who neither of them was. Merely that they were connected. And that capital created interest. Objects were bought and sold. Articles were comforts, accessories worn. Pets were pleasures and flowers galore; a maid to make things easier. Candy, cupcakes, diamonds, sin. Limits stretched and obliterated. What else was joy? What little was he? What was the cost of an accoutrement, the sacrifice for a smile? Some simplicity, some satisfaction to demand? Another hour in the sun. A boy to own.

On what market were ethics for sale? In what currency was autonomy capital?

"They say money is zip to happiness and I say rubbish. If money is beauty—which it is—and beauty is happiness—which *it* is—then the corollary stands as stated." She sighed and pressed back her shoulders. They exited the park and headed for home. "The ensemble is unlike any I own, Daniel. It was easily the gem of last month's shows. Naeem Khan. You have heard of him?"

Danny halted. William opened the door and Marina bounded through the foyer. She stood next to Harold holding an envelope in her hand, turning it between her fingers as Danny doubled to catch up. He reached the lobby, pale, as Harold turned away.

"Daniel," she said, offering him his due. He went for it and she snapped it back. Danny looked up. Marina was waiting for him. They stood there for endless moments with her breath on his neck and the scent of her hair in his nose until she tilted her head, lifted to her toes, and whispered contentedly like a schoolgirl passing a secret into his ear. "There will be no more second chances." Then she smiled and walked away.

* * *

"Literally?" Una said, crossing her legs on a bench in the middle of Union Square. "It just means 'high sewing' and Paris actually has claim to it. To the term, the fashion." Danny watched as she sipped her carrot-beet-pear-ginger juice. The way she puckered her lips. The way she lifted her brows. He grinned. "But it can also mean the clothes and the designers who make them. There are houses in New York and London, too, that use the term and make the clothes. But that's semantics. And you know the French."

"You're saying there's someone who decides this stuff? Who's in and who's out? Who's good enough and who's not?"

"Mm . . . mm." She handed back his orange-apple-coconut-kale. "Mine's better. It's something like the chamber de commerce de industry de Paris. I wished everyone would just speak Italian. Anyway, I looked it up once. A whole catalog of requirements. Everyone thinks it's anyone who shows, but Lagerfeld shows and he isn't *haute couture*; he's *prêt-à-porter*. The same with pretty much all of them—Gucci, Tommy, Prada—they're just standard fashions at exaggerated prices. The big guns, the real superpowers are the Chanels. The Diors. Galliano is *haute couture*. Givenchy, Anne Valérie Hash, Stephanie Rolland, Elie Saab. Yves Saint Laurent was. Laroche and Ralph Rucci were. It must be a total bitch to maintain. Financially. Artistically. Emotionally. Of course, they all make ready-to-wear, too. They pretty much have to."

Danny unwrapped a sugar-free, non-dairy, all natural cookie. "And who buys it?"

"Who buys it? How should I know? Who buys Rembrandt? Georgia O'Keefe? Who eats at Aquavit and shops at Harry Winston?" She shrugged. "People."

Danny looked up as two little girls wearing pink and white berets and matching cashmere coats skipped by. Their dresses swirled as their heels clicked the concrete and the pearls at their necks leapt about. Danny thought of Kimmy and Kelly. He pictured them sleeping side-by-side, probably cold, probably hungry, piles of clothes on the floor. He wondered if they were getting the socks, the underwear, the earmuffs and mittens he'd been sending, the paper and crayons and messages they still couldn't read and perhaps never would tucked inside. The girls stopped in front of him and danced as they pleased. His sisters would have danced just the same.

"What are you thinking about?"

He sighed as they capered on through the leaves. "I don't know."

Una moved closer and unwrapped her cookie. "These people, Danny, they're not all New Yorkers. Or Canadians." She

winked. "Most of them aren't. They're Turks. They're Brazilians. Monacan princes and twelve-year-old daddy's girls from
Hong Kong or Abu Dhabi who can't figure out what else to do
with all their time and credit cards." Una put her cup under the
bench and lay back in Danny's lap. She wiggled her shoulders
and hips along the bench and even then, horizontal, remained
fully unchanged—her neck, her lips, her cheeks, even her hair,
impervious to gravity.

"So? Milan? Paris? You still haven't told me. How were
they?" He couldn't decide what to do with his hands. Everywhere he put them felt awkward and amateur. "See a lot of
bored, newborn millionaires at the shows?"

Una smiled. Her neck craned long and Danny stretched his
arms out sideways. "Exhausting. Stressful." She looked down
at her feet. She exhaled and her smile faded. "Milan and Paris;
Paris and Milan: fashion's eternal love-hate capitals. Same as
always. Never-ending. Castings here, castings there. Streets,
time—it all blurs. An actual *meal* is unheard of. Studios are
packed, everyone's sweating and the air's all tense and fuggy.
More models than you can count. More languages and competition than the Olympics. Selections are ruthless. Tempers are
short. Expectations are fucking impossible. Really, they're
insane. The scheduling alone is mad. You make it to a dozen
castings in a day and miss just as many but you still have Balmain at six, Zucca at seven, Akris at eight. And you're starving.
But of course Balmain won't finish with you until well *after*
eight so you've missed Zucca and you're late for Akris. And
you've got Nina Ricci at nine. The rest of the world is leading
a relatively sane life, finishing dinner, watching sitcoms, making
love, and you're running somewhere through the middle of
Paris trying to change shoes so you don't break a heel on a cob-
blestone, not even sure of where you're going. Or why.
Because you *like* to be degraded? Because you *like* to be hungry? Is that it? Maybe you like the commands. Maybe you like
the pressure or the security or the guilt. The loneliness? The

lights? The masks and costumes you wear, the people you become? Maybe you like the ideal even if you know the reality. Maybe you can't help but believe your reality *is* the ideal. Even when you know it isn't. Or maybe there's no reality at all. And no ideal either. And though your life is nothing more than one big show you go on, skipping the intermissions. Whatever it is, the sun has set and there you are, still going, still running along, crisscrossing the arrondissements more drained and hungry and rejected than ever and yet somehow—God only knows—determined."

Danny furrowed his brow. A leaf fell to Una's stomach. She twirled it in silence, then poked him with it playfully on the chest. "So which do you do?"

"Which what do I do?"

"Come late to Akris or show up early at Nina Ricci?"

"Oh. Early at Nina?"

She whirled the leaf across his nose. "Is that your final answer?"

"That's my final answer."

Una paused in playful suspense. "*Oooh! So soorrry!* The correct response is, '*Late . . . to . . . Akris.*' Early to jobs, late to castings—unless you have an excuse."

Danny laughed, and thought of a few.

Una lifted her head and her hair and sobered. Danny felt himself drawn to her—her voice, her sincerity, her passion, some sort of air of warmth that emanated from her. "Really, there *are* parts of the industry that I like. Even in show season. The energy. The creativity. I do, I just . . ." She turned her head in his lap. He admired her profile, her contours, how her chest rose and fell, millimeters at the most, but plenty. She turned back to him abruptly. "Did you work the Betsey Johnson show?"

"Una, I worked so many I doubt I'd remember it if I did."

"No, trust me, you would. You'd remember. My friend Mei told me all about it. She was in it. They all wore these porkpieish, bowleresque hats with violent bright blue and yellow and white wigs underneath where the bangs came right down to the eyebrows and all the rest hung around the earlobes like Uma's in *Pulp Fiction*. Nothing matched. There was everything from sweater-nightgowns with ducks and beach balls to leotards with skulls and crossbones. At the beginning they wore mini bowties with bathing suits and concertina sleeves pretending to dance and flit and fly like fairies, sucking lollipops, swinging lunch boxes, and fluffing their wigs as they spun all ditzy-like. Then there was a pirate . . . Would I *lie?* Up and down the runway he went. The girls did their thing and sometimes he was there and sometimes he wasn't! Mei said it was bizarre and felt like Halloween. At one point they were all in these white tulle something-or-others which Mei called 'naughty-nurse-meets-lingerie-wedding-dress'—*handcuffed!* Who, Danny, who puts handcuffs on models and calls it ready-to-wear? She said she felt like a hooker in a circus. Oh, and the finale had them all traipsing out tied to balloons!"

"Balloons?"

Una rolled her eyes. "Bal*loons*. Balloons! Honestly, I'm all for experimentation. I'm all for new and unique and different. But just because you throw paint on a canvas doesn't mean you've made art. It just doesn't work that way. There has to be a purpose. There has to be a process. There needs to be a vision and some expression *of* that vision, an attempt at one at least, no matter how good or bad or liked or disliked the end result is. But communicate! Say something more than just gobbily-gook. *Tell* me something." She sighed. "Who knows, maybe there's this whole artistic dialogue going on out there and I'm the only one not getting it. But even still, does that magically make it fashion? And if it does, what makes Fashion Week the place for it? Nursery rhymes and lullabies might be music but no one sings them at the Grammys."

"True, but maybe that's her take on style."

"It's a mockery."

"It's a show."

"Balloons, Danny? Handcuffs? Lollipops?"

"And spotlights? Music? They're not part of fashion either."

"Why do I even care? We're just conduits, right, just some blank, soulless bodies. We don't add to the art. We don't contribute. We're just a bunch of disposable dolts. Designers, photographers, what do they need us for? Use mannequins. Use robots."

Danny looked at her. Her eyes, conspicuous yet unassuming, wandered fluidly. Her eyebrows and hands and lips did too. She exhaled with a grunt.

"I know," she said. "I know, I know. I hate it when they discard us and I hate it when they exploit us. Either we're empty and mindless or we're shocking and mindless. But why? Why does it have to be one extreme or the other? Why can't sophistication sell clothes? And why can't the clothes show a little sophistication? Why is everyone trying so hard and not accomplishing anything? Not just in fashion. Look at Hollywood. Look at the music industry. Look at painting and literature and architecture and design. Movies cost millions and fall flat; the scripts suck. Singers can't write, they can't dance, they can't play, and they can hardly even sing. Hey girl you so beautiful I just wanna fuck you and fuck you and fuck you for real but wait lemme flex for the camera first and show off this expensive gold chain I don't even own or this pimped ride either but lemme fuck you good and your sister too damn everyone come pay ten ninety-five for this single so I can make more porn and call it music. Give me a break!" She shook her head. "Literature is just as weak—the ideas, the words, there's no challenge, no excitement. The same with all the condos and offices, all repeats, all predictable. And if Ikea hasn't sent furniture six feet under then someone tell me what has." She flicked the leaf again. Danny watched the sheen on her knuckles skid round as she twirled it. "I know, I *know*, there will always be an exception. But exceptions just highlight trends. And right now the trend is to throw darts in the dark and resurrect the eighties and send models down the runway like hobos on vacation. Bernhard Willhelm. Junya Watanabe. Jeremy Scott. What happened to organic and inspired and honest? Why is eccentric the trend and accessible the exception?"

Danny watched New York walk by. Self-expressions covered the continuum of every category—men looking like women, wealthy like poor, liberals like conservatives, young, old, religious, secular, the expected, the unexpected, the opposite of each.

"Can you see anyone from down there?"

Una smiled. "I see you."

Danny blushed. "I thought we came here to people-watch."

"We are. I am . . ."

He blushed more. He looked away.

They sat there in silence. Then Una shot up. "Have you seen it?"

"Seen what?"

She grabbed his arm. "The spread! *Our* spread!"

Danny had all but forgotten. So much had happened since. Even more hadn't. Time felt eternal but the memory vivid— the sounds, the smells, the clothes, the intensity. His adrenaline jolted. They headed north on Park Avenue to the closest magazine shop carrying copies of *GQ*, *Penthouse*, *Sports Illustrated*, and a dozen others in the window. Inside, next to the cigars and the cashier, Danny saw an outsized magazine with a pink **W** stamped sleekly in the upper left corner. He recognized the actress on the cover but in his excitement couldn't recall her name, or notice it in block print across her chest.

Una pulled it from the rack and flipped forward. Danny stood behind her with his chin over her shoulder and his hands pressed deep, deep in his pockets, tapping his thighs and craning his neck as they scanned the Table of Contents.

"There," Una said, and dented the page where she pointed. "Woman's World—182." She fanned it back, excited, more so, Danny knew, for him than for herself. The font was bold and defined, silver and red with the credits in italics below. To the right, Una strode strong. She aimed directly at the lens, though seemed unaware that she was. Her hair was curly and emphatic, flowing with volume. It floated above the garment— alpaca fur in tobacco brown, the coat left powerfully open. It was lined to the knee with the same fatty fur that plumed at the collar, and with a shell that was fiercer and sleeker in waxed olive leather. She wore a shirt and a skirt in robust, mimicking military hues, the former a shade lighter in lamb, the latter much the same but in stonewashed denim. Brown continued to her feet. Boots towered to her knees. The fabric fell back at the heel as a trio of straps swayed at each side. Around her waist she wore a belt in bole brown, over her collar beads in tan brown, on her left wrist a matte bracelet in near-black brown, and in her right hand she carried a clutch in pink. She was turned away from a building and somewhere behind her, lingering in the distance, dwarfed in the contrast, still holding the door through which she walked, was Danny.

Una turned the page. Two more pictures revealed similar scenarios. She turned the next, and the next, and in each image there was Una—forward, focal, commanding—and somewhere behind her, or peripheral, illegible, supporting but never immediately, contributing but never completely, was Danny.

*   *   *

He read the email once more, and hit send. Then waited for Luke's reply:

danny if you want us to explain every pic we cant theres just way to many dude.. but its not about you its about how we market you to clients.. two pics is great theres lots of guys that test get none.. 08102600018 and

08102600114 and some in that last look are def good your right we just dont think there what you need not now but well hold them you never know.. Gabis great but next time tell us first your shooting and well tell you what we need so you don't waste your time..

sorry about w its an editors choice it happens..

for $$ if you need an advance talk to accounting cause clients have 90 days..

He didn't know how long he stared at it, feeling as empty and foolish as a puppet on strings, but he still was when Xavier and Isis came in, abundant with Spanish and gifts and energy he couldn't comprehend.

"Danny!" Xavier put down their bags. Isis took off her coat. Festivity suddenly filled the apartment. "Danny?"

He didn't move. The couple looked at each other, baffled. Xavier called again, and a few moments later Danny looked up.

"What's the matter?" Xavier said.

Danny didn't respond. He looked lethargic, unwilling to fight. He simply stared, almost comatose, then stood and turned toward Jeremiah's room.

"Danny, what the hell's going on?"

He stopped. He turned. "Nothing," he said, his tone like the glaze in his eyes. "Nothing at all. Just . . . dreams."

Xavier turned to Isis, then back to Danny. "You know," he said, "a lot of people only ever talk about dreams. A lot of others don't even have any."

"Not those kinds of dreams," Danny said. "Maybe somebody's, but not mine."

Xavier folded his arms. Isis sat down on the sofa. "Honeymoon's ending?"

"*Honey*moon?" The word hit every wall. Danny's face turned vivid and shocked. "What honeymoon? There was no *wedding*, no engagement. There was never any *love!*"

The room was silent. Xavier looked torn. "You're thinking of stopping?"

"Did I ever begin?"

"Maybe you should get away for a bit. Go down to Miami, check out another market. People jump when you say you're from New York. Besides, it's Models' Law: make yourself unavailable and everyone wants you."

Isis nodded. "Is true, Danny. Is true."

"Xavier, I can't just . . . I can't . . ." He clenched his jaw and looked away.

"Not forever. For a season. A week. It doesn't even have to be work-related. You could come with me to Europe for the holidays!"

Danny closed his eyes. He dropped his head against the wall. "I know you're just trying to be nice, Xavier. I appreciate it. But it's like—it's like teasing. Talking about it. I can't afford that. I'd be flat out broke if it wasn't for this model apartment."

Isis sat up. "Model aparmen?" Xavier turned to her, wide-eyed. But too late. "Danny, dis here no model aparmen."

Everything stilled. Danny turned slowly to Xavier. "Then what is it?"

Xavier sighed. "Danny, it's not like you were never supposed to know."

"What *is* it?"

"They're not free, Danny. The agencies aren't just some guilds of philanthropy. They're not havens with open-door policies. You pay. Sooner or later, you pay."

"What . . . is it?"

"It's Remmy's," Xavier said. "Not the agency's. He owns the whole building."

Danny looked puzzled. Then entirely aware. "He wants something from me . . ." He shook his head. "What's he want from me?"

"What? Don't be crazy, he's doing the agency a favor. Every apartment was full but they wanted you so Remmy said you could stay here until a bed opened up."

Danny looked at him skeptically.

"Everything's cool, trust me. You're fine here. If Remmy wanted you gone, you'd be gone. I promise."

Danny turned.

"Where are you going?"

"To bed," he said.

"It's six o'clock."

"I know." And he headed hopelessly down the hall.

"You're *fine* here, Danny. Trust me. Kinzie misses rent all the time."

He climbed into bed, and in minutes was asleep. It was still dark when he woke to giggles and shrieks and to loud, foreign profanities. He looked at the door with a glare, then saw a note slipped under it. He stepped down, groggily, from the loft.

Ever had Glühwein? I got you a seat on my flight. My treat! Merry Christmas!

                                        X.

Chapter Twenty-One

NIGHTS STARTED COMING EARLIER. Days began to shorten. Birds ventured south and subways strained to forgotten extremes as the increasing cold sent the sane underground. Shoulders tightened. Thighs plumped. Taxis stuffed every avenue. Ice skating returned to Rockefeller Center and nut vendors lined the streets. Restaurants formed coat-checks. The holidays lingered.

Una worked incessantly. Cozumel. Mazatlan. Twice in the Keys and Caribbean. In New York more times than Danny could count. When she was home they went out. She took him to concerts, promotions, art galleries, nightclubs, to Ditmars for potlucks and the East Village for Spoken Word, birthdays of friends who lied about their age and her favorite designer's Just Because party, a Rangers game at the Garden, *The Lion King* on Broadway, the top of the Empire State.

Danny tried not to dwell on the disparity. He knew Una preferred not to discuss their careers—and in turn, who bought what for whom—but it seemed that regardless of what they did or where they went, he was reminded of it. He was reminded by the people around them; he was reminded by the novelty of every event; he was certainly reminded by the appreciation he felt. Whether they went to a supermarket and he bagged groceries as she paid or they cooked dinner thereafter and he listened to her commentaries on Asia or art or inequality, he was reminded of it. He didn't want her to change but he wanted desperately to contribute. And in a society that expected nothing less, yet a profession that permitted nothing more, it vexed him.

He did what he could to endure. He woke up each morning at six and reached Marina by seven, worked until eight and returned home by nine. Mid-month he worked another editorial, with Mert & Marcus and a dozen other boys who looked just like him, and the following week worked a couple's piece for Cole Haan for *Women's Wear Daily*. Thanksgiving came and he traveled back to the Poconos, and he worked more. Some of the guests were different—the Italians were missing; Donald was with another woman—but the night was otherwise routine: the mingling, the indulging, the systematic behaving; the staff drinks that followed; the unconsciousness that came. The work was the same, yet incredibly harder. The knowing made it so. The bracing for it. The dreading of it. The surrender to it. The clock inside his head. The storm inside his stomach. He knew how it would unfold. He knew exactly how it would happen. That mild, titillated flush; and she'd line the glasses. That inflated ease; and she'd fill them. Her eyes would greet and her smile would warm but together they'd torture. She'd raise her glass and gleam and say "Cheers!" but he'd hear "*Fuck* me. *Fuck* me." All he'd hear is "*Fuck* me."

Without looking he'd know. He'd shut his eyes and raise his glass and he'd tilt it. He'd take it. The clock inside his head would stop, the storm inside his stomach would settle. And every memory, every moment, every hurt and hatred and happiness that lingered, every silence and suffocation, every touch and torment, every fear and hope and burden and betrayal and every morning and every evening and every absence in between would shut down, and the world he knew would vanish.

Nothing would matter, because nothing would be.

"You look . . . unwell, Daniel," he'd hear her say. It wouldn't matter if she had. It wouldn't matter if she hadn't. He'd hear it. He'd know it. "Perhaps you should rest? Go, Daniel. Rest. I shall check on you . . ."

And like a bat to his cave or a ship on the horizon he'd be gone, and all that he'd know was the things that he wouldn't. He wouldn't know how he ascended the stairs, how he found his room or opened the door. He wouldn't see the walls or the windows or feel contact with the quilt as he hit the bed. He wouldn't sense the pillows on his cheeks and wonder if they were the softest pillows his cheeks had ever touched. He wouldn't sweep his arms and legs across the mattress, over the sheets or under them or tucked tight between, like he had once in the snow. He wouldn't smell them either, or recognize them if he had.

A knock at the door, he wouldn't recall. He wouldn't know that a curtain of light had swept over his body, up to his nose, and returned quickly to dark. He wouldn't hear the intimations about him—soles along the carpet; ice inside a glass. He wouldn't know how long he'd been watched, or how closely, if at all; or by whom. He wouldn't know subtlety or intent or intuition. Shadow. Breath. Presence. Desire. He wouldn't smell her, or her perfume.

Gone—comatose-gone—he wouldn't stir, he wouldn't flinch. The buttons would come undone and the skin across his chest, his nipples, exposed to the air, would stiffen. He wouldn't feel the air. He wouldn't know the buttons had been opened or that a nose or a nail or a tongue had touched him. He wouldn't know it. Later, he wouldn't recall it. But his skin would. His neck and his collar, every goose bump down to his belly button, and his hips would.

And the ice that melted on his neck and pooled in the pillow above his shoulder.

The lipstick.

The fingerprints.

He wouldn't remember his hips rise. He wouldn't remember them fall.

He wouldn't know how his pants had creased as they had, or how they'd dropped. He wouldn't know how the hairlessness of his thighs felt against the brush of lashes, lips, articulate breasts, or that they'd been brushed at all. He wouldn't know how his fingers, his face, his toes never curled, or how he had simply lain there—gone, flat, frozen—nothing but his briefs aroused.

He wouldn't remember them move, steadily. First up. Then down. Or the sound of the smack once they did. Like a belly flop.

He wouldn't feel fingers. He wouldn't feel palms. He wouldn't feel warmth or wetness or have any sentience of his own exaggeration. He wouldn't feel himself stretch. He wouldn't feel himself pull, hard, as he lay there, gone. He wouldn't be as entertained; nor entertained at all. He wouldn't be humiliated; and he wouldn't rage or riot or resent. Nor would he enjoy; he wouldn't exult; he wouldn't roll his eyes or plow his head or arch his back, curl it and arch it, curl it and arch it, find pleasure or pain, punch the mattress, pull his hair, suffocate on his fist or bite it. He wouldn't writhe or moan or sweat or see. He wouldn't look. He wouldn't feel. He wouldn't hear how skin stroked against skin, how it slid and how it stopped, how it tickled and how it teased. How it stroked again. How it slid again. How it tickled and teased and stroked again. He wouldn't know how it felt, outside or in. Outside like a garden. Like sun. Like rain. Like tulips in the wind. Inside like a rocket ship.

Ten. He wouldn't sense it.

Nine. He wasn't meant to.

Eight. Some things just happen.

Seven. Some things just don't.

Six. Everything was gone!

Five. More gone than he?

Four. When wealth is a fetish.

Three. When beauty is a drug.

Two. She pulled back her hair.

One groan, one grope, one glance around the room—a single sprain of the skin and he knew. Not where or when or how or who. But he knew. He smelled it in the air. He felt it on his chest. He tasted it with a grimace on his lips. He thrust his cheek against the pillow and he heard it on his neck. And in the silence that weighed upon him.

He sat up. He tried to. But his shirt, his pants, his entire presence was a tangle. He was his own web, his own trap—his clothes, his body, his coherence and his faith.

Sober, stunned, he unlaced his shoes. He took off his socks. He treaded in place by the side of the bed and the brim of the light, shifting his weight from foot to foot like a child needing to pee, but slower, narrower, calmer, unaware of urgency, odium, or shame, unaware of himself, simply distant and dazed, robotic until his pants fell to his feet and his underwear followed; and he shadowed himself to the bathroom.

In the darkness, the dimness that stalked, he looked at himself. Arid. Impassive. Mute. Blank as though still senseless, he looked. His hair unmoved, his eyebrows intact, his face so sterile and distracting of a body that was anything but clean, he simply looked. His reflection was elementary, just as obscure: object of experience; avenue to others; some life or Life or lives outside him, desires and motives that were born beyond him, fostered free of him, at the least unaware of him, and yet matured toward him, at him, into and throughout him. All the people who permeated him, all those who penetrated—he looked at them inside him; he looked at them all over him. He looked but he didn't see what they saw. He didn't feel what they felt or want what they wanted and he didn't understand what would make them. He looked at his arms and he saw pallor, his collar and saw blame. He looked at his ribs and his stomach and he saw fragility fending void, shame around his neck, passivity upon his chest. He looked at his jaw and he saw tire, timidity, his lips so little to say. Nose, ears, eyes—he looked and looked away.

He turned on the shower. He turned the dial to hot. The water fell like pencils or pins from boxes of billions, pricking the tiles he was too dull to see and leaping without pause into plumes of condensation. There was comfort in the sound. He hardly heard it but there was serenity, there was security, some return of potential or hope.

He turned back to the mirror. Faint wisps of moisture stroked evenly up the glass. He stood stationary but watched as he sank. His body faded. The fog reached his chest and wiped it casually away. It gripped his neck. It smeared his chin. It buried his lips. He glanced into his eyes and like a house of cards he collapsed to the floor in madness.

Chapter Twenty-Two

SUN AND SNOW MIXED GENTLY as they fell. Pilots maneuvered planes amid the glare as baggage trucks laid tracks between them. Men wrapped in headsets and neon jackets paced to and fro in the wind. Glints of red and green flashed instructions behind them. The twinkle, the patterns, the evanescence in the air, like the operations on the ground, conveyed some grandeur of aplomb.

Danny turned around in his seat. A cloud from his breath fogged the window. "I've never been on an airplane," he said.

"I don't know how you put up with the dress code in this country," Xavier said. "It doesn't matter how long I—you never what?"

Danny was looking ahead, already surveying the other Berlin-bound passengers. "Been on a plane," he said. "What do you mean, dress code?"

Xavier stared at him. "Never? Not once?" Danny shook no and kept searching. Xavier looked incredulous. "Well . . . well, what do you see?" he said at last.

Danny shrugged. "Jeans?"

"Look higher."

"Shirts?"

"Yes, and what's on them?"

"Is this another one of your lessons?"

Xavier smiled. "What's *on* them?"

"Words."

"Precisely. And what do they say?"

Danny rolled his eyes.

"Better yet," Xavier said, finding a pen and paper, "go write down what you see."

Danny looked at him. He mumbled something about always being so difficult, then moved about the gate examining the brandings. It wasn't long before he realized. Nearly everyone was labeled. *Puma. Gap. Gap Kids. Calvin Klein. Ralph Lauren. Armani Exchange.* Three, four, five *Nike.* Six. Seven *Nike. J Crew. American Eagle. Abercrombie & Fitch.* He wrote down every brand and how many there were of each, then went back to Xavier whose T-shirt read: **goat milk?**

"You've got an opinion about everything, don't you?" Danny said.

Xavier shrugged. "Would you drink it?"

"Would I drink it? Xavier, that's gross."

"Maybe from a donkey? From a cat?" Danny grimaced. "Of course they're not as exploited. Their milk's not as advertised. So why would you? Why be different when you can be the same? There's no celebrity out there telling you how cool you'd be if you jumped on the bandwagon and started stealing from your dog. No athlete suggesting that *you too* could be free advertising space for buffalos and horses and their enslaved sisters. No industry feeding you fat, sugary lies about the benefits of lactose from a camel, a yak. Pasteurized? Homogenized? Condensed? Raw, skim, evaporated? Poor burly yak just isn't good enough. Not enough hormones. Not enough cancers or quadruple bypasses. Not enough commercial branding or economy stimulating or ethics violating or—"

"I get it, I get it! I'll try the almond milk."

Xavier smiled. "And the shirts?"

* * *

It had been days since they arrived and the first time since visiting every museum, monument, night club, and beer garden that they did nothing but wander, at their leisure, through the city's most outstanding Christmas market, full of wreaths, full of evergreens, full of Zwetschgenmännle and soldier Nutcrackers and assorted stained glass ornaments, incensed candles, gold-foiled angels and heart-shaped Lebkuchen adorned with the drifts of Stille Nacht, O Tannenbaum, vanilla-roasted pecans swirling through thoughts of snow and prayers for peace. Windows were aglow. Necks were bundled. A tube of gift wrap pierced through every shopping bag that passed by.

The Glühwein was affectionate. They sipped and they sat and as Danny asked himself about hope, about truth, about the things that inspired him and all the holidays not worth remembering, Xavier recounted Christmases from Paris, those of high school and college with cousins in Park Slope. As a model in Rio, Rome, once over the Pacific. He spoke fondly about his travels, about the summer that turned to fall before a semester that formed years between degrees at Columbia, the people he met, the jobs he worked, the cities he saw, all the parties and possibilities and promises and lies, how different it was and how essentially the same. "Bookers used these things called Telexes," he said. "Models used answering services. We checked in constantly. Always communicating. In the agencies, nothing was digital yet, and every model's chart was kept on a wheel, like on the game show. There was no way one booker could rep eighty guys on his own. Things were smaller. In a way they were faster, how we'd race like a flock of journalists to the nearest phone. We all knew each other, too. And we knew our bookers. Not this Facebook stuff, I mean we really *knew* them and we . . ." Xavier paused. "Danny?"

"Huh?" His eyes glistened, fixed on the lights. A whiff of apple cider blew by, and somewhere, someone started playing a recorder. The wind was gentle but cold. Danny didn't move. "Do you think . . . we each have a destiny?"

Xavier crossed his legs academically. "Define destiny."

Danny paused. There was a sort of spiritualism, some reflection in the lights. "What am I doing with my life?"

Xavier sighed. "Modeling. You're a model."

"Am I? What makes me? What have I *done* to become one?"

"Yes, Danny, you are. You do—so you are."

"It's just not what I . . . It's not what I thought it would be."

Xavier set down his wine. He reached for Danny's shoulder, but withdrew.

"I thought I was starting something better with my life. There would be money. Freedom. An open door somewhere. But there's not." He shrugged as if to apologize. To the glow. To himself. To anyone who would accept. "I really thought I was coming to New York to model but all I'm . . . all I . . ." He closed his eyes. The lights, the cider, the recorder carried on.

"Danny, you're an artist. You're a brand new artist in a near-forsaken economy. Artists work numerous jobs. They struggle. In New York it's implied."

"So the girls aren't artists?" Danny glared at his wine. "Because none of them bartend or cater or . . . I started *before* the economy crumbled. And you and Remmy and Kinzie have all done fine."

Xavier shook his head. "Contrast," he said, "but never compare."

Danny folded his arms, irritated at the Christmas joy.

"Try to imagine something," Xavier said. "Imagine you're one of the first poets, or painters, or any artist. But instead of it being many centuries ago, it's hardly decades. And instead of it being a society focused primarily on survival, more and more people have more and more money, and the more they spend the more they support your work. But imagine these people aren't always people. They're companies, they're corporations, and they have even more money than real people have, and more control over the success of your new art. Now also imagine, as all

221

these factors are uniting, mass communication is budding and your medium is directly affected. Because your medium is a product of it. Modeling is an art but the modern use of it is sheer business. It was built on technology with economics in mind, and no other art or artist, Hollywood included, can say the same. The public will always pay to be entertained, but it will never demand another billboard. The modeling *we* know is still pubescent and it's only now reaching its first reality check. After the war everything was hot. Modeling mushroomed. Marion Morehouse was huge. Lisa Fonssagrives was worldwide. Dorian Leigh topped six figures a *year* and Dovima made models one-name wonders. Suddenly there was Twiggy, Penelope, and Veruschka. Then Patti, Janice, and Iman. By the eighties models had gotten so big that Fashion reincarnated the Trinity: the Christy, the Naomi, and the holy Linda. By the nineties models maxed out. Claudia and Cindy were giants, Kate was a queen, and even guys gained attention. People knew that Hoyt meant Richards; that Tyson meant Beckford. But then what? Then who? Gisele slipped in at the end but otherwise supermodels died with the century. The status is *gone*. The celebrity is *gone*. It's been just about ten years and no one's gone on talk shows, no one's landed movie roles, no one's dated royalty. No one is kept around long enough to try. The industry has gone ADD with the rest of us and no one notices or cares. Globalization has saturated Fashion and all the competition has forced rates to dive. Victoria's Secret is the only client that still pays. Fashion shows have turned into internships. Campaigns have become nothing more than good editorials. Magazine covers and cosmetics companies are reserved for celebrities. Hollywood has colonized Fashion. Designers themselves are better known than the models they book. Photoshop has brought back nearly every old-timer looking younger than ever and taking whatever work still exists. Everyone new comes in thinking modeling is one big party. No one has an ounce of preparation. Suddenly the bubble bursts and the game is over. *I'm* fine. Remmy is fine.

Kinzie—well, he's another story . . . But we got in years ago and we were groomed and we diversified, we stayed realistic. That one day it would end. That some parts of it are beyond our control. That it was never even ours to begin with. And unless you accept it for what it is and enjoy it for what it teaches you, you'll be gone as fast as the rest."

Danny shook his head. "So you're saying the girls aren't artists."

"I'm *saying* this context never existed. This phenomenon is completely new. There's never been an art *this* dependent on capital. Not on wealth, but corporate capital. And there's never been an art so fast and subjective and undefined that on any unforeseen day you could rise or fall and never know why. Some of it you can control. Most of it you can't. You can't control your sex. You can't control your age. You can't control the fact that patriarchy and chauvinism and outrageous insecurities have created a culture that tells men to use women as distractions from their own imperfections and tells women to be nothing but perfect. And as a guy living in a society in which men eclipse women while working in a profession—the *only* profession—in which women eclipse men, leaving all the misogynistic reasons aside, you have to realize that *we* are second class, that two industries are operating as one, that we wouldn't exist without them, and that even if you never become a one-name icon you can still be exceptional at what you do."

A couple stopped at one of the booths in front of them. Danny flicked at his coat. "Xavier, have you . . . Have you ever . . ."

Xavier squinted at the couple. "Have I what?"

He bunched it in his hand. "Has a photographer . . . Has one ever . . . tried . . ."

But Xavier stood up. "Handerson?"

A sprightly, captivating man (6'2"; 166; 40L; 15-34; 31x33; 11; salt/pepper; blue) about Xavier's age with a pregnant woman beside him turned in the thickening darkness. Danny exhaled.

"*Ach du Scheiße!*" Xavier raced to the couple, the man animated with disbelief. They hugged and laughed and gripped each other's arms as the woman waited patiently. Then Xavier turned and shook her hand all smiles. He draped an arm around his friend, and led them jovially back to Danny.

"Danny, this is my very dear friend, Handerson. We go way, *way* back! *Mann, wie lange ist das denn schon?* Hugo Boss?"

"Time flies," Handerson said.

"And this is Julia, his wife, and their soon-to-be *baby*."

The two men were already chatting when she reminded them of her breaking back and swollen ankles. They rode back to the couple's apartment, not far from Xavier's, and the two friends carried on the entire way about agents, agencies, models, photographers, designers they thought they had forgotten. They talked about nights in foreign countries and flights they nearly missed, jobs and parties and contracts that wouldn't end and things that made Danny wonder if he'd ever become friends with someone in one city, and later meet them in another; if he'd ever have experiences so unique, so memorable, that he'd have equal enthusiasm recalling them.

When they got to the apartment, Danny and Xavier sat down in the living room while Handerson changed and Julia got into bed. Handerson joined them minutes later carrying a small container and a pack of folded papers. Without his scarf, Danny noticed the tattoo on his neck: a clothes hanger inside a circle, a diagonal line running through it.

Handerson opened the container. He pinched at the contents, then sprinkled them into one of the papers. "What are you talking about?"

Xavier picked up a beer. "Fluffing . . ."

"Fluffing?"

"You know—*fluffing*. Underwear. *Full*ness. The photographer fluffs a little . . ." Xavier gestured vaguely with his hand.

"It wasn't fluffing," Danny said.

"How do you know?" Handerson rolled a filter.

"I just do," he said, looking at Xavier, unable to believe he had already forgotten the day he detailed his entire body to him. Surely, he knew he didn't need to be fluffed.

"Who was the photographer?" Handerson smoothed out the cone. He lit the tip. He held the opposite end to his lips, and breathed deep.

"Gábi," Xavier said. "He's still newish. Think Rick Day, but more powerful."

"So what was it, if it wasn't a fluff?" His voice was suddenly thicker, heavier.

"Not *it*," Danny said, and wished he'd kept his mouth shut.

"What, like more than once?"

Danny took the joint from his host, flicked a whorl of ash into a tray and inhaled hard. Then harder. He quickly felt cloudy yet clear, even yet elevated, and passed it.

"I forgot my glasses so I went back. The door was open, living room was empty. I looked into the bedroom and saw Gábi—*fluffing* Kinzie. Coke everywhere."

"Kinzie's gay?"

"Kinzie's desperate. If I ever wrote Kinzie's biography," Xavier said. "I'd call it *Memoirs of a Male Model: the Cities I Saw, the Runways I Walked, the Agents I Fucked, the Photographers I Blew, the Money I Made, and the Little I Have to Show for it.* Or maybe just *Wasted.* He's done some great work but he's the ultimate freeloader."

"He wasn't enjoying it," Danny said defensively.

"Not *that* part," Xavier corrected.

"Oh, what? And you've always been a saint?" Handerson let a rill of smoke slide out from his lips. He offered the joint, but Xavier refused.

"What's that supposed to mean?"

He forced it into his friend's hand. High and suddenly sober, Xavier looked at it, inept like a football player cradling a violin or a violinist fumbling a football, then took it, smoked it, and passed it back. "Golden Beach? The fat man himself?"

"Handerson . . ."

"I'm not judging."

"Yeah, but how should I have known?"

"Fine. But what did you book later that month?" They stared, sober and stoned, awkward and unaware. Handerson killed the joint. "And who shot it?"

*   *   *

Both nights of Christmas passed, and the following evening Danny and Xavier went to Handerson's for a leftovers-potluck with a mix of expat actors who were thrilled to call each other family and twice as many locals who were just as thrilled for an excuse to get away from theirs.

Danny wasn't used to the vibe. He was accustomed to models, to a sort of stasis of inexcitability. But he was suddenly surrounded by actors, and the norm of impassivity he knew became a dynamism he didn't. Both, he believed, were sharp. Both were savvy. Actors, however, were a little less attractive, a little less scripted, greatly more energetic, and always verbose. They quoted Molière and Kafka and translated them and laughed. They wore color. They ate food. They drank wine instead of Vodka, and Coke instead of snorting it, and they danced. They sang flamboyant songs and made broad, sensational, unflattering facial expressions, exaggerated flicks of the wrist, sweeping dips of the head, a sporadic gyration or leap. As a model never would.

But he enjoyed it, this difference—the feel, the intimacy, the reality, the candor. The lack of pressure. There was ease in the way they interacted, artlessness unchecked, some informality like the kind he shared with Una and noticed signs of in other models during rare occasions of privacy and forfeit.

There was personality. There was essence. There was volume and there was the word on Xavier's shirt: **freality**. There was relief. And individualism. And apathy to status quo.

Or perhaps, there was simply acting. Acting of another sort. A louder approach. Active instead of passive. Theatrical rather than discreet. Variations he didn't recognize. Acts so distinct they couldn't have been contrived. But were still acts.

The night was moving swiftly with novelty and Danny couldn't imagine what else was still possible. He had already shared a bottle of Półtorak with a couple from Kraków. He had survived propositions by a Parisian in red, and a Swede who mildly terrified him; audited a partially translated disquisition on the differences between weed and hash and completed both tutorials appropriately; eaten halvah for the first, second, and third times with a jocose daughter of Turkish immigrants; and entertained countless questions about modeling, New York, Broadway, and the myriad references to all things *Sex and the City*. He had mingled with everyone—had "let go," as Xavier often suggested. He had learned new words like *Schauspieler* and *Besetzungschef*, sampled homemade latkes and blintzes, preserves and applesauce. He had listened to a dramatized history of the Komische Oper, learned to open a beer bottle with nothing but another, attempted to understand a theory in quantum physics that speculates a particle smaller than an atom yet one strong enough to move matter solely by way of thought, how to count to six in Korean, ten in German, and on occasion found himself telling stories more glamorous than he remembered them. He had just reached for more marzipan and walked to the window for air, feeling high, when he noticed Handerson.

"Sweet photo . . ." Danny nodded at the wall.

"Thanks." Handerson was equally stoned. "It's old. Ten years?"

"You took it?"

"I did. I took it."

Danny looked back at the photo, liking it, loving it, but unsure why.

"I made the frame, too."

"You didn't."

"I did. I made it. I bought every little piece at the *Flohmarkt*. The flea market. You've been? The one by the *Tiergarten*?" Danny shook no. Handerson lit a cigarette. "Better than any museum."

Danny watched as he took a drag and shed the ash. He wondered if the ashtray were also self-made, the table supporting it, the rug below it. He wondered what other abilities he might possess. Anyone. Everyone. Himself.

"You know photography"—Handerson inhaled—"isn't that old." He offered the cigarette to Danny, then inhaled it again and blew the smoke upward in widening rings. "Hundred, two hundred years. More or less. Sometimes I study it and think, *This* is art? Clicking a button on a contraption that someone *else* designed and someone *else* built?" Danny wasn't sure if he was still stoned or not, or if he could handle much more thinking after discourses on theatrical psychology and robots in war, but Handerson was engaging without proselytizing or even acting, and Danny enjoyed it. "But I still study it," he said, and rolled another joint.

"Modeling can't be an art," Danny said, cloudy and clear. "Photography maybe, but not modeling."

"Yeah? Why?" Handerson spoke so slowly he made Danny feel twice as high.

"Because you can't study it. It's just *you*."

Handerson put the joint to his lips. He inhaled hard. "Because no one has tried or because it's not possible?"

Danny felt light years away.

"What about writing? What about singing? What about dancing and acting? Lots of arts are *just you*. But we've figured out ways to study them."

*   *   *

Xavier was sleeping when Danny left. He found a map and some fruit, slid a note under Xavier's door, and walked across Berlin.

It was hours before he reached it, just as Handerson had described. It stretched as far as a football field, row after row of tents and tables all teeming with buyers and sellers and wayfarers from around the world who had come to admire, to bargain, to photograph the tables and tubs and racks of relics that Danny never imagined he'd walk so far to see.

There were irons—soapstone and terracotta; sad and electric; charcoal box irons; and mangle boards. There were eye glasses. There were baby carriages made of wicker, candle holders of crystal; pearl necklaces all fake. There were turbans woven in Tunis, wigs once worn in Odessa, fur hats from St. Petersburg that looked like soiled wheels of hay and smelled of moth balls, dish rags, and cold pee. There were rugs: wool rainbows of halite, malachite, cinnabar, and talcum, patterns of paisley and plaid, striped and spiral, Turkoman and Mehrab hanging from chords and piled like pancakes at Sunday brunch. There were porcelain tea pots, silver platter sets, utensils too many to count. There were issues of *Der Spiegel* dating forty, fifty, sixty years stationed alongside antique cabinets, bronze door knobs, and centuries-old mirrors caked in ways no cleanser could ever clean. There were bookshelves, wind chimes, walking canes, and irreparable grandfather clocks; Lederhosen, Lederhosen, and Lederhosen; armies of Barbie Dolls and Hulk Hogans, Minnie, Mickey, bootlegged video cassettes—*Star Trek*; *Boogie Nights*; *Belle de Jour*—portraits of other people's poodles, of Karl Marx, of Rainer Rilke behind faded posters of Marilyn Monroe, Grace Kelly, Bugs Bunny, and Godzilla; John Wayne and Dean Martin in *Rio Bravo*, a dapper Roger Moore in *Octopussy*. There were coins, bills, and stamps, pins and patches, scissors, hammers, axes, bullets, and transistor radios. There were tiles that weighed more of glue than of ceramic, and compasses that were no longer magnetic. There were vinyl records by the cartload: Captain Beyond; Acid Jazz; The Mersey Beats; George Harrison's *All Things Must Pass*. There were T-shirts washed and worn to rags that read "Puma" and "Opel" and "We Can Do It" and blue jeans made by Levi Strauss or prepubescent girls in Mexico. There were children's books titled *Tom and Jerry* and *Was Machen Wir Heute?* and *Gut Freund mit Tieren* laid out along collapsible tables and stuffed into Dole and Bajella and Golden B boxes below and beside them: *Licht auf Yoga* and *Der Kalte Krieg*; *Advanced Management Accounting Problems*; and Dee Browns' *Wondrous Times on the Frontier*. There were landline telephones like boxes with ears—large, dial-front faces. There were voltage adapters for a euro, extension cords for less, binoculars in broad, bulky leather cases, padded and rugged and inscribed in Slovakian or Czech or a combination of both, Virgin Marys with broken noses, Virgin Marys with missing teeth, Virgin Marys that had been fondled and fondled and fondled since birth, Nutcrackers the witnesses of world wars, bells polished hard, ashtrays polished harder, guitars and flutes and wind-up recorders, harmonicas, accordions, pipes and wine glasses, table cloths and letter openers, and coffins adorned with everything but bodies.

Danny picked up a Lego. It was plastic, scratched, not much heavier than paper. He jostled it momentarily in his palm, then tossed it back into the container of thousands, and wondered why. Legos. Doll houses. Packages and packages of thermal underwear. Cookie cutters shaped like stars. Scraps of fabric, threadbare. It all seemed so evident, so natural. And yet cryptic and bizarre. A knife. A sword. Who would ever want one? Copper buttons. Knitted socks. Medals bled for by others.

But who wouldn't? Handerson bought wood. Danny saw forests. He saw trees, or remembrances of them. But not tables. Not chairs. Not picture frames made by hand.

He stayed for hours. He tried on cowboy boots. He flipped through oil paintings. He browsed unpublished plays in languages he didn't read. He looked at stethoscopes, stuffed animals, decoy ducks, and all the congregants who horded them, and he wondered what else he couldn't see. The beauty? The benefit? The beginning to something more? He turned over some wood, jagged and undefined, and he wondered if art was just that: the manipulation of resource. The vision and the creation, and the aim to make them one. Did it have to be beautiful? Did it have to have meaning?

He wanted standards. He wanted science. He wanted certainty and consistency or something that would make sense. He wanted proof in attraction, reasons in temper. Yet art was aloof—brief and undefined. He sat down at the opposite end of the market. He looked back at its plentitude and wondered if it wasn't the absence of a standard that plagued him, but his inability to create one. Handerson had said that all standards evolve, that none stay static. "The difference between standards in science and standards in art," he said, "is that standards in science change in relation to findings, while standards in art change in relation to feelings." Danny wanted to be sure. He recalled their conversation, the three of them, stoned, sitting at a café talking about beauty and stereotypes and Gia, about what it meant to be intelligent versus possess intelligence, to be beautiful versus possess beauty, if there were boundaries or even choices involved; and what, if not all, was imposed by others.

"You can be both and have both," Xavier said. "But no one will permit it."

Danny thought of Marina. Then sensed a lecture.

"Here we go!" Handerson exclaimed. "Get ready for Montezuma's Revenge—dissertation style. Hello, Mario Livio! Hello, Sir Leonardo da Vinci!" Xavier chuckled. Danny was sure he was high. "Divine Proportion! Golden Ratio! Fibonacci Sequence! One plus the square root of five divided by two and *voilà!* From seashells to sunflowers, the pine cone to the Pantheon!"

Danny didn't know what any of it meant but Xavier seemed to enjoy the banter, Handerson certainly to provide it. He mocked, professor-like, exaggerated in pomposity as though acquainted with one. "Let's hear it, Xavy! The etymology. Some quotations. Was it Burke or was it Stendhal? Beauty: *'la promesse du bonheur!'* Oh, but the great Xavier Legard disagrees! Romanticists be gone!" The weed was almost frightening. Xavier clutched his stomach in laughter. Handerson, now histrionic academic, played on. "Emerson and Thoreau—morality, wholeness, and virtue. Godard and Gibran—*crap!* Ovid and Camus—fragility and illusion. Goethe and Voltaire, that freak poet, Poe, too—sensitivity, revelation, a process of the soul. Plato! It is harmony that fashions integrity! Schlegel! The simultaneously attractive *and* sublime!" Handerson paused pretentiously. "Who isn't taking notes?" Xavier lay his face on the table trying his hardest not to roar. Danny resigned himself to ignorance. "Lessing? Wilde? The luminous John Ruskin? Sondheim of course—what the eye arranges. But Kant! But Hume! Diderot, Ockham, Santayana. Augustine and Aquinas, Heidegger and Shakespeare. A quandary—"

"*Stop!*" Xavier held up his hand and gasped.

"A quandary: *When*—I'd write this down if I were you, though clearly I'm not—*when* does manipulation cease to be art? At what point does the truth become a lie?"

"Han-der-*son!*"

"A man portrays a woman on stage. A mask is worn in a movie. The lie is truth. The show goes on. Persona is acquired and the difference undone. But when truth is lie, when markets are made and realities are broken, what then? What more can be claimed? Idealists shout, *Eternity!* But pottery's glaze won't last forever. And neither will the pot."

Chapter Twenty-Three

JANUARY WAS INTERMINABLE. Another Fashion Week loomed and agents were curt, flustered, and myopic. Models bombarded the city. Castings were indefinite. The snow stacked higher, the clouds hung lower. New York was dreary and tame. Danny returned feeling rejuvenated and booked a job in Miami the following day. It wasn't long though, before comfort surrendered and routine was restored. Marina was also back from abroad. And the holiday pounds had to go.

"Have you looked at me, Daniel?" She marched perfectly beside him. Her hair was up, her shoulders back, her clothes electric and trim. "I look like a baby elephant. Like some obese mastodon dreadfully in need of a laxative. Balderdash! Liposuction! Dubai, Daniel—how terribly pleasing a place. Oh, to be slim! To be hollow and wan, like some exiguous tubercular resting mindlessly in her garden of lilies. Yet look at me. Tanned. Full. Robust. A pregnant little piggy, ready for the roast."

Danny didn't respond.

"I nearly invited you, Daniel."

He turned to her. "To Dubai?"

"Well, not to Dubai per se," she said vaguely. "Simply, to play . . ."

He didn't want to know. But his curiosity was nailed. "Play what?"

"Roulette," she said.

"*Roulette?*"

"Airport Roulette."

Neither said a word. This game, the implications of it just lingered between them like a gun on the floor until she smiled valiantly and explained.

It was a daredevil's dream. It was sick and it was sinister and it was entirely true. He wondered if she lived her life based off of movies, or if movies were based off of her. He couldn't fathom how she found so little meaning and contentment in her limitless life, that she needed to reach so eagerly for any possible extreme. All he wanted was security. All he wanted was honesty. He wanted nothing to do with what this woman was after, and when she suggested he take part in the next year's "follies," that he experience what it felt like to abandon one's banalities and storm blindly into the sadism of the unknown, he declined without a moment's hesitation.

"Oh, but it is a mind-fuck!" she exclaimed.

Danny quickened the pace.

"I would compensate you, of course, Daniel."

He kept his head held high.

"And what would you do instead, visit Mum?"

"She's not my mom," he said. "And I happened to spend the holidays in Europe." That word. It sounded so classic, so vast and reassuring. He could have been anywhere.

"Europe?"

"Berlin."

"Why, Daniel," she said, as if amused, "how urbane, how truly cosmopolitan."

He sensed her disdain and waited for more. He waited for some jaunt about how she wouldn't have expected such sophistication, such a hip and intrepid choice as Berlin. But she said nothing more.

"Have you been?"

"Daniel, it is beautiful. Of course I have been."

Danny shrugged.

"Very well, Daniel. You *are* a model."

"What?"

"Why, Daniel," she said, as though he were the only one who hadn't heard. "Beauty cannot identify beauty. It holds no recognition of self."

He paused. "Is that a compliment or an insult?"

"Neither, Daniel. It is but a verity, a simple *verity*—nothing more, nothing less. True beauty is not contaminated by understanding; it is not marred by intellect or intent. Beauty itself is pure, and contemplation is a stain. Within beauty, within *actual* beauty, there is only absence, only emptiness, the being some hollow shell, a crust without a core. *That*, Daniel, is why models cannot be artists: artists cannot *be* beautiful, for if they were, they could not and would not *create* beauty. Artists *seek* beauty. They yearn for it. And one cannot yearn for that which one already possesses. They desire beauty because they lack it, and their desire stems from a depth that no beautiful being can comprehend, and one which none contains. Compliment or insult—I do not know, Daniel. But another lap to be sure."

"How can you . . . You don't really . . ."

She looked at him, loose and unaffected.

"This might come as a shock to you, Marina, but beauty is only empty because average is insecure."

"Is that so, Daniel?"

"What *I* want to know," he shot back, "is why art even has to be beautiful! And who decides? How do they know? Like there's some gauge somewhere that measures it. Measures *what*? A freckle? A wrinkle? A gray hair? And concludes? What about *me*? Am I beautiful? Why, because I'm simple? I'm empty and nothing's contaminating me? What, like a baby? Like a bird? Like the sky? So what happens when I walk into a wall and my face looks like an iron? What then? Do I stay void or do I develop a core since my crust's been contaminated? The face is gone so the head and heart kick in? I finally think and feel? Like my face was some sort of barrier? To the world? To myself? And what *about* my face, anyway? I could *be* a baby minus the fat, and some models are even skinnier! Their eyes, their necks, their ears—they look like aliens! What's so *beautiful*? What's being *measured*? A photograph? Is that it? I photograph well, so *that* makes me beautiful? Lights and lenses say I am? The lens of a camera, but not the lens of an eye?"

He looked at her with the repulsion he felt. He expected some smack of censure, some tyrannical offensive. But earned none.

"Vigilance," she said, slowly. "Or you may jeopardize your own appeal."

*   *   *

It had been weeks since their return from Berlin. Xavier had gone back to Harlem and Danny never saw him or had the chance to truly thank him. He spent his days in an office, his nights with Isis, and the few times he came home it was to change clothes or to swap books or to meditate. Danny had gotten busier as well—with Una; with castings; reading more than ever—and though he had thanked Xavier plenty it irritated him that he hadn't yet demonstrated it. So as the semester began and Berlin risked being forgotten, he headed to Harlem, to take Xavier to lunch.

He took his time wandering the halls, sensing all the opportunity and purpose and direction around him. He caught pieces of lectures. He peered eagerly into classrooms. He read every bulletin on every board as though each one had been posted for him—announcements for fellowships, for programs abroad, for guest lecturers and new courses, even more in search of research assistants, summer interns, anyone interested in joining the Philosophy Club, the Classics Club, the Chess Club, a magazine called *The Gadfly*, another called *Tablet*, and organizations named Earth Coalition and Democracy Matters and CU Smile among others that both saddened and inspired him.

In the halls he passed students as equally as intriguing as the clubs they formed. He watched them go plainly about their lives and more than anything he wondered how they had gotten there. He wondered how they prepared, with what paradigm. A mother? A father? Unconditional and always positive? Were there bedtime stories? Were there science projects? Were there hugs in the contract? Was there sports and music and art? Foods and languages and lands all foreign? Senses sparked? The imagination its own invention? He wondered if they knew what he knew: that childhood is a chance; that opportunity has limits; that education counts many among its distant admirers.

He looked at them as they walked by. Not in the way they looked at him—*on* him and *upon* him—but into them, inside them, their lives, their upbringings, their influences an assortment of challenges, motivations, stimulants, and gifts; investments planted deep, obstacles just right, communities to encourage. How fortunate. How blessed. How safe they were to be intellectually elite in a world that wanted brilliance. How *safe* they were to be more than a frame or face or façade, to be more than a spectacle at which to smile, an aesthetic to fancy or fondle.

Their eyes met and he wondered, too, what they saw. When his burrowed deep and theirs swept like sails in the wind—what had they seen? Him? And looked away? Were they preoccupied? Were they unmoved? Were they too arrogant or too alarmed or too bothered by inferiority? To look into him? Perhaps it was cultural. Perhaps social. Perhaps they had learned not to stare and he hadn't. Perhaps they had learned little of life and he had learned more. Perhaps they only spoke when spoken to. But they did look—for a moment at least—and he wondered what they saw. Beautiful idiot? Dumb model? And when they looked promptly away, he wondered, too, if *they* wondered what *he* saw. Ugly intellects? Embarrassing squares?

Xavier's voice was suddenly in Danny's ears. Students gathered in the hallways; classes were soon to end. Danny crossed his legs on the floor and he listened, impressed, to the eloquence of his roommate and to the articulation of so many of his own thoughts.

"Don't write," Xavier said. "There is no need. The questions cannot be found. Discovered, maybe, but not in the space between your pen and paper, or nails and keys." Xavier paused. The seminar, "Ethics and Aesthetics: Examinations of Art and Beauty," was his first, despite the many pieces Danny had already heard of it. Now was different. Xavier spoke slowly, carefully, professionally. And Danny felt proud.

"*What*," Xavier said, "is beauty?" Danny pulled his knees to his chest and smiled. "What is art? Is the latter necessary? Is the former innate?

"Is all art beautiful? Is all beauty artistry? Is one the very foundation of the other, and are there differences between? Creation. Manipulation. Evolution. Design. Synthesis. Complete. Does theology hold the answer? Does science?

"Is art imitation? If so, whose? Of what? How? Is interpretation even relevant? Has Plato been proven or disproven?

"Life's necessities—are *they* beautiful? Food. Shelter. Clothes. Rain? The sun? Are trees beautiful? Is birth? Is death?

"Can the same three necessities be art? *May* . . . the same three necessities be art? 'Cuisine.' 'Architecture.' 'Fashion.' Should they be? Should they never be?

"Can art be math? Can it be science? Can math or science be art?

"Religion?

"What predicates value? What determines worth? What is that of beauty, of art? Which implies the other? The value implies the beauty, or the beauty implies the value? And when does essence interfere?

"Why, *how*, as Avedon said, can beauty be as isolating as genius, or deformity? Is there a relationship between the beautiful and the mad?

"Does art threaten? Does beauty threaten? Do they inspire or do they mislead?

"Are art and beauty, the artist and the beautiful, the artistic and the beautified, superior or inferior to their alternatives? Is there a moral obligation to advertise or censor art and beauty? To encourage them or to deny them? Is use of time an issue of ethics?

"The body? The being? Beautiful? Artistic? Is there one entity or are there two? Face. Figure. The timbre of the voice, the fragrance of the skin, the touch of the tongue. And everything else, accessible to the senses but beyond their categorization. Character. Constitution. Integrity.

"In beauty, is there a difference between what is natural and what is artifactual? Why do we antagonize? Why do we laud? What informs us? Politics? Gender? Ego?

"Was Kant correct? Is there a bifurcation of aesthetic—beautiful and sublime? And if so, are his categories accurate? What falls beyond either-or?

"Is blood beautiful? Is snow? Is a color, more so than another? What about age? Justice? Geometry? A word. A sound. Silence. By way of virtue, or by default?

"Listen."

There was silence.

"Listen."

There was an unnerving pause. Danny waited. He wanted more. He wasn't sure if he wanted questions or answers or merely the continued comfort of being understood, but more. To discuss is at least to perceive.

"As you've already seen in the syllabus," Xavier said, his tone more conclusive, his tempo not as measured. "In each of the first three weeks you'll write a short exercise. One thousand words maximum. A combination of creativity, philosophy, and analytics. They're warm-ups, no more, to the assignments to come. For next week you'll write *one* of the following: An interview with Oscar Wilde's Lord Henry Wotton. A conversation between Goethe and Schiller—German or English is fine—see the syllabus for details. Or a eulogy for the sun, the wind, or the rain. Are there questions?"

Danny had drifted with Xavier's "listen" to some distant clarity. Then he jumped as the sounds of feet rushed forward and the door slammed opened. Students trickled by, each glancing at him and away, until no one but Xavier was left.

"Danny!" Xavier slid on his coat.

"I'd—I'd take your class," Danny said. And wished he could.

Chapter Twenty-Four

C ASTINGS ENDED AS SHOWS BEGAN. Danny got optioned for Mackage, Lacoste, and Domenica Vaca, and booked for Custo Barcelona. His elation quickly deflated, though, when no sooner than his three options were released, staff at Barcelona recalculated costs and the designer was forced to cancel each of the four male models originally confirmed. Danny told Derek he would have walked for free but didn't realize that when wealthier, more celebrated designers were paying models with coupons to McDonald's and shoes sold at Florsheim's, his offer was moot. He was hardly the expense.

Shows began in early February. Una was booked every day. Danny returned to the Tent in all black and aside from anticipating her, he watched the routine unfold. Celebrities sat comfortably at the front. Agents squeezed helplessly at the back. Guests rejoiced and lamented the final season of shows in Bryant Park—as they had the season before and likely would again the next. The lights dimmed and the atmosphere cooled. Music and a blinding glow filled the tent, and as models marched plastered in makeup, the tempo, the ordering, the synthesis of the artistries moved brilliantly with the clothes. From the classic to the futuristic, each was sublime.

For Danny though, the aura abated. He focused solely on the models. Show after show—William Rast; Sergio Davila; 1909 Victorinox—he watched them. Their posture. Their lips. Their ambiguity and dearth. Everyone told him he had it. Everyone assured him he did. From agents to photographers, confidence abounded. Yet he didn't book. He didn't work. And this image, this look, this "heroine-chic"-turned-"androgy-amore" and the designers, the branders, the clients who loved epicenes whose lives and careers no paparazzi knew and whose features made Danny's look valiant, this obsession with the slight, the wan, the ephemeral, and this selfish, ominous, stubborn sickness of ideal which Xavier wore sardonically across a shirt—**hunger for success**—this grayness, this elusiveness, this absence of interstice as though male and female, god and goddess, Hermes and Aphrodite were one, he knew, wouldn't last forever. And neither would he.

3.1 Phillip Lim was underway, and Danny wondered if Fashion was anything like Academia. He'd been thinking about the students he saw at Columbia, wondering if they ever thought about their situation the way he was learning to think of his. About excess. About essence adorned. About exclusivity and select for select and about the palavering that produced more. About the rest of the world's untold idealizations, their resentments, their misunderstandings, and stereotypes. About their respective routines, how mundane and foreseeable, the unforgiving scrutiny and the looming, if not inveterate, exams, opportunities to build confidence crushed, and the parties too, their surest consequences. He wondered if there was as much pretense and politics for college students as there was for models and if the former could possibly compare. To what extent did they conform? To what extent did they truckle? Had they ever dared to cheat or lie? And if they fucked a professor, did they want to?

The audience cheered. The finale ended and the designer waved wide with a bow. Danny's phone vibrated in his pocket.

The crowd dispersed and he checked the message. "Call me," she said.

He replied with a text: "I'm working."

Seconds later she called again. Again he checked his voice-mail. "Do I strike you as the texting type, Daniel? *Call* me."

The Tent was now empty. He took his coat from backstage and stepped outside, shivering in the wind as he dialed.

"Can you drive?"

"Can I drive?"

"Beep-beep, Daniel! Can you *drive?*"

"Yeah. Of course." He hadn't thought of Jimmy in months, of his Oldsmobile and how his weekend drunkenness became Danny's education. Danny drank with him, but always stayed the soberer—law and license be damned.

"Splendid, Daniel. Go to the Lowell and tell Boris you want Bentley II in white. It is now eleven. Be here by noon."

"I'm sorry? Marina, I'm working. You can't just call when-ever you want like—Marina . . . ? Marina!" He looked at his phone. The screen faded blank. "Fuck! *Fuck!*" He threw his arms in the air. The wind spun in circles. Models crisscrossed around him and for a moment he simply stood there, furious and defiant. Then he closed his eyes. He inhaled the snow. He scorned himself for even contemplating it, yet assured himself no one would know. No one checked on him. Una was already at her apartment resting for Calvin Klein, showing outside the park. And Marina would pay him. Handsomely. As always. He glanced at the street. He turned back to the Tent. He hated what she did to him. He hated what she did *for* him, by way of him, how she diminished him, turned his life into her own and made money all that mattered, used his weakness as her bait but neither reeled him in nor let him go, simply watched as he suf-fered, writhing on her line. He hated the way she knew it, the way she calculated it, how uncaringly she executed it. He hated her entitlement, her exploited heirarchy, her born-and-bred pomp. He hated that she wasn't the only one, and that neither was he: even if he broke free, even if he healed and ascended and shouted Truth to the world, there would still, always, be others—other Marinas, other Dannys, other struggles and strangleholds and master-model dilemmas. He hated that he was anything but alone. And yet completely alone.

He breathed deep, and stepped slowly, silently away.

*   *   *

William held the door as Harold scampered out to do the same. Marina followed comfortably in black leather boots to the knee, black velvet gloves to the elbow, a single weave of wool-cashmere tartan in black, cream, and tinseled stone to the elbow and calf, Giambattista Valli from head to toe as if she'd purchased the entire ensemble right there off the runway in Paris.

"Good day, Daniel." She situated herself in the seat behind him, hints of winter and Guerlain swirling to a standstill. "How agreeable of you to join me. I pray no one caviled you whilst collecting the car?"

He didn't answer. He simply looked at her, patient, through the rearview mirror.

"I have a *most* divine day planned, Daniel. Though how dreadfully it began—some sonic drill boring itself into my skull. Oh, it was savage. Heinous to say the least. You received your pay I presume; I sent it down on the lift. Daniel, do drive, would you; the day will be gone by tomorrow." And on she went: the evening; the wine; the bottles and bottles of wine, and the reasons she hadn't shown, again, that morning. Eric Ripert and his kumamoto. Eric Ripert and his kampachi. Eric Ripert and his wild osetra caviar culled straight from the Caspian Sea. "His ganache, Daniel—my word, there *is* a god!" And the wine that wouldn't end. Adrian and Ferran and the wine that just wouldn't end. The dusk that turned to dawn and the ice cubes, the strawberries, the wine—"Marina"—the broken glasses— "*Marina*"—the melted chocolate—

"MARINA!"

Their eyes met in the mirror. Neither moved. They sat there, staring, perplexed, neither sure of what to say nor entirely sure of what had been. Marina's chest rose wide. Danny loosened his grip on the wheel. He exhaled without a sound.

"Where," he said, apologetic but firm. "Drive where?"

Still, neither moved.

"*I* have a divine day planned, Daniel. I vacated my schedule. I took my triptans. I went back to bed and when I woke up, *I planned a divine day.*"

He closed his eyes. "*Where?*"

"*Dee-vine.*"

He shook his head in defeat. He dropped his hands from the wheel and gazed out the window. Her glare eased at last and as the seatbelt buckled behind him and the sound of probing came from her purse, he glanced at her, mumbling, "Where? Drive where?" And for a second he remembered: he was a model in New York, driving a Bentley down Central Park. He lowered his chin, and suppressed a smile.

Undirected, he drove. Fifth Avenue bustled. Painters sold prints. Horses pulled carriages. Tourists ogled outside Tiffany's and FAO Schwartz and Abercrombie & Fitch with all its boys, Danny's more muscled associates working shirtless in winter for flattery or health care, or to avoid an otherwise impecunious end.

He kept south without asking. Marina seemed satisfied, and the car was a gem. He drove easily around taxis, potholes, breezed into the Forties and for a moment felt untouchable until he came to the Tent and nearly crashed.

"Daniel!" she exclaimed.

"There . . . was a squirrel!"

"Bloody hell, I *eat* squirrel!"

He calmed and continued. He passed the Empire State Building and was approaching Broadway and the Flatiron when she directed him at last.

"A right at West 21st Street, Daniel. The store is called Da Vinci."

"Art supplies?"

"Naturally, I would have had the items delivered directly, but I have not painted in a month of Sundays and . . . well, time has had its way. Regardless, I perused the place last week with the aid of a most delightful collegiate fellow. Acrylics. Chamois. Palettes. His jaw was as smooth as varnish, and I wish to make my purchase."

She stepped out and walked stately into the store. Danny drove in circles until half an hour later she called him back, chattering about gesso and impasto and tortillons and the edible boy with the slick jowl. She continued on even as he pulled up beside her and she sat down behind him. "I'm right here," he said, and closed his phone in her face. But she hardly paused. And Danny drove west by default.

Jeffrey from Jeffrey New York had called. "He is holding a Dries Van Noten," she said. "He claims it is a must, Daniel, though we both know the season's collection was *vastly* unadventurous. Nothing like the last. There is not a critic I—"

"Straight or right?"

"—know who . . . Daniel, are your ears blocked?" The light turned green. A car behind him began to honk. "*Jeffrey.* We are going to *Jeffrey*."

"Jeffrey is not a direction, Marina. It's not an address."

She gazed softly out the window. "You flummox me, Daniel. You flummox me. A model, and you do not know Jeffrey. Do you jest?"

The car honked louder. Others joined in. "For Christ's sake! Straight or right?"

"How you flummox me . . ."

"*Marina!*"

"Flummox, flummox, flummox."

He drilled the gas. The tires shrieked and they barreled across Eighth Avenue. No sooner than they cleared the intersection, she sighed: "14th Street, Daniel, off Tenth." He stared at her. She gazed quietly. He clenched his teeth and navigated without reply. Minutes later, as though the spot had been reserved for them, he parked outside the store. The doorman escorted Marina into the building and Danny laid his head against the glass, closed his eyes, and fell asleep.

An hour later, not a toe through the door, she woke him. "Christian Louboutin!" she exclaimed. "The man is not *human!*" Danny stretched his neck. Marina sat down, leaned jubilantly forward, and insisted he behold her latest peep toe platforms—blue with near-five-inch heels and a scaly glisten that all but made her orgasm.

"Uh-huh." He sped off, and Marina slid back.

"Heaven," she sighed, and sat there slouched and hypnotized while Danny took it upon himself to head north via the West Side Highway. They were well into the Thirties before she picked herself up. "Oh. Splendid, Daniel. To 57th."

She sounded so innocent, he couldn't help but ask, "What's on 57th?"

It was too late. He regretted it immediately. Without even seeing, he sensed her. He could have taken the word right out of her mouth. And the daydream that followed.

"Jewelry . . ."

She said it with such certainty and such élan that his foot fell intuitively heavy. He drove faster. He arrived sooner. He listened less. Pianegonda. Visconti. Teno. What did they mean? What difference did they make? What was a stone marked two, ten times the rent he didn't pay? What was a metal, a mineral, a crystal he couldn't eat? Crivelli didn't sell rings at the dollar store. Nanis wasn't accustomed to bargain-hunters. Staurino Fratelli? How many did she already own? At what point was plenty too much? When did excess diminish value and what was so wrong with temperance?

"Do you donate?" he said suddenly. She looked at him. "Do you? Money? Time? Anything?" She simply looked at him.

247

She returned impassively to the window, and remained there until Danny sighed and wondered who she was when she was alone. If she reflected. Repented. Or refused and moved on.

She stepped out at the store, and he drove submissively away.

Half an hour later she called him back. "Tea time, Daniel! 69th and Madison." She set another bag beside her.

"Ito En?"

"Why, Daniel, you are not a ewer after all! At least not an empty one."

He turned right on Fifth Avenue.

"Though your navigation is appalling. *North*, Daniel. Not south."

"We're not going to Ito En," he said.

"Oh truly, Daniel, and the London Bridge is not in London. Turn this car around. Turn it around and cease this rubbish straight away." But he didn't. He turned onto 55th, then onto Seventh, and thought she had fallen asleep or decided it was all amusing when out of nowhere she stormed forward. "*What*, Daniel Ward, are you doing?"

"Taking you to McNulty's!"

"And what, pray tell, is that?"

"A tea shop," he said. "The best in the city."

"No, Daniel. No. You are *driving* to Ito En and you are *doing* so immediately. Truly, Daniel, what have you been smoking?"

"Come on, don't be so—" She lunged for the wheel. The Bentley swerved wide. "Jesus Christ, Marina! Are you insane?"

"Daniel Ward, turn this car *around!*" She lunged again. Again they swerved. Arms tangled in knots. The car swooped and shimmied. Brakes shrieked and as the city spun he broke free of her at last, jolted and dumbfounded, and pushed her firmly away. Then forced himself, nervously, to laugh.

"Fuck, Marina, you're crazy! You're going to get us killed over a damn tea bag?" He checked his mirrors and breathed. "Jesus."

"You are treading tender lines, Daniel Ward. I bid you caution. *And yes . . . tea.* I do not know at what desideratum you aim but I purchase my tea at Ito En. *Only* Ito En. You may contrive and connive as you please, but you will do so in vain."

"Marina," he said, still whiplashed with disbelief. "I've been to every tea shop there is. Podunk. Porto Rico. Tea & Sympathy. Lady Mendl's—"

"Lovely, Daniel."

"—Franchia, Grace's, Alice's, Yaffa's—"

"Daniel!"

"Una loves tea." He paused. "McNulty's is the best and if you don't think so, then . . . well . . . well then today is free. And the tea is on me."

"Oh, is that so, Daniel?"

He focused on the road. He wondered why she cared. He wondered, more so, why he cared. "Yes," he said. "That's so."

He continued down Seventh Avenue until he passed 23rd and Marina asked where this place McNulty's—"it *sounds* Irish"—was located.

"Christopher Street. The Village."

"The *Village?*" He'd never heard her so shocked. "Daniel, I do not travel south of 14th Street. SoHo if I am blindfolded. Turn around, Daniel. Ito En. I will not be seen in such boorish parts."

"I guess you've never tried the chocolate at Jacque Torres," he said, driving on. "Dumbo *is* in Brooklyn."

"Daniel *Ward* . . ."

They crossed 14th Street and she released something of a gag or a choke, took out her new Lady Claude Pythons and stroked them. Minutes later he stopped the car.

"Not that one," he said, pointing with a smirk at a Leather Man shop. "That one."

"You will regret this." She slapped him with a glare. Then exited like a queen attempting a slum. He watched her step inside, and he drove off, quietly, in prayer.

It was nearly an hour before she called.

"Well?"

"The Lowell," she said.

"McNulty's?"

"Yes? What about it?"

"Well what did—" He pulled away. "The Lowell . . ."

She patted her hair. "Teuscher first. I want chocolate."

He felt vindicated. He could have recommended anything—a new dish detergent, a better brand of toilet paper. The category was irrelevant, except that she liked tea. Otherwise it was what lay beneath, what her approval meant, and how he perceived it.

"Dear God," Marina said. "Is that Kinzie?" She stared in awe out the window. Danny tried to find him but failed. "It is! Why, what a fascinating look he has achieved. At first glance he looked worse than a bloody forest fire, simply parched and consumed, even ashen. But at second something more. Something faint and ethereal. Translucent!" Danny hadn't seen Sasha since before leaving for Berlin. And with his shoot in Miami, spending time with Una, walking Marina, and all the castings between, he hardly noticed. It was usually that way, living alone with three roommates he saw more often at random than in the apartment they shared. But Sasha concerned him. He always had.

Marina sighed. "It is a faint and unfair line—that between beauty and death."

"Death?" Danny froze.

"Like pleasure and pain. A faint line indeed."

Danny turned again but too late. Marina shook her head. She sighed something about the misfortune of his timing, about fashion's increasingly dull political correctness, models all balloons before long, and Danny drove somberly in thought.

Marina bought champagne truffles as desired, and they reached the Lowell at last. Danny checked the clock. He could be home by seven and still have ample time to relax before meeting up with Una. All he needed was his money.

"And *how* would you propose I return home, Daniel?"

He knitted his brow. "Walk?"

"*Walk?*"

"Yes—*walk*. That thing we do every morning . . ."

She looked at him oppressively. He sank in his seat. "I shall return by eight. Immanuel is bringing Eduardo and I am having double lomilomi. *You*, Daniel, shall wait. *Then* you will drive me home. *Then* you will return the car. *Then* you are dismissed."

She stepped out without pause as Danny waited, again, for Marina to pleasure herself. She returned two hours later, her hair combed but disheveled, her posture as soft as the glow in her cheeks. Danny looked away. He started the car. Neither said a word. It began to snow as they reached the condo. Marina leaned forward. She set an envelope on the passenger's seat, then a long, black, narrow box beside it. Danny glanced down, hardly moving an eye.

"What is that?"

She collected her bags. "Or for whom."

The door closed and she faded elegantly across the sidewalk, under the awning, and into the condominium. Danny looked at the box. He reached for it. He hesitated. He looked back at the building, at the splendor, at the void, at the snow falling gently, then drove back to the Lowell and caught the subway home.

The envelope, its contents, the precise pay was irrelevant. It would be no more, no less, and he put it away without looking. The box he examined. He was already late but time never pardoned him anyway. Five, ten, twenty minutes he sat there, stared at it, strained to accept it. He knew. She needled him right to the nerve. She knew just where to prod and just when to stop, how much to offer and how often to give. She studied him and tested him and always made sure he could pass, that he would. But his innocence, his need, his nerves—something was wearing; something was thin. His heart begged no, and he opened it at last.

Diamonds.

He closed it immediately. He pulled his knees to his chin, and he rocked.

Chapter Twenty-Five

MARCH CAME UNNOTICED. Its predecessor was frenzied. Rumors circulated that Monica was ill. Una worked everywhere. Sasha was in and out of the hospital more often than a doctor and Danny was discomposed. Marina was careless with his time, his thoughts, her money—calculated if there was a difference. Shows and parties proved only temporary distractions. Autonomy continued to evade him. He was groped by an editor leaving a bathroom in Midtown. He was followed by a casting director on his way into another. He watched models interact with designers and photographers, socialites and their associates, and he fought hard not to be suspicious or envious or secretly proud. He was marred by reminders of shame. The more he knew, the less he understood.

It was the first of the month and nearly night. Danny sat in the hallway of a hotel waiting to enter his first-ever casting on a Sunday. Elsewhere—L.A., Miami, abroad—clients held castings as they pleased: weekends; holidays; midnight if necessary. But not in New York. In New York, while shoots were planned freely and could last indefinitely, castings were held during business hours only, and infuriated models when they weren't.

The clients were young and wealthy and had flown in from Dubai. They sent out requests earlier that week but either by way of the economy or word of who was shooting drew three times the number they specified. There was, of course, no way to prevent the casting crashers from showing. But an effort could have been made to turn them away.

Instead, the line grew, and bursts of laughter coiled from the suite down the hall. Models walked out mumbling. They shook their head, rolled their eyes. The hints were clear and led a smattering toward the back to leave upon arrival rather than wait hours to be seen by clients who didn't look. Most, however, were too desperate.

Danny knew the frustration. He had been to these castings before. He had waited quietly, respectfully, as clients skimmed—more so fanned—through scores of portfolios, opened them at the back, leafed in reverse, skipped pages as they went, sometimes bored, sometimes angry, then quickly withdrew a card, glanced at it or didn't, smiled or didn't, said thank you or didn't, and made everyone hate life. Occasionally, someone spoke up. And when she did, it was tremendous. It was explosive. Like a downpour in a desert. Something Danny knew he'd never dare.

It was nearing nightfall by the time he met them: two men in their thirties chatting volubly in a language he couldn't decode and felt impolite to interrupt.

"Hello . . . ?"

He entered, but stopped. A hand waved him forward and the two men continued to chat. Danny sat down in the chair in front of them. He laid his portfolio on the table, offered his hand in greeting, then steadily, uneasily, retracted it.

The men talked at length until the leaner of the two gestured vaguely at the book. The second man, louder, on Danny's right, as though feeling for a light switch in the dark reached a hand out in front of him and patted the air in search of it. The cover, at last, kissed the table, and the conversation ensued. The opening photo was a portrait by Yuri. The composition was exquisite and easily Danny's favorite. He stood beside a

window, staring at the sun. His pupils felt like they were melting but his face stayed undisturbed. He never blinked, never
cried, never yielded or protested or claimed the endeavor
absurd, the picture impossible. He simply accepted, fought,
and persevered.

But the picture was passed, unseen, and Danny had to
remind himself to breathe. His shoulders softened. His lips
parted. The second and third pictures came into view. They
too, were bold and coaxing. Yet the slimmer man gave them no
more than a glance and the louder man never looked. He
merely continued to talk, to turn, fluid and absent and altogether galling until more pages had been passed and he fanned
to the back—talking—removed the first composite he
touched—talking—closed the portfolio at last—talking, talking—stacked it on a pile of numerous others, and fluidly,
absently, gallingly, continued talking.

Danny sat stone-still. He couldn't remember the last time
he felt so disregarded. He didn't know if he should stay or go,
if they'd acknowledge him or dismiss him, take his picture, confirm his measurements, ask him to try something on or care if
he left without saying goodbye. He didn't even know if they
knew he was there, or why, and it burned him so badly he
wanted to rage. He wanted to shout, "You rich arrogant
pricks!" He wanted to shove his middle finger in their face and
tell them to go to hell, to fuck off, to waste someone else's time.
He wanted to swipe back his card and force them to stare at it,
then rip it into thousands of pieces and scatter them around the
room. He wanted to live up to the stereotypes he knew they
had of him, just as they lived up to the very ones he had of
them: *rude pompous bastards!* He wanted to be affected. He
wanted to emote. He wanted to rant and rave and lower himself to their level with curses and insults and precisely the same
puerile behavior the world expected of him—callow, crude,
impulsive.

No.

He picked up his portfolio. The men continued talking. He cringed as he walked ahead. Four more, three more, two more steps and he'd be out the door, the next model inside, lessons learned, order maintained. Soon enough it would happen again, another casting, another client, another foot to the stomach, and he, like everyone, would walk stolidly away, wondering how some people could get life so miserably wrong, and who, if anyone, booked these mystery jobs for which dozens were requested but few ever seen. How ironic was an industry that was visual yet blind. Fabrics were felt. Perfumes were smelled. Drinks were tasted. Products were perceived this way or that but the model, expressly, was seen. Only. And if not? If he wasn't? What was he if never seen?

Danny spun suddenly around. He was already across the room with his portfolio open and on the table by the time the men had turned, silenced, and stared. "Do you have *any* idea what it took to get some of these shots? Any at all?" He plunged his finger into a page of plastic-covered-paper. "This picture. Do you know what went *into* this picture, how long we *worked* on it? Getting it? Not *good*. Not *really* good. Fucking-*awesome*-good." He turned the pages. "There's no campaigns. There's no Prada or Gucci in here. No Missoni. No Dsquared2. No covers from *Cream*. I've never shot with Chad Pitman or Junji Hata. My book isn't filled from front to back and I don't have stacks of tears from million-dollar budgets or absurd editorials from Milan. What I *do* have though—what I have a-goddamn-*plenty* of—is *this* . . ." He smashed his fist against his heart. "*That's* what's in this book. *That's* what's in these pictures."

The room was silent. No one moved. Danny felt his legs start to shake, his chest start to tighten. He didn't know what he had said but only that it was over and with some revival of consciousness or concern he turned and left, unsure if he'd ever model again.

*　　*　　*

255

First thing Monday morning he went into Edge prepared with pleas and apologies. Yes it was stupid. Yes it was unprofessional. Yes, he *did* understand, and no, he did *not* want to risk his reputation *or* that of the agency. He would, of course, write to the client and no—*no*—he would *not* let it happen again. Ever.

The secretaries were all rapidly accepting and transferring calls when he entered. He forced a slight nod, a defective smile, and received three of the same in return amid the standard Monday morning spell. He passed the receptionists but instead of turning right at the semicircle and continuing to the Men's board he stayed left toward the nearest bathrooms and with his hand on the door he stopped.

"What, it's just *over?* Just like that?"

"For Christ's sake, Kinzie, you could have *died!*"

"Yeah, I could've, Carla, and where the fuck were you?"

"Kinzie, have you looked *around?* Would you open your eyes?"

"Same old shit, Carla. The *same* old shit."

"Lately! That's all it ever is!"

"And what the hell do you want me to do about it?"

Danny prayed to God no one was in the bathroom, or on their way. He felt pitiful for listening but couldn't pull away.

"I don't have the time for this, Kinzie."

"Time for *what*, Carla?"

"For *this*. For *you*. For *any* of it."

"Oh, so it's all champagne and caviar when we're booking and fucking and high, and the money's—"

"That was years ago, Kinzie!"

"Which *part?*"

"Just take the month off. Get yourself together. Call me when you're clean."

"A month? I can't afford a month!"

"Well I can't afford *you*, Kinzie. Either book out or find another agency."

"So it's just like that? It's that simple?"

"For Christ's sake, Kinzie! I don't have the time for this senti-mental bull shit!"

The silence was piercing, the moment eternal. Danny stood motionless as Sasha appeared like a rain cloud around the corner. He blew straight past him, dark and chilled, then oddly, eerily, without a hint of recognition, he turned.

"Hey."

"Kinzie, I was just . . . I just . . ." Danny looked at him. "Are you OK?"

Sasha rubbed his forehead. His eyes were hollow, his cheeks sunken. He looked like he might vomit, or die. His hands shook but whether from withdrawal, shock, anger, or shame, Danny couldn't tell. He'd never gotten to know Sasha more than superficially, and though he knew pieces of his roommate's past, he tried not to judge.

"Can I borrow some cash?" Sasha never bothered with niceties.

"Kinzie, I . . . I'm broke. I wish I—"

"You quit fucking Marina?"

"What?"

"Bitch regurgitates quicker than a cow."

"Kinzie, I was never—"

"Let me tell you something," Sasha said, his eyes, his cheeks, his words all bare. Danny nodded. He tried not to stare, he tried to stay calm, however immoral it might be. Sasha looked like an oyster pried of its pearl. There was no sparkle. No spirit. No lift. Just weight. Life. The thanklessness of gravity. He looked down, quivered, and without warning slammed the heel of his hand over Danny's shoulder into the door behind him. *"That's* how quickly it starts." He slammed it again. "And *that's* how quickly it ends." Danny turned stiff as a board. Sasha held his glare, then crumbled instantly to the floor. Danny looked about. He didn't know if he should pick him up, let him be, call for help; but as heedlessly as Sasha sank, Danny joined him, trying his best to keep his cool.

"You're sure you're OK?"

Sasha sat painfully, sprawled like trash. His neck was twisted, his legs contorted. His spine curled sideways against the wall. His entire being spoke honesty and despair. He mumbled like a drunk, with solitude exposed.

"Light bulbs. All we are. One burns out, screw the next one in. Xavier's high on work ethic, what to do-wear-eat like anyone gives a shit and he's never dropped his pants for fuck. *We* were friends. Don't *tell* me it was the drugs. Yeah, I know—*always* drugs. Well it was Armani and Guess *before* the homotography! Paris, Milan like we owned it. Carla was barely a gopher. Junior booker with braces and everyone fucking knows it. *She* came to *me*. Skiing, sucking, fucking. She *encouraged* it. Blow the photographers! Blow the casters! Fucking ecstatic when the phones are ringing, there's cash in the bank, we're off stone-stupid somewhere with our books, our G-Stars, our dicks tucked away like we don't know up from down, Pope if we saw him. Not a goddamn clue. And it's the sons of bitches *going* to the castings that never get booked. Preaching to the choir. You're out at every goddamn cattle call there is, client's on the phone with some booker somewhere holding onto her balls trying not to nut over some model she's never seen, couple tests if she's lucky, but no, he's working, Mexico, Miami, can't make the casting when everyone knows he's out buying more blow, girlfriend's waiting while the booker he's fucking, dude's boyfriend too, he's wrapping up the whore's fifth fucking campaign that season while you and the rest are standing in some slow-ass elevator in Chelsea plucking nose hairs in front of pocket mirrors. Not a damn clue that *I'm* the one to hate. And *she* tells *me* she doesn't have the time. *All I did!* For years! For her! Little cunt. 'You could have died, Kinzie, you could have died.' *I have died!*"

Tears filled his eyes.

Every word quaked in Danny's ears. They sat there on the floor like two old men who had nothing left to say, who knew

themselves and the other and the world with such certainty that
they knew they knew nothing at all and to say anything would
only prove it. Danny was distressed in ways he didn't even realize. Thoughts trained through his head and collided from
every direction. He focused nervously on the floor. He studied it, frantic and in denial and wondering how long he could
keep from looking up at the weight of Sasha's empty face.

Minutes passed before Danny decided he just wouldn't let
Sasha out of his sight. He'd monitor him, cook for him, get
him healthy again; he'd do whatever was necessary. But just as
his conviction surged he remembered where he was and why.
His phone rang and Sasha stood up, mumbling "light bulbs."

Danny stood faster and told him not to leave. He steadied
him as he took out his phone, then stopped as he saw the number.

"Oh, fuck . . . Kinzie!" But Sasha was already distancing.
"*Shit!* Kinzie!"

His heart drilled. He slipped into the bathroom, rehearsed
every apology in a blip, and answered the phone.

"I'm up to my eyeballs in emails," Carla said. "You're on
option from yesterday. The client should be calling back by
afternoon. It shoots tomorrow night in Central Park just in
case you . . . *Oh, for the love of*—I have to go . . . Kinzie, what
do you think . . ." She hung up the phone. Danny stared
dumbstruck at the door.

*   *   *

His call-time was six o'clock for a shoot projected to run
late. At a quarter of, and hardly seconds after he exited the subway, a mile from Marina's, she called.

"Where are you, Daniel?"

He lowered his head. "Marina, please. Don't do this."

"Where *are* you, Daniel?"

"I'm at East 86th. Why?"

"Be here by seven. That should be more than ample time."

"What? Marina, I'm headed to a job."

"I truly astound myself sometimes, Daniel—seven fifteen."

"I am *going* . . . to a *job*."

"You really *can* be a difficult one, Daniel. What is the rate?"

"I'm not telling you the rate. I don't ask about your money."

"What is the *rate?*"

He swallowed and sighed and shut his eyes.

"I will double it."

Danny halted in the middle of Park Avenue. He didn't move until a Hummer came charging and he bounded to the curb.

"I said I will *double it*."

"Marina, no. Stop. Don't do this. What do you even . . . Why do you keep . . . Damn it, Marina, do you have any idea what you're asking? Just not show? No reason? No notice?"

"Oh, Daniel," she said, her tone unbearably flippant, almost bewildered but blunt. "I am not asking you. I am telling you." And without pause she hung up the phone.

For months it had built. Deviously, it grew. Time and again he felt it, refused it, kept sanity in its place. He breathed deep, deeper with resolve. And he lied if he had to. But now this struggle, this chaos, this panic-filled shame erupted from the last remaining peace he could retain and like a drug or a monster stormed through his body. It ruptured his intestines. It suffocated his lungs. It paralyzed his limbs and shattered his spine, smothered itself mercilessly across every inch of his face, and it stabbed and stabbed and stabbed at his heart. It clobbered. And he broke. There in the middle of New York, surrounded by Navigators and Escalades, five-figure garments and four-story homes, Central Park just ahead and the stress of adoration, expectation, perfection, impossibility, inadequacy, failure, silence, desperation, competition, risk, self-loathing, indifference, sheer desensitization—as a model—coupled with the convenience, simplicity, security, perks, possibilities, extravagances, money, money, money, more, the weight of reliability, the excess, the demands, the manipulation, confusion, indecision, excruciating discord—as a male model, a non-model, a boy toy—all grabbed him at the throat, pummeled him in the ribs, clubbed him on the knees, and as he had been so vigilantly forbidding himself for so long from doing, yet quietly wishing he long-since had, he broke.

Tears stung his eyes. Snot traced his lips. Some foreign, some anonymous self like one he had seen and stared at just the day before in Sasha, repeatedly in Charlene, many he had in pity called lonely and crazy now ripped at his hair, sent his fists flailing, tore bellows from his chest, tugged wildly at his clothes, and curled his body into a quiver on the sidewalk.

It was some time before the pockets of onlookers dispersed. The blood drained from his cheeks, the tears dried with the snot, his clothes and hair and limbs all settled. And shortly before eight o'clock, a doorman he didn't know but who clearly knew him stood blindly aside as he continued to Marina's condo thirteen floors above.

She opened the door, and for a moment said nothing. She simply stood there, observed him. She didn't declare his belatedness. She didn't mention his appearance. She didn't ask any questions but simply watched as his gaze fell everywhere she wasn't. Their eyes never met but he knew, and he knew that she knew he knew. For every sign, every variable, every smell and sound and undetectable haze indicated it. The phone call, if nothing else, indicated it. The transaction. Why they were there. What he was selling. What she was buying. The cost, the sacrifice irrelevant. A craving satisfied. That alone. She looked and she waited with incalculable patience; she allowed him every opportunity to think, to feel, to know. And he did. The moment was eternal until at last she softened, she straightened, she smiled in a way he would have never wanted to see, and in a voice he had no choice but to hear, she welcomed him. "Good evening, Daniel."

He swallowed. His chest caved. His neck locked. His eyes swam vacantly about and with a tremor, hardly more than a whisper, he replied. "Good evening."

He stepped inside. She closed the door. And nothing more was said.

He followed her to the bedroom. Nothing seemed real. Nothing seemed itself. The paintings were lackluster. The lights scarcely shined. The carpets were coarse and the furniture, the curtains, even the view that once stunned him were all undistinguished, black-and-white, bland if not blank. Marina turned around. She stood in front of him, clutched his hand in hers, and lifted it, slowly, slower, the slowest she possibly could with only his index finger exposed and everything but the heat of her hand still detached from what it really was. He closed his eyes, and he was gone. She stood inches in front of him, watching him, studying him, something like hesitation in her eyes as though awed by the achievement of so long a journey, processing the transition from fantasy to reality while lifting higher, slowly, higher, her hand so steady it nearly shook, his finger guided and everything around him still dull, his eyes still closed, only her hand and his of any significance until almost imperceptibly, infinitely softly, with the slightest but slightest of touch, as from the tinniest tip of a feather, the smallest droplet of water, the faintest whisk of the wind, one more delicate than any he had ever illustrated and any she had ever felt, the very center of his finger touched the very outskirt of her shoulder and with the flavor and heat of a desert waft she exhaled onto his neck.

Her eyes fluttered closed. His opened in a flash. The paintings were suddenly masterful, the lights bright, the carpet supple. Everything was its original and more, and she moved his finger so slowly and tenderly down the length of her arm that he could actually see each hair respond with arousal as he passed it.

Another thick, humid zephyr escaped her lips, smothered itself across his neck, flushed over him instantly, and with a shudder that felt like a surge he closed his eyes, again, and was gone.

No drink. No drug. No misunderstanding or lack of consent. No lack of control. Quite simply, quite consciously, he was gone.

When his finger reached the dint, just above her elbow. When it lingered there—a moment, an eternity—then continued increasingly upward. When it drifted back down, back up, back down, impressively, patiently, slowly. And then, as well, when it stopped. When it traveled inward, traced the hairlessness of the vein that divided bicep from tricep and finally reached her wrist, her palm, the knuckle and nail of every finger and returned up again, incredibly, gradually, delicately, and reached her collar. The dip. The bone. The agreement of one to the other. He was gone. When he outlined it. When his finger aroused it. When it continued to her neck. When it traveled to her ear, her cheek, her chin, the lateral of her lips and every atom of her face, over her jaw, the bank of her neck, the opposite collar, its bone, its dimple, and when she relayed his finger from one hand to the other to begin an equal journey of the retired arm. He was gone when she rotated. When she circled her hand and his finger to the zipper between her shoulders, lowered it down, blade by blade, silently, properly, spectacularly, and her dress fell to the floor. He was gone when she maneuvered her arm over her head, when his finger brushed the fuzz along her neck, when it grazed left across the top of one shoulder, then right over the top of the other, so . . . *so* . . . slowly, and when she maneuvered back again and it toured every knob of spine, every slant of rib, every stretch of skin, and when at last it lowered its lowest and followed the inner crevice and camber of her rump, lower, deeper, forward; and paused there, so . . . *so* . . . lightly. Gone, he was gone when she backed toward him, led his finger around to her front and guided it between her breasts, over her abdomen, past her navel to the brim of her pubic hair, north again, south again, scarcely, precisely, perpetually, and gone when it rounded each breast, again, again, again, circling smaller, spiraling in, imperceptibly tighter and forever around until her nipples needled like nails. Gone when his finger felt her hair. Gone when it tiptoed inside. Gone when it retracted. And gone when it continued on. Gone when she let go. Gone when he guided himself. Gone when thighs, knees, ankles, and toes and every space between quaked and quivered. Gone when she widened. Gone when he heightened. Gone when she dripped.

And he was gone when she returned it—the touch, to his body—just as exactly with her tongue.

Hours passed. Tremors stirred. Words were yet to be spoken and the night—the phone call, the breakdown, the decision—started circling in Danny's head. It happened unforeseen. A glance in the mirror. A glimpse of them in bed. He looked away. But moments later he looked back, and he stared. Not at her but at him, at everyone he had once been and everyone who had been him. He recalled nights and emotions he hadn't in years and others it seemed he'd never escape. He looked at himself like a middle-aged man, a belt, a bottle, a briefcase in hand, suddenly aware of years past, routine rehearsed, some comfort in the uncomfortable or delusion within. He looked at himself, and he peered straight through.

Marina reached across the bed. She took a condom from the nightstand and put her teeth to the tip. Danny turned. He looked at it. Then at Marina. And for the first time since seeing her that morning they looked at each other. They met each other. Nothing about their encounter was anything like the untold others he'd known, and yet nothing about her was new. She was feral yet feminine, aroused yet composed. She was as savvy as always and inconceivably bold, but the aura of expectation he invariably saw in her, had grown. To certainty. And Danny, at last, refused. He ambled on his knees across the mattress, found his underwear, and like a little boy who had just peed through the previous pair, put them on.

"Daniel?"

He pulled on his pants. He shook his head.

"Daniel, what are you doing?"

"No," he said. He slid his feet into his shoes, stuffed his socks in his pockets.

"*Daniel.* It is all or nothing, quid pro quo."

It was all he could say: "No." He pulled his shirt over his head and he trembled.

Marina stepped off the bed. "Daniel Ward, look at me this moment and tell me *what* you think you are doing."

He didn't answer. He didn't acknowledge her. On or off, something had clicked, and in some steady, pure, definitive way, quiet but audible, introspective and articulate and the maximum he could utter, he shook his head, picked up his bag, and said it again: "No." Again: "No." Again and again as he walked out the door, cowered at the elevator, shaking, breaking, dying. "No . . . No . . . No . . ."

*   *   *

The night refused to end, and in the earliest rays of conscience something raw felt unfinished. He understood that it was over. He accepted his choice. He knew there was nothing to confirm or explain, nothing to correct or undo, that freedom had its own set of certainties, that responsibility was one of them. All of this was clear. Still, he returned. He had been programmed to feel guilty, and always to apologize.

The reasons, he reminded himself, were ample. He transgressed her. He misled her and offended her. He should have never strayed into a world so rugged and volatile. He should have never been so naïve, so young and hopeful and attractive and poor. There was no one to blame but himself. He baited her. And she required him.

But apologizing would have to wait. He entered the foyer and stopped.

"I was instructed to give this to you," Harold said, and handed him an envelope. Danny stared at it, speechless.

Two hours later the call came as expected.

"Tell me. Plainly. *What* happened last night . . ."

He had rehearsed it. He knew exactly what he'd say. Like an athlete envisioning his success, he was prepared. But confronted, he froze.

"What . . . *happened?*" she said. Still he didn't answer. He simply stood there aphonic with the events of the night swirling in his head and the words he intended to say mixed up inside. "It's five past nine and I've just listened to *six* messages from the client asking where you were. 'Carla, it's six fifteen and Danny hasn't shown.' 'Carla, did you give Danny the right location?' 'Sorry, Carla, if you're checking voice mail could you please call Danny?'" There was an unending silence. "Well? The client wants to know. *I* want to know. *Where* were you?"

"I . . ." But the words wouldn't come. "I . . ." He tried again, anything—a lie, the truth. Nothing.

"You *what*, Danny?" Her initial calm had evaporated. He pictured her sitting there, flicking her pen between her fingers, then drilling it like a woodpecker, hard into her desk. "I hope you're listening, Danny, cause I'm only saying it once. Your contract is up in May and right now half this board couldn't care less. *Monika* is still undecided. She just happens to be out sick today so consider it a favor I'm not making her worse." She huffed with amazement. "Wardrobe never showed either. No model, no clothes—what are the odds! Not only *that*, the client has a permit for two more nights and says they want you if—'if he isn't unwell or already booked.' I don't know what's going on and I'm not even sure I care anymore but if you're not in that motor home by ten to six with a foolproof apology and an attitude of gold you can consider yourself finished."

That night, more determined, more disciplined, more alluring and adept and persuasive than ever, his energy acute and intuitive and in sync with the photographer's, inspiring her, discerning her, welcoming and executing her instructions, her creativity, and integrating his own unique attributes, smiling with his eyes, talking with his neck, tempting and shocking and baffling with his every transformation, every manipulation, his chin, his hips, his hands, his feet, teasing but not hurtfully, loving but not lastingly, shunning but not honestly, himself even as he wasn't, all that was in him and the more that lay beyond, fraction and whole, broken and reborn, everyone and no one and someone unknown, he shot.

They didn't finish until the park closed, well past midnight, and a few hours later he returned to nearly the same spot, where Harold handed him another envelope.

He went back again the following morning and the one after, and each thereafter for the next two weeks until on the first day of spring he arrived punctually as usual and instead of receiving her envelope, he received her.

"Daniel." Her lips were narrow, her tone nondescript.

"Marina, I . . ."

She continued past him. He followed instantly. He all but ran just to catch her, and she was nearly at the park by the time he did.

"Marina, I've been coming here every morning because I wanted—"

"Oh, it is a splendid day indeed." She inhaled vigorously. Danny looked at her. "Perhaps we shall see a crocus by April. Perhaps the Warblers are underway."

Time suddenly repeated itself. The whip cracked in his ear. Neither said a word and he floundered in thought, wishing she'd speak but hoping more so that she wouldn't; wondering why he was there but knowing it wrong not to be; believing, as with the client, that everything had been forgotten, that somehow sanity had been restored yet well aware it never existed. It

267

was this thing—belief—that plagued him most. It was his reluctance to think defensively, rationally; his inability to. It didn't matter how many times faith had failed him, he never abandoned it, hardly even questioned it. Others became cynics; Danny became blind. He knew what she wanted and how she sought it, what she would do to acquire it, any of it, and yet he told himself it wasn't so.

"Daniel," she said, now halfway around the reservoir. "Are you a virgin?" It was all she had said since mentioning crocuses and Warblers, and her tone was equally polite.

"Do you have *any* manners?"

"Do you have any excitement?"

"What kind of a question is that?"

"It is a question, Daniel. Are you a virgin?"

It wasn't simply that he was offended, but more so that he genuinely didn't know what to say; and in his silence she asked again.

"A virgin, Daniel—*are* you?"

He couldn't believe he was even entertaining such a foray. "I guess that depends on how you define *sex*."

"Oh, do not be complicated, Daniel."

"*I* thought I was simple."

"Only as one *does*, Mr. Ward."

"And is done unto?"

"Experience is *sought!*"

"And opportunity is limited!"

"Limits are for cowards." She turned with ease. "Modeling is not a meritocracy. It is a commerce. Capitalism helps those who help themselves."

"Yeah, and I'd say you treat me like a dog, but that would be a compliment."

"Oh, Daniel, do not be so moral, you are a model."

"What does that *matter* to you?"

"What does it matter to *you?*"

He refused to respond. A moment later she went on.

"Are you queer?"

"*Queer?*"

"Yes, Daniel, *queer*, or must I delineate 'man' and 'attraction' as well?"

"*No!*"

"The ire, Daniel—why? I adore queers, their lovemaking above all."

"I said *no*."

"You seem vexed, Daniel, ill at ease."

"I'm fine."

"Flimflam! You are not!"

"Yes, Marina, I *am*."

"Truly, Daniel, the Mongols made Baghdad look better than you. Haunted houses on Halloween are more cheerful than you. Why, I would sooner listen to Jesus thunder upon the cross than entertain your toxic attitude. Oh, Darth Vader! Oh, Hannibal Lecter! Freddie Krueger, Norman Bates, Jack Torrance! Anton Chigurh, I beg you! Save me!" Then quietly, plainly, she turned toward Danny, her expression arid and underwhelmed, and stared. He looked ahead and eventually she did too, but cried, "Oh, Tony Montana! Phantom of the Opera! Keep me from such sobriety and rue!" She turned to him again, even and orthodox, and stared.

Danny said nothing. They turned away from the water, back to the condominium, his jaw clenched in a mix of resentment and chaos, some immobility beyond negotiation. He had abandoned her, insulted her when he dressed in her bedroom trembling, No, No, and like some impish augur she foresaw his return. She predicted his apology and raised his pay, and Danny didn't know whether to laugh or cry.

He could see no end: either he would yield to her desire, be paid unprecedentedly, then replaced for the next; or he would continue to deny her, engage her eccentricity, and never break free.

Either way he would suffer. Either way, succumbing to her desire or diminishing his own worth, she would dictate every term and he would hate himself incalculably. Either way, he remained her folly.

Sometimes he wondered if it was the events or the circumstances he loathed more, if he might view everything differently had he been raised differently, aspired differently, worked for a different woman, a lady, more altruistic, less mercurial, someone who might at least keep a conscience. But he wondered, too, why he cared. About her, her actions, what they meant to him. And how much money he would require to stop.

"No," he said suddenly. "Don't define queer. Define *cheating* . . ."

"Oh, great day—he is alive!"

"Define it. What is it? Obviously not looking or listening. I assume not smelling or touching or tasting either. So where's the line? What crosses it?"

"Jonathan loves me, Daniel."

"And do you love him?"

"We have an agreement."

"Oh, I'm sure you *do*."

"He is *impotent*, Daniel."

"So *what!*"

"It. Turns. Him. On."

"Give me a break! It turns *you* on. You don't give a damn about him or anyone and you know it. You live up here in your little castle with your chocolate and your men and your million-dollar shoes and you don't give two shits about the rest of the world. You're just like everyone else in this city, but worse! You think you're so sophisticated, so sensitive because you live here. Nothing could possibly happen that you haven't seen. If it's not good enough for New York, then it's not good enough for you. Isn't that right, everything the world has to offer is right here and if it isn't then you don't want to know about it. You're like every other elitist New Yorker, so cosmopolitan you're provincial. You only leave town for thrills. You only go anywhere for your joyrides and you make a mockery of anyone who can't. When

was the last time you lived—really *lived!* Not this crap about airport roulette and lomilomi and oh, Darth Vader!, oh, Freddie
Krueger!, and whatever else you do to hide. I mean *living.*
Being a part of the world, a part of society. Start a foundation.
Teach someone to read. All the things you could do but never
will, and it makes me sick! Here *I* am, no parents, no siblings, no
one with a care in the world about me except a girl I adore and
constantly envy, trying to *do* something with my life, just save a
dime, maybe go to school one day, and you can't do anything but
tease me with it! I don't even have a credit card and you're in the
back of a Bentley crying over tea bags and the umpteenth expan-
sion of your condominium. Well piss on someone else! This is
*bull*shit! This ring-around-the-reservoir like you don't have a
hundred trainers and twice as many pimps. I'm over it!"

"Why, Daniel, how umbrageous. Impassioned indeed.
Cute. That was cute."

Danny stopped just ahead of Fifth Avenue and jelled. "It's
over."

Marina guffawed heartily. "Why, Daniel, we've not yet
begun!"

Her tone was so clear and irrefutable, so calm and yet so
eager, he stepped back.

"*I* am not for sale," he said. "I'm not some doll, some
gigolo."

She moved toward him so fast he nearly fell. "*You* have
already been *bought!*" Her entire being was nonnegotiable.
"What do you know of wealth? You dream and that is all!
When money means nothing to me and everything to you and
no greater currency exists, what leverage can you possibly possess? When you need what I have and I have all of what you
need, *you . . . will . . . return.* You will *always* return."

He was frozen in a hypnotism of terror—of Marina, of her
hedonism, her malice; but more so of her words, their potential.
They suffocated like a noose around the neck. They stung like
an ocean in the eyes.

"There is," he said, faintly but decisive. His cheeks were limp. His feet tripped backward beneath him but his heart held firm. "There *is* a currency greater than money. And there's a difference between need and want."

Chapter Twenty-Six

UNA CALLED IT A CITY, but Danny had seen similar sorts. With a population forever tiptoeing toward ten thousand and an economy buttressed by catfish, a mental institution, and a steel mill owned by a company from Brazil, Danny thought "bush" or "boonies" might more accurately depict the place.

"Well," she said, "there's only one New York."

"And only one Selkirk . . ."

He liked the little town. He liked it as a respite at least, and certainly with Una. She showed him her high school. They lingered by the river. Neighbors waved excitedly and smiled with compliments on some recent campaign or spread they had seen of her before subduing and asking the very questions that they themselves had just answered. Sometimes groups gathered, young girls talking vividly about their own promising future as a model, young boys not talking at all. Parents were as interested in Danny as they were in their hometown hero and after the second or third had proven acquainted with him— his name, agency, how they met, information that neither of them had offered—Una's blush became fixed. Danny simply nodded and marveled at the enthusiasm.

Friday night they drove down to Winnipeg and Saturday they went up to the lake. Sunday was Una's birthday. Her mother had baked all week, refrigerating pies and cakes at neighbors' and relying on friends to bring anything they could carry. She had, at first, only invited a few guests. "But it just grew, baby doll! I tell one person you're coming home—that it's your *birthday*—the next thing you know everyone from Stonewall to Steinbach is driving up Main Street!" It certainly seemed so. Una posed for more pictures in one afternoon than she did on a full day of editorial and when the flashes and the hugs and the stories all ended and the sight of all the gifts to be opened became visible at last, they retired to her childhood bedroom.

Danny took a small glass pipe and a bag of weed from Una's dresser and sat down on the bed beside her.

"Hold it in," she said. "Hold it in . . . Now say 'weed.'"

"Weed," he said. It came out deep and deliberate. Una giggled and did the same. They smoked it dry and Una took a piece of cake in her fingers and fed it to him.

"Don't swallow, don't swallow . . . Say 'cake.'"

"Cake," he said, and started to laugh, moist and muffled with a mouth of mush.

"Give me some, give me some!" He fed it to her. "Cake," she said, then snorted and wheezed. She was gasping for air when she spotted a balloon. She opened it and stuck it between Danny's icing-covered lips. "Breathe in. More . . . Now say 'helium.'" It came out like a squeak, and they fell over like trees, panting, laughing like children. They caught their breaths at last and ate as much as they could swallow.

"I sayr a Gahd," Una said, her hands just as full as her mouth. "A soon a I sop mahd-uh-ing I'm affing a birffay ery-ay or a res a my ife."

"Oh, yeah? Every day?" He cut another sliver as Una licked her hands.

"See, this is why I'm not a zero. Maybe if I did a little more coke and a little less weed I wouldn't be so hungry."

Danny rolled his eyes. "Did you have a good birthday?"

"I was kidding!"

"Did you have a good *birthday?*" He was perfectly high.

"I did," she said. "*Thank* you. But what am I going to do with all those presents? You can't even walk through the living room!" She studied him. "Were you in on this? You know all I wanted was some peace and quiet."

Danny raised his hands, palms of icing out. "Totally innocent."

"You better be!" She reached out and drilled him with tickles. Danny snapped forward. He fell on top of her. He tickled back. Una shrieked. Her mouth caught Danny's chest which muffled her as she laughed harder and squirmed wilder. She snuck her hand around his back, just below the scars, and without warning or remorse sent him into hysterics. The volley went on, silly and unrestrained, until at last she tore so exactly into his armpit that he nearly rolled them off the bed before seizing a bedpost and flipping them in the opposite direction. Una landed face up, her hair sprawled across the pillows, her eyes even with Danny's above her. Neither moved. They just stared. They heaved. Their breaths mixed in the pocket of heat between them. Danny's arms began to ache. Traces of sweat filled Una's forehead. "Don't . . . don't go back . . . to the other room."

Xavier had called it the longest courtship in the history of human civilization. Sasha was certain they were lying—"like bunnies in spring, for sure." And Jeremiah said the whole world would hear it when the deed at last was done. Danny ignored the banter. He knew he would know when the time was right, and Una hadn't hinted. They enjoyed each other in manifold ways—their curiosities, interests, talents—and both were aware, enough, of the other's experiences, their associations, their fears: their bodies; the pain. Others could rush. They'd take their time.

"Don't . . ." she said again, so softly the words hardly left her lips. "Don't go."

Danny didn't say a word. He leaned forward, as slowly as he could, cautious of her request, of what it meant, of what it would; conscious of every glance, every breath, every whisper. His heart drummed. His shoulders strained. His veins ran like rivers overflowing in his hands, deep in the mattress. Still he leaned slowly, closer, and like dabbing a ball of cotton on an open wound he kissed the sweat from her brow.

Una closed her eyes. He kissed her cheeks, her temples, the outsides of her ears. He stroked her hair and kissed her neck, back and forth, side to side, over her shoulders, up her arms, then down the entirety of her body, carefully, nervously, lovingly removing every article of clothing until she lay naked in front of him breathing harder than before. He stepped back from the bed. Her eyelids fluttered. Clothed only in a blanket of kisses she watched him back away, then stop, and gaze, with something ethereal in his eyes, and almost as slowly as he undressed her, watched as he undressed himself.

Midnight passed. The sheets were stained and drying with fluids wildly pungent, with chocolate cake, with worn out balloons, Danny and Una wrapped somewhere inside. They lay facing each other, silent, discovering details they never had. Una traced a finger over his face, his hair, his neck, as his eyes yielded to her touch.

"Danny?"

"Hmm?"

"What are you thinking about?"

He opened his eyes. She laid her hand on his arm and he knew if he'd tell anyone he'd tell her, and if he didn't then he never would. "About how . . . when I tickled you, and you laughed, you reminded me of my sisters. Just happy and how I've wanted . . ." He looked at her. "They're not really my sisters. My mom—she's not really my mom."

She smoothed his cheek with her thumb. Danny breathed and told her everything: Houston; his birth-mother; the diagnosis. An aunt in Roswell and her drunken boyfriend. The nights. The noise. The neighbor who found out. Then Santa Fe, the "group home." Its pastor and his sins and a woman named Eve whose were worse. Without explanation, Topeka. The year there uneventful and eventually Bo, Linda, their house, his new school and the vacations they took and how perfect it all was. One day the counselor's office. The solemnity. The details. The funeral and the pain and all the hatred and confusion, the days and the weeks that would never end and the wills that were never honored, the lawyers, the psychologists, the family members, everyone with a say, an idea, an interest. Kansas City in the interim. Another "home." Another man who liked to touch. "Daniel. He always called me *Daniel*. 'Come into my office, *Daniel*. How are you today, *Daniel*? You're a good *boy*, Daniel.'" The room was silent. His words circled freely in the dark. He stared at her—focused and detached—at her neck, her chin, the outline of her mouth, anywhere but where she could see him and he wouldn't see her cry. "So then . . . so then came Frank and Charlene. Frank was driving trucks. Charlene was answering phones. She wanted a baby so bad. They tried but just couldn't. I don't know why they adopted a twelve-year-old but they did, and I liked them. We lived in Lawrence and everything was fine until one day Frank starts talking about Gary, Indiana and the next thing I know we move. Then Charlene finds out she's pregnant. That was the happiest day of her life. She glowed straight through summer but Frank . . . Something wasn't right with Frank. He started drinking, started talking about money, about having two kids. Then one day, when I was turning thirteen, Charlene found out it was twins. And Frank disappeared."

Una had been stroking his hair, and stopped.

"Charlene, well . . . Charlene basically lost it. She started blaming me for things, things I never . . . She called me a jinx. She said I cursed her. That nothing would have turned out the way it had if I—"

"*No*, Danny. That wasn't your fault. Look at me, Danny. None of it."

"She . . . well, she calmed down some, after the girls were born. But it didn't last. She started drinking, getting to work late. There was this daycare center the girls went to. They knew. They must've. This one woman came by on the weekends. Never spoke. Just handed me apple juice, little bags of Cheerios and cut-up grapes. Then walked away. She brought diapers too and I changed them. I made sure they had socks, warm blankets. I couldn't really read much until high school, but I brought home books from the library and tried. They slept in my room, and I tried. "Not every day was so bad but some . . . Like my back. The scars. That wasn't a good day. That wasn't a very good year really. The girls . . . I mean, it was my fault because if I just stayed out of it, if I just let them cry, but they weren't even a year yet and I couldn't take it. They just wanted someone to hold them and they were sitting right there next to her and I kept saying, 'Charlene, the girls. The *girls*, Charlene.' But she was drunk and so I just picked them up. I just walked over and scooped them up and then . . . the bottle. She broke it. She . . . she smashed it and she . . . I was walking away and all of a sudden it cut into me. Like teeth. Like scissors. I screamed. I ran into the bathroom. I put the girls down so fast I dropped them. Blood was everywhere. I blasted the bath. Water, Charlene, she's pounding '*Danny, Danny!*' The girls were shrieking like I never heard, my head bursting, I'm biting through towels not to explode, and Charlene keeps pounding and pounding. '*Open*, Danny! *Open*, Jinx! *Open*, Danny! *Open*, Jinx!'"

He quaked in horror as Una flung herself over him. She pulled him to her as tight as she could, squeezing and smothering and protecting him as he struggled, exhaustedly, to break free. She didn't utter a word but she held him, rocked him, her tears in his hair, his snot on her collar, until neither was able to move, and they slept.

*　　*　　*

It was barely nine in New York when Una's phone rang in Selkirk. They hadn't slept more than a couple hours and it wasn't until her agent's second try that she woke. Danny's head hit the pillow as Una turned, then tumbled out of bed, her knees knocking as her feet found the floor. Her hair was explosive. Her eyes were swollen and mottled. Her belly and breasts were crisscrossed like a road map with the markings of the sheets, her nails mashed deep with chocolate. Her neck was encrusted with Danny's snot and her thighs were rubbed raw in the only way possible.

She patted sleepily for the phone. She slid a shirt over her head, propped herself against the wall, and studied the smudges on her hands as she waited.

"Nicole. Hi. It's Una. Can I talk to Sam? . . . I'm fine . . . Oh . . ." She cleared her throat. She sat down at the foot of the bed, unknotting the cake from her hair as she waited to be connected to her agent.

"Hey, it's Una. Did you call?" She went to cross her legs and froze. Her face filled with shock. She turned quickly around. "Thanks. Twenty. I know, I'm ancient." She looked down at her legs. She turned again and looked at the sheets. "I did. It was. My mom invited a few friends and half the province showed up." She lifted her leg high above her head. Her mouth opened as wide as her eyes. "Oh, yeah? And what's that?" She lost her balance, and slipped off the bed. "No, I'm here! I just . . ." She went to pull herself up and stopped. "I *did? . . .* It *is? . . .* It *isn't! . . .* Sam, *yes . . .* Yes, I'm sure! Of course I'm sure, I'll call you from the airport . . ." She tossed the phone on the bed. "Danny, wake up! We have to go!" She shook his legs and raced out of the room.

Danny sat up with a moan. He was about to roll back over when he looked down at the sheets and gaped. He lifted them up, held them high, then dropped them in a flash. He looked around the room. He saw the pipe, the balloons, the tray of chocolate cake. He saw their clothes in a heap on the floor and remembered.

He threw on his jeans and followed the sound of running water to the bathroom. It didn't matter that her silhouette was barely visible behind the curtain or that they lay tangled and naked the night before. He waited at the door.

"Una, I'm sorry about the sheets. We'll get you new ones. I had no idea—"

"Danny, my booker called. We have to go. We've got to get back to New York. I'm flying to Prague."

Danny looked incredulous. "What?"

"I booked Herbal Essence! TV, print, everything!" She pulled back the curtain after an unusual silence. "You can say something. It's only enormous."

"I thought you booked out."

"Of course I booked out."

"But you're taking the job."

She reached for a towel. "Are you still high?" Her body was back to its original. The bags, the lines, the chocolate, every blotch and discolored encrustation washed away. She bent forward and wrapped her hair, then reached for another towel and dried off.

"No, but I thought booking out meant booking out."

"It does, Danny, but when your booker calls and tells you a client wants to fly you four thousand miles and put you up for a week to shoot a national ad with massive usage do you turn around and say, 'Oh, sorry, Booker Bob! But take another look at my chart. I'm booked out in Selkirk, Canada . . .' Or do you say, 'I'm on my way,' and haul ass?" She stepped out of the shower and was brushing her teeth a moment later. He stood there watching her, still astonished by the turn of events and the alacrity with which they spun. He didn't know what to say. It wasn't the first time this had happened, not the second or the third that she was there one moment and gone the next. But however common it was, this time was different. They had

traveled together. He met her mother, her whole town, celebrated her birthday with her. They shared intimacies that
couldn't be underestimated. At the end of it all they fell asleep
together and hours later, as though unaffected, she was racing
to change flights and fly across continents. No agent had ever
asked him to jump; he wasn't in the habit of asking how high.
Only Marina gave those types of commands. Yet if the orders
came from agents, would he respond just the same?

She turned on the sink, spat, rinsed, and dried, then walked
past him to her room. "Turn down a job, Danny, and see if
your booker keeps fighting to get you more."

"It's not that. I *get* that. It just amazes me how much you
work, how you're—"

"I *knew* you were jealous."

"No I'm not!"

"Right, Danny, you're not jealous—so then what are you?
Proud? Overjoyed?" She started pulling clothes from her
closet. "Every time I book something big or far or semi-glam-
orous you get like this, all somber and stuff like it should be you
and not me. If I'm shooting catalog in Milwaukee or Dallas
somewhere you're cool as a cucumber. But I book Herbal
Essence on hours notice in Prague with usage from here to the
moon and you act like you don't even know my name. But no.
You're not jealous. Not at all."

"I'm *happy* for you, Una. *Incredibly* happy for you. But you
. . ." He groaned. "You don't know what it's like on the other
side."

"Excuse me?"

"Una, we walk into a club and you're a queen! The bounc-
ers, the bartenders—they accept me because *you* accept me;
they think I'm something because being with you makes them
think I am. But I'm not. *You* take *me* to dinner. *You* take *me* to
the movies. Everything we do is because *you* make it possible.
Because *you* have the connections. *You* make the money. And I
just wish for once that I could have a month half as good as

yours or book something big enough to take *you* out, take *you* shopping, make *you* happy. Let *me* be the guy and *you* be the girl."

"Oh! There it is!" She threw up her arms. "The guy-girl thing—how many times have I heard this!"

"What guy-girl thing? Not from me you haven't." Danny still wasn't packing. He stood there in his jeans, watching her rush around the room as their first honest fight unfolded in front of him. "I don't know what you're talking about but if you had any *idea* what it's like to be a guy in this industry you might appreciate what you have."

"Cry me a river, Danny! Appreciate? You think I don't *appreciate?*"

"It is *ten* times harder for us and you know it. Yeah, you outnumber us but your opportunities are endless. You walk into a casting and you know damn well if you don't book it there'll be a dozen more that week. *I* walk into a casting and *that's* my casting. That's it! Either I book it and I breathe, or I twiddle my thumbs and I wait for the next. But you—you work constantly, your rates are higher, you're always principal, you—don't roll your eyes, just count the magazines! How many girls do you know working night jobs, Una? How many do you know who can't get by modeling? Plus the perks? All the free-bies? Develop a drug problem, an eating disorder, something serious and everyone's got something to say. But a guy? A male model? No one gives a rat's ass! No one cares! No one expects it so no one believes it and no one does a goddamn thing to cor-rect it. Because he'll never earn enough, end of story! And when was the last time a photographer grabbed you, Una? When was the last time an editor or a casting director followed you into a bathroom? When was the last time you had a fling with your booker to make sure the other girls on the board wouldn't get booked before you? Right—never! Because there isn't the same pressure. Not the same competition. You don't have to! And because anyone who'd be so *stupid* to try—anyone from the greatest photographer to the sick rich fifty-year-old fuck jerking off all day in his Tribeca penthouse paying off promoters to get into model parties—any of *them* would get put away. But what if it was one of the countless gay men or straight women in the industry who isn't even interested in you? Guys can't be harassed? Guys can't be assaulted? Only women can be victims? Maybe in the real world, but not in this one. Nothing's *ever* real in the modeling world."

Una spun around so fast she threw her bag in the air, the rage boiling out of her. "Welcome to *my* world! Welcome to *my* reality! For Christ's sake, Danny—sue me! Sue every girl who's ever made it as a model, the few who get a break from the bullshit. We didn't set the standards and we didn't set the exception either. The *one* exception! The one profession in this misogynistic world where we out-earn you. Big fucking deal! What, so you don't feel *adequate?* You don't feel like a man? Because I earn more? Because you're not the center of attention? The attention you *want?* You feel like shit when someone treats you like shit and you think I don't know how that feels? Just being part of this industry makes me sick— knowing I'm making some CEO filthy rich off the countless women spending half their paychecks to look like me. Women ridicule me every day, Danny! It's not physical but it still hurts, it still stings. Not just what they say but what they feel, what they believe. About me, about themselves, about the industry. But *I'm* not the problem. The industry isn't either. Society is."

She picked up her bag and walked out of the room. Danny followed immediately. "You're always going to do this. You're always going to be just a phone call away."

"You would be too, Danny! Don't act like you wouldn't take the money."

He paused, jolted. She picked up the phone.

"Are you coming or not?"

"Why would I? It's not my job."

"Why would you stay? It's not your home."

He sat down in the living room. He ran his fingers through his hair. It wasn't that she was leaving. It wasn't that she could and always would. It was that she was leaving *now*. That she didn't see how he felt, that she didn't understand what she meant to him. Suddenly the drapery, the façades, the grown-up faces were gone and they were children. They were emotional. They were real, themselves—people they didn't know.

Chapter Twenty-Seven

J UST MONTHS EARLIER—when he had returned from Berlin, then again from Miami—everything had felt the same. The agency was still belligerently glamorous. The Village was still cramped and asymmetrical. The F train was as listless and fickle as ever, and still shrieked its dreadful *eeeee*. Brooklyn was still stupidly far, the entire west side was still boisterously gay, and Times Square was still the quagmire of the world. Manhattan, as attractive as it was repellent, still felt like a blood transfusion. From Chelsea Piers to Alphabet City, Washington Square to Central Park, nothing, save Danny, felt different. New York had simply waited for him to return.

Now it was the reverse. Now it was the city that changed and Danny who waited. He felt lonely and out of place and mindful of everything—every detail, every banality, every platitude and plagiarism and red that passed for pink, every gray called white and bird that wouldn't sing. He felt his own dullness in everything around him. He sensed his own disdain. And the more he shunned the world, the more he anticipated her return and wondered when and where and with whom he would see her. What would he say? What would she? At a casting. On the street. His need to know, some aspect of closure became a burden he couldn't bear. He had lost all interest in socializing and being seen, but his dissonance grew and he stormed every club he could think of. Every prey and predator and New Yorker who required a drink or a drug or a dream to get by, he found. But not Una. And no matter how desperately he had to see her, it had to seem by chance. He refused to call.

He receded further. He gravitated to Derek and Jen and however much he could, stayed clear of Carla. He spent more time examining himself, studying the stranger who scrutinized him back. Would his hair look better longer; were his shoulders misaligned? He set up Jeremiah's camera and tripod and timed pictures repeatedly. He held poses, changed the light, altered nuances so subtle he had to print them to detect the difference: cheeks, lips, his eyes softer, jaw tighter, less profile of the nose. He shifted in shadows. He shifted in his clothes, took them off, varied the mood in his hands, his feet, his collar, and reflected on each image anew. He looked at those of others in magazines and books, watched fashion shows online, placed a mirror opposite the video camera, and walked.

The more he withdrew, the more requests, more options, and more jobs he gained. He tested with photographers who were adamant to have him. He met with designers who were suddenly fascinated by him. He shot an editorial with Yuri for *V Man*, worked with women who worked every day, and knew beyond all doubt that he should have been happier. His portfolio was improving. His name, his face was disseminating. Praises were being extended and he progressed at what he came to do. It was only later that month when Jen called and told him he had been booked for Malo—"*Malo*, Danny, *Ma-lo!*"— that he realized. He put down the phone. And he ached to pick it up again.

He read more than ever. He kept away from all the places he frequented with Una and he stayed later and later and later at the library. He read essays by Orwell, novels by Fitzgerald, short stories by Poe. He remembered the list he once requested from Xavier and he read *The Picture of Dorian Gray* like it had been written under an alias for God. He read its preface repeatedly, every aphorism even more. He defined so many words that long before the artist's death he began a new notebook. He found its views insulting, the dialogue showy, the characters maddening, and he couldn't get enough. Eventually, he bought it, and in the margins jotted ideas about youth and beauty, arrogance and art, about revealing and concealing, needing and wanting, criticizing and complimenting. About perception. About society. About inclination and attitude and trust. "A picture," he wrote, "is the falsest truth. Lies become pictures, and pictures always become truth." The next day he crossed it out: "<u>Truth</u> becomes pictures. Pictures become <u>lies</u>." But he crossed that out too, and at the end of the book wrote: "Dorian is sick. Everyone should know him."

Danny read constantly. But he stopped on the subway. He liked to as a passenger but the more he rode the less he traveled. The train reached the end of its line and he sat. He waited. Then rode back without reason. For the simplicity perhaps. The assurance. Pelham Bay Park to the Brooklyn Bridge. 207th to Far Rockaway. The S more times than he knew. Each line, each station, each hour had its own idiosyncrasies, each ride its own demographic. Teachers. Bartenders. Medical residents ending another thirty-hour shift. Runaways with bandaged wrists. Men in suits. Men in uniforms. Men in drag. MTA employees commuting, cleaning, repairing. Conversations in Spanglish. Sobbing. Praying. School kids fighting. Guide dogs. Tourists. Homeless and Broadway's best. They got on. They got off. And Danny rode. Station to station. Borough to borough. Early morning or late at night. Miles and miles of reminder.

Sometimes there was music. The opera singer on the evening L. The fiddler on the Q, the Manhattan-side 7. There was the flutist on the noon-time 6, the hip-hop artists on Central Park locals, the Hispanic Klezmer duo at Essex and Delancey. Union Square was musical mayhem. After midnight, on occasion, he heard an oboe in the Bronx.

There was a regular at West 4th he had grown fond of. He wore corduroys and thermal shirts and on weeknights from eight o'clock on he played the guitar, sometimes the keyboard or the harmonica or sang acoustic on the south side of the mezzanine. He started playing there at the beginning of the year and Danny started acknowledging him soon after, altering his path and letting the coins clink as he passed.

The exchange continued for months until one night in April, shortly after he had found out about Malo and thought solely of Una ever since, he was walking up the stairs and heard a song he knew. He used to dance to it with her, in the night clubs all electric, the DJ empowering, everything but the two of them irrelevant.

But now it was slower, softer, like a lullaby or a lover's lament. The singer's eyes were shut. He stood hunched and he swayed. His fingers moved like they were divorced from his hand, each partnered to its own string and arcing gracefully from fret to fret. He sang with an honesty transcendent of language. And Danny wondered if it were possible to sing any sadder. He came closer. Commuters dropped coins as they passed. He heard the chime of metal on metal, the flatness of a thud as they hit the velvet-lined leather case and the clarity of each note that seemed to be seeping into the tiles, the concrete, the heart of every passerby with a vitality Danny had never heard. He stopped near the musician and without realizing it he sat down, laid his head against the wall, and closed his eyes.

He wondered if she were there. In New York. Back in Selkirk. Still in Prague. Maybe somewhere in between. Another job. Another hotel. Maybe taking a bath. Maybe going to bed. Was she out with friends? Making new ones? Had she already? Was she high? Was she strung out somewhere? Some plush white sofa? Some balcony? Some floor? Did she know where or who she was? Did she want to? Was she walking, right then, above him? Was she sad? Was she sadder than he? Was she sitting alone, thinking of him, missing him, wondering if she had made a mistake? Was she wondering if he missed her too? If she asked, if she called, if he'd come for her. If he'd run to her. If he'd meet her halfway. Or if he wouldn't.

"You OK here?" The musician crouched down beside him, his guitar all packed. "It looked like you were having a dream."

Danny rubbed his neck. "What time is it?"

"About one." He set the guitar between them. "I see you a lot. You tip me."

Danny shrugged. "You sing well . . ."

The musician reached over the guitar. "My name's Zeke."

"Danny," he said, and moved suddenly to stand. "I—I have to go . . ."

He barreled up the stairs. But it was, in fact, just a dream.

* * *

Two nights later he returned. The musician was tucked into his usual spot picking the bills out of his case and sweeping the coins to the side.

"You stopped early." Danny sat down beside him. "Busy night? Make a lot?"

"Money?" The musician shook his head. "No, it's not mine. I don't keep it."

"None of it?"

Zeke pulled out a container the size of a soda can and let the coins tumble into it. "My mother died last year. I don't earn very much—I'm just a teacher—but I decided I'd raise money whenever I could and donate it to this organization that's researching what she had. It's the effort," he said with a shrug. "It makes me feel better, too."

Danny slouched against the wall. "I'm really sorry. What did she—"

"A blood disease. It's pretty rare. She got dizzy sometimes, got these headaches. I don't know how many times I told her to go see a doctor. She'd just smile." He shook his head. "She never did go to the doctor. And I loved her too much to insist."

The next week Danny met the musician three more times, and always longer than he expected. Zeke asked him what he did—"Model? You're a *model?*"—and the answer lasted days. Zeke asked for every detail and had a question for every answer. Danny had the time and found their conversations cathartic. He told him about his trip to Chicago, about the agency's model search. He told him about his roommates and other models, about how different they all were and how differently they each approached their work.

He told him about Edge, all the agents, the politics and dynamics and how he wondered almost daily if and when he would be dropped. He told him about castings and shoots and what was real and what wasn't, who cared and who didn't, all the hurry-up-and-wait, the counterfeit perfection, the artificial ease, about how everyone assumes that because you're attractive you fuck everything in sight. "Because you can? Because you should? Because morality, apparently, is the inverse of beauty?" He talked about anomaly and about hypocrisy and he told Zeke about Una and Marina, about how he met them and how they parted, everything he liked and everything he didn't, what they had taught him, how he had grown, the happiness he trusted and the money he earned but how in the end he wasn't either's priority, and wasn't sure he ever would be—always second to a career, always the object of another.

"You need to call her," Zeke said.

"Which?"

"Which? Una! Danny, Marina's done, she's finished. No more."

Danny sighed. "I just wish I felt equal to her. Maybe then the disappearing acts wouldn't bother me. We'll never be close to equal but I still think about it. Trying to be. Then I think about Marina. I think about sacrifice . . ." He rubbed his face.

"What do you mean?"

"Money is an amazing thing. The way we obsess over it. The things we do for it. There are a lot of men and a lot of women with a lot of money in this city, a lot of young, attractive, *scared* boys, too, who will . . . who are willing . . . who just refuse to give up." He closed his eyes, he shook his head. "When the price is right, morality is just a word." He could practically taste her as he said it.

"So work at a bar! Work at a restaurant! Why sex?"

"It happens, it just happens! Your *job* is to *make* people want to sleep with you. Every instant becomes this dance, this flirtation, whether you want it to be or not or even realize it's happening, it just does. You see it, you feel it, you fight it like the devil but they hunt you. They prey on you. They're hungry and they're lonely and they're rich, and if you're attractive and starving, if you're a model—a male model—and you still haven't figured out that you're *not* just an object, that you *do* have a soul, they find you. If they're socialites, they offer money. If they're in the industry itself, they offer work. They offer the *idea* of work, regardless of whether or not any exists. And because you know your industry is more fickle than the stock market and you know the only thing that counts is now— this very moment—you jump. You hope. You think: there might not be a tomorrow. And you believe what you've been told—that you'll be washed up even if there is. A tomorrow. It's no different than the way men treat women in the real world. Double standards. Intimidation. Innuendos. Every guy going around like he's got what every girl needs. The world would be very different if more guys experienced what I do. Being a male model is like having a backstage pass to the life of a woman. Believe me—if models could talk, Fashion wouldn't sell."

"So—so get out," Zeke said. "Leave. Start something new."

Danny gazed at the passersby about him. "There's this psychology. It's so hard to explain. It's like asking why anyone would stay in an abusive relationship. But you—you just keep thinking it'll get better. You're already at the bottom. There's no other . . . Even if it wasn't so trapping, I don't have a degree. I have no qualifications, no contacts, no security to fall back on. I'm like a ghost. I'm here but I'm not. More than a dream; but less than a reality." He leaned back against the wall. "I *am* saving. I'm trying to. I'd been thinking maybe, maybe I'd go to college one day. I want to succeed, you know. At something. Anything! Not just tomorrow. Today. Right now that means modeling. I want to know I did my best. And I know I can still do better."

"Yeah, and how will you know?" Zeke said. "When some 'authority' tells you? When all the world agrees? What if there's just no such thing as success in modeling? For you. For guys. What if it's just not tailored that way?"

Pedestrians dispersed and Danny found himself staring abstractedly at a billboard across the mezzanine. "The world doesn't agree on anything except that men make more money and women buy more clothes. Right or wrong doesn't matter. The world agrees. In fashion that means girls work and boys watch. Una's right. Modeling is for girls like life is for men. The only difference between a working model and a non-working model is sex. And that's the truth in more ways than one."

*   *   *

Early the next week he was nearing the end of his fourth reading of Oscar Wilde with virtually every page annotated when the same nagging thought he'd had all weekend returned. He put down the book. He took a box from his dresser, then scribbled a note on a piece of paper. He put the box and the note in a small paper bag and that evening, headed for the subway.

He was halfway underground when he heard Zeke's voice, gentle yet powerful, singing a song he didn't know. It sounded like raindrops on a window sill, the eloquence of the wind. Danny slowed, instinctively.

You could be happy, and I won't know
But you weren't happy, the day I watched you go
All the things that I wished I had not said
Are played in loops till it's madness in my head

He swiped his card at the turnstile. Zeke stood facing the opposite direction, but from the hunch and the sway in his posture, the slow roll of his head and the swell of his voice, Danny knew his eyes were closed.

Is it too late to remind you, how we were
But not our last days of silence, screaming, blur
Most of what I remember makes me sure
I should have stopped you from walking out the door

Coins tumbled and tinkled into the case at Zeke's feet. Dollar bills fluttered into the mix. A dimpled girl in a flowy spring dress sang as she spun across the mezzanine. A couple joined hands as they passed. There was something in his voice, in the words, maybe the sorrow or the understanding or the impossible optimism clinging desperately to every note that brought everyone within earshot together.

You could be happy, I hope you are
You made me happier, than I'd been by far
Somehow everything I own smells of you
And for the tiniest moment it's all not true

Danny paused. He smiled. He laid the bag on the keyboard, and unencumbered, walked away.

Do the things that you always wanted to
Without me there to hold you back, don't think, just do
More than anything I want to see you, girl
Take a glorious bite out of the whole world

He stood by the stairs, waiting and watching to see that what he left was received. Zeke repeated the lines. He sang them again and again, louder, and softer, and healthier, with each repetition. The entire station felt at peace, and Danny was certain he had done the right thing.

Zeke quieted at last. The notes began to settle. There was a faint echo of soles, the clarity of completion. More passengers left tips and Danny watched as the musician opened his eyes, noticed the bag, and looked inside. Then back up and in every direction. He pulled the note out with care.

It's mine but it doesn't belong to me. I'm just doing what the owner should have.

Zeke looked up once more but quickly returned to the bag. He took out the box, slender, black, and obvious. He looked up again, nearly trembling, and for a moment seemed as though he might not open it, afraid or overwhelmed or simply lost in disbelief. But he did. And he shook. And as the trains rumbled swiftly below and his eyes welled with the ache and the purity of gratitude, love, of loss and regret, he looked directly to where Danny had been watching.

Chapter Twenty-Eight

CARLA WAS THE ONE who called. After all, it was she who most wanted him out, and she who convinced Monika to want the same. She said he was unpredictable. "Erratic." She said she needed professionals on her board, models she could count on, could trust. She wasn't a babysitter. She wasn't a psychologist and she certainly wasn't a magician. She also said the market was changing—"fast, practically overnight." His look was no longer wanted. He no longer applied.

Jen emailed that afternoon on behalf of Derek, Surya, and Terry, to whom Danny had tried but never warmed. Edge wasn't like other agencies, she wrote. Its boards were divided based on clients, not models. Because of their size, unanimity was never easy. They had campaigned for him though. They liked him and they knew he'd be successful. Carla had her own issues, her own agenda, and there was nothing they could do about it. "And for the record," she wrote. "Malo loved you. I'll get you the pics. I promise."

It all happened on a Friday, the first in May. It wasn't until the following week when Danny had at last regrouped and decided to start setting up appointments with all the agencies he could think of that he got a text from Jeremiah: "Left agency last week. Know they dropped you. Don't sign with ANY-ONE. Talk soon."

Danny called back but Jeremiah didn't answer. He called Xavier but hadn't heard from him in weeks and knew he wouldn't until finals were finished and grades turned in. Sasha wasn't available either. Danny hadn't heard from him since shortly after their talk at Edge, and even if he were around he was in need of more help than Danny could give. More than anyone, of course, he wanted to talk to Una. He couldn't explain how days had turned to weeks, now a month or more since they last spoke; how he had let it happen or why he hadn't foreseen it. Each day he missed her more and each day he told himself, or allowed himself—he no longer knew which—to resent her.

Zeke's words rang sharp: "Done. Finished. No more!" Off and on, he agreed. And yet distress can make prudence look stupid. And habits are like termites to the will. Once again, Danny boarded the uptown F.

He told himself to apologize. He'd intercept her as she was leaving the building, and he'd simply apologize. Whether or not she was even walking that morning, whether she had changed her time or hired a new partner, whether she'd lambast him on the spot or bid him upstairs—for tea, a bath, a painting—none of this had occurred to him.

It was nearly seven when he exited the subway in Lenox Hill. It had been a while since he had. It was all still rich and comfortably tame. The five-story townhouses were still set twelve steps above the sidewalk and still occupied by single families of four with just as many maids; they were still padded by black iron gates and state-of-the-art alarms, a cop at every corner; still adorned with gilded walls and nineteenth century curtains, statues of lions and hundred-pound urns and tall red geraniums lining the balconies and their festooned flower pots. There were still Town Cars and M5s and cyclopean QX56s, still emblazoned corner boutiques with names like Chopard, Graff, Domeinco Vacca, and Roberto Cavalli. There were still bagels selling for three ninety-five.

But the clouds hung ominously low. And though the wind was warm in his face, the trees were quiet, the birds all elsewhere.

There was an odor in the air. It was faint, inaccessible, yet it thickened as Danny continued toward the park. It smelled of plastics and heavily polished woods, rug fibers centuries old. It smelled of linens, of flowers, of brick unexpectedly pungent, though the more he sniffed the less he identified. The scene on the ground teemed with distraction. Pedestrians weren't frantic or hurried, but for the early hour, the crowds were growing, and moving in the wrong direction.

Approaching Madison he heard honking, then saw the avenue wedged with taxis, SUVs, and overachieving tour buses all attempting to turn left but forced further uptown. The west side of the street was barricaded. Officers directed traffic and made little effort to contain the pedestrians zigzagging across the gridlocked intersection.

Danny could see Fifth Avenue ahead. A throng of onlookers faced south, spreading freely into the unoccupied street and anywhere else they could without crossing the bands of yellow tape that begged their safety. Video cameras recorded everything. Dogs barked in circles. Phones were open and on, passersby talking, texting, tweeting about the little they knew. Police cars, fire trucks, ambulances, and unidentified vehicles all invaded the scene. Reporters sought a story.

"What happened?" Danny asked the doorman standing cheek by jowl beside him as he strained for a clearer view.

"Fire." The man shook his head. "Top floor. Lady's dead."

Danny looked up. Plumes of smoke drifted overhead. He couldn't see the scene in question but something told him it was hers-to-be.

"I lived in a building where there was a fire once," the doorman said hopelessly. "Fire's bad enough. But the water damage below . . ."

Danny continued to strain. He looked up and down Fifth Avenue. The residents were easy to identify. They paced or they huddled or they gave interviews in bathrobes, night gowns, slippers or sneakers on their feet and keys clutched tightly at their chest. Some hugged. Some cried. Some stood back in horror or amazement as though it were surely a dream. They called friends. They smoked. One simply sat there. Motionless. Danny spotted her at last. And the look on her face raised goose bumps about his body.

*   *   *

He didn't expect to ever talk to anyone at Edge again save to collect what was his. He certainly didn't expect to talk to Carla. Yet a week after she released him, he did.

"Technically you're still with the agency until the end of the month," she said. "But if you take the booking or not, it's up to you. It's a charity event so it's unpaid—one of those Jeffrey fundraisers for Hetrick Martin or Lambda Legal. I really don't care. You're on your way out." Her tone was vague. He couldn't tell if she was embarrassed, humored, or indignant. Or as indifferent as she claimed. "Should I email the details?"

The event was four days away and Danny made use of every one, watching model after model, show after show: Evandro Soldati for Perry Ellis; Eddie Klint for Miu Miu; Lyle Lodwick for Yigal Azrouël; Baptiste Giabiconi, over and over and over for Chanel. There was Jon Kortajarena for Salvatore Ferragamo; Danny Schwarz for Rag & Bone; Michael Gstoettner for Iceberg; and Will Chalker carrying a tiger for Dolce & Gabbana. There was Sean O'Pry walking for Moschino; Vincent Lacrocq for Yves Saint Laurent; Philip Huang for Versace and Belstaff; and Noah Mills for Diesel and Dsquared2 and Giorgio Armani—both women and men. There was Garrett Neff for Rock & Republic. There was Stan Jouk for Michael Kors. There was Matvey Lyvok for Patrik Ervell. And there was Mathias Lauridsen and Jesper Lund for them all.

Danny watched. He watched their ease. He watched their gait, their expression, their posture and their poise, not simply each in itself but as an ensemble and complement to the music, the lights, the clothes above all. He watched them repeatedly, every detail, turning, pausing, blinking, breathing. He watched the bend in their knees, the distance of each step, how much or how little they swung their arms, the position of their head.

He studied them every morning, then copied them every evening. He thought of the shows he'd seen at Fashion Week and while he knew his wouldn't attract their equal, he was determined to be prepared for anyone, whether agents, editors, or Jeffrey himself. With even more patience and precision than he had for the past few weeks, he walked. He arranged both the mirror and the video camera simultaneously—the former at Sasha's side of the apartment, the latter at his own—and watched himself from in front as well as from behind. He walked naked. He pulled wardrobe from every closet and he walked shirtless in shorts and sandals. He walked in boots. He walked in suits and overcoats, sweaters and skinny jeans, each item adapting his mood and everything that came with it. He found one of Xavier's many self-made T-shirts, the connotations of which he never truly, until then, understood: **sex, drugs, and rock & role models**. He put it on. He put on a pair of straight leg jeans he had received from his shoot for *Numéro Homme* and a soiled pair of Jeremiah's deserted pre-Nike-owned Converse All Stars. He took the two largest dictionaries from Xavier's shelf, held the French-Spanish-Italian at one side, the ancient Greek at the other, filled a small plastic cup halfway with water and placed it on his head, turned on the apartment iPod, balanced, and walked, studied, and walked.

He arrived at the gallery fifteen minutes ahead of call-time. A registration table was being prepared and a sign was being hung. Fellow male models dressed in all black were carrying boxes between makeshift bars, setting glassware fastidiously behind them. Much of the space was empty and unadorned, minus a thin, gray carpet covered in plastic running lengthwise from the back through the gallery. Assistants wearing headsets and electricians on ladders fixing lighting, checking speakers, relayed instructions as a lanky group of models—those walking, not serving—congregated cordially in a corner opposite the egress.

Danny sat down in his own corner and read. More models trickled in. The studio became increasingly animated with greetings, directions, music off and on. A half hour had passed before a forty-something-year-old man with well-cropped hair wearing jeans and a blazer entered the gallery from the back. He fixed his glasses as he assessed the state of affairs, then turned to the sprawl of models and smiled. A shaggy blonde with blue eyes was closest.

"Boyd!" he exclaimed and rustled the model's hair. "Have I seen you since *Milk*? I loved it! I loved it, loved it, loved it!" Danny stood up. The sprawl slowly condensed. The man began to connect with every model he saw as though he knew them better for their work than for who they otherwise were; yet heartfelt and accurate in every accolade. "Matvey, that was some publicity piece you had in the *L. A. Times*. Reid, geez almighty, how many *GQ* editorials can one man do? Brad, *The Silent Film* was just too adorable. Please tell Karl I said hello. Oriol, I'm telling you, your Bvlgari Aqva is *still* my favorite. Those eyes; those *eyes!*"

The commendations continued. Danny watched from the far side of the huddle, all the while wondering if he was the only one the man didn't know, or if, in fact, he did, and if Danny was the only one who didn't know him. *How did I book this*, he thought, and the man carried on: Stan for *Surface*; Blaine for *Flaunt*; Chad for *Arena Homme +*. He praised Garrett for *L'Uomo Vogue*; Lyle for *Dazed & Confused*; Jamie for *Upstreet*; Terron for the *V Man* Special; a different Danny for *Esquire*; and Adam for his acting in "The Hills." He congratulated Lars on his work with Koto, introduced himself kindly to Travone, inquired into Philip's real estate and Evandro's capoeìra, and said thank you, thank you, *thank you* to Noah, Mat, and Sean.

"Don't tell me. Don't tell me." He stood in front of Danny, his hands pressed in prayer down the center of his face. He shook them forward. Danny smiled, embarrassed. *"L' Officiel Hommes?* With Milan?" Danny shook his head, he parted his lips. "No, no! Don't tell me . . . *Velvet?* No. Something with Terry? *Numéro Homme?"*

"With Yuri," Danny said. "But it's not out yet."

"Yes." He clasped his fingers and turned his prayer into a pistol. He stood there. Looking. Just looking. "Danny Ward," he said, "Danny Ward," and tipped the barrel to his lips, the hammer under his chin. "Danny Ward . . ."

He backed away. A crowd of various staff, about half the number of the models, had gathered in the vicinity behind him. Someone motioned for the music to be lowered, and as it was he addressed the models.

"Before I say anything, please know how much your presence here tonight means. Fashion could not exist without you. And this event would not be the *same* without you. Your time, your professionalism, your support—they're all essential to tonight's success. Some of you have participated in our fundraiser fashion shows before. They are *fun* . . . The clothes are *fun* . . . The guests are coming for the auction, of course, but also for *fun*. The show is light, it's informal. We're not asking for somber faces. No Fashion Week stares, no dark or blank expressions. We're also not asking you to skip down the runway or smile from ear to ear. But the audience will be very close to you, the lights and music will be energetic, and little smirks, slight eye contact, a peppier walk are all perfectly OK. Call it pleasant professionalism. Anyway, tonight's event is an auction with all proceeds being donated to the Empire State Pride Agenda. Most of you know Jeffrey has raised thousands for various LGBT organizations. The event is also intended to help publicize next month's 40th anniversary of the Stonewall Riots. Of course we're not asking you to be our spokespeople, but after the auction and fashion show are over you're all welcome to stay and schmooze and enjoy the refreshments. Are there questions so far?"

The models glanced at one another.

"Jeffrey will be here soon. We're going to run you through the show even though it's relaxed and you've all done this a hundred times. When we're finished you'll check your outfits. Styling is simple. Most of you have just two looks, some of you have three. Remember, pleasant professionalism. And again, *thank* you. We love you.

Two hours later the studio was chock-full. Danny sat behind the divider listening to the audience bid on gift certificates, box seats, sapphire necklaces, and ten-day cruises as a woman with purple ink needled across her neck applied foundation to his cheeks. Models talked quietly beside him. Jeffrey's staff steamed clothes or paced back and forth with walkie-talkies and a finger pressed visibly to their lips. Danny looked in the mirror. He could only wonder if his career was over.

"Finished," the makeup artist said. "I'm telling you, your skin is just gorgeous."

"Thanks," he said. He started toward hair and at the same moment was stopped by a voice he'd never forget.

"Sweetie, I ain't seen that pretty face since it stole my sista woman's heart away." Danny turned. Oman spun a comb toward the sky, then spanked the seat beside him. "*Get* your scrawny ass over here and give Mama a hug." They met each other halfway with Oman laughing volubly before snapping away some dozen reminders of silence. "Look at you," he said, the volume of his voice, though not its enthusiasm, contained. "Ganymede *must* have had a twin and *that* is all I got to say about *that*. Now sit down and tell Mama everything you know."

"I booked *Numéro Homme*," Danny said. "And Malo."

Oman massaged his hair. "What I tell you—separated at birth!"

"Both should be out sometime in summer."

"Mm-hm, and won't I know it, too." He reached for a spray bottle.

Danny sobered. "Edge dropped me . . ."

Oman wiped off a comb. "Fall down, get right back up, sweetie! That's what my great aunt Gigi Mae always said and she died smiling near ninety-nine years old."

"I know, sometimes it just . . . I was in Canada with Una. For her birthday."

"Oh, sweet, *sweet* Jesus! I never thought I'd hear the words!"

"But we're not together anymore."

Oman stopped. Danny looked down. "Excuse me?" Danny shrugged. "Sweetie, this chair don't swivel but I will *make* it spin! Now look me straight in the eye and talk before I do something scary with these scissors."

Danny sighed. "I don't know. I don't *know!*"

"What you mean, you don't know? Cause I'll call a sista right now and find out!" He took his phone out of his pocket.

"Oman, please. *Please.*"

"Well what's she got to tell me that you can't?" He paused, put the phone away, and reached for a container of wax.

Danny sighed again. "Nothing," he said. "Nothing, I don't think. It's just . . . It's just that it's complicated. That's all. It's complicated."

"Sweetie," Oman said, pinching and pressing as necessary through Danny's hair. "Listen good cause this right here is what it *all* comes down to: *Life* . . . is complicated. What *you* got to do is figure out how to *simp*lify it. That's what my great aunt Gigi Mae always said and it's as true as the good Lord's day is long. Simplify it. You hear me?"

"I hear you."

"Amen," Oman said, and continued about his work. He didn't say another word, just nodded occasionally as though in agreement with some conversation inside his head. Danny watched him. He watched his hair take shape, the strands coaxed but not forced, all arranged in a matter of minutes, the styling, as Jeffrey's assistant had said, "simple." The word was frustrating; it was contradictory: it was plain *and* sincere *and* classy *and* humble *and* ignorant *and* unsophisticated. It was something different in every context and to every person. It was the sought and the unattainable, yet the mocked and ignored. Simple was the accessible, the original, the undivided, and unadorned. It was essence but also ignorance. It was completion but also deficiency. It was the modest to the sublime. It was everything he was raised to be, encouraged to be, and tried his hardest not to be.

Simple. Tonight it was beauty. It could have been the opposite.

He finished in hair and found a corner to himself. A man carrying a clipboard walked around whispering, "First looks in five, first looks in five." Opposite the partition the auctioneer called for higher bids. Makeup artists and hair stylists attended to the last of the models as those who were finished headed to the racks. Danny flipped his phone in his fingers. He turned it over and over without realizing it. More items were sold. More models moved into wardrobe. The man with the clipboard came back. "It's time."

"I'm coming," Danny said. He turned around and faced the wall. He dialed her number for the first time in six weeks, but it didn't ring. The call went to voicemail and suddenly he forgot all the simple things he had planned to say.

There was a beep, and then silence. ". . . Una . . ." He closed his eyes and leaned into the wall. "Una, it's Danny . . ." He paused again and sighed. "Are you . . . I'm not even sure if . . . Una, there's so much I want to tell you but I'm at this fashion show right now at Milk Studios and I shouldn't even be on the phone but I saw Oman and we . . . well . . . well, we were talking about you and I . . . I just realized that . . . I just really . . ."

Someone tapped him on the shoulder. He turned around.

"We need you in your first look."

"I'm coming. Una, I have to go. The point is . . . Well, it's simple. I miss you. And it kills me."

He turned slowly, somberly around. A moment later he was across the room undressing with the others as a girl his age in a plaid polyester shirt introduced herself.

"I'm your dresser tonight," she said.

"My what?" Danny took off his pants.

"Couldn't agree more, but better safe than sorry. And your second two looks are pretty close together." She handed him a pair of dress shorts that stretched hardly a foot from belt loops to cuffs. "Thom Browne," she said. "Pull the socks up to your knees. The shoes might be slippery, especially with that roll-out. I stuck some tape near the toe for you. A little extra grip."

Danny hardly listened. He put on the shirt, the tie, the smoke-gray suit. He found a mirror and stared. He looked like he was wearing daisy dukes to a business function.

It was a half hour later when Mat opened the show. They had been standing there patiently, waiting in line like the jobless outside an unemployment office when suddenly the crowd opposite the divider hushed, the lights slowly dimmed, then burst back on, and the speakers followed suit. The makeup artists and hair stylists rushed to the front with their respective supplies making last-second checks and adjustments.

Danny peered ahead as the man with the clipboard tapped Mat on the shoulder. He disappeared through the split and without a moment of hesitation the guests erupted with hoots, whistles, and applause. Some combination of exhilaration and helplessness came over him. The energy from the lights, the music, the heretically ebullient mob infiltrated his spirit and lifted him. He felt confident, galvanized, and yet equally undone. A show was not a shoot. There was no security of a photographer guiding, encouraging, no opportunity to take the picture again, to perfect it as necessary, to "correct" it at will.

And though the focus of a fashion show, in theory, was clothes, the fashions being shown already had been. Critiques were past. The items were in stores. The show was "fun," with the models the entertainment and while Danny was invigorated he felt like a piece of art—finished, raw, exposed. Available for evaluation; at last to be hung, or hanged.

The line moved forward: Oriol followed Mat; Boyd followed Oriol. Mat emerged from the opposite side of the egress and as soon as he cleared it, rushed to the racks. Within moments he was bare to his briefs. His dresser helped him into a pair of pants, then put on his socks and shoes for him as he tucked in his shirt. It hardly took a minute and he was back in line five looks behind Danny, a stylist fine-tuning everything.

Danny turned around and was suddenly third. Oman tweaked his hair and told him the gods were at war. A makeup artist powdered his nose and jaw, then stood aside. The man with the clipboard grabbed a hold of his lapel, tugged hard on his sleeves, pinched the knot in his tie, then for the slightest moment froze, waited, listened, and said, "We're walking in three . . . two . . . one," tapped Danny on the shoulder and without falter or reflection he walked.

He had practiced it untold times. He had walked the length of his apartment more often than he could count and watched the models about him even more. But no number of rehearsals could simulate the real thing. The intensity of each variable was too unique, and as a whole far greater than the sum of its parts. There wasn't the safety of his walls. There wasn't the comfort of a camera as his audience. There wasn't the cruel supremacy of the lights or the muscle of the music. There wasn't the pressure.

For a moment everything seemed surreal. Everything seemed lost of meaning, inexplicably slow, euphoric, and prodigal. He felt weightless in some liminality of fame, a transition of self. He walked with a selection of the most acclaimed models of his time and no one knew the difference. He didn't allow it. In his mind it was all just a dream, all odd and unpredictable. But to his body, what they saw, what he showed: command; articulation; ease.

He offered only the slightest, tantalizing hint of recognition; otherwise he walked just as he practiced. He reached the end of the carpet. He stopped. He didn't unbutton the jacket to show some inner intricacy that didn't exist or cock his head this way or that for fear of an awkward symmetry. He simply stopped, stood, and impressed the persona of the ensemble he wore. His eyes read geek-chic. His lips spoke country cowboy. His nose knew the nightly bottle and his cheeks claimed Normandy.

He turned. And sixteen seconds later he exited. Arms and legs were everywhere. Clothes looked like rags about the floor. Models and dressers stumbled silently in circles as all care and courtesy vanished.

Danny joined the outskirts of the commotion. He undressed swiftly but patiently, unassisted with minutes to spare. He got back in line wearing Veronique Branquinho from top to bottom, garments of a single summer red that no department store had dared to buy. He stood toward the back letting many of those whose first look had followed his now file in front. Garrett, Noah, Stan, and Travone comprised a swimwear contingent. Six other models also queued ahead in muted linens with unsynchronized accessories.

Danny led a wave of color. He moved forward in all red as he was accompanied by Lars, Jamie, Matvey, and Adam in outfits of teal, lavender, lemon, and Egyptian blue. His shirt was short-sleeved with the collar cut wide, others in polos or button-downs with pants mostly similar. Each wore sunglasses by Number (N)ine and sleek white loafers looking like a rainbow out of order. In a heartbeat Oman fixed his hair, a makeup artist smoothed his brows, the man with the clipboard ran his palms across his shoulders, yanked hard at his pockets, froze, waited, listened—"three . . . two . . . one"—tapped him on the shoulder and Danny turned through the split with a smile in his eyes.

There was a smattering of applause, an "ow-*ow!*" and a "woooh!" He heard them mix with the music and wanted desperately to turn. But even if it were possible, again, everything flushed surreal: time, place, perception, self—each redefined with indifference at best and fettered him to a trance of grandeur.

He stopped. He posed. He turned. And sixteen seconds later he exited.

It was look thirty-four. Thirty-five was heading back, thirty-six was heading out, thirty-seven was being adjusted, and thirty-eight being primped. The sunglasses, T-shirt, and loafers came off in a heartbeat. The pants were unbuttoned by the time he reached the racks. The line moved forward. His pants were off, the next pair on. He lifted a foot, and a sock slid up his ankle; he pointed it, and sank into a shoe. The line moved forward. He lifted the other foot as the shirt swirled across his back, his arms through the sleeves, and button, button, button—the line moved forward—button. Tuck, clasp, buckle, zip. One shoe was tied. He left the other in place and straddled wide for the vest and cravat. The dresser stood up and slammed her head between Danny's legs. Danny fell sideways. The line moved forward. The rest of the room stopped. Everyone stared. The dresser clutched her mouth in dread as models awaiting the finale winced. Danny rolled over and nearly everyone backstage rushed toward him panicking. Just as quickly, he stood up.

"One inch closer," he said, "and I'd be sterile for life."

Everyone exhaled. The line moved forward. In some five to ten seconds the vest was on, buttoned short, the cravat around his neck left loose, his pants brushed clean, jacket set casual, every hair, facial feature, and article of clothing tweaked and approved, with time enough to breathe.

"Three . . . two . . . one . . ." He disappeared through the split.

*   *   *

The gallery teemed even more than he had realized. By the time he had changed the carpet had been pulled away, the bars bombarded, and the music replaced by a drone. Danny didn't bother to strain. The swarm was too dense and the odds too slim.

He headed for the closest bar. It had been a while since he had had any alcohol, since he had even socialized among so many people. He had, of course, learned long ago to drink alone; it was New York that taught him to drink en masse.

He asked for a beer, but walked away with vodka. He turned to leave the bar and before he could spill the first drop a familiar voice called his name from behind.

"Yuri! What are you doing here?" He smiled and gave his favorite photographer a hug.

"I *do* live down the street. Or have you already forgotten since becoming Mister 'I-do-charity-events' Model?"

Danny chuckled. "Yeah, right . . . So are you a friend, a donor?"

"Jeffrey lets me borrow. And I let him know who's up-and-coming."

Danny hesitated, wondering if he even wanted to know. "Did . . . Did you . . ."

"Did I what?"

But there were suddenly hands masking his eyes from behind.

"Guess who!" Xavier said.

Danny turned around to find two of his three roommates. Xavier wore a T-shirt that read: **Reduce (me). Reuse (me). Recycle (me).** Jeremiah shook Danny's hand, then handed a business card to Yuri.

"Well done, Danny! Well done!" Xavier said.

"Why didn't you tell me you'd be here?"

"Finals. Getting evaluated. Looking for a new place."

"You're moving?"

Xavier grinned. "With Isis."

"Wow," Danny said. "And Remmy? Will he find someone new?"

Jeremiah leaned in. He gave Danny a card. "I was going to call it Men's Board," he said. "But then I thought, in case it's true—that no agency in New York can survive without women—a name like that wouldn't be the best way to recruit them."

"You're starting your own agency?"

"A-List," he said. "I've got the contract if you've got a pen."

"You—you want me on your board?"

"Danny, are you crazy, you're going to be huge. Valentino-with-Lindbergh huge.

Burberry-with-Testino huge. Milan, Tokyo, Taipei. Are you kidding me?"

He didn't know what to say. He'd been thinking more and more about his future, a degree, maybe Community College. Even if he didn't enroll that fall, he was finding it harder and harder to get excited. Everything was talk. Everyone in the city knew how. Words were as free-floating as the wind. Promises were the very backbone of dejection. Danny had heard it all a hundred times: this booker has connections here; that booker can get you in there; no one books boys like Carla . . . It was tiring. It was overwhelming. He felt like a doll being torn by toddlers. Yet it was adults, not children, who pulled. And they were stronger and savvier and more ruthless than any two-year-old. No one was without an interest.

But Jeremiah had never let him down. He had always kept his word and always kept Danny confident. That he could succeed. That he would. Even if it was all part of some broader, unspoken agenda, it had never worked against him.

"I've got a booker named Beth who'll be running the agency . . ."

Danny lit up. Then sighed. "Can we talk about it tomorrow? It's just loud and I've got a lot on my mind."

"Certainly," Jeremiah said. "But just so you know, I'm converting the apartment. With Xavier moving out and Kinzie in rehab and you hopefully—"

"Rehab? Kinzie's in rehab?"

Xavier and Jeremiah looked at each other. "Does Una live on another planet? Where have you been, Danny?"

His demeanor suddenly softened. "I don't even know where to begin," he said. "We sort of crashed around her birthday and haven't talked since. That was March."

"Well, she's here," Xavier said.

"She is?" Danny turned, and in a moment was gone. He lifted his head, his heels, maneuvering among the crowd as he crisscrossed the studio. It was virtually impossible to move. Guests were half drunk, gesturing theatrically and modeling overbearingly—shoes, a purse, the pockets on a pair of pants. It took him twenty minutes just to cover half the floor, and somehow reconnected with his roommates twice along the way. When he passed them the second time, she was there.

Danny stopped. Xavier saw him and gestured to Jeremiah. Like older brothers or best friends they smiled and disappeared into the crowd. For a moment, neither Danny nor Una moved. They were close enough to see each other, yet far enough to be divided. The guests mingled between them, fantastic and unaware of the reunion they intersected. Danny stepped forward. Without a smile or signal or any acknowledgment of the crowd he kept his eyes fixed to hers and slowly narrowed their distance.

Una waited as he neared. She held her hands serenely in front of her, the color of her dress the same shade as her eyes. Her neck was pronounced with her hair up, her face unadorned the way Danny preferred. He could see her chest rise and fall, slight flutters, but otherwise firm. Her shoulders were set square, her collars like speed bumps on a road too tender to tread.

Danny met her at arm's length and stayed there, admired her, free of interference, then despite the rage around him he whispered. "I missed you."

She stood taller than he remembered, in sandals without heels. Her chest filled. Her collar spread. "I was underground when you called."

His lips parted as if to smile, then sobered. He looked at her—her lips, her eyes, her cheeks unrevealing, and they stood there waiting. For what, though, it wasn't clear. There was so much to say, so much to satisfy. And yet again—at last—so much time. This couple that wouldn't race.

Una closed the remaining distance between them. She stood inches from his face, kept her gaze on his eyes, and whispered what he already knew. "I missed you, too." And they embraced like neither ever had.

Minutes passed. They walked outside and without a word about Selkirk or time or the things they already understood, Danny told Una about *Numéro Homme* and Malo and A-List, about the musician he met and a tea house he found and a book he nearly memorized. Una told him about Herbal Essence, about Prague, about the time she spent in Paris doing the things she always wanted to, thinking about the things she needed to, and not once picking up her phone except to call her mother and tell her agent she was still alive. They dallied there for a while as guests trickled by. The temperature had dropped and neither was warmly dressed, nor saw any reason to stay.

"I just have to pee," Una said.

"I'll go back in with you. I never did meet Jeffrey."

Una was already at the door. "Another time? I can introduce you whenever."

He stood there at the foyer, now completely puzzled. It could have been anyone. It could have been Carla. It could have been Jeremiah. It could have been Yuri or some other unsuspecting photographer. Of course, it could have been chance, a valid request—unlikely but possible. Less likely than

Una in Europe, talking to no one yet promoting him nonetheless? He wasn't sure he wanted to know. If he "owed" someone. If he was indebted to someone.

"And I supposed you had absconded, Daniel, without even a greeting."

He stopped in his tracks, then turned speechless to the door.

"Why, surely you *knew* I would be here."

"Marina . . ." He fumbled for words. He thought suddenly of their last encounter, the fire, the necklace. He thought of Una inside. "How—how are you?"

"Aside from wet, I am well." She seemed ever-so-slightly different. Calmer. Less erect. Not so tumescent. "I imagine you heard. A mere fortnight before the condo is to be ours, it burns. And she dies."

"I did hear. I—I should have called."

Marina shifted dismissively. "Yes, and what would that have done, Daniel? Brought the old beast back to life? Restored ash to original?"

"Well, no, but . . ."

"You have been busy," she said, nodding indiscernibly. He shot a glance inside the studio. "You have been working. This is good."

"How . . . did you know?"

"Oh, Daniel, how vastly you have changed. And yet how little."

"Have you changed, Marina?"

She sighed. "The key to self-betterment, Daniel, is emulating the lies we tell others about ourselves."

He stiffened. "I'd say the truth is more shocking."

"Only a fool knows the difference."

"So you haven't . . . changed . . ."

"I, Daniel, was never a constant." She walked past him along the curb to her car. Then turned. "Do you still have the necklace?"

He shook his head without a word. His heart pounded violently. She looked at him with a long, meditative stare.

"Good night, Daniel." She stepped casually inside. "You *may* still surprise me." The driver shut the door. The engine began to purr. He stood there, unmoving, colorless and ashamed. And as the car pulled away a cool breeze blew, and a shiver passed over his spine.

Epilogue

I T WAS MIDNIGHT in late spring in a condominium on Central Park. A middle-aged woman with an appetite for extremes straddled wide over her bed and a boy. She planted her knees at his waist. She paused in control. Then she lowered herself, hard, to entirety. The boy closed his eyes. The woman breathed deep. She arched her back. She moaned. The bed began to rock. She moved slowly and evenly in effortless aches until her thighs flexed tighter, her panting came quicker, and she stared glazed with a smirk in the mirror. Her breasts and buttocks bobbed wildly with enhancements as her hair slapped across her face, splashing sweat and saliva at the man filming everything beside them.

The night continued until the sheets were soaked and the woman was satisfied. Without a word, she strolled naked from the bed through the condo. She set an envelope by the door, fixed her favorite martini, then took her time in the bathroom as the man fell asleep and the boy dressed in silence. The following morning, each returned to society. The man ordered scotch aboard a flight to Los Angeles. The woman walked comfortably through Central Park. And the boy, red-eyed, unkempt, clutching a brand new portfolio, sat quietly in the corner of a casting— waiting, watching, thinking about things few would ever imagine, before bringing his envelope to the bank.

CPSIA information can be obtained at www.ICGtesting.com
Printed in the USA
265818BV00001B/1/P